PENGUIN BOOKS

SCOUNDREL

Before becoming a full-time writer Bernard Cornwell worked as a television producer in London and Belfast. He now lives in Massachusetts with his American wife. He is the author of the hugely successful *Sharpe* series of historical novels.

Penguin publish his bestselling contemporary thrillers *Sea Lord*, *Wildtrack*, *Crackdown*, *Stormchild* and *Scoundrel*, and the historical novel *Redcoat*. Penguin also publish his myth-imbued Arthurian romance, *The Warlord Chronicles*, which consists of *The Winter King*, *Enemy of God* and *Excalibur*.

For more information about Bernard Cornwell's books, please visit his official website: www.bernardcornwell.net

BERNARD CORNWELL

———

SCOUNDREL

PENGUIN BOOKS

PENGUIN BOOKS

Published by the Penguin Group
Penguin Books Ltd, 80 Strand, London WC2R ORL, England
Penguin Group (USA) Inc., 375 Hudson Street, New York 10014, USA
Penguin Group (Canada), 90 Eglinton Avenue East, Suite 700, Toronto, Ontario, Canada M4P 2Y3
(a division of Pearson Penguin Canada Inc.)
Penguin Ireland, 25 St Stephen's Green, Dublin 2, Ireland (a division of Penguin Books Ltd)
Penguin Group (Australia), 250 Camberwell Road, Camberwell, Victoria 3124, Australia
(a division of Pearson Australia Group Pty Ltd)
Penguin Books India Pvt Ltd, 11 Community Centre, Panchsheel Park, New Delhi – 110 017, India
Penguin Group (NZ), 67 Apollo Drive, Rosedale, Auckland 0632, New Zealand
(a division of Pearson New Zealand Ltd)
Penguin Books (South Africa) (Pty) Ltd, 24 Sturdee Avenue, Rosebank, Johannesburg 2196, South Africa

Penguin Books Ltd, Registered Offices: 80 Strand, London WC2R ORL, England

www.penguin.com

First published by Michael Joseph 1992
Published in Penguin Books 1993
Reissued in this edition 2011

2

Copyright © Bernard Cornwell, 1992
All rights reserved

The moral right of the author has been asserted

Printed and bound in Great Britain by Clays Ltd, Elcograf S.p.A.

Except in the United States of America, this book is sold subject
to the condition that it shall not, by way of trade or otherwise, be lent,
re-sold, hired out, or otherwise circulated without the publisher's
prior consent in any form of binding or cover other than that in
which it is published and without a similar condition including this
condition being imposed on the subsequent purchaser

ISBN: 978-1-405-92921-9

www.greenpenguin.co.uk

MIX
Paper from
responsible sources
FSC™ C018179

Penguin Books is committed to a sustainable
future for our business, our readers and our
planet. This book is made from paper certified
by the Forest Stewardship Council.

Scoundrel is for
Jackie and Jimmy Lynch

PART ONE

August 1, 1990 was my fortieth birthday. Sophie, my lover for the past three years, left me for a younger man, the cat fell sick, and the next morning Saddam Hussein invaded Kuwait.

Welcome to the best years of my life.

Three weeks later Shafiq asked if I could deliver a boat from the Mediterranean to America. Hannah, my part-time secretary, had taken Shafiq's telephone call and late that afternoon she came to the fishing harbour to give me the day's news.

"Who called?" At first I thought I must have misheard her. I was working in a trawler's engine room with the motor going. "Who called?" I shouted up through the open hatch again.

"Shafiq." Hannah shrugged. "No other name, just Shafiq. He said you know him."

I knew him all right, knew him well enough to wonder just what the hell was coming next. Shafiq! For God's sake! "He wanted what?"

"He wants a boat delivered."

"When?"

"He doesn't know."

"From where in the Mediterranean? France? Spain? Italy? Cyprus? Greece?"

"Just the Mediterranean. He said he couldn't be more specific."

"And I'm to deliver it where?"

Hannah smiled. "Just America."

I shut off the engine. I had been testing the trawler's hydraulic pumps, making sure that some scumbag hadn't lowered the pressure by half a ton to disguise a bad valve or a weak hose. I waited for the noise to die away, then looked up at Hannah. "What kind of boat?"

"He doesn't know." She laughed. Hannah had a nice laugh, but since Sophie had taken off every woman seemed to have a nice laugh. "I shall tell him no," she said, "yes?"

3

"Tell him yes, yes."

"What?"

"Tell him yes."

Hannah adopted the patient look she used when she was trying to save me from myself. "Yes?"

"Yes, *oui, ja, sí.* That's what we're in business for." Or at least that was what my letterhead said: Nordsee Yacht Delivery, Services and Surveying, Sole Proprietor, Paul Shanahan, Nieuwpoort, Belgium; though in the last few years the servicing and surveying had taken over from the delivery.

"But, Paul! You don't know when or how or what or where! How can I commit you to something so stupid!"

"When he phones back, tell him the answer is yes."

Hannah uttered a very Flemish noise, a kind of glottal grunt which I had learned denoted a practical person's scorn for an impractical fool. She turned a page in her notebook. "And a woman called Kathleen Donovan called. An American. She wants to see you. She sounds nice."

Oh, Christ, I thought, but what is this? A man turns forty and suddenly his past comes back to haunt him, and I had a swift filthy image of Roisin's blood on the yellow stone, and I thought of betrayal and of unhappiness and of love, and I hoped to God that if Roisin's sister was looking for me that she never, ever found me. "Tell her no," I said.

"But she says —"

"I don't care what she says. I've never heard of her and I don't want to see her." I could not explain any of it to Hannah who was so very practical and so very married to her plump policeman. "And tell Shafiq I want to know why."

"You want to know why?" Hannah frowned at me. "Why what?"

"Ask him why."

"But . . ."

"Just why!"

4

"OK! I'll ask!" She threw up her hands, turned, and walked along the quay. "I think the cat has worms!" she called back.

"Give it a pill!"

"It's your cat!"

"Please give it a pill."

"OK!" She gave the finger, not to me, but to one of the fishermen who had whistled at her. Then she waved to me and walked out of sight.

I went back to work, surveying a trawler that was being sold across the North Sea to Scotland, but my mind was hardly on the boat's hull or its engine or its hydraulics, instead I was wondering why, out of nowhere and on the very same day, the ghosts of danger past and love betrayed had come back to haunt me. And, if I was honest, to excite me too. Life had become dull, predictable, placid, but now the ghosts had stirred.

I had waited four years for Shafiq to remember me, to summon me back to the darker paths. Four years. And I was ready.

"It has been four years, Paul! Four years!" Shafiq, indolent, thin, kind, sly and middle-aged, sat on a deep, cushion-rich sofa. He had taken a suite in the Georges V in Paris and wanted me to admire his opulence. He was also in an ebullient mood, and no wonder, for Shafiq loved Paris, loved France, and the more the French hated the Arabs, the more Shafiq approved of Gallic good taste. Shafiq was a Palestinian who lived in Libya where he worked for Colonel Qaddafi's Centre to Resist Imperialism, Racism, Backwardness and Fascism. At first I had refused to believe any such organisation existed, but it did, and Shafiq was on its staff, which was doubtless why he had such a taste for European decadence.

"So what do you want?" I asked him sourly.

"I have never known Paris so hot! Thank God for the

invention of air-conditioning." As usual we spoke in French. "Have a cake, please. The *mille-feuille* is exquisite."

"What do you want?"

Shafiq ignored the question, instead opening a small, brightly enamelled tin of cachous and slipping one under his tongue. "I am pretending to be a Greek. I have a diplomatic passport even, look!"

I ignored both the fake passport and Shafiq's delight in possessing it. Shafiq's contribution to resisting imperialism, racism, backwardness and fascism was to act as a messenger between Libya and whatever terrorist groups were the flavour of Colonel Qaddafi's month. At first sight he seemed an unlikely secret agent for he was too childlike, too flamboyant and too likeable, but they were perhaps the very qualities that had let him survive so long, because it was impossible to imagine a man as risible as Shafiq being associated with the polluted wellsprings of political evil. "What do you want of me?" I asked him again. Whatever he wanted I would probably give him, but after four years I had to play a reluctant role.

"You would like a Gauloise? Here! Take the pack, Paul." He tossed the cigarettes to me.

"I've given up. What the hell do you want?"

"You've given up smoking! That's wonderful, Paul, really wonderful! The doctors say I should give up, but what do they know? My brother-in-law is a doctor, did I ever tell you that? He smokes forty a day, sometimes fifty, and he's fit as, what do you say? A fiddle! As a fiddle! You'd like some tea?"

"What the hell do you want, Shafiq?"

"I want you to deliver a boat to America, of course, just as I told your secretary. Is she beautiful?"

"As a rose in morning dew, as a peach blossom, as a Dallas Cowboy cheerleader. What kind of a boat? From where? To where? When?"

"I'm not sure."

6

"Oh, great! That's really helpful, Shafiq." I leaned back in my overstuffed armchair. "It's your boat?"

"It is not mine, no." He lit a cigarette, then waved it vaguely about as if to indicate that the notional boat belonged to someone else, anyone else, no one of importance. "How is your love life?"

"It doesn't exist. I've just been junked for a married French pharmacist. I got custody of the cat. Whose boat is it?"

"You lost your girlfriend?" Shafiq was instantly concerned for me.

"Whose boat is it, Shafiq?"

"It belongs to friends." Again he gestured with the cigarette to show that the ownership was unimportant. "How long will it take you?"

"How long will what take me?"

"To deliver the boat to America, of course."

"That depends on what kind of a boat it is and how far it's going and at what time of year you want it delivered."

"A sailboat," he said, "and soon, I think."

"How big a sailboat?"

"With a big lead keel." He smiled, as though that detail answered all my queries.

"How big?" I insisted.

He sucked on the cigarette, frowned. "I don't know how big, so give me, what do you Americans call it? A ballpark guess? Give me a ballpark guess."

I cast a beseeching look towards the ceiling's ornamental plasterwork. "Three months? Four? How the hell do I know? The bigger the boat, the quicker. Maybe."

"Three months? Four?" He sounded neither pleased nor displeased with my ballpark guess. "Is she blonde?"

"Is what blonde?"

"Your secretary."

"She's got brown hair."

"All over?"

"I don't know."

"Ah." He was sad for my ignorance. "Why did your lover leave you?"

"Because I want to retire to America one day and she doesn't, because she says I'm too secretive, because she finds life in Nieuwpoort dull, and because her Frenchman gave her a Mercedes."

"You want to live in America?" Shafiq asked in a tone of shock.

"Yes. It's home."

"No wonder you are unhappy." Shafiq shook his head, I think because Sophie had walked out on me rather than because I was an American.

"If I'm unhappy about anything," I assured him, "it's because of this meeting. For Christ's sake, Shafiq, you ignore me for four years, then you drag me to Paris to tell me you want me to deliver a boat, and now you can't give me a single Goddamn detail of the job."

"But it's business!" he pleaded.

"After four years?" I sounded hurt.

He shrugged, tapped his cigarette ash into a crystal bowl, then shrugged again. "You know why, Paul, you know why." He would not look at me.

"You didn't like my deodorant, Shafiq?" I mocked him.

He raised his eyes to meet mine. He did not want to articulate the old accusation, but I was putting him through the wringer and he knew he would have to endure the ordeal. "They said you were CIA, Paul."

"Oh, shit." I leaned back in the chair, disgust in my voice.

"We know it isn't true, of course." Shafiq tried to reassure me.

"It's taken you four years to make up your minds?"

"We can't be too careful, you know that." He sucked on the cigarette, making its tip glow bright. "Our business is like modern sex, isn't it? Practise it safely or not at all, isn't

8

that right, Paul?" He laughed, inviting me to join in his amusement, but my face did not change and he shook his head sadly. "It wasn't our side that accused you, Paul, it was the girl! Your girl! What was her name? Roisin?" He even pronounced it properly, Rosh-een, proving that he remembered her well enough. "She was your girl, Paul."

"My girl? She was the office bicycle, Shafiq. Anyone could ride her."

"That's good, Paul, I like it! The office bicycle!" He chuckled, then made a dismissive gesture. "So you understand, eh? You see why we could not trust you? Not me, of course! I never believed you were CIA! I defended you! I told them it was a ridiculous notion! Cretinous! But they wanted to make sure. They said wait, wait and see if he runs home to America. I guess you didn't run home, eh?" He smiled at me. "It's good to see you again, Paul. It's been too long."

"So this sailboat," I asked coldly, "what kind of business is it?"

"Just business."

"Is it to do with Iraq?"

"Iraq?" Shafiq spread hands as big as oarblades in a gesture suggesting he had never heard of Iraq or its invasion of Kuwait.

"Is this to do with Iraq?" I asked again.

He gave me a smile of yellowed teeth. "It's just business."

"The business of smuggling?" I asked.

"Maybe?" He offered me a conspiratorial smile.

"Then the answer is no." It was not, of course it was not, but if I yielded too easily the price would be low, and I wanted the price for this job to be very high, so I laid on the objections. "I don't smuggle things, Shafiq, unless I know what I'm smuggling, and how it's hidden, and why it's being smuggled, and where it's going, and who it's going to, and how much, and when, and who benefits, and who might be trying to stop it, and how much they propose paying me to get it past them."

"I told them you'd say that!" Shafiq sounded triumphant.

"They?" I challenged him.

"The people who want you to go to Miami tomorrow," he answered coyly, hoping that the mention of Miami would sidetrack my question.

"They?" I said again.

"Your old friends," he said, confirming what I had suspected.

"They're in Miami?" That did surprise me.

"They want you there tomorrow." He stuffed a slice of almond cake into his mouth, then mumbled, "They're expecting you, and I have your ticket. First class even!" He made it sound like a treat, like a red carpet into the lion's den. Not that I needed such an enticement. I had waited four years for someone to rescue me from hydraulic systems and fibreglass osmosis and rotted keel-bolts.

So I telephoned Hannah at her Nieuwpoort home. It was a Sunday afternoon and she sounded sleepily warm and I wondered if I had interrupted the plump policeman's revels. "Cancel this week's appointments," I told her.

"But, Paul . . ."

"Everything," I insisted, "is cancelled."

"Why?"

"Because I'm going to Miami," I said, as though it was something I did every month and thus no occasion for her surprise.

Hannah sighed. "Kathleen Donovan phoned again. She says she's visiting Europe and she promises she doesn't need much of your time, and I told her you would be –"

"Hannah! Hannah! Hannah!" I interrupted her.

"Paul?"

"Make sure the cat takes its damn pills, will you?" I asked, then I put the telephone gently down and, next morning, flew to Miami.

*

Little Marty Doyle was waiting for me at Miami International where, despite the heat, he was jumping up and down like an excited poodle. "It's just great to see you, Paulie! Just great! It's been years, hasn't it? Years! I was saying as much to Michael last night. Years!"

Marty is a nothing, a lickspittle, an errand boy. Officially he works for the Boston School Committee, while unofficially he gophers and chauffeurs for Michael Herlihy. Herlihy never learned to drive because he suffers from motion sickness and his mother always insisted he had to sit in the back of the family car, and ever since he's ridden about like Lord Muck. These days Marty is his dogsbody and driver. "So what the hell are you doing in Miami?" I asked him.

"Looking after Michael. He's not happy because of the heat. He's never liked the heat. Makes him itch. Is that all your luggage?" He gestured at my sea-bag.

"How much do you want me to have?"

"I'll carry it for you."

I lifted the sea-bag out of his reach. "Just shut up and lead on."

"It's been years since I seen you, Paulie! Years! You don't look any older, not a day! That beard suits you. I tried to grow a beard once, but it wouldn't come. Made me look like that Chinaman in the movie. Fu-Manchu, know who I mean? So how are you, Paulie? The car's this way. Have you heard the news?" He was skipping around me like an excited child.

"The war has started?" I guessed.

"War?" Marty seemed oblivious to the American-led build-up of forces in Saudi Arabia. "It's about Larry," he finally said, "they reckon it's healed, see? He'll be as good as new!"

"What's healed?"

"His heel! He had surgery on it." Marty giggled at a sudden dawning of wit. "His heel's healed. Get it?"

I stopped in the middle of the terminal and looked down at Marty's bald head. I was tired, I was hot, and Marty was yapping at me like a poodle in heat. "Who the hell is Larry," I asked, "and what the hell are you talking about?"

"Larry Bird!" Marty was astonished at my obtuseness. "He missed the end of last season because of his heel. It had a growth on the bone, or something like that."

"Oh, Christ." I started walking again. I might have known that the most important thing in Marty's world would be the Boston Celtics. The Celts were a religion in Boston, but somehow, perhaps because I now lived in a small harbour town on the Belgian coast, my devotions to the old hometown religion had lapsed.

Yet it felt good to be back on American soil, even in Florida's unfamiliar tropical heat. I had been away seven years. I had never meant the time to stretch so, but somehow there had always been a reason not to fly the Atlantic. I had bought tickets once, only to have the lucrative chance of delivering a brand-new boat from Finland to Monaco change my plans. Nor did I have family reasons to go home for my parents were dead and my sister was married to a buffoon I could not stand, and so, these last years, I had worked in Nieuwpoort and nursed my dreams of one day going home and living a long, easy retirement in the Cape Cod cottage I had inherited from my father. I was saving up for that retirement, and that savings account had been another reason for not spending money on expensive transatlantic air fares. But I had still been away for too long.

"Michael's waiting for us." Marty held the back door of the limousine open for me. "And there's a fellow come over from Ireland to meet you. Brendan, his name is. Brendan Flynn. He arrived yesterday."

"Brendan Flynn?" That did surprise me, and it chilled me. Brendan was one of the Provisional IRA's top men, maybe third or fourth in the movement's hierarchy, and such men did not travel abroad for trivial reasons. But nothing about this odd deal smelled trivial; it was transatlantic air tickets, suites in the Georges V, a white limousine at Miami International. I had walked into it eagerly enough, but the mention of Brendan's name gave the whole business a real blood smell of danger.

"It must be something big, Paulie, for a fellow to fly all the way from Ireland. And you've travelled a few miles too, eh? From Paris!" Marty was fishing for news. "So what do you think it's all about?" he asked as we swung clear of the airport traffic.

"How the hell would I know?"

"But you must have an idea!"

"Just shut up, Marty."

But Marty was incapable of silence and, as he drove north, he told me how he had seen my sister just the week before, and that Maureen was looking good, and how her boys were growing up, but that was the way of boys, wasn't it? And had I heard about the New England Patriots? They had been bought by the electric razor man, but they were still playing football like amateurs. A convent school could play better, so they could. And who did I think would be up for the Super Bowl this season? The Forty-Niners again?

Marty paused in his stream of chatter as we neared the Hialeah Racetrack. He was looking for a turn-off among a tangle of warehouses and small machine shops. "Here we are," he announced, and the softly sprung car wallowed over a rough patch of road, turned into a rusting gate that led through a chain link fence topped with razor-wire, and stopped in the shade of a white-painted warehouse that had no identifying name or number painted on its blank anonymous façade. A stone-faced man sitting in a guard shed beside the warehouse's main door must have recognised Marty for I was casually waved forward without any query or inspection. "You're to go straight in," Marty called after me, "and I'm to wait."

I stepped through the door into the warehouse's shadowed, vast interior. Two forklift trucks stood just inside the door, but otherwise I could see nothing except tower blocks of stacked cardboard boxes. The air smelt of machine oil and of the newly sawn timber used for the pallets, or like machine-gun oil and coffin wood. I was nervous. Any man summoned by Brendan Flynn did well to be nervous.

"Is that you, Shanahan?" Michael Herlihy's disapproving voice sounded from the darkness at the far end of the huge shed.

"It's me."

"Come and join us!" It was a command. Michael Herlihy had little time for the niceties of life, only for the dictates of work and duty. He was a scrawny little runt of a man, nothing but sinew and cold resolve, whose idea of a good time was to compete in the Boston marathon. By trade he was an attorney and, like me, he came from among Boston's 'two-toilet Irish'; the wealthy American-Irish who had houses on the Point and summer homes on the South Shore or on Cape Cod. Not that Michael was what I would call a proper attorney, not like his father who, pickled in bourbon and tobacco, could have persuaded a jury of Presbyterian spinsters to acquit the Scarlet Whore of Babylon herself, but old Joe was long dead, and his only son was now a meticulous Massachusetts lawyer who negotiated trash-disposal contracts between city administrations and garbage hauliers. In his spare time he was the Chairperson of Congressman O'Shaughnessy's Re-election Committee and President of the New England Chapter of the Friends of Free Ireland. Michael preferred to describe himself as the Commander of the Provisional IRA's Boston Brigade, which was stretching a point for there was no formally established Boston Brigade, but Michael nevertheless fancied himself as a freedom fighter and kept a pair of black gloves and a black beret folded in tissue paper and ready to be placed on his funeral casket. He had never married, never wanted to, he said.

Now, in Miami's oppressive heat, he was waiting for me with three other men. Two were strangers, while the third, who came to greet me with outstretched arms, was Brendan Flynn himself. "Is it you yourself, Paulie? My God, but it is! It's grand to see you, just grand! It's been too long." His Belfast accent was sour as a pickle. "You're looking good in yourself! It must be all that Belgian beer. Or the girls? My God, but it's a treat to find you alive, so it is!" He half crushed me in a welcoming embrace, then stepped back and gave my shoulder a friendly thump that might have felled a bullock. It was rumoured that Brendan had once killed an IRA informer with a single flat-handed blow straight down on the man's skull, and I could believe it. He was a tall man, built like an ox, with a bristling beard and a voice that erupted from deep in his beer-fed belly. "And how are you, Paulie? Doing all right, are you?"

"I'm just fine." I had meant to reward four years of silence with a harsh reserve, but I found myself warming to Brendan's enthusiasm. "And yourself?" I asked him.

"There's grey in my beard! Do you see it? I'm getting old, Paulie, I'm getting old. I'll be pissing in my bed next and having the nuns slap my wrist for being a bad boy. God, but it's grand to see you!"

"You should see me more often, Brendan."

"None of that now! We're all friends." He put an arm round my shoulders and squeezed and I felt as though a hydraulic press was tightening across my chest. "But, my God, this heat! How the hell is a man supposed to stay alive in a heat like this? Sweet Mother of God, but it's like living in a bread oven." It was no wonder that Brendan was feeling the heat for he was wearing a tweed jacket and a woollen waistcoat over a flannel shirt, just as if Miami had a climate like Dublin. Brendan had lived in Dublin ever since he had planted one bomb too many in Belfast. Now he dragged me enthusiastically towards an opened crate. "Come and look at the toys Michael has found us!"

Michael Herlihy sidled alongside me. "Paul?" That was his idea of a greeting. We had known each other since second grade, yet he could not bring himself to say hello.

"How are you, Michael?" I asked him. No one ever called him Mick, Micky or Mike. He was Michael, nothing else. When we had been kids all the local boys had nicknames: Ox, King, Beef, Four-Eyes, Dink, Twister; all of us except for Michael X. Herlihy, who had never been anything except Michael. The X stood for his baptismal name, Xavier.

"I'm good, Paul, thank you." He spoke seriously, as if my question had been earnestly meant. "You had no problems in reaching us?"

"Why should I have problems? No police force is watching me." I had aimed the remark at Brendan who was a noisy and notorious beast, not given to reticence, and if he had travelled here with his usual flamboyance then it would be a miracle if the FBI and the Miami police were not inspecting us at this very moment.

"Stop your fretting, Paulie." Brendan dismissed my criticism. "You sound like an old woman, so you do. The Garda think I'm at another of those Dutch conferences where we discuss the future of Ireland." He mocked the last three words with a portentous irony, then began excavating mounds of corrugated cardboard and foam packing from inside an opened crate. "I took a flight to Holland, a train to Switzerland, a flight to Rio, and then another plane up here. The bastards will have lost my footprints days ago." His echoing voice filled the warehouse's huge dusty space, which was lit only by what small daylight filtered past the roof's ventilator fans. "Besides, it's worth the risk for this, eh?" He turned, lifting from the opened crate a plastic-wrapped bundle which he handled with the piety of a priest elevating the Host. Even Michael Herlihy, who was not given to expressing enthusiasm, looked excited.

"There!" Brendan laid the bundle on a crate and pulled

back its wrapping. "For the love of a merciful God, Paulie, but would you just look at that wee darling?"

"A Stinger," I said, and could not keep the reverence from my own voice.

"A Stinger," Michael Herlihy confirmed softly.

"One of fifty-three Stingers," Brendan amended, "all of them in prime working order, still in their factory packing, and all with carrying slings and full instructions. Not bad, eh? You see now why I took the risk of coming here?"

I saw exactly why he had risked coming here, because I knew just how highly the IRA valued these weapons, and just what risks the movement would take to acquire a good supply. The Stinger is an American-made, shoulder-fired, ground-to-air missile armed with a heat-seeking high-explosive warhead. The missile and its launcher weigh a mere thirty pounds, and the missile itself is quick, accurate and deadly to any aircraft within four miles of its launch point. Brendan was gazing at the unwrapped weapon with a dreamy expression and I knew that in his mind's eye he was already seeing the British helicopters tumbling in flames from the skies above occupied Ireland. "Oh, sweet darling God," he said softly as the beauty of the vision overwhelmed him.

The Provos had tried other shoulder-fired anti-aircraft missiles. They had used Blowpipes stolen from the Short Brothers factory in Belfast, and Russian-made Red Stars donated by Libya, but neither the Blowpipe nor the Red Star was a patch on the Stinger. The big difference, as Brendan had once told me, was that the Stinger worked. It worked just about every time. Fire a Stinger and there is a multi-million-pound British helicopter turned into instant scrap metal. Fire a Stinger and the Brits cannot supply their outlying garrisons in South Armagh. Fire a Stinger and the Brits have to take away their surveillance helicopters from above the Creggan or over Ballymurphy. Fire a Stinger and every newspaper in Britain, Ireland and America sits up and takes notice of the IRA. Fire enough Stingers, Michael Herlihy believed, and there would be a bronze statue of a scrawny Boston garbage lawyer strutting his way across St Stephen's Green in Dublin.

"It will be the most significant arms shipment in the history of the Irish struggle," Michael Herlihy said softly as he gazed at the unwrapped weapon, and if his words were something of an exaggeration, it was forgivable. The Libyans had sent the IRA tons of explosives and crates of rifles, but neither bombs nor bullets, nor even the green graveyards full of the innocent dead, had yet budged the Brits one inch from Ulster's soil. Yet Stingers, Herlihy and Brendan fervently believed, would scour the skies of their enemies and so shock the forces of occupation that, just as glorious day follows darkest night, Ireland would be freed.

There seemed just one snag. Or rather two: both of them thin, both tall, both dressed in pale linen suits and both with dark smooth faces. Michael Herlihy made the introductions. "Juan Alvarez and Miguel Carlos." They were not names to be taken seriously, merely convenient labels for this meeting in an anonymous Hialeah warehouse under the clattering exhaust fans that flickered the dusty sunlight. "Mr Alvarez and Mr Carlos represent the consortium that acquired the missiles," Michael said unhappily.

"Consortium?" I asked.

The one who called himself Alvarez answered. "The fifty-three missiles are currently listed as US Government property." He spoke without irony, as though I would be grateful for the information.

"God, but it's beautiful," Brendan muttered. He stroked the Stinger; caressing its olive-green firing tube and folded acquisition array. The missile itself was invisible behind the membrane that sealed the firing tube.

"And the consortium's price?" I asked Alvarez.

"For fifty-three weapons, *señor*, five million dollars."

"Jesus Christ!" I could not resist the blasphemy for the

price had to be extortionate. I had been away from the illegal arms business for four years, but I could not believe the cost of a Stinger had escalated so high, not since the United States had been giving Stinger missiles to the Afghan mujaheddin, which surely meant there had to be other Stingers available on the black market. Yet these men expected five million bucks for fifty-three missiles?

Alvarez shrugged. "Of course, *señor*, if you are able to buy the same quality for less elsewhere, then we shall understand. But our price remains five million dollars." He paused, knowing just how deeply the Provisional IRA lusted after these weapons. "The five million dollars must be paid in gold coins, here, in Miami."

"Oh, naturally," I scoffed.

"And naturally, *señor*," Alvarez went smoothly on, "a small deposit will be required."

"Oh! A small deposit now?" I sneered.

"The cost isn't your business, Paul, so shut up," Brendan snarled. He was in love with the missiles and thought them worth any price. He took me by the arm and steered me out of the Cubans' earshot. "The point of this, Paul, is that we already have the gold. It's all agreed. All we need do is bring the gold here."

I understood at last. "In a boat? From the Mediterranean?"

"That's right."

"The Arabs are giving you the gold?"

"And why not? Considering how rich the buggers are? They've got all that oil and all poor Ireland has is a bogful of wet peat. What's gold to them, Paulie?" Brendan's grip on my arm was hurting. "But the point of bringing you here was so you could see the Stingers for yourself. Shafiq said you'd not help us unless you knew just what it was all about, so now we're showing you. You always were a careful man, Paulie, were you not?"

"Except in women, Brendan?" I asked the question sarcastically, probing a four-year-old wound.

"She was more trouble than she was worth, that one."
He spoke of Roisin, but his casual tone did not entirely
disguise the old hurt. He let go his bone-crushing grip and
slapped my back instead. "So will you fetch the boat over?
Will you do it now? Because it'll be just like the old days!
Just like the old days."

"Sure," I said, "sure." Because it would be just like the
old days.

In the old days I had been the Provisional IRA's liaison
man with the Middle East. I was the guy who made the
deals with the Palestinians and who listened for hours to
Muammar al-Qaddafi's plans for world-wide revolution. I
was the Provos' sugar daddy who brought them millions in
money, guns and bombs until, suddenly, they decided I
could not be trusted. There was a whisper that I was CIA,
and the whisper had finished me, but at least they had left
me alive, unlike Roisin who had been executed on the yellow
hillside under the blazing Lebanese sun.

The Provisional IRA's leaders claimed that Roisin had
betrayed a man. Roisin had tried to shift the blame on to
me, and that brush of suspicion had been enough to cut me
off from the IRA's trust. They had let me run the odd
errand in the past four years, and once or twice they had
used my apartment as a hiding place for men on the run,
but they had not shown me any of their old confidence –
until now, when suddenly they wanted a boat delivered and
I was the only man remotely connected to the movement
who understood the intricacies of bringing a boat across the
Atlantic.

"We would have asked Michael to bring the boat over,"
Brendan explained, "but he gets sick just looking at the
sea!" He laughed, and Herlihy gave him his thin, unamused
smile. Michael did not like being teased about his chronic
motion sickness, which seemed an unsuitable affliction for a
black-gloved soldier.

Brendan poured me a whiskey. We had gone back to his room in a waterfront Miami hotel where, bathed in blissful air-conditioning and with a bottle of Jameson Whiskey standing on the low coffee table, Brendan was explaining to me why it was necessary to bring the yacht from Europe to America. "The Cuban bastards insist on gold, so they do, and Michael tells me it would be next to impossible to find the gold over here."

"Treasury regulations," Herlihy explained. He was not drinking the whiskey, but had a bottle of mineral water instead. "Any transactions involving more than ten thousand dollars must be reported to the Treasury Department. The legislation was enacted to track down drug dealers."

"So your old pals the Libyans obliged us," Brendan took up the tale again. He was standing at the window, puffing at a cigarette and staring down at the pelicans perched on the sea-front pilings below. "I've seen them in the Phoenix Park zoo, so I have, but it's not the same, is it?"

"The Libyans are giving you the gold?" I wanted to make sure it was Libya, and not Iraq.

"We don't have that kind of scratch ourselves," Brendan said happily, "but we did manage to raise the deposit. Or Michael did."

"You raised half a million bucks?" I asked Herlihy in astonishment. The folks in Boston, New York, Philadelphia and the other cities where the Irish-Americans lived could all be generous, but they were not usually wealthy and their donations were mostly small. And those small donations had been shrinking thanks to the politicians from the Irish Republic who had been touring America to preach that the IRA was an enemy of the south just as much as it was an enemy to Britain. Now, suddenly, Michael Herlihy had raised half a million dollars? "How the hell did you do it?"

"It's none of your business," Herlihy told me sourly.

"Your business, Paulie," Brendan said, "is the five million in gold. The Libyans are putting it up, God bless them, but they're insisting we make the arrangements for moving the gold from there to here, and that's when we thought of you." He smiled happily at me. "Can you do it now?"

He sounded genial enough, but Brendan always sounded genial. Many men had died misunderstanding Brendan's open, happy face and bluff, cheerful manner. Beneath it he was implacable, a man consumed by hatred, a man whose every moment was devoted to the cause. If I turned down this job he would probably kill me, and to the very last moment he would smile at me, appear to confide in me, call me 'Paulie', hug me, and at the end, murder me.

I took a sip of whiskey. "Has anyone found out how much five million bucks in gold weighs?"

"A thousand pounds, near enough," Brendan said, then waited for my response. "Say three big suitcases?" I was not worried about the space such an amount of gold would take up, but what its weight would do to a sailboat. However, a thousand pounds of extra ballast would be nothing to a decent-sized cruiser. "Well?" Brendan prompted me.

"I can carry a thousand pounds of gold," I said.

"How?" Herlihy snapped.

"None of your business."

Brendan laughed at the hostility between us. "And of course, Paulie, there'll be a good wee fee in this for you."

"How much?"

"The half-million deposit that we'll get back when the gold arrives. Does that sound good to you?" Brendan glanced at Herlihy as though seeking confirmation and I sensed that the two of them had not agreed on that fee beforehand. I also saw Michael Herlihy blench at the amount and for a second I thought he was going to protest; then, reluctantly, he nodded.

"The point being" – Brendan beamed at me – "that I know a boat filled with gold could be a hell of a temptation, even to a man as honest as yourself, Paulie, but I look at it this way. If you try to steal the gold then you'll have made an enemy of me, and one day I'll find you and I'll make your death harder and slower than your worst nightmares. Or you can keep the faith and walk away at the end of the job with a half-million dollars, and I reckoned that half a million should be enough to keep any man honest." He smiled, as if pleased with his reasoning, then turned back to the sun-bright sea beyond the tinted glass. "Look at the size of those fowl! Can you eat them now?"

"Half a million sounds good to me," I said as equably as I could.

"Not that we're utter fools, Paulie" — Brendan was still staring at the pelicans — "because we'll be giving you some company on the trip. Just to help you along, so to speak."

"To be my guards, you mean?" I asked sourly.

"To be your crew." Brendan turned back to me. He was keeping the tone of the conversation light, but that was because he knew I could not turn him down. By just coming to Miami I had agreed to whatever he wanted. "Say two of my lads to be your crew?" he went on. "Work them hard, eh?"

I shrugged. "Fine." And why, I was wondering, if the Libyans had insisted that the Provisional IRA transport the gold, had Shafiq approached me first? And why had Brendan and Michael not agreed on my fee before they met me? Or perhaps they had agreed, but Brendan, with his usual enthusiasm, had suddenly decided to quote a much higher figure because he wanted to tempt me. But that suggested he also had no intention of letting me live long enough to collect the money. I suspected the half-million-dollar fee was nothing but a bait to make me take the job, and that Brendan's two guards would chop me down the moment the voyage was done.

Indeed, the whole affair seemed oddly ragged. The Provisional IRA had learned from too many past mistakes and these days they did not launch half-baked schemes, and they certainly did not leave details like an unagreed fee dangling in the wind, which suggested that this operation was being planned hastily, perhaps in the single short month since an Iraqi army had stormed across the defenceless frontier of Kuwait. "The important thing now," Brendan went blithely on, "is to choose the right boat, and you're the best fellow to do that."

"If I'm going to sail it across the pond," I agreed, "then I want to choose it."

"So would you mind flying right back to Europe?" Brendan asked. "The Libyans are in a hurry to ship the gold, so they are."

"We're in a hurry," Michael Herlihy amended the explanation, then added a reason for the haste. "Next April is the seventy-fifth anniversary of the Easter Rising and we'd like to give the British a bloody memorial to mark the occasion, and we can't ship the Stingers to Ireland till you've brought us the gold."

"You want me to fly back tomorrow?" I asked Brendan, and sounded surprised. I had hoped for a chance to fly north and visit the Cape Cod house that I had not seen in seven years, and maybe to visit my parents' grave in Boston, but Michael and Brendan were in too much of a hurry.

They were in even more of a hurry than I suspected. "Not tomorrow," Brendan said, "tonight," and, like a conjurer, he produced the air ticket from a pocket of his tweed jacket. "To Paris, then on to Tunisia. First class, Paul!"

They were trying too hard, I thought. They did not need to entice me with first-class tickets. It smelled as though they were persuading me to do something I did not want to do, and surely they should be treating me like a volunteer? The discrepancy was just another unlikely ragged edge to add to my disquiet, but also to my curiosity. A lot of people were going to a lot of trouble to make me accept this job, and that much effort suggested there could be a huge reward hidden among the details, so I said I would fly out that night.

Brendan went with me to Miami Airport. "It's grand to be working with you again, Paulie, just grand."

I ignored the blarney. "You couldn't find anyone else with the right qualifications, was that it?"

For a half-second he looked blank, then laughed. "Aye, that's the truth of it."

"So you're being forced to trust me again?" I could not keep the bitterness from my voice. Little Marty Doyle was driving us and I could see his ears pricking with interest at our conversation.

"You know the rules, Paul," Brendan said awkwardly. "It only takes a touch of suspicion to make us wary."

"Wary!" I protested. "Four years of silence because some bitch accuses me of being in the CIA? Come off it, Brendan. Roisin invented fairy stories like other women make up headaches."

"We know the girl lied about you," he admitted sombrely. "You've proved it. You could have betrayed us any time in the last four years and you haven't. And besides, Herlihy had a word with his people in Boston and they said the girl was fantasising. There was no way the Yanks were running an operation like she said. All moonshine, they said. It was a good wee story, though. She could tell a good wee story, that girl. She was good crack."

I wondered who Herlihy's people were, and supposed they were Boston police who could tap the FBI who, in turn, could call in a favour from the Central Intelligence Agency. So someone had run a check on Roisin's allegations, and I had come up snow-white. "Did Herlihy's people check on Roisin as well?" I asked.

"She was a one!" Brendan said in admiration, carefully not answering my question. "Jesus, she was a one. She had a tongue on her like a focking flamethrower. You could have used her to strip varnish!"

"But was she CIA?" I asked.

"Just a trouble-making bitch, that's all." He was silent for a few seconds. "But she was a lass, wasn't she?"

I had always thought that Roisin and Brendan had been lovers, and the wistfulness of his last words brought the old jealousy surging back. Roisin had been a gunman's groupie, a worshipper of death. She would have bedded the devil, yet still I would have loved her. I had been besotted by her. I had thought the world revolved about her, that the sun was dimmed by her, the moon darkened by her and the stars dazzled by her. And she was dead.

I caught the night flight to Paris.

Shafiq was waiting for me at the Skanes-Monastir Airport. He was wearing a suit of silver-grey linen with a pink rose buttonhole which on closer inspection turned out to be plastic. I was a shabby contrast in my crumpled, much-travelled clothes. "So how was Miami?" Shafiq asked me.

"Hot."

"And the girls?"

"Exquisite. Ravishing. Limpid."

That was the answer Shafiq wanted. The poor man dreamed of Western girls, especially French girls and, in the old days, he had insisted on making our summer rendezvous on the Riviera so he could stroll the promenades and stare down at the serried rows of naked French breasts displayed on the beach. It never bored him, he could gaze for hours. The casual display of nudity fed Shafiq's fantasies and once, sitting in the café of the Negresco, he had shyly told me his ambition of finding a French bride. "Not a whore, you understand, Paul? Not a whore. I have enough whores." He had paused to cut into a Napoleon-kake, then carefully scooped the creamy custard which had oozed from between the pastry layers on to his teaspoon. Shafiq loved sweet things, yet stayed skeletally thin. "I am tired of whores," he said when he had licked the spoon dry. "I want a fragile Parisian girl, with white skin, and small bones, and short golden hair, who will smile when I come through the door. She will play to me on the piano and we shall walk our dog beside the Seine." I later discovered that Shafiq had a fat dark wife and three moustached daughters who squabbled in a small Tripoli apartment.

Now he escorted me to the parking lot where his rented white Peugeot waited. Out of sailing habit I cocked an eye at the weather. The day was cloudless, while the wind was in the north and cool enough to make me glad I had brought a sweater. "Where are we going?"

"The marina at Monastir." Shafiq unlocked the car.

"There are boats for sale there, Western boats. You should see them, Paul! They sail into the harbour and the women wear bikinis so small that they might as well not have got dressed at all. They are, how do you say it? Almost in their birthday clothes?"

Shafiq was filled with an irrepressible verve, like a lover in the first freshness of passion. I had seen other men thus animated, men going on their first bombing mission to make a new Ireland out of dead bodies; but I could not understand why Shafiq, who had grown middle-aged in the service of violence, should find buying a western yacht such an energising experience. He accelerated out of the parking lot, spitting a stream of Arab profanities at a taxi driver who had dared to sound a protesting horn at the Peugeot's irruption into the traffic stream. "We are going to meet someone," Shafiq announced, as though he had arranged a great treat.

"I thought we were buying a boat?"

"We are, we are, but you are going to meet someone first. His name is Halil!"

"Halil." I repeated the name with none of the enthusiasm with which Shafiq had invested the two plain syllables. "So who is Halil?"

"He is in charge of this end of the operation. Just as Mr Herlihy is in charge of the other."

Herlihy was in charge? Not Brendan Flynn? I tucked that oddity away as just another slight dissonance that made this whole affair so strange. "So who's Halil?" I asked. The name was clearly a pseudonym, but in the past, with a little pushing, Shafiq had often been ready to betray such confidences.

But not this time. "Just Halil!" Shafiq laughed, then raced past a truck loaded with piled crates of squawking chickens. "But Halil is a great man, you should know that before you meet him." Shafiq's words, friendly enough, were nevertheless a warning.

"Is the gold ready?" I asked.

"I don't know. Maybe? Maybe not. I don't know." There were chicken feathers stuck under the Peugeot's windscreen wipers. Shafiq tried to shift them by flicking the wipers on and off, but the feathers obstinately stayed. Abandoning the attempt he lit a cigarette and grinned conspiratorially at me. "You saw the Stingers?"

"I saw one."

"What a weapon! What a weapon! Now you understand about the boat, yes?"

"No."

"Paul! You don't want the heroic fighters of Ireland to have Stingers?"

"I'd like them to have battle-tanks and rocket artillery, but I don't think it makes sense to pay for the weapons by stuffing a boat with gold and sailing it across the Atlantic. Haven't your people heard of cheques? Or bank drafts? Or wire transfers?"

Shafiq laughed. "Paul! Paul!" He spoke as though he were chiding me for a familiar and lovable cantankerousness, then he fell silent as the Peugeot threaded the traffic close to the harbour. Above us towered the turrets and castellated walls of the Ribat fortress, while next to it, from loudspeakers installed in the minaret of the Grand Mosque, a tape recording called the faithful to prayer. We turned a corner and there, spread beneath us in the October sunshine, was the marina. The Mediterranean sailing season had not yet ended and so the pontoons were thick with boats, many of them flying big elaborate race flags so that the ancient harbour looked as if a fleet of mediaeval war vessels had gathered under its gaudy banners. "Halil is waiting on the boat," Shafiq said, suddenly nervous.

"The boat? I thought I was choosing the boat?"

"Halil has found something he thinks is suitable. It might be best if you agreed with him." Shafiq was palpably anxious. Clearly Halil, whoever he was, had the power of life and death and Shafiq was trying to impress that fact on me.

I was determined not to be impressed. "Halil is an expert on crossing the Atlantic?" I asked sarcastically.

"He is an expert on whatever he chooses to be," Shafiq squashed me. "So come."

We walked past the security men and down one of the long floating pontoons. Shafiq was so apprehensive that he scarcely spared a glance for the sun-tanned women in the cockpits of the moored boats. Instead he led me towards the pontoon's far end where a handsome sloop was moored. "That's the boat!" Shafiq had paused to light a cigarette. "You like her?"

"How can I tell?" I said irritably, yet in truth I did like the white-hulled *Corsaire*. The name was painted across the swimming platform of her sugar-scoop stern above her hailing port, Port Vendres, which was the French Mediterranean harbour nearest to the Spanish frontier. *Corsaire* looked a handsome boat, expensive and well equipped, effortlessly dominating the smaller and scruffier yachts further down the pontoon. She was not the product of any boatyard I knew, making me suspect that she had been custom designed and specially built for a wealthy owner who had his own particular ideas of what made a good cruising boat. This man had wanted a fractional rig, a centre cockpit, and a long low freeboard on a boat some forty-four feet long. The design, I grudgingly admitted to myself, did not look like a bad choice for a transatlantic voyage. So long as she was in good condition.

"Why is she for sale?" I asked Shafiq.

"Her owner left her here last winter. Tunisia's winter rates are cheaper, you understand, than in France? But he's since fallen ill and he needs to sell her." Shafiq raised a hand in greeting to the two young men who sat in *Corsaire*'s cockpit beneath a white cotton awning that had been rigged over her boom. He spoke to them in Arabic, gesturing at me, and they grunted back brief replies. I had seen such men before: thugs plucked from the Palestinian refugee camps, trained to kill, then given guns, girls and the licence to strut like heroes among their exiled people.

"Is one of them Halil?" I muttered.

"They're his bodyguard." Shafiq replied in a low voice, then smiled obsequiously as the two young men gestured us to climb aboard. Then, while one stood guard, the other ran quick hands across our bodies to make certain neither of us was armed. If any of the Western yacht crews saw the intrusive body search, they ignored it, for Tunisia, despite its Western trappings, was still a Muslim and Arab country and a man did well to leave its customs and barbarities unremarked. One of the bodyguards relieved me of my sea-bag, then pointed me towards the main companionway. "Be respectful, Paul!" Shafiq hissed at me. "Please!"

I ducked down the steep stairs. To my right was the chart table and instrument array, to my left the galley, while ahead was the spacious saloon with its comfortable sofas and fiddled shelves. The saloon seemed very dark after the bright sunlight, but I could just see a young man sprawled on the furthest sofa. At first glance he looked no more prepossessing than the two brutes in the cockpit, and I assumed he must be a third bodyguard protecting his master who would be in the forward sleeping cabin, but then the young man took off his sunglasses and leaned his elbows on the saloon table.

"I am Halil."

"I'm Shanahan."

"Sit." It was a command rather than an invitation. Behind us the washboards were slammed into place and the hatch slid shut, imprisoning me in the *Corsaire*'s belly with the man called Halil. It was stuffy and humid in the boat, and something in the closed-up hull reeked of decay.

I sat on the starboard settle. My eyes were slowly adjusting to the gloom, yet I could still see nothing noteworthy about the man who raised such fears in Shafiq. Halil looked to be in his middle thirties and had a dark-skinned, unremarkable face. His black hair was thick and brushed straight back, and his only idiosyncrasy was a thin moustache like a 1940s bandleader. He was wearing a white shirt, no tie and a black suit. He looked strongly built, like a peasant, while his left hand, the only one visible, had short square fingers. A burning cigarette rested in an ashtray on the table and beside it was a packet of Camels and an expensive gold lighter. "The owner wants 650,000 French francs for this boat," Halil said unceremoniously. "Is that a fair price?"

"If she's in good condition," I said, "she's a bargain."

"She is frivolous." Halil brought his right hand into view to lift the cigarette. He sucked deep on the smoke, then restored the cigarette to the ashtray. His right hand, I noticed, had been shaking so that the cigarette smoke trembled.

"Frivolous?" I asked.

The dark eyes flicked towards me and I began to understand Shafiq's nervousness, for there was something almost reptilian in the blankness of this man's eyes. "Boats, Shanahan," he lectured me, "should serve noble purposes. They can be used to bring fish from the sea, or to carry goods, or to be gun platforms for fighting, but only a frivolous people would build boats for pleasure." He spoke English in a deep-toned voice that invested his words with authority. "You think such a frivolous boat is worth 650,000 francs?"

"I think she's worth more."

"I shall offer 600,000," he said flatly. But why was he making the offer, I wondered, and not the Provisional IRA? Brendan Flynn had insisted that the Irish were responsible for transferring the gold, yet this dark-voiced man was quibbling over *Corsaire*'s price as though it would come from his budget and not the IRA's.

"You'd best make no offer till I've inspected the boat," I told him, "and I'll want her hauled out of the water so I can see her hull."

I could have been speaking to the wind for all the notice Halil took of me. "She has already been inspected," he said, "and declared fit for your journey. She is thirteen and a half metres long, four and a quarter metres wide, and has an underwater depth of one and three-quarter metres. Her keel contains 3,500 kilos of lead. What more do you need to know?"

"A lot," I said, noting how heavily *Corsaire* was ballasted, which suggested her builder had been a cautious man.

"There is no time to be particular." Halil spoke very softly, but there was an unmistakable menace in his voice. I wanted to argue with him, but felt curiously inhibited by a sense that any opposition to this man could provoke an instant and overwhelming physical counterattack. He seemed so utterly sure of himself, so much so that, even though his vocabulary had proved he knew nothing of boats, he nevertheless had spoken of *Corsaire*'s sea-going qualities as though his opinion was final. Yet his next question showed how much he still needed my expertise. "How long will it take you to cross the Atlantic with her?"

"Leaving from here?"

He paused, as if unwilling to admit anything. "From near here."

"Going where?"

Again the pause. "She will go to Miami." Where, I thought, her delivery skipper would be murdered; one more anonymous body which would be ascribed to the drug trade's carnage.

"When will the voyage be made?" I asked.

"That does not matter," Halil said disparagingly, though in fact it mattered like hell. Any Atlantic passage undertaken before the trade winds had established themselves would take much longer than if I waited till the new year, but I

33

sensed this man was not amenable to detail and so I made a crude guess.

"Three months."

"That long?" He sounded horrified and, when I did not modify the answer, he frowned. "Why not use the engine? Can't you put extra fuel on board and motor across?"

"A boat like this one will only go as fast as her waterline allows." Again I spared him the detail, and instead offered him a helpful suggestion. "Why not buy a big motor-yacht? One of those will cross much faster."

He made no reply, but just lifted the cigarette to his lips and this time I saw that the fingers of his right hand seemed crooked, as though the hand had been injured and never healed properly. The hand shook, so much so that he had difficulty in putting the cigarette between his lips. Water slapped at *Corsaire*'s hull and reflected the sunlight up through the portholes to make a rippling pattern on the saloon's ceiling. I was soaked with sweat, though Halil seemed immune to the close humidity inside the boat. He lowered the trembling cigarette. I thought he was considering my suggestion of using a motor-yacht to transport the gold, but instead he suddenly changed the subject, asking me whether I believed America would fight to liberate Kuwait. It seemed an odd question in the context, but I nodded and said I was sure America would fight.

"I hope so," Halil said, "I hope so." He spoke softly, but I sensed how badly this man wanted to see a great Arab victory in the desert. Was that why he had asked me the question, simply to satisfy his curiosity? Or was his query somehow related to this boat, and to my recruitment, and to a Stinger missile in a Miami warehouse? Those were questions I dared not ask. The truth of this operation, if it ever emerged at all, would appear in grudging increments.

Halil was still worrying that America would not give the Iraqi army its chance of immortal glory for he suddenly took a folded sheet of newsprint from his suit pocket. "Your politicians are already trying to escape the horrors of defeat," he said. "Look for yourself!" He pushed the scrap of newspaper across the saloon table. It was a recent front page story from *The New York Times* which told how House Representative Thomas O'Shaughnessy the Third had introduced a bill to Congress which, if it passed, would forbid the employment of American military forces in the Gulf for one whole year. O'Shaughnessy was quoted as wanting to give economic sanctions a chance to work before force was used. "You see!" Halil's voice was mocking. "Even your legislators want peace. They have no courage, Shanahan."

I shook my head. "You know what they call O'Shaughnessy in Boston? They call him Tommy the Turd. They say he's too dumb to succeed, but too rich to fail. He's a clown, Halil. He's in Congress because his daddy is rich."

Thomas O'Shaughnessy the Third was less than thirty years old, yet he was already serving his second term in Congress. Michael Herlihy was one of O'Shaughnessy's staff, helping the Congressman cultivate the IRA sympathisers in his Boston constituency. I suspected Michael had been behind one of Tommy's early crusades which demanded that the British government treat IRA prisoners according to the Geneva Convention. The campaign had collapsed in ridicule when it was pointed out that the Geneva Convention permitted combatant governments to execute enemy soldiers captured out of uniform, which meant Tommy's bill would have given American sanction for the Brits to slaughter every IRA man they took prisoner, but the proposal had never been seriously meant, only a proof to his constituents that Tommy's heart was in the right place, even if his brain was lost somewhere in outer space.

I offered the cutting back to Halil. "Congressmen like O'Shaughnessy will make a lot of feeble noises, but the

American public will listen to the President and, if Saddam Hussein stays in Kuwait, you'll get your war."

"May God prove you right," Halil said, "because I want to see the bodies of the American army feeding the desert jackals for years to come. In the sands of Kuwait, Shanahan, we shall see the humbling of America and the glory of Islam."

I said nothing; just held the cutting across the table until Halil leaned forward for it. He reached with his good left hand and, as he did, I suddenly knew exactly who this man was and why Shafiq was so terrified of him, and I felt the same terror, because this man, this unremarkable man, this ignorant stubborn man, this hater of America and self-proclaimed expert on boats, was wearing a woman's Blancpain wristwatch.

He was il Hayaween.

The Blancpain watch was an expensive timepiece enshrined in a miraculously thin case of gold and platinum. Except for its small size the watch did not appear particularly feminine; instead it looked what it was: a delicate and exquisitely elegant wristwatch. It was also a very expensive wristwatch. I knew, for I had bought it myself.

I had bought it five years before in Vienna where Shafiq had met me in the café of the Sacher Hotel. It had been an early spring afternoon and Shafiq was lingering over a *sachertorte* until it was time for him to leave for the airport. We were probably talking about Shafiq's favourite subject, women, when he had suddenly dropped his fork and cursed in Arabic. Then he switched to panicked French. "I am supposed to buy a gift! Oh God, I forgot. Paul, help me, please!" He had gone quite pale.

There had followed a desperate few hours as we searched Vienna for a jeweller who might stock Blancpain watches. I had derided Shafiq's urgency until he explained that it was the legendary il Hayaween who had demanded the watch, and Colonel Qaddafi himself who wanted to be the watch's giver, and then I understood just what the price of failure might entail for Shafiq. Yet our search seemed hopeless. Blancpains were not like other watches, but were genuine old-fashioned hand-made Swiss watches, powered by clockwork and without a scrap of contaminating quartz or battery acid, and such rare timepieces needed to be specially ordered. The shops began to close and Shafiq was nearing despair until, in one of the little streets close to St Stephen's Cathedral, we found a single specimen of a Blancpain watch. It was a rare specimen, it was expensive and it was beautiful, but it was also a woman's watch. "Do you think he'll know?" Shafiq asked me nervously.

"It doesn't look especially feminine," I said, "just a bit on the small side."

"Oh, dear sweet Christ!" Shafiq liked to use Christian blasphemies, which he thought were more sophisticated than Islamic imprecations. "If it's the wrong watch, Paul, he'll kill me!"

"And if you take him no watch at all?"

"Then Qaddafi will cut off my balls!"

"We'll take the watch," I had told the shopkeeper, and proffered him my credit card.

Now I had seen that same watch on Halil's wrist, and I knew who he was : il Hayaween. Not that il Hayaween was his real name, any more than Halil was, or even Daoud Malif, which was the name usually ascribed to him by the Western press when they did not use the nickname. Il Hayaween was an Arabic insult meaning 'the animal' and its first syllable was pronounced as an explosive breath, but no one would dare explode the word into Halil's face for, in all the shadowy world of terror, he was reckoned the most famous and the most lethal and the most daring of all the deadly men who had ever graduated from the refugee camps of the Palestinian exiles. In the pantheon of death il Hayaween was the Godhead, a ruthless killer who gave hope to his dispossessed people. In the gutters of Gaza and the ghettos of Hebron he was the leveller, the man who frightened the Israelis and terrified the Americans. Children in refugee camps learned the tales of il Hayaween's fame; how he had shot the Israeli Ambassador in a tea garden in Geneva, how he had bombed American soldiers in a Frankfurt night club, how he had ambushed an Israeli schoolbus and slaughtered its occupants, and how he had freed Palestinian prisoners from the jails of Oman. Whenever a misfortune struck an enemy of Palestine, he was reputed to be its author; thus when the jumbo jet fell from the flaming skies over Scotland the Palestinians chuckled and said that he had been at work again. Some Western journalists doubted his very existence, postulating that anyone as omnipotent as il Hayaween had to be a mythical figure constructed from the lusts of a frustrated people, but he lived all right, and I was talking to him in the saloon of a French yacht in Monastir's marina.

Where I was not thinking straight; not yet. Terrorists live in a skewed world. Their view is dominated and overshadowed by the cause, and every single thing that moves or creeps or swarms on earth is seen in its relation to the cause, and nothing is too far away or too trivial or too innocent to escape the cause. Thus, to a man like il Hayaween, a game of baseball is not an irrelevant pastime, but evidence that the American public does not care about the monstrous crime committed against the Palestinian people; worse, it is evidence that the American people deliberately do not want to consider that crime, preferring to watch a game of bat and ball. Therefore a scheme to kill baseball spectators would be a justifiable act because it could jolt the rest of America into an understanding of the truth. Terrorists believe they have been vouchsafed a unique glimpse of truth, and everything in the world is seen through the distorting lenses of that revelation.

So perhaps, in such a skewed world, paying for weapons with a boatload of gold makes sense.

And risking the gold by sailing the boat across the Atlantic makes sense.

And allowing a Palestinian terrorist to choose the sailboat makes sense.

And involving the Palestinian's most notorious killer in the purchase of Stinger missiles destined for Northern Ireland makes sense.

Or maybe not.

Halil pushed the folded newspaper cutting into his pocket. The cigarette had gone out, so now he lit another before staring into my eyes again. "Shanahan," he said with a tinge of distaste. "You moved to Ireland when you were twenty-seven. Is that right?"

"Yes."

"You lived in Dublin for one year and in Belfast for two."

"Yes."

"You joined the Provisional IRA?"

"That was why I went to Ireland."

"And the Provisional IRA asked you to live on mainland Europe?"

"Because it would be easier to liaise with foreign groups from mainland Europe than from Ireland."

"Yet six years later they ceased to use you for such liaison. Why?"

I understood that this man already knew the answers and that the catechism was not for Halil's information, but to make me feel uncomfortable. "Because of a woman," I told him.

"Roisin Donovan." He let the name hang in the stifling air. "An American agent."

"So they say," I said very neutrally.

"Do you believe she was CIA?"

I shook my head. "No."

"Why not?"

"Because I assume the CIA choose their operatives more carefully. Roisin was impulsive and angry. She had a hair-trigger temper. She was not a person you would choose to keep secrets."

"And you?" Halil asked.

I laughed. "No government would trust me to keep a secret. I'm a rogue. Civil servants choose people like themselves; dull and predictable and safe."

Halil raised the trembling cigarette. His hand quivered as he inhaled the comforting smoke and again as he rested the cigarette. "But these agents she spoke of, they were different. They were not predictable."

I said nothing.

He watched me. I could hear the halyards beating on the metal mast, I could even hear the slight noise of the chronometer's second hand ticking away above the chart table behind me.

"These agents" – Halil broke the long silence – "would be sent from America and would have no ties to home. They would stay away for years, never talking to their headquarters, never reporting to an embassy, never behaving like an agent, but just watching and listening until, one day, they would disappear." He made an abrupt gesture with his good hand. "They would go home with all their secrets and never be seen again."

"That was Roisin's fantasy," I said.

"Fantasy?" He made the word sinister.

"She made things up. She was good at it."

"She accused you of being such an agent . . ." He paused, searching for a definition. "An agent who does not exist," he finally said.

"I told you, she made it up." Roisin had indeed accused me of being one of the secret secret agents. It had been a clever and compelling idea. She claimed that the CIA had sent agents abroad who had no links with home. There would be no threads leading back to America, no footprints,

40

no codenames even, no apron strings. They were one-shot agents, untraceable, secret, the agents who did not exist.

"She made it up," I said again. "She made the whole thing up."

Halil watched me, judging me. I could understand the terror that such a concept would hold for a terrorist. Terrorism works because it breaks the rules, but when the authorities break the rules it turns the terror back on the terrorists. When the British shot the three IRA members in Gibraltar a shudder went through the whole movement because the Brits were not supposed to shoot first and ask questions later, they were supposed to use due process, to make arrests and offer court-appointed defence lawyers. But instead the Brits had acted like terrorists and it scared the IRA, just as il Hayaween was scared that there might be traitorous members of his organisations who could never be caught because they would never make contact with their real employers. The agents that did not exist would behave like terrorists, think like terrorists, look like, smell like, be like terrorists, until the fatal day when they simply vanished and took all their secrets home with them.

Now il Hayaween worried at that old accusation. "Your woman claimed the CIA had infiltrated a long-term agent into the Provisional IRA with the specific intent of exploring the IRA's links with other terrorist groups." He paused. "That could be you."

"She was desperate. She was ready to accuse anyone of anything. She wanted to blind her own accusers with a smokescreen. And how the hell would she know these things anyway?" I saw that question make an impression on Halil, so I pressed it harder. "You think the CIA told her about the agents who don't exist? You think maybe she read it in *Newsweek*?"

"Maybe you told her in bed."

I laughed. There was nothing to say to that.

He considered my laughter for a few heartbeats. It was

not wise to laugh at Halil because he was a man whose pride was easily hurt, and a man who repaid hurt with death, but this time he let it pass. "She blamed you for the man's betrayal."

That was an easy accusation to rebut. "I didn't know where Seamus Geoghegan was, so I couldn't have betrayed him. I was in the Lebanon when it happened, and he was captured in Belfast." Seamus was the Provisional IRA's star, the il Hayaween of Ireland, and Roisin had given him to the British. Or so the Brits had said, and that accusation had finished Roisin. Her response had been to blame me, but she was the one who died.

Yet still her accusation echoed down the years. These men needed me, or rather they needed my sailing skills, yet still they worried that I might not be what I seemed. I tried to reassure Halil. "I've held my secrets for four years, even though I had no prospect of being fully trusted again, so surely, if I was one of those CIA agents, I would have given up and gone home long ago?"

"So the girl was lying?" Halil wanted to believe my denials. Not that I would have been allowed within ten miles of him if he seriously believed the old story, but he wanted to make sure.

"Roisin saw plots everywhere. She was also a very destructive woman, and that was why she betrayed Seamus Geoghegan."

He frowned. "I don't understand."

Dear God, I thought, but now I had to try and explain psychology to a terrorist? "Seamus is frightened of women. He's the bravest man ever born in Ireland, but he doesn't have the courage to ask a girl for a dance because he thinks all women are perfect. He thinks all women are the Virgin Mary. I suspect Roisin tried to seduce Seamus, failed, and so she punished him." I could think of no other explanation. Seamus had been one of my closest friends – and perhaps still was, though it had been four years since I had last seen him. He was now in America, a fugitive from British vengeance. He had been betrayed, arrested, tried and sentenced, but a year later, in a brilliantly staged IRA coup, he had escaped from the Long Kesh prison camp. By then Roisin was dead, for her betrayal of Seamus had earned her a bullet in the skull.

"You saw her die?" Halil asked.

"Yes." She had died in the Lebanon where she had been attending the Hasbaiya terrorist training camp. It had been Roisin's keenest ambition to have the IRA send her on that course, and her eagerness had been transmuted by suspicion into an accusation that she planned to betray Hasbaiya as well as Seamus. Thus, as a favour to their Irish allies as well as to themselves, the Palestinians had arranged her execution.

"You didn't try to stop the killing?" Halil asked me.

"Why should I have done?" I even managed a small callous laugh.

"Because you loved her."

"But she betrayed my friend," I said, and I saw, in the sudden poisonous recurrence of memory, the split second when the vivid blood had spurted from Roisin's punctured skull to splash among the yellow stones. I had been wearing a red-and-white checked *keffiyeh* which I had wrapped about my face because the hot wind was blowing gusts of powdery sand off the hill's crest. The *keffiyeh* had prevented Roisin from recognising me, a small mercy. For a few moments, as the flies had gathered thick on the bloody margin of her death wound, I had suspected that I too was about to be shot for the heinous crime of being an American, but instead I had been curtly ordered to bury her. Afterwards the Palestinians had questioned me about Roisin, trying to determine how much she had known and how much she might have betrayed to her masters in Washington. I had given them what reassurances I could, and then, shriven of her accusations but still not wholly trusted, I was cast into the outer darkness and given nothing but trifling jobs.

Till now, when it was Halil's turn to assay my guilt or innocence in the shadowy scales of an old suspicion and, as he stared at me, I wondered once again why a man of his reputation was caught up in such a small matter as the six occupied counties of Northern Ireland. The death of a few Brits in that wild damp island could hardly count for much in il Hayaween's wider world, and certainly not at a time when the Arab world had found a new champion to flaunt Islam's banner in the face of the hated Americans.

And perhaps Halil sensed his interest was raising an unhealthy curiosity in me for he suddenly waved a dismissive hand. "Look at the boat," he said off-handedly, "and tell me your opinion." It seemed my suggestion of using a powerboat had not met his approval and so, under the silent gaze of Shafiq, Halil and his two bodyguards, I clambered about *Corsaire*. I did not have nearly enough time to make a proper survey, but I decided she was a handy craft, well made and well maintained. Her mainsail was furled inside her aluminium mast, while her vast genoa was stored below to keep it from the ravages of sunlight. Her hull was fibreglass and her deck was teak. A sturdy inflatable dinghy was folded away in an aft locker, together with an electric-powered pump to inflate it. She was a sensibly designed boat, and the only feature I disliked was her engine which, though capable enough at sixty horsepower, was fuelled by gasoline, but at least the motor banged into healthy life as soon as I connected the batteries and turned the ignition key.

I poked and pried through the accommodations below. Many of the French owner's belongings were still aboard; thus in the aft cabin I discovered a sweater, a half-bottle of brandy hidden behind the pilot books, a copy of *Playboy*, two tins of sardines, a can of sugar, a sleeping bag, the top half of a bikini and a broken pair of sunglasses. I lifted the main cabin sole to find the bilge filled with flexible water tanks between which was the decaying body of a rat; clearly the source of the boat's foul stench. Rat poison lay in white chunks on top of the shiny keel-bolts. I lifted the stinking remains of the rat and, to Shafiq's shuddering disgust, carried it topside where I chucked it into the harbour.

"You like the boat?" Halil asked me.

"I'd prefer a diesel engine."

"Why?"

"Gasoline fumes explode. Diesel is safer. But she'll do." The engine compartment was well ventilated and equipped with an automatic fire-extinguisher slaved to a gas-alarm so that, even in the unlikely event of a fuel-fire, *Corsaire* would probably survive. "She's not a bad boat." I spoke unfairly for she was better than that; she was an elegant, nicely built craft and, judging from her broad beam and deep cabin, she would probably prove a stable sea boat. She had clearly been equipped for long voyages because she had a single sideband radio mounted with the expensive instruments above her chart table.

"You can take her to America?" Halil asked me. He was sitting in the centre cockpit, close to the big destroyer wheel.

"Sure," I said cheerfully, "as long as she's prepared properly."

"Meaning what?" Halil was suspicious.

"For a start I need to get her out of the water and have her hull scrubbed down. She'll want a couple of layers of good anti-fouling paint. Then she's got to be equipped and stocked for a three-month voyage. I'm told there are two Irish lads going with me, so I'll need food for them and –"

"Make a list," Halil interrupted me.

"She needs a liferaft, charts . . ."

"Make a list," he said impatiently.

"And there's paperwork!" I warned him. "I'll need a bill of sale, a Tunisian clearance permit, insurance papers –"

"Make a list!" he snapped at me again.

45

Shafiq laid a tremulous hand on my arm. "Paul. It might be wisest if you just made the list? And we shall send for you when the boat is ready."

"Why can't I prepare the boat?" I asked. "I'm sailing it!"

"We shall prepare it," Halil answered, flat and unyielding. "Make a list, Mr Shanahan."

So that night I slept on board *Corsaire* and next morning made the list. It was a huge one, encompassing not just the victuals needed to carry three men across the Atlantic, but also the safety equipment and chandlery that would complete *Corsaire*'s inventory. Halil came at sunset and glanced through my handwritten pages. Most of the items were obvious: food, water, fuel, sleeping bags and navigational equipment; but some of the items made him frown. "Glassfibre mats? Resin? White paint?"

"That's how I hide the gold. By making a false floor under the cabin sole."

"Water tanks? Three-inch flexible piping?"

"We'll be hiding the gold where the present water tanks are placed, so we'll need new ones specially shaped for their areas. You don't want a customs agent wondering why we've got tube tanks in a square locker. And I need the tubing to run the water aft."

"Lead weights?"

"We're altering the boat's trim, so she'll need rebalancing." I had mixed the lies with the truth so easily, but then I was as practised at that game as il Hayaween, maybe more so. We all have our secrets, which is why trust is such a rare coin.

"It will all be ready," he promised carelessly.

I slept on board *Corsaire* one more night. Next morning I again offered to stay and help prepare the boat, but Halil was adamant that my presence in Monastir would arouse suspicion. It would be better, he insisted, if I waited at my home in Belgium. "I shall send you a message when the shipment is ready."

"How long will that be?"

"It might take a month to collect the coins. Maybe more, maybe less." He spoke carelessly, yet I remembered Brendan Flynn assuring me that the gold was already safely collected, and Michael Herlihy enjoining haste on me so that the deadly Stinger missiles could be deployed in Ireland as an Easter present for the Brits. Halil's offhand words only added more dissonance to the cacophony of strange noises that surrounded the Stingers.

Yet the nervous world was already full of discordant sounds. In Iraq and Saudi Arabia the sabres rattled, and on the West Bank and in Jordan the Palestinians ululated for their coming victory beneath the crescent flags of Islam, while in Northern Ireland the drab-green helicopters clattered through the wet grey skies. Everywhere, it seemed, the world was preparing for war. I flew home to Nieuwpoort.

Once back in Belgium I slept off the jetlag of two Atlantic flights, then told Hannah that I was closing down Nordsee Yacht Delivery, Services and Surveying.

"You're doing what?" Hannah asked.

"I'm tired of working, Hannah. I need a rest. I've decided I'll buy a sailboat and become a sea-gypsy."

"This is Sophie's doing, yes?" Hannah had never approved of Sophie and clearly believed my ex-lover had left me with addled brains. "But what of the Rotterdam surveys?" The Flemish mind could hardly encompass such irresponsibility. To abandon work for pleasure!

"I'll do the trawlers." They were two boats in Rotterdam that I had agreed to survey, and I needed such work while I was waiting for Halil's summons, but once that summons arrived I wanted to be ready to leave instantly.

"And what about that Mr Shafiq?" Hannah asked suspiciously.

"If you mean will I do his delivery job? Yes."

"You'll want me to send him an estimate? Put dates in the diary?" She waited with pencil poised, though really her efficiency was a mask for curiosity. Hannah was dying to know who Shafiq was, and why I had flown halfway round the world for him, but I could explain none of it to Hannah. That old world of IRA men and Libyans and midnight boat deliveries and gunfire in dry valleys was something she knew nothing about, and I intended to keep it that way. I also intended to make my fortune in these next few weeks, but that too must stay secret from her. I really was retiring, I really was going out of business, but I could not tell Hannah any of it.

Instead I gave her custody of the cat, closed down my bank accounts and began searching for my boat. I was looking for something very specific, a forty-four-foot boat which was registered in America but for sale in Europe, and to find her I faxed messages to yacht brokers in half a dozen countries and searched the small advertisements in the back pages of every European yachting magazine. I dared not specify American ownership for fear of prompting an unwelcome curiosity about my motives, but by asking the boat's hailing port I was able to weed out every nationality except the American vessels. I thought I had found what I wanted in the German port of Langeoog, but the boat, though owned by an American, lacked either a State Registration Certificate or any Coastguard documentation. "Does it really matter?" the broker, a stout Frisian, asked me. "Over here we're not so particular."

But I was being very particular, and so I went on searching until, just before Hallowe'en, a brokerage in Cork, Ireland, sent me details of an American cutter moored in Ardgroom Harbour off the Kenmare River.

I gave Hannah my apartment keys and made her promise to check the fax and the telephone answering machine each day, then I flew to Cork where I hired a car and drove west to Ardgroom Harbour. I borrowed a fisherman's dinghy and sculled myself out to the yacht.

She was called *Rebel Lady* and I almost dared not inspect her in case my first impression turned out to be false. My first impression was that she was perfect.

Rebel Lady was an American-built, American-owned, forty-four-foot cutter with a double-ended dark green hull that had been battered by rough seas and streaked with an ocean's dirt. She had clearly been designed for long voyages for a windmill generator whirled at her stern beside an elaborate self-steering vane. Gulls had streaked her with their droppings and weed grew at her black-painted bootline, yet, despite her shabby condition, she looked almost brand new. A pathetic hand-lettered 'For Sale' sign was attached to her starboard shrouds, while her hailing port, lettered like her defiant name in elegant black and gold, was Boston, Mass. *Rebel Lady* even had her Massachusetts registration number still painted on her bows, which meant that if her papers were intact then, for my purposes, she would be ideal.

I found her keys hidden in the locker where the broker had told me to look and let myself into her saloon, which smelt of stale air, sour clothes and salt. The boat appeared to have been momentarily deserted by her crew, for a kettle stood on the galley stove and two plastic plates had been abandoned in a sink half full of water. A sneaker lay on its side by the portside bunk while a sweatshirt advertising a restaurant in Scituate, Massachusetts, had been discarded on the cabin table. Arched across the coachroof's main beam was a row of handsome brass instruments: a chronometer still ticking obediently away to Greenwich Mean Time, a barometer, a thermometer, and a hygrometer for measuring the air's humidity as a gauge of the likelihood of fog. There was a depth sounder over the chart table, a VHF radio, a log, a wind-speed and direction indicator, a fluxgate compass and an expensive Loran receiver. Also above the chart table, among a row of books, I saw the traditional yellow jacket of *Eldridge's Tide and Pilot Book* and the sight gave me an almost overwhelming pang of homesickness. I could not resist taking down the well-thumbed book and turning the familiar pages with their tables of high and low water at Boston, the current table for the Cape Cod Canal and the charts of the tidal currents in Buzzards Bay and Nantucket Sound. The book reminded me that I had been away from my home waters for much too long; seven years too long.

I sat in the swivel chair of *Rebel Lady*'s chart table and thought how she would make a fine boat for Cape Cod; a good boat to sail down east to Maine or hard south to the Chesapeake Bay. I closed my eyes and heard the water splash and ripple down her flanks, and the sound somehow reminded me that this would also be a lonely boat. God damn Roisin, I thought, for all the dreams she had broken, because forty-four feet was too long a boat for a lonely man. All I needed was a small shoal-draft cat-boat to sail single-handed around Nantucket Sound, but *Rebel Lady* was the boat I would buy and *Rebel Lady* would one day be my retirement boat, my lonely home away from my Cape Cod house.

I called the broker from the public telephone of a bar in Ardgroom and learned that *Rebel Lady* belonged to an American doctor who, taking a summer's sabbatical, had sailed with his three sons to search for their family's Irish roots. Instead he had learned that the summer pastime of sailing in sun-drenched Boston Harbor did not easily translate into enduring a stinging force-nine gale in the mid-Atlantic. Seasick, shaking, terrified and with a broken wrist and a fractured rib, the good doctor had made his Irish landfall and sworn he would never again set foot on a small boat. He and his sons had flown home in the comfort of an Aer Lingus Boeing 747 and left the *Rebel Lady* swinging to a mooring in Ardgroom Harbour. "He'll take whatever you've a mind to give," the Cork broker told me with a refreshing honesty, "but it would be a criminal shame to give the man less than seventy-five thousand punt. She's a fine boat, is she not? But it's a pity she's green." He was lamenting her colour for, in Irish superstition, green was an unlucky colour for a boat.

I did not care about Irish superstition, only about American bureaucracy. "You're sure you've got all her papers?"

"As I said before, I've got every last one of them. They certainly like their paperwork in America, do they not? I've even got the original bill of sale, so I have. The boat's a mere two years old, and she's only ever had the one owner."

"What's the owner's name?"

"O'Neill. A Dr James O'Neill. A grand man is the doctor, but a better physician than a sailor, I should think." It was a delicate judgment, very Irish in its balancing of a criticism with a compliment.

"I'll be paying you cash," I said, "if that suits you."

"I think it might," he said cautiously. My God, of course it suited him. Tax evasion is Ireland's national sport and I had just given him a championship year. "Say seventy thousand?" I said, just to spoil it a little.

He paused for just a second, then accepted. "It's a bargain, Mr Stanley." I had given my name as Henry Stanley.

I drove back to the harbour where a sudden west wind was flicking whitecaps across the sheltered grey water and slanting a sharp rain off the ocean. I sculled myself back to *Rebel Lady*, chucked the pathetic 'For Sale' sign overboard and, using my rigging knife, prised away the manufacturer's plate from the side of her coachroof. I copied the hull identification number from her transom and the serial number from the engine, then, my oilskin drenched from the sudden cold rain, I drove back to Cork where, in a smoky bar, I treated the broker to a pint of stout and paid him seventy thousand Irish pounds for the boat. It was a steal, but undoubtedly Dr James O'Neill would be well pleased to be rid of the cause of so much of his discomfort. It was an old story; men bought boats as a fulfilment of their dreams, only to have a single ocean passage turn the dreams into nightmare. Atlantic islands like the Azores or the Canaries were notorious for the bargains their harbours offered; yachts abandoned after just one leg of a long-planned voyage.

The broker, who was doubtless on a generous commission, counted the pile of notes happily. "You've bought yourself a good vessel, Mr Stanley," he said as he forced the folded pile of banknotes into a jacket pocket, then he watched hopefully as I counted another stack of punt bills on to the table. "And what would they be for, Mr Stanley, if I might ask?"

"I'm paying you to look after her. I want the mast off her, and I'd like her brought ashore and scrubbed down.

Then cover her with tarpaulins. I'll send you word when I want her launched and rigged again, but it may not be till next summer."

"No problems there." The broker eyed the punt bills.

"And I want a new name painted on her stern," I said.

"Changing a boat's name?" He sipped his stout, then wiped the froth from his moustache with the back of his hand. "That means bad luck, Mr Stanley."

"Not where I come from." I pulled a beer mat towards me and wrote the new name in big block capitals on its margin. "*Roisin*," I said the name aloud, "and she needs a new hailing port, Stage Harbor. And no 'u' in harbor. You can do that? I want it in Gaelic script, black and gold."

"It shouldn't be a problem." He thumbed the edge of the punt bills. "But if there is a snag with the work, then how can I reach you?"

"That money's my guarantee that you won't have any snags."

"So it is, so it is." The notes vanished into a pocket.

As I left the bar I scorned myself as a sentimental fool for painting a dead girl's name on the backside of a green boat. I caught a glimpse of my bearded face in a hatstand's mirror in the hallway of the bar and, for a change, I did not look quickly away. Instead I frowned at the reflection as though I was looking at a stranger. I did not like what I saw, I never had. The face was hag-ridden, redolent of too much bad conscience. I remembered Seamus Geoghegan sitting in a car with me on some wet dawn; after a long silence, he had sighed and said that thinking never made a man happy. He was right, and mirrors made me think of myself, which was why I owned so few of them. It was better not to think, not to remember, and not to wonder what I had made of a life in forty years.

That night I phoned Namur in Belgium and left a message for an old friend called Teodor, and the following morning, with *Rebel Lady*'s papers safe in my sea-bag, I flew to

Barcelona. My business there took two days. I telephoned Hannah, as I had on every night of my trip, to discover if any summons had come from Tunisia, but there was no message. "Except that American girl is still trying to reach you," Hannah said.

"Kathleen Donovan? I've told you I don't want to meet her."

Hannah sniffed her disapproval. "So when will you be back?"

"Late tomorrow. Real late. I'll see you on Thursday."

Next morning I flew north to Brussels, collected my car from the long-term car park, then drove to Namur where Teodor was waiting for me. He needed to take photographs; one for the false Massachusetts driving licence and another, with different clothes and subtly different lighting, for the false American passport. Teodor was the finest counterfeiter in the Low Countries and had been supplying me with false papers for over ten years. He insisted he would only work for people he liked, which I took as a compliment. He was an old man now and, as he worked in his shirtsleeves under a bright magnifying lamp, I saw the concentration camp number tattooed on his forearm. He would talk about anything except that wartime experience, though once he had told me that he dreamed about the camp at least three times a week. "You're going on a journey, Paul?" he asked me now.

"Yes."

He reached for tweezers and a can of spray adhesive. "Why do I sense this is the last time I'll see you?"

"Because you're an emotional and maudlin old fool."

He chuckled, then held his breath as he sprayed a tiny jet of adhesive on to one of the photographs. "There's grey in your beard. You're growing old, Paul, like me. Ah, good!" He pressed the photograph into place. "You're going home, aren't you?"

"Am I?"

"You've had enough, Paul, I can tell. You're like an athlete facing his last and biggest race. You want to win, but you want to stop competing even more. Is it a woman?"

"Mine just left me. She went off with a rich married frog who promised to give her an apartment in Antibes."

"You need a woman, Paul. You're a very private man, but you can't be so different from the rest of us. What do you plan to do? Settle in America and learn to play golf?"

"I'm too young to play golf." That made him laugh. "Besides," I went on, "who says I'm retiring?"

"I do. I know these things." He bent close over his work. He had once told me that he had been a fine soccer player in his youth, but now Teodor had a withered right foot, a hump back, and a pencil drawing of his wife. She had died in Treblinka and all the photographs ever taken of her had been destroyed by the Germans. Teodor, years after the war, had gone to a police identikit artist and had patiently assembled a picture of his lovely Ruth which now hung framed above his work bench. "Of course she was not so pretty," he had confessed to me, "but I remember her as even more beautiful." Now he shot me a glance from under his thick white eyebrows. "You've been in Europe how long now? Almost ten years? Not many people last ten years, not in your kind of work."

"You don't know what kind of work I do, Teodor."

He laughed softly. "I have deduced you are not an accountant. Nor are you one of those bureaucratic shits who live in Brussels off the taxes I take care not to pay. And despite what this passport says, Paul, I do not think you are a doctor. No, you are a man who keeps secrets, and that can be a very tiring profession. Not that it's any of my business." He straightened up. "Now come here, I need Dr O'Neill's signature. Three times, and with different pens. I have even made you a Visa card as a parting gift, see?"

I peered at the card under Teodor's strong worklamp. "How the hell did you manage the hologram?" I asked in genuine admiration.

"Mere genius, Paul, mere genius. But it will all be for nothing unless you collect a few items to support the fiction. Buy some medical journals and send yourself a couple of letters addressed to Dr O'Neill." He held up a defensive hand. "I know! I know! I am teaching you to suck eggs. And let me give you this." He fumbled through a drawer to find a pasteboard card printed with the American telephone number of an Alcoholics Anonymous group. "That always helps a doctor's disguise, Paul. I use Alcoholics Anonymous for medical men and policemen, but if you were pretending to be a lawyer I would supply you with the business cards of massage parlours. These details count. Now, practise the signature before you sign. You're a doctor, remember, so you scribble, you don't write. Good. Again. Again. Better! Again." Teodor was a perfectionist. "I can sell you a real credit card that will be good for nine months?" he offered. "Its owner is in a French prison and will take fifty thousand francs?"

I left him two hours later with a whole new identity safe in my pocket, then, in a rainy darkness, I drove across country to Nieuwpoort. The autumn wind had gone into the north-east to bring the Low Countries a foretaste of winter. I drove fast, but even so it was almost midnight before I reached home and parked the Opel in the alleyway opposite my apartment house. When I switched off the engine I could hear the clatter of metal halyards beating on the masts of the yachts berthed in the South Basin. It was such a familiar sound, and one I would miss when I left Nieuwpoort. The wind gusted down the street, bringing the smell of sea and shellfish. I locked the car, ran across the road, and pushed open the apartment block's unlocked front door.

"Is that Mr Shanahan?"

"Oh, Jesus Christ!" I reeled back from the shadow which suddenly rose inside the dark hall. Someone was waiting for me, someone who knew my name, someone who spoke in

English, and I remembered my old training which had taught that, before making a kill, it was prudent to make the victim identify himself just to make certain it was the right person who was about to die.

"Mr Shanahan?" It was a girl's voice, American and unthreatening, which lack of menace did not mean she was not holding a silenced gun in the shadowed hallway.

"Who the hell are you?" I was crouched in the porch, holding my sea-bag as a shield to protect my chest from the half-expected bullet.

"I'm sorry. I didn't mean to frighten you. It's just that the light bulb was broken in here, so I had to wait in the dark."

"Who are you?" I straightened up, sensing I was not to be shot.

"Your secretary said you'd be back tonight. She's real nice. Gee, I'm sorry. I really am. It's just that I had to see you because I've got an Apex ticket and I can't afford the penalty to change it, so I have to fly back to the States tomorrow and this was my last chance. I didn't mean to scare you. I'm real sorry." The girl seemed to be more upset than I was. She had come to the doorway so that the streetlamp lit her face and I knew who she was, oh God, I knew who she was, and the venomous memories whipped into my consciousness. She looked so like Roisin, so achingly like the dead Roisin.

"Who are you?" I asked again.

"My name's Kathleen," she said, and thrust out a tentative hand as though to shake mine. "Kathleen Donovan." Even her voice was like her sister's, like enough to bring a mocking ghost to shadow the rainswept darkness. I did not shake her hand. "I just wanted to see you," she explained weakly, and took her hand back.

"What about?" I asked the question harshly for, though I knew the answer, I had to pretend otherwise. "Christ! Do you know what time it is?"

"It's late, I know. I'm sorry. It's just that . . ."

57

"You've got an Apex ticket." I finished the sentence, then pushed past her into the hallway. "If you want to talk to me, Miss, what did you say your name was?"

"Donovan. Kathleen Donovan."

"Miss Donovan. If you want to talk to me, then let's talk where it's warm."

I did not want to talk to her, but she looked so like Roisin that I could not say no. I wanted to probe the old wound. Christ, I thought, but why did it happen? How could a woman turn a man's blood to smoke and leave him forever miserable?

Kathleen Donovan followed me up the uncarpeted stairs and edged nervously into my apartment. She looked tentatively around, as if judging my soul from the bare furniture, scraped linoleum, and half-empty shelves. "Coffee?" I asked her. "Or something stronger?"

"Do you have decaffeinated?"

"No."

"Then just a glass of water, please."

I fetched her a glass of water and poured myself a whiskey. I took my time in the kitchen, for I needed to re-establish my equilibrium. God damn it! Why now, of all times?

I carried the two tumblers back to the living room where I gave her the water, put down my whiskey, then drew the curtains against the chill Belgian night. I lit the gas fire. "Sit down." I spoke more gruffly than I intended, but I did not want her to know how she was unsettling me. She took off her coat and folded it over the sofa's arm, then nervously perched herself on the sofa's edge. She looked to be in her late twenties and was dressed in a sober tweed suit, a high-necked blouse and a string of plain blue beads. She wore no other jewellery, and I remembered how Roisin had hated glittering baubles. Kathleen had the same dark red hair as Roisin and the same long jawline and the same hesitant expression that suggested she was perpetually puzzled by

58

the world. Indeed, Kathleen looked so horribly like her sister that it hurt just to be in the same room. "If you want me to make a marine survey," I told her carelessly, "then you're too late. I'm closing down the business."

"No." She shook her head vigorously. "I don't want to see you about boats." She hesitated. "Doesn't my name mean anything?"

"Donovan?" I shook my head. "I'm sorry, no. The only Donovan I ever knew was a priest in Fort Lauderdale, and the whiskey killed him twelve years ago."

She looked stricken, almost as though I had struck her hard about the face. "I had an older sister," she explained to me, then corrected her tense, "I *have* an older sister called Roisin. I think you knew her. In fact I'm sure you knew her."

Knew her? My God, but they were hardly the adequate words. The first moment I had ever seen Roisin was in a Dublin pub and I had known I would never be happy until I loved her, and when I loved her I suspected I would never be happy again. After she had left me a friend said there was such a woman for every man, but most men were lucky and never met their fate. But I had, and Roisin and I had loved in a sudden incandescent blaze of lust, until, just as suddenly, she had stalked away from me for another man. Later, months later, I had watched her die, and her ghost had haunted my life ever since. Now her younger sister was asking if I had ever known her. "I'm very sorry," I said calmly, "but I've never even heard of her. What did you say her name was? Rosheen? How do you spell it?"

Kathleen Donovan ignored my questions. Instead, for a few seconds, she just stared at me as she tried to gauge the innocence in my voice, then she tried to jog my memory. "She lived in Ireland for a while," she said, "in Belfast. Just off the Malone Road."

"She was a student?" I asked. Lots of students lived near the Malone Road.

"No, not really." Kathleen began searching through her handbag and I watched her, marvelling at the resemblance. Roisin had been thinner than Kathleen, and had harboured a pent-up energy that could be terrifying in its intensity, but the two sisters had the same Irish green eyes and the same pale, vulnerable skin, though Kathleen seemed much calmer, more at peace with herself. Her eyes seemed to hold wisdom where Roisin's had held nothing but an unpredictable wildness. Indeed, I suddenly thought with a pang of dread, Kathleen was just what I had hoped Roisin might become, and I uttered a silent prayer to a merciful God that he would keep me from falling in love. Especially now, for this was a time when I needed to be like Michael Herlihy, a sexless monk, devoted to the cause and to death; but I knew my weakness, and no one had exposed that weakness more ruthlessly than Roisin Donovan. "Here's a picture of her." Kathleen held a snapshot towards me.

I glanced down at the photograph, forced my gaze away and sipped whiskey. "I'm sorry," I tried to sound careless, "but I've never seen her."

"You lived in Belfast, didn't you?" Kathleen asked me.

"Yes, but that was ten years ago."

"In Malone Avenue?" she asked.

"Near enough," I said vaguely, "but so what? People were always coming and going in that area. It was a place for students, nurses, itinerants. I didn't live there long, but I do assure you I lived there alone." I forced myself to pick up the photograph. It showed a younger Roisin than I remembered, but the camera had perfectly caught the blazing intensity of her hunter's eyes. "Sorry," I said again, and tossed the picture down. I found I had finished my whiskey so poured myself another.

Kathleen momentarily closed her eyes as though what she was about to say was very difficult and needed all her concentration if she were to articulate it properly. "Mr Shanahan," she said at last, "I know it must be hard, because I know what Roisin was, is, and that means you can't tell me everything, but I want you to understand that our mother is dying and she wants to know if Roisin is alive or dead. That's all." She stared at me with her huge green eyes that were sheened with tears. "Is it so very much to ask?"

I swallowed whiskey. A car sped down the street outside, its tyres splashing on the wet tarmac. I was feeling foully uncomfortable and wishing that I had never given up smoking. "Tell me about your sister," I said, "and I'll see if anything jogs my memory." I knew I should dismiss this girl, that I should send her unhappy and dissatisfied into the rain, but another part of me, the insidious part, wanted to keep her here so that I could torture myself with this revenant of Roisin.

Kathleen bit her lip, took a breath, talked. "We grew up in Baltimore, but our parents were born in Ireland. In County Kerry. They emigrated in 1950. My father's a plasterer, a good one, but there wasn't work in Ireland." She hesitated, as if knowing that she was straying off the subject. "Mom and Dad never regretted moving to the States. They wanted to forget Ireland, really, but Roisin was obsessed by it. I mean, really obsessed. I don't know when it started, back in high school, I guess, but she was really mad at Mom and Dad for living in America. She wanted to be Irish, you see."

"I know the syndrome," I said.

"She learned Gaelic, she learned Irish history, and she learned Irish hatreds. Then she went to live in Ireland." Kathleen hesitated and frowned up at me. A tear showed at the corner of one eye. "You know all this, don't you?"

I shook my head. "I told you. I know nothing."

Kathleen began to cry very softly. She made no noise, the tears simply brimmed from her eyes and ran down her cheeks. She fished in her coat pocket, found a shred of tissue, and angrily cuffed the tears away. "I'm so tired," she said, "and I just want to know what happened to her. I want to know if she's alive."

I tried to sound sympathetic. "I wish I could help."

"You can help!" Kathleen insisted. "She mentioned you in her letters! She said you had a house on Cape Cod! She said you were a yachtsman!" She sniffed and wiped away her tears. "I'm sorry. I'm just tired."

"Paul Shanahan isn't such an unusual name," I said.

She dismissed that feeble evasion with an abrupt shake of her head. "I've spent three weeks in Ireland, talking to people who knew Roisin. They kept mentioning you. They said —" She checked.

"They said what?" I encouraged her.

"They said you might have had links with the IRA." She spoke defiantly, challenging me with her unlikely truth. "They said that's why Roisin wanted to be with you, because you were her introduction to the IRA."

"Me?" I sounded wonderfully astonished.

"And one person I spoke with," Kathleen pressed nobly on against my obduracy, "said you were in the IRA for sure. He said you were one of their best-kept secrets."

"Oh, Lord help us." I turned to pull the drapes aside and to stare down into the wet street. "The Irish do like their stories. They love to gossip, Miss Donovan, and they do it better than anyone in the world, but it's only in Dublin bars and bad novels that Americans play heroic roles in the IRA. I went to Ireland to learn about traditional boatbuilding skills, and I stayed there because I liked the country, but I moved on here because I couldn't make a living in Ireland." I let the drapes fall and turned back to her. "I'm a marine engineer and surveyor. I'm not in the IRA, I never was, and I never knew your sister."

Kathleen stared at me, her eyes huge, and I wanted to cross the room and hold her tight and tell her all the truth and beg her forgiveness for that truth, but instead I stayed where I was. I could see the struggle on her face, the struggle of belief and disbelief. On the one hand I had sounded so very convincing, while on the other she had a mass of evidence that contradicted me. "I heard another story," she said.

"Go on," I said carelessly, implying that all the stories in creation would not jog my memory.

"I heard a rumour that Roisin is dead. That she was executed for betraying the IRA. I spoke to a policeman in Dublin and he said he'd heard she was working for American intelligence and that she'd been sent to Ireland to discover who in America was sending guns to the IRA. He'd heard that she'd been shot in the head and buried in Ravensdale Forest."

I shrugged. "I'm sorry. None of it means a thing."

My denial had no effect. "The policeman told me it was Roisin who betrayed Seamus Geoghegan. You've heard of him, haven't you?"

"He's the fellow the British are trying to extradite from America, right?"

"He's a friend of yours," Kathleen accused me.

I laughed. "Let's be serious? I'm a boat surveyor!"

"I met Seamus Geoghegan's brother, Mr Shanahan, in Derry. He was the one who told me about you and the IRA, and that wasn't bar gossip. He told me his brother stayed in your apartment in Belfast once, and he said his brother met Roisin at your apartment. He told me!" The last three words were a protest at my obduracy.

I shook my head wearily. "I'm sorry," I said, "but I don't know Seamus Geoghegan and I've never met his brother and I don't know your sister, and I'm really sorry."

Kathleen dismissed my denials with an abrupt gesture. "Maybe it's all true, Mr Shanahan! Maybe she was in American intelligence and did betray Geoghegan! But does that make you a member of American intelligence too? Is that why you can't talk to me?" She paused, eyes bright, desperate for an answer. "For God's sake," she went on, "my mother's got a year to live! Maybe less! All she wants is to know the truth, that's all! To be certain. Do you know what it's like to grieve for a child, but not even to know if you need to grieve? Mom keeps thinking Roisin will come home, that she's alive somewhere. For the love of God, Mr Shanahan, I'm not a security risk! I just want to know, that's all! You don't even have to tell me anything! Just give me a nod, that's all!"

The gas fire hissed. Kathleen stared up at me. I took a deep breath. "I really can't help you," I said.

"Oh, you bastard!" Kathleen Donovan said tiredly.

"I think you should go," I said gently. "Can I drive you somewhere?"

"You can burn in hell." She snatched up her coat and stood. For a moment I thought she was going to spit at me, then she turned and walked away. The front door of the apartment banged as she stormed out and, a moment later, I heard her footsteps clatter away on the pavement outside.

Oh dear Christ. I sat on the sofa, leaned my head back and closed my eyes. Roisin, Roisin, Roisin. God damn it. I remembered her smile, her laughter, her moments of tenderness, but she was dead, and I was a bastard. I could have told Kathleen the truth, all the truth, but I had long schooled myself against the truth. The truth makes a man vulnerable. The truth betrays. Lies are a shield, a fog, a maze in which to lose the curious. I told myself Kathleen Donovan could have been a stooge for British Intelligence, or even for the Provisional IRA. Maybe Brendan Flynn had sent Kathleen to see if I would betray my membership of the IRA, thus marking myself as a security risk and not to be trusted with the Libyan gold. And if I had so betrayed myself then Brendan would never have dared leave me alive with my knowledge of a missile in a Miami warehouse, and soon a Provo hit squad would have come to Nieuwpoort to leave my bullet-ridden body floating in the River Yser.

So, I reassured myself, I had been right to tell Kathleen

nothing, because the first rule was to trust no one and the second rule was never to tell the truth, ever, for the truth is like gold. They were good rules, even if they did mean having to send a girl away in tears into a wet windy night, and even if it did mean drinking the rest of the bottle of Jameson to smear away the memory of Kathleen's hurt face, and even if it did mean adding another sin to the tally of rotten sins.

Oh dear sweet God, I thought, but let the memories go away.

I heard nothing from Tunisia in November. December came and in the streets of Nieuwpoort the Christmas lights struggled to shine through the winter rains. I lived frugally and wondered if the whole deal had collapsed. Perhaps the Cubans had found other buyers for the Stingers, or perhaps Halil had found another yachtsman to deliver *Corsaire* to Miami. When Shafiq had first contacted me everything about the Stinger deal had been urgent and exciting, while now the whole scheme had slowed to a crawl, if not to utter immobility. Perhaps, after all, this was proving to be just another operation gone sour in the planning, only to be abandoned. Most operations ended like that. They began with a rush of enthusiasm that was slowly eroded by reality, but I did not break security by contacting Dublin to find out. Instead I just waited patiently and hoped that I had not destroyed my business for nothing.

Kathleen Donovan did not try to contact me again. Some nights, lying alone in the cold apartment, I regretted not telling her the truth, but took solace from my suspicion that she had been sent to prise me into indiscretion. Maybe, I told myself, the British had sent her, and maybe she had not been Roisin's sister at all, but merely a lookalike recruited by the Brits. The British were ruthless bastards; too many IRA men had simply disappeared, vanished without trace from their homes on either side of the Irish border. I began to convince myself that British Intelligence, coming four years late on my cold trail, had sent the girl to trap me into indiscretion. And it had been a clever touch, I thought, to bring in Seamus Geoghegan's name. Did Seamus have a brother? He had never mentioned one, but even if he had, would such a brother say I was in the IRA? I told myself Kathleen Donovan's story stank like rotting fish, but then I would recall her stricken eyes and my conviction of her falsity would waver. There had been an innocence about her that rang very true, yet I told myself that in the world of secrets the false always rang true.

The winter nights drew ever longer and still I heard nothing from either Tunisia or Dublin. If Michael Herlihy had paid the deposit on the Stingers then it was looking like a lost cause, unless, of course, the Libyans had found another way to deliver the five million dollars. That seemed the likeliest answer; that common sense had afflicted everyone involved and persuaded them of the stupidity of committing five million dollars to a small boat in a wide sea.

I eked out my own cash. I still made a little money surveying boats, but the waiting and the inactivity were eating into my savings and, as Christmas neared, I began to think of selling *Rebel Lady*. I had bought her for a song and, if I fetched her from Ireland to the stronger market of mainland Europe, I might be able to make a pretty profit on her even in a recession.

Then, just before Christmas, I was woken in the middle of a cold night by the chatter of the fax machine. I walked naked to the living room, switched on the light, and saw the message. I was requested to make a survey of a cruising yacht presently laid up in Marseilles. Would I please send an estimate of my travel costs and a statement of my usual fees to M. Jean Piguet. That name was the key, the ciphered message which meant *Corsaire* was ready, and that the golden voyage would happen after all.

I felt a pulse of excitement. I had not felt that surge of adrenalin for a long time. It was the seductive kick of danger and the anticipation of risk. The time had come to vanish.

I did not sleep any more that night. Instead I packed my sea-bag with what few belongings I wanted to carry into my new life, then waited for the winter dawn. At nine o'clock I went to one of the fishing harbour cafés and used its public phone to call Barcelona, then I made a long call to Brussels. Afterwards, the dice thus irrevocably thrown, I threw my sea-bag into the back of the car and, just as Teodor had suspected, left Belgium for good.

Shafiq was again waiting for me at the Skanes-Monastir Airport. He was jittery with excitement, craning to catch a glimpse of me over the heads of the arriving passengers. "Did you think we had forgotten you?" he asked archly.

"I thought you'd found someone else to do the job," I said.

"Paul! Paul!" he chided me. "It just took longer than we expected to assemble the gold, nothing else. Is that all your luggage?"

"I don't need more."

"One small bag to cross the world?" Shafiq laughed and led me out of the terminal. It was a brisk day with a north wind and a sky of high scudding clouds and Shafiq was in a mood to match the weather; capricious and nervous. He was doubtless relieved that the operation was at last beginning, but that beginning only increased his terror that something could now go wrong. "So what did you make of Halil, Paul?"

"A dangerous man." I spoke with a careful neutrality.

"A dangerous man! Merely dangerous!" Shafiq threw my sea-bag and heavy yellow oilskin jacket into the boot of his hired car. "Is a tiger dangerous? Does a hawk kill? Ha! Dangerous." He mocked the inadequacy of my description, then accelerated into the airport traffic. "He is a great man," Shafiq said solemnly. "One day they will name a city for him in Palestine, a great city! Built on the bones of the Jews."

"What happened to his right hand?"

Shafiq mimed a pistol being fired. "He was shot in the wrist. The bullet severed some nerves and tendons. He can still use the hand, but clumsily. It happened in Lebanon, near the Israeli border."

"Thank Allah it was his right wrist" – I spoke in a very matter-of-fact voice – "and not his left. It would have been a shame to have lost that pretty watch."

Shafiq glanced at me, smiled, then roared with laughter. "That's good, Paul! Very good! You are not so blind, eh? But you will say nothing. You understand me? Nothing! Halil has a long reach and a lethal grip." I noted how Shafiq still used the pseudonym 'Halil' rather than the nickname il Hayaween. Both of us might know Halil's identity, but it would be risking fate to admit it openly, even to each other.

"Am I going to meet Halil today?" I asked.

"Not here, not in Monastir, but he will bring you the gold."

"Where?"

"At Ghar-el-Melh. It's on the north coast and will be safer, much safer. Not so many eyes watching."

"Do I pick up my crew there?"

"No. They came yesterday." Shafiq sighed and I suspected he was glad that I was taking Brendan's two gunmen off his hands.

"What are they like?" I asked.

"They are young," he said grandly, and as if that quality forgave all their sins. "It is a pity," he went on, "that we could not have sent Palestinians to help you, but such men would surely have raised suspicions on their arrival in America."

"I think that's a fair statement," I said drily.

"So these two will suffice." It was a grudging judgment.

"Have you met them before?"

"Never." He looked more lugubrious than ever, then gave a brief shake of his head. "It isn't like the old days, Paul. I don't deal with Ireland any more, and I hear nothing from anyone. These days I just work at the Centre and run a few errands. I go to Marseilles sometimes, but never further north." His mood had plunged as he made the sad confession and I supposed that poor Shafiq must have been tarred by Roisin's accusation that I was one of the deep penetration CIA agents; the ones whom Halil had described as 'the agents who did not exist'. What a clever story she had told! If an agent did not exist then he could not be detected, which meant anyone could be an agent, even Shafiq, so poor Shafiq had been relegated to the minor leagues, sowing discontent among French Arab immigrants by carrying messages to mad-eyed clerics in backstreet Marseilles mosques. Then, when it was decided that I was the perfect man to sail Halil's gold across the Atlantic, Shafiq must have been reactivated as the person most likely to recruit me. No wonder he had seemed so pleased to be in Paris; it must have been Shafiq's first visit to his dream city in four years. "Just errands," he now added in a self-pitying echo.

"But you must be important, Shafiq," I sounded him out, "if they trust you to work with Halil."

"Ah, yes! They trust me." He tried to sound confident, but failed. He shrugged and lit a cigarette. "Things change, Paul. Things always change."

"What I don't understand," I said, looking away from Shafiq into the monotonous flicker of an orange grove, "is why a man as important as Halil, and a man as experienced as yourself," I added that sliver of flattery to prime him, "should be dealing with a matter as trivial as Ireland. Nothing that Brendan Flynn is doing will bring the destruction of Israel one day nearer, yet your movement is devoting its best men to his ambitions! It is all so" – I paused as though searching for the exact word, then launched it like a killer blow – "so unsophisticated, Shafiq!"

I had known the accusation would goad Shafiq who, sure enough, shook his head angrily. "What we are doing is just one tiny part of a massive operation, Paul. You see only a, what do you call it? A cog! You only see a cog while all around us, unseen, great millwheels are turning." He was pleased with the metaphor and embellished it by taking both hands off the wheel and churning them vigorously in the air. "Halil is the planning officer for the world-wide punishment of Iraq's enemies! And the enemies of Iraq are the enemies of Palestine! And wherever those enemies might live, Halil's work will be seen! That is not unsophisticated!"

I stared at him in silence, knowing I dared not ask the obvious questions, but would have to glean what scraps I could. "Stingers? In Ireland?"

Shafiq waved a dismissive hand. "Everyone knows that Britain does America's bidding, and that America is Israel's master, so Britain must be made to suffer. Your anti-aircraft missiles will hurt Britain, but they are only a small part of the pain the West will feel as a punishment for opposing the legitimate demands of Iraq and the Palestinians." He had become quite angry as he trotted out the well-worn propaganda.

"Oh, I see now!" I said, in a tone that suggested I had been culpably obtuse. "We had to wait for the gold to arrive from Iraq! What is it? Gold captured in Kuwait?"

Shafiq waved a hand in a gesture that I could translate as an affirmative, but which also suggested he knew he had revealed too much.

"What I still don't understand" – I was pushing my luck to see if I could tempt Shafiq into further indiscretion – "is why Halil sends money by boat when he might just as well send it electronically."

"Ha!" Shafiq accompanied the scornful exhalation by once more throwing his hands into the air. The Peugeot wandered towards the oncoming traffic, provoking a chorus of horns. "Everyone knows," Shafiq said when he had regained control of the car, "that the Americans can now monitor every electronic transfer of money in the world! It is the computer that does it! So instead we shall be old-fashioned. We shall smuggle gold like a pirate! I thought that would please you, Paul. Does it not please you?"

"Oh it does," I said, "it truly does." But it pleased me even more that I had been given a glimpse of the truth, il Hayaween's truth, that the Stingers were not just meant to make Britain weep, but were a small part of the world-wide campaign of terror that Saddam Hussein had sworn to unleash on his enemies. And that il Hayaween was the co-ordinator of that threatened slaughter which had provoked governments across the world to guard their airports, harbours and military installations. So Brendan Flynn, I realised, had not been dealing with Tripoli, but with Baghdad, and Baghdad's urgency would explain why the price of the Stingers had gone so high; because a world-wide terror campaign would hugely increase the demand for illicit weapons, and that increased demand would be reflected in inflated black-market prices. It all made sense, so much sense that I wondered why I had not understood the equation earlier.

Shafiq was suddenly scared that he had been far too indiscreet. "I have said nothing you can repeat, Paul! Nothing!"

"Shafiq!" I said earnestly and with a hurt expression in my voice. "Shafiq. You and I are old friends. We have endured much together. We have taken risks for each other and protected each other. We have trusted each other." I was laying it on with a gold-plated trowel for I knew it would all be music to Shafiq's ears and, sure enough, tears showed in his eyes as I went on. "We have been fellow soldiers, and do you think I am the kind of man to betray an old comrade? My dear friend, I have heard nothing today that I had not already guessed, and I have heard nothing today that I will ever repeat to another soul. May my mother die of worms if I tell you a lie."

"Thank you, Paul, thank you." Shafiq took a deep breath as if to contain his emotion.

We turned into Monastir's marina. It was winter, and the pontoons looked drab. There were plenty of yachts, but most were under wraps, their sails unbent, waiting out the winter months until the Mediterranean spring fetched their owners south again. There were a handful of liveaboards in the harbour, but not as many as usual for the prospect of war in the Gulf had scared people away from Muslim countries. Only *Corsaire* looked fully ready for the sea, even to the extent of having two crewmen sprawled in her cockpit. "Are they my guards?" I asked Shafiq.

"Your crew." He sounded hurt that I should be so distrustful. "I hope you like them."

"I'm sure I will." I plucked my oilskin and sea-bag from the boot, then went to meet the two men Brendan had sent to guard me and, I suspected, to kill me when my usefulness was done.

My God, I thought when I got aboard *Corsaire*, but was this the best the Provisional IRA could drag up? It was no wonder that Shafiq had sounded so unenthusiastic about Liam and Gerry, for they were hardly the stuff of legends.

Liam was a skinny youth with a starved wan face, red hair and jug ears. He had timid, furtive eyes, suggesting that for all his short life Liam had been surrounded by stronger people who had left him pinched, resentful and ratlike.

The only ratlike thing about his companion was a small pigtail that decorated the nape of his thick neck. Gerry was a beefy, red-faced man whose cheap shirt strained across his plump back and bulging stomach. He had a massive chin, small eyes, and cropped black hair. He greeted me with a surly nod, as though trying to establish a pecking order at our very first meeting.

I chucked my sea-bag into the after cabin and ordered them to tell me about themselves. "We can't be strangers and shipmates," I said cheerfully, "so tell me your stories. How old are you for a start?"

They were both twenty-three, both born and raised in Belfast, and both now living in Dublin. They pretended to be battle-hardened veterans of the Irish Troubles, but their boasting was uncomfortable and unconvincing. They had the restricted vocabulary of deprivation, the fouled lungs of

73

chain-smokers and the thin minds of ignorance. Liam and Gerry were the cannon-fodder of riots and revolution, the spawn of decaying industrial cities, and they were supposed to be my shipmates for the next three months. I asked if either had ever sailed before. Liam shook his head, though Gerry claimed to have spent some time aboard an uncle's lobster boat. He was vague on the details, but bridled indignantly when I asked if he was competent to steer a simple course. "I can look after myself, mister!"

Liam was far more apprehensive. "We're crossing the Atlantic in this wee boat?"

"Yes."

"Fock me." He went pale.

"It'll do you good," I told him. "Put some colour in your cheeks. By the time you reach Miami you'll be a competent seaman."

"But I get focking seasick, mister!" Liam said.

"You what?" I asked in horror. Flynn had sent me seasick crew?

"I told Mr Flynn that, but he said it didn't matter! He said this would be like a focking cruise, so he did."

"The aeroplane was real good," Gerry said accusingly, as though *Corsaire*'s accommodation was a real disappointment after their charter flight from Dublin. For both boys it had been their very first aeroplane flight, but neither was looking forward to their maiden yachting voyage with quite the same excitement.

Shafiq, relieved that I had taken responsibility for Liam and Gerry, gave me Halil's written instructions. They were simple enough. I was to take *Corsaire* to the north Tunisian port of Ghar-el-Melh where we should wait for the gold. Once the coins were concealed aboard *Corsaire* we were to sail for Miami. "And who the hell do I contact when I reach Miami?" I demanded of Shafiq. I could not believe I was simply supposed to call Michael Herlihy's Boston office and risk being overheard by the FBI.

74

"They know who to contact." Shafiq pointed to the two Irish lads.

"You do?" I challenged them.

"Yes, mister," Gerry said.

"What a way to run a revolution," I said unhappily. "So let's get on with it."

I stowed my few belongings, put my sextant in a drawer of the chart table, then rummaged through the supplies which il Hayaween had arranged to be put aboard. It took me two hours to check the boat, but everything seemed to be present, including thirty feet of flexible plastic tubing that I thrust out of sight in a deep cockpit locker, then, with nothing to hold us under the battlements of Monastir, I started *Corsaire*'s engine and singled up her mooring lines. The Palestinian influence had ensured that there were none of the time-consuming bureaucratic procedures that usually accompanied a Tunisian departure; instead, after bidding Shafiq farewell and shouting at Liam and Gerry to stay out of harm's way, I cast off, reversed from the pontoon and motored towards the open sea.

At the very first surge of the waves Liam belched, gripped his belly and his cheeks turned a whitish green. I told him to stay on deck, for the last thing I wanted was to have the boat's interior stinking of his vomit. He lay flat, groaning and unhappy, as we plugged head on into the persistent north wind. "Have you ever heard of Michael Herlihy?" I asked Liam, who shook his head miserably. "He's much worse than you," I said cheerfully. "He gets seasick just looking at a boat."

"Oh, Jesus." But he could not have been feeling too unwell, for he managed to light himself a cigarette. "How long till we get to wherever we're going?" he said miserably.

"Two days to Ghar-el-Melh," I said cheerfully, "then two or three months across the Atlantic."

"Months?" He stared at me, saw I was not joking, so crossed himself. "Christ help me."

The morning turned cold as we headed north into the Gulf of Hammamet. Liam's seasickness got no better, yet he insisted on sharing Gerry's enormous midday meal of eggs and bread fried in bacon fat and washed down with the sweet cola they had bought in Monastir. Liam fetched the meal back up in seconds. Gerry frowned at the bucket I had managed to thrust on to his friend's lap. "Waste of good food, that."

I asked them more about themselves and heard the all-too-familiar Belfast story of children born into bleak housing estates and growing up into the hopelessness of chronic unemployment. In another society they might have found menial jobs, but there were not even floors for them to sweep in Ulster, and the pointlessness of their lives had scraped their souls to a bedrock of hate that could only be appeased by the twin pleasures of drink and reducing other people to their own level of misery. Uneducated, unskilled and bitter, they were good for nothing except to be the foot-soldiers for Ireland's Troubles, but even that calling had turned sour. Somehow, they were vague about just how it had happened, their names had been given to the security forces. Warrants for their arrest had been issued and so Liam and Gerry had been forced to flee south across the unguarded border with the Republic of Ireland and there, in what they called the Free State, they had found a refuge in a Dublin housing estate every bit as bleak as the Belfast ghetto from which they had fled.

"How do you like Dublin?" I asked Gerry. Liam was almost comatose, but Gerry seemed to be enjoying the afternoon. We were under sail, chopping north and east into a steep head sea that threw up great fountains of salty spray. I was sailing to save gasoline, and planned to tack back towards Cap Bon after nightfall. I was still not used to the boat which seemed clumsier than her lines had suggested. She was riding low in the water and making heavy work of seas that a boat of her length should have soared across. Her previous owner had over-ballasted her, perhaps out of nervousness, and doubtless he had made her into what he wanted: a safe docile boat that would have been comfortable enough on a fine summer day, but *Corsaire* was ill suited to this choppy and windy winter work and I dreaded to think how she would behave with an extra thousand pounds of weight in her belly. Still, short of beaching her and cutting a chunk of lead out of her keel, there was nothing I could do, and better a too heavy boat lumping across the waves than a lightweight bouncing across.

"Dublin's focking terrible," Gerry answered my question about how he liked living in Ireland's capital, and Liam groaned agreement.

"Why is it terrible?" I asked.

"Because no one focking cares about us in focking Dublin," Gerry explained indignantly. Like Liam, he used the word 'fock' as a modifier, an intensifier, and as an all-purpose replacement for any other word that momentarily escaped his restricted vocabulary. "Dubliners don't focking care!" he went on. "I mean, Jasus, we've been risking our focking lives for Ireland, so we have, and the focking Dubliners couldn't give a monkey's toss what we've done! The focking Garda came round, didn't they just, and they said they knew who we was and why we was in Dublin and if we so much as lifted a little finger they'd take us inside and beat the focking Jasus out of us. It's your focking Ireland I'm fighting for, I told the focking policeman, and you should be focking grateful to me, but was he shit? He told me to fock away off!"

"It's tough," I said with careless sympathy. In my own Dublin days I had seen how IRA activists fleeing from northern arrests had come south expecting to be treated as heroes, only to find an utter indifference and even a distaste for their actions. One Dubliner, after listening to a northerner for a whole evening, had wearily told me that Britain's best revenge on Ireland would be to give Ulster back to the Irish.

It took the lumbering *Corsaire* three days to reach Ghar-el-Melh, which turned out to be a small harbour surrounded by ancient fortifications. The harbour entrance was silting up so that I was forced to creep over the bar at what passed in the Mediterranean for a high tide. My pilot book told me that this dying port had once sheltered the feared Barbary pirates, but Liam and Gerry only cared to know whether or not the village under the deserted castle battlements might shelter a pub. "Probably not," I said.

"No focking booze?" Liam, recovered from his seasickness by being safely anchored in port, asked in a horrified voice.

"Not a drop."

"So how long are we going to be here?"

"Till the gold arrives," I explained.

"Have you really got fock all to drink on board?" Gerry wheedled.

"Not a drop," I lied. In fact I had hidden two bottles of Jameson Whiskey that I was saving for Christmas Day. I had hoped we would spend the day at sea, but Christmas came and the gold had still not arrived and so we just stayed at anchor in the deserted harbour.

Our Christmas dinner was Spam fritters, tinned peas and French fries. Afterwards I brought out the surprise Jameson's and the three of us sat in *Corsaire*'s saloon and, with their tongues freed up by the whiskey, Liam and Gerry told me the old and familiar Belfast tales. At first, trying to impress me, they spoke of their own heroic exploits; of bombs ripping British patrols apart or flattening whole sections of the city centre, but the stories were lifeless and bereft of Belfast's sharp wit, suggesting that the truth was somewhat less colourful. I finally punctured their bombast when I told them I had lived in Belfast myself, and that during those years I had given shelter to Seamus Geoghegan when he was first on the run from Derry.

"You know Seamus?" Liam asked incredulously.

"Sure. Very well." I saw my reputation soar in their eyes. Liam and Gerry were already wary of me, for I was a very strange creature in their starved eyes. I was foreign, bearded, tall, competent and taciturn, but now that they had discovered I knew Seamus, I became almost as godlike as Seamus himself.

"You really know him?" Gerry asked.

I crossed two fingers. "Like that."

"Jesus." He half smiled at me, then frowned, and I wondered if he was contemplating the difficulty of eventually killing me. Killing a stranger is easy compared to killing a man you know, and neither Gerry nor Liam, for all their bombast, struck me as men who would find a cold-blooded killing easy. Bur perhaps their job was merely to escort me to Miami where my death, if it was indeed ordained, would come from the hands of others.

As Christmas night wore on the stories of Gerry and Liam's prowess were replaced by better and funnier tales. Liam told the night's best story, that of the young boy who threw the nail bomb. "He was only a wee thing" – Liam stubbed his cigarette into the mess of gravy, butt ends and cold peas on his plate – "he can't have been more than ten or eleven. It happened up in Turf Lodge, so it did. There was a riot one evening, nothing special, just something to pass the time like, but the focking Brits had sent a focking patrol up there to break a few heads, so the lads took the wee boy aside and asked him did he want to throw a nail bomb?" Liam paused to light another cigarette. "He said yes, of course he did, because all the wee boys are just waiting for the chance to do their bit, like. You know what a nail bomb is, mister?"

"Of course he focking knows!" Gerry said. "He lived in Belfast, didn't he?"

"I know what it is," I assured Liam. A nail bomb was a length of metal pipe crammed with explosives and plugged at either end with four-inch nails. It was thrown like a stick grenade and, when it exploded, it scattered a lethal shower of nails among the enemy.

"So they take the wee fella behind a house, right, and he's shown the bomb, and he's told that if he throws it properly then he'll be given other jobs, like more responsible jobs, know what I mean?" Liam was enjoying telling the tale. "So they give the wee boy the bomb, light the focking fuse for him, and tell him to run like fock. Go, boy, they tell him, go! So the wee kid, he runs like fock, so he does, and he throws the focking bomb at the focking Brits, then he turns and focking sprints away like the devil himself is up his arse. But he's just forgotten one thing, so he has." Liam paused to increase the suspense of the tale's telling.

I was pretending not to have heard the story. "He's forgotten something?" I asked innocently.

"His focking dog!" Gerry could not resist interfering with Liam's story. "He's forgotten his focking dog!"

"Who's telling this focking tale?" Liam's indignation overcame his timidity.

"Keep your focking hair on!"

"Dog?" I asked.

"Aye!" Liam looked back to me. "The wee fella's got a dog, see, and the dog focking worships the wee fella, and the dog sees this bomb sailing away towards the focking Brits and the dog thinks, that's a stick, so it is! He thinks it's a game of fetch, see? So the dog runs after the bomb, because he thinks it's a game. But it isn't! It's a focking bomb! And the fuse is smoking and even the focking Brits are laughing by now! And the crowd screams at the focking dog, leave it alone, fock away off, but the dog's got the bomb in its teeth now, see, and it's carrying the bomb back to its wee master, and the crowd is all running away, so they are, and the dog's wee tail is wagging like mad, and the wee boy is running like fock, and his ma is screaming at him to get a focking move on before he's blown to focking bits, and the harder the wee boy runs the quicker the dog runs after him." Liam paused to cuff tears of laughter from his eyes. He was laughing so much he could hardly articulate the punch line. "And then the focking bomb goes bang!"

"Oh, Mother of God, but did it fock!" Gerry put in.

"There was focking dog-scraps everywhere!" Liam was still half helpless with laughter. "There was bits of dog on the focking roofs! There was dogmeat everywhere!"

"Oh Christ, but did we laugh!" Gerry slapped the saloon table in applause for his friend's story.

"No one was hurt," Liam said.

"Except the dog," Gerry said, and started laughing again.

"The wee fella forgot about his dog, you see?" Liam wanted to make sure I had understood all the tale's nuances. Above us the wind sighed in *Corsaire*'s rigging and stirred the ketch's long white-painted hull and slapped a halyard in mournful clangour against the aluminium mast. The companionway hatch was open, giving me a view of the high stars and a single wisp of elongated, moonlit cloud.

Gerry took a long drink of whiskey, then poured himself another mugful. "It's funny you being an American," he said at last.

"Is it?"

"Aye, it is," he said truculently. "I mean you going to live in Ireland and all that. Jasus, if I had the chance I wouldn't leave America, not to go to Belfast! No way! I'd stay in America. Get a job, make some money, eh?" He seemed to realise that he had already destroyed any hopes he might ever have possessed of making a normal existence; hopes of a job, a wife, children, of the small happinesses that make the world go round.

"I had a cousin that moved to America." Liam, emboldened by the success of his last story, spoke in the expectant tone of a man telling a joke. "Landed at the New York Airport, so he did, and his uncle met him off the plane, and they was walking out of the airport door and there was this hundred-dollar bill lying on the pavement.

Just lying there, so it was! 'Well, pick it up!' his uncle says. 'Go on, lad, pick it up!' And my cousin looks him straight in the eye and he says, 'I've only just got here and you expect me to start work already?'" Liam waited for me to laugh, then grinned proudly when I did.

Gerry flickered a dutiful smile, but the thought of America and all its bright hopes that were beyond his reach had depressed him. "We used to make a lot of money off the Yanks," he said wistfully. "We used to sell them rubber bullets! They'd pay a lot of money for a rubber bullet to put on their mantelpiece." The black bullets, thick phallic missiles designed to incapacitate rather than to kill, were fired by British troops on riot control duty and had become a prized souvenir of the Troubles. I remembered a canny man in Derry who had set up a useful garden-shed business carving fake rubber bullets from old truck tyres. He claimed to have sold a couple of hundred of the counterfeits before the Provisionals, realising they were losing market share, had threatened to put real bullets in his kneecaps if he did not stop his trade. "And there was a game we used to play with the Yanks," Gerry said after a while.

"A game?" I asked.

"You know, mister, with the Yanks who used to visit Belfast to see a bit of the Troubles. I mean they were good fellas, so they were! They gave us money, but of course they wanted to see a bit of the action, didn't they? There was no focking point in flying all the way to Northern Ireland not to see a wee bit of aggravation."

"So what was the game?" I knew the answer, but they were enjoying their moment of telling me tales and it would have been churlish to deny them the pleasure.

Liam, the more articulate of the two, took up the story. "We used to meet them in a bar, right, and ask if they wanted to meet the IRA. They didn't know we were the IRA, did they? How could they? I mean, if you told every stray Yank that you was in the movement then you might as well tell the focking Brits. So of course the Yanks would always say yes, I mean why else were they there? They'd come all the way from Boston or Chicago to give us a wee bit of support, to pat us on the back, like, and slip us a dollar or two, so of course they wanted to meet the Provisional IRA soldiers. So we used to tell them, go to such-and-such a house at ten o'clock next morning. We'd give them the address, it was always an abandoned house, one of those that had been half burned out like, and we'd say that some of the boys were meeting there before going off to plant a bomb or shoot a soldier."

"You could tell a Yank anything," Gerry put in. "They'd believe you!"

"They wanted to believe, you see," Liam, who did not want me to feel slighted, explained helpfully.

"So what happened?" I asked, as if Seamus Geoghegan had not told me this exact same story ten years before.

"Well, they'd go, of course," Liam said, "and sometimes their wives with them, because the women are just the same. They'd be all excited like! I mean they were going to meet the real IRA! They were going to meet the heroes! But what they didn't know was that we'd phoned the focking Brits on the security line, you know what the security line is?"

"Of course he focking knows!" Gerry put in. The security line was a telephone number that anyone could call to lay anonymous information against the terrorists. A machine answered the call and no names were asked, which meant that more than a few personal scores were settled courtesy of the security forces.

Liam grinned. "So we'd phone the focking Brits and we'd say that some Provos were meeting at such-and-such a house at quarter past ten the next morning, and then we'd ring off. Well, you can imagine what happened!"

"Tell me."

"The Yanks would turn up" – Liam was grinning at the

sheer cleverness of the ploy – "and they'd wait there, and the next thing they'd know there was a focking patrol of focking Brits, all scared out of their focking wits because they thought it might be a focking ambush, and the focking Brits would hammer into the house like it was D-Day and all they'd find was the Yanks there! But the Brits wouldn't know they were Yanks, not straight away! They thought they were our lads! So they'd knock them about a bit, you know, give them a focking good kicking!" Liam laughed and shook his head. "It always worked! The Brits fell for it every focking time, and of course the Yanks would go home and say how focking brutal the focking Brits was, and they'd never know it was the IRA that arranged the kicking for them! And when they got home they'd send us even more money! Especially if one of their womenfolk got a hammering! Jasus! It was like stealing sweets off a baby." He chuckled, then looked wistful. "They were good times. The best."

Gerry sloshed the whiskey round his mug. Despite the open companionway the cabin was foul with cigarette smoke and reeking of unwashed bodies, whiskey and stale food. Gerry leaned back on the berth cushions. "The Provos must have made focking thousands of pounds out of having the Yanks given a focking good kicking. And others too, of course. The Dutch, now, they always wanted to be in on the thick end of it. Especially the Protestant ministers, because they wanted to prove they loved Catholics, see? But it was mainly the Americans, so it was." He fell silent, evidently remembering the good days of home and thuggery, then, as a sudden thought blew across his mind, he frowned at me. "Is it really five million dollars we're waiting for?"

I nodded. "It truly is."

"In gold?"

"In gold," I said.

"Fock me," Gerry said wonderingly, and I knew for a second or two he was thinking of stealing the money, but then the stern call of duty made him shake his head in self-reproof. "Brendan said it was the most important mission we'd ever perform. For the movement, like?"

"I'm sure it is," I said, "I'm sure it is," and, the very next morning, in a cold north wind, the gold arrived.

Il Hayaween arrived before the gold. He came in a black-windowed Mercedes and was accompanied by his two dark-suited bodyguards who commandeered a fisherman to ferry all three men out to *Corsaire*. Il Hayaween sharply ordered Gerry and Liam to stay out of earshot below then sent his two bodyguards to wait on the foredeck. He looked at his precious Blancpain watch. "The trawler should be here by noon."

"Good."

He sat on the cockpit thwart after fastidiously wiping it with a linen handkerchief. He seemed awkward, but I put that down to his unfamiliarity with boats. "Is she suitable?" He waved his good left hand around *Corsaire*.

"She's a pig."

"A pig?"

"She wallows like a pregnant sow. She's too heavy. But I can get her to America, if that's what you wanted to know."

"And quickly," he said in his harsh voice.

I shrugged. "There's a chance the Stingers will reach Ireland by April 24, but I wouldn't bet on it. Not unless someone makes arrangements to ship them before the gold gets to Miami."

"April 24?" Il Hayaween frowned at me.

"The seventy-fifth anniversary of the Easter Rising. Isn't that what Flynn and Herlihy want? To give the Brits an anniversary Easter egg?"

He blinked as if he did not really understand what I was talking about, then shook his head. "The war will come sooner than that."

"In Kuwait?" I asked.

"Of course." He paused, staring at the withies which served instead of buoys to mark the harbour's uncertain entrance. "We shall be relying on your organisation to support Iraq's defence against the imperialist aggression."

I wondered what the hell I was supposed to say. There had been a time when I would have been the main conduit for passing such a message to the Provisional IRA's Army Council, but Roisin had ended that responsibility. Nevertheless il Hayaween seemed to expect some response, so I nodded and promised to pass the message on.

He angrily shook his head as though he did not need my help to communicate with the Army Council, then laboriously raised his maimed hand to light a cigarette. "We have already received pledges of support from Ireland. But will they keep their word?" He glared at me as he asked the question.

"I'm sure they will," I said truthfully. I was hardly surprised that the Provisional IRA had promised to support Iraq with a campaign of violence because for many years now the Arabs had been the major supplier of the IRA's needs, and the Army Council could hardly turn down such a request from so generous a benefactor. What did surprise me was that il Hayaween was telling me of the Army Council's promise, but his next words went some way to answering my puzzlement.

"Reactionary forces in Damascus and Tehran have suggested we should wait and see how effective Iraq's armed forces prove before we launch a world-wide campaign of terror, but we have refused to condone such timidity." He sucked on the cigarette as though taking strength from its harsh smoke. "We expect action, Shanahan."

"I'm sure you'll get it," I said, but inside I was noting the true import of il Hayaween's message. If Damascus and Tehran were preaching caution then there had to be deep rifts within the Palestinian ranks. Some fighters must be siding with Syria, others with neutral Iran, while yet a third faction, which il Hayaween led, was sticking with Saddam Hussein. Yet the rift plainly threatened the success of his plans for a global campaign of terror and, as those plans collapsed, he was desperately trying to keep his surviving troops in line. He was even desperate enough to seek my opinion of whether the Provisional IRA would keep their word, but I doubted he really needed to worry. The IRA's strongest Arab link was Libya, and Libya still seemed fully committed to Saddam Hussein's ambitions. "You'll get your big bang from the Irish," I reassured him.

"I want more than bombs." He paused. A catspaw of wind skittered over the harbour and whipped his cigarette smoke towards the shore. "What's wrong with the Russian ground-to-air missiles that Libya supplied to the IRA?" he suddenly asked me.

"As I understand," I said, "they're too slow to accelerate, which gives the British helicopters time to drop decoy flares. Also their range is not very great and their launchers are too heavy, which makes them awkward to move about. They're also unreliable, sometimes they don't fire at all."

"But even such an unsatisfactory missile, if it works, could destroy a jumbo jet as it climbed away from London Airport?"

Christ in his benighted heaven, I thought, but I dared not show my horror. Instead I just nodded. "Oh, sure, yes."

"If it was fired from close to the airport? Maybe from a house nearby? Or from a parked truck? Is there a suitable launching place for such a missile? You have surely been to London Airport?" Il Hayaween's questions sounded so banal, but evil so often did.

"I'm sure it's feasible," I said, and tried to sound enthusiastic.

"You're saying there is such a launching place?" he insisted.

"There is, yes." I was thinking of the industrial estates not far from Heathrow's runways, and I imagined a rocket streaking up from a roofless truck to tear an engine from a jetliner's wing and bring the great machine down to explode in sliding horror on the ground. "There are plenty of suitable places," I said equably.

"Then I shall tell your Chief of Staff that a Jewish or a British jumbo jet would be an acceptable gift in exchange for all the weapons we've donated to your revolution. And I can say that an expert opinion tells me that such an attack is feasible, yes?"

"Oh, indeed yes," I said warmly, though I doubted that the Army Council of the Provisional IRA would listen to my expert opinion. It was not that such men were squeamish about civilian deaths, indeed the visionary structure of their new Ireland was built on the graves of such dead, but men like Brendan Flynn were exquisitely sensitive to the effects of bad publicity in the United States, and they knew only too well that even a handful of slaughtered American airline passengers might cause a fatal dose of realism to infect the American-Irish. The dollars of American supporters had dwindled over the years, but they were not so paltry that anyone in Belfast or Dublin would willingly abandon those donations.

"You have been very helpful to me," il Hayaween said with an awkward and seemingly unaccustomed courtesy, and I wondered why a man of his satanic reputation was taking the trouble to condescend to me, and I decided that it was a symptom of the real disaster threatening Iraq's world terror plans. Il Hayaween's reputation was threatened by dissension from Syria and Iran, maybe even Libya was having second thoughts about Iraq's chances of victory, but he would not give up. He would press on to the bitter end, dreaming of airliners exploding, of all the undeserving dead whose corpses might balance the injustices of history.

Moments later a trawler crept across the harbour's outer bar and anchored just inside the sheltering sandbank. She carried no flag and bore no identifying number on her bows, but il Hayaween confirmed that she was the vessel carrying the gold. I hoisted *Corsaire*'s anchor, went alongside the ancient, rusting fishing boat and put Gerry and Liam to work carrying the heavy bags of coin from one ship to the other. As the first bags arrived I cleared *Corsaire*'s cabin sole and lifted her floorboards to reveal the empty belly of the boat, which looked like an elongated fibreglass bowl studded with the chunky bolts holding her massive lead-filled keel in place. It was into that long bowl-like trough that we poured the gold coins, settling *Corsaire* even deeper into the water as the extra thousand pounds of ballast chinked into her shallow belly.

It took two hours to make the transfer. We needed no special precautions to hide our activities for there was no possibility of interference from the Tunisian authorities, but even so the trawler's crew seemed relieved when their job was done. Perhaps it was il Hayaween's baleful presence that unnerved them, or maybe it was the Uzi sub-machine-guns that his two bodyguards openly carried. Whatever, as soon as he decently could, the trawler's skipper put back to sea.

Il Hayaween satisfied himself that the coins had been bedded down in *Corsaire*'s bilge. "They will be well hidden?"

"I've hidden a score of cargoes this way," I reassured him. "I'll glass the gold into the boat and no one will be able to tell the new floor from the old."

"You promise?"

"I promise. Isn't that why you're using me? Because I'm good at this sort of thing? So stop worrying."

"I am paid to worry," he said, then snapped his fingers to summon his two bodyguards. Once they had reached the cockpit he held out his hands for their two sub-machine-guns. "These are for your crew." He laid the guns down on the cockpit thwarts.

"Not for me?" I asked jocularly.

"Your job is to hide the gold and carry it to America.

Their job is to guard it." By which he meant that their job was to guard me. "Throw the guns overboard before you reach Miami," he ordered Gerry and Liam.

"We will, sir, we will." Even though there was nothing extraordinary in il Hayaween's looks or manner, Gerry still seemed to realise that the Palestinian was a very Archangel of Satan while he himself, like his friend Liam, was at best only a minor imp.

"If you fail me," il Hayaween said to the three of us, "then I shall pursue you to the last hiding place on earth, and when I find you I shall kill you, but not quickly, not quickly at all." He grimaced at us, perhaps meaning it to be a smile, then turned towards the fisherman's boat that had been summoned from the quay. None of us moved as he clambered over the gunwale. I was wondering how many men, women and children il Hayaween had killed. He raised his maimed hand in a gesture of farewell as the fisherman poled the bright-painted wooden skiff back to the quay.

I put Gerry and Liam to work again. I inflated *Corsaire*'s dinghy and sent Gerry ashore to collect buckets of fine sand that I poured to fill the voids between the gold coins. Then, when the sand and gold were riddled firm and smoothed over so that their top surface was a shallow reflection of the original curve of the bilge, I covered the mixture with layers of glassfibre mat and cloth strips. Liam helped me, but his capacity for even such a simple task was short-lived. "It's focking boring," he complained to me, then retreated to the cockpit where he lit a cigarette and stared balefully at the grey-green harbour water.

I finished the job myself; first mixing the resin and its foul-smelling hardener, then brushing the mixed liquid on to the prepared fibre mat. That job done I went back to the cockpit to wait as the fibreglass hardened and dried. I made idle chatter with Liam and Gerry, but my thoughts were elsewhere. I was being struck by the sheer amateurishness of this operation. How was it, with all the resources of Iraq and the Palestinians behind us, and with the cunning and practice of the IRA at our side, we were still reduced to this laborious method of smuggling gold? And were these two sour boys the best guardians that the IRA could find? And was *Corsaire* the most reliable transport at Iraq's disposal?

"What are you thinking, mister?" Gerry flicked a cigarette butt into the water.

"I'm thinking that the resin should be dry soon," I lied.

As darkness fell I mixed the white gelcoat with its hardener and brushed it on to the cabin sole. By midnight the new work had dried hard and the gold was thus hidden beneath a false floor. The white of the new floor was not the exact same shade as the rest of *Corsaire*'s interior fibreglass, but the new work would be hidden by the cabin flooring and any searcher might conclude that the shallow bilge had been left with a deliberately rough and discoloured finish simply because it was out of sight. I laid down the wooden sole, covered it with the saloon carpet, then hoisted *Corsaire*'s anchor. I used a flashlight to steer a cautious course across the shallows of the harbour entrance until, at last, clear of the bar and with the weight of the gold making her even more sluggish than before, *Corsaire* plunged her bows into a short hard wave and made Liam dive for the starboard gunwale. His gun clattered on to the cockpit's teak grating as he retched miserably into the sea.

I raised the yacht's sails, shut off her motor, and took my ramshackle enterprise into the night.

We sailed into the winter Mediterranean, a sea of short grey waves, spiteful winds, and busy sea lanes. I headed far north of the African coast, out beyond the busiest stretch of sea where the giant ships plunged blindly east and west between the Straits of Gibraltar and the Suez Canal, but even in these less trafficked waters there was filth on every wave; mostly plastic bottles and bags. I remembered a friend claiming that it was possible to navigate the Mediterranean by understanding the sea's currents and reading the town names from the plastic bags that floated out from every shore.

My two guards, realising that their responsibilities involved wakefulness, had imposed a crude watch system on themselves which meant that on our first afternoon out from Tunisia Gerry was trying to sleep in the forecabin while the seasick Liam was slumped in the cockpit where, with an Uzi on his knee, he was trying not to show his abject misery. "If you ate less grease," I told him, "you wouldn't be so sick."

"Fried food is good for you," he said stubbornly. "It lines the belly, it does."

"With what? Sump-oil? And you should give up smoking."

"Oh, come on, mister! What do the focking doctors know?"

"You're so eager to die young, Liam?"

"My grand-da, now, he smoked like a focking chimney, he did, and he had a proper fry-up every morning! Blood pudding, fried bread, bacon, eggs, 'taters, sausage, tomatoes, the works, and all of it fried in bacon fat, and he lived to be seventy-three!"

"That's not old."

"In this focking world it is." Liam drew hard on his cigarette, then half choked as a spasm erupted in his gullet. He twisted round to vomit and the Uzi clattered on to the cockpit sole.

"I hope that gun's safety catch is on," I said when he'd finished retching.

"I'm not a focking amateur," he moaned unhappily, then raised red tired eyes to the towering triangle of *Corsaire*'s mainsail. "I could murder someone for a piece of soda bread right now," he said, and the thought of that Irish delicacy immediately sent another spasm of sickness bubbling up his throat and he gagged again, chucked away his cigarette and twisted over the gunwale to spew helplessly into the bubbling sea.

"I can cure your seasickness," I said when the latest bout was over.

"How, for Christ's sake?" He was crouching out of the wind to light a fresh cigarette.

"A bottle of cod liver oil and a bottle of whiskey, both drunk straight down, followed by thirty-six hours of absolute agony, but after that I promise you'll never be seasick again."

"Oh, my God. Oh fock." He turned again. I had once made the same offer to Michael Herlihy, who had similarly turned it down. Michael and I had been teenagers and I had cruelly forced him into a small cat-boat and brought him ashore two hours later looking like a dead wet squirrel. I doubted he had ever forgiven me.

Liam flopped back on the thwart and watched as I opened the engine hatch and took a wrench to the boat's exhaust system, disconnecting the outlet pipe from the muffler. We were under sail, so the engine was cold and quiet. Then I took the thirty feet of flexible tubing from the cockpit locker and connected it to the top of the muffler with a jubilee clip. I fed the pipe's free end through the engine compartment's forward bulkhead and thus into the starboard lockers of the saloon. Liam, recovering from his last spasm of sickness, frowned at the serpentine loops of tubing that filled the engine hatch and cockpit floor. "What are you doing?"

"Running a blower through the bilges to dry off the gelcoat we put on top of the gold."

"Very wise," he said, as if he knew what I had been talking about, "very wise."

I put the boat under the command of the Autohelm, then went down to the saloon where I opened the lockers, pulled the hose through and introduced it into the boat's bathroom where a shower tray had a water activated pump under its outflow. A grille in the bathroom door allowed fresh air to circulate from the saloon to keep mildew from growing too thickly in the shower stall, and the grille made the bathroom perfect for my purpose. I cut off the excess tubing which I carried back to the cockpit and tossed overboard to add to the Mediterranean's pollution. "There," I said comfortingly to Liam, "all done."

"Will it take the stink out of the boat?" he asked. "Because it focking stinks down there, it does."

"It's the resin-hardener. It'll pass."

"Smells like a whore's armpit."

"You hire the wrong whores, Liam."

He looked sour at the implied criticism, then freshened as he remembered what rewards were waiting at our destination. "They say American girls are real nice."

"They're clean!" I said encouragingly. "And they like their men to be clean too. They're particular about that."

"I had a swill off before we left home!" he said indignantly.

"You'll slay the ladies," I assured him. "Especially in Boston. They love their Irish heroes there. You'll be the Grand Marshal of the St Patrick's Day parade and Congressman O'Shaughnessy will want his picture taken with you. It won't be like Dublin, I promise you."

"It'll be grand, so it will." Liam, his face pale as milk, watched in misery as I unfolded a chart. "Where the fock are we?" he asked.

"There." I pointed to a spot just off the Tunisian coast.

He looked round the horizon, trying to spot land. "Can't see a focking thing."

94

"We're just out of sight of the coast," I explained. In fact we were much farther north, but Liam did not really care. I could have sailed the *Corsaire* down the throat of hell and he would have been too sick to notice.

My two guards ate sandwiches that night, washed down with sticky Tunisian cola and cheap instant coffee. I gave Liam four powerful sleeping pills to help his drowsiness overcome the stench of the hardener, then sent him to his bunk in the forecabin. Gerry sat with me in the cockpit for a while, but soon became bored with the darkness and the inactivity and so took his precious Uzi below. He loved the small gun. He caressed it and kept it always close. It gave him status. I watched him from the cockpit and saw him tracing the gun's workings with his fingers. "I'm going to have to close the companionway," I called down after a while.

"I need the fresh air," he whined.

"The light's wrecking my night vision. So either switch the damn lights off, or close the hatch."

He chose to shut the companionway. I waited till my eyes had adjusted to the darkness, then went to the foredeck where I tripped the catch on the half-open forehatch. As I softly closed the hatch I could hear Liam's rhythmic snores. I went back to the cockpit and waited.

I was beating north-west, taking *Corsaire* into the open waters between Sardinia and the Balearics. It was a chilly night, and dark. The heavy boat was sluggish, its extra weight making awfully hard work of the small seas, and the awkward, choppy motion seemed to reflect my mood. I was nervous. My heart felt raw and sick, an actual feeling in my chest which I suspected was the physical manifestation of conscience. I wondered if, over the years, I had become careless of death, and that sense of a skewed and wasted past made my whole future seem as bleak and dark as the seas ahead. The short waves thumped on *Corsaire*'s stem, smashing white over her bows and draining noisily from her scuppers. Just after ten o'clock I saw a container ship steaming eastwards, her stack of lights as bright and tall as an office block, but once she had sailed beneath the horizon we were again alone in the harsh darkness.

At midnight, with my heart thumping like a flabby bladder, I turned on the engine. The starter whirred, caught, and the motor steadied into a regular and muffled beat. I left it out of gear as though I was merely running it to charge the batteries. The sails hauled us into the seas. I heard nothing from the saloon and suspected that Gerry, like the half-drugged Liam, was asleep. After a while the water-activated pump beneath the shower tray clicked on and spewed water outboard for a while. Still no one woke below.

I let the motor run as *Corsaire* thumped and dipped into the Mediterranean night. Her bow wave shattered white against the dark waters, foamed briefly, then faded behind. The stars were shrouded by clouds and we were far from the powerful loom of the lighthouse on Cape Spartivento and so I steered by compass and kept a rough log, noting after each hour my estimate of miles run. Six, five and a half, six again, and each small increment of nautical miles carried *Corsaire* and her dying cargo north-west towards Europe. I was supposed to be racing along the Muslim North African coast to the Straits of Gibraltar, and from there south-east to the Canary Islands from where we were supposed to let the trade winds carry our cargo of gold across the Atlantic, but instead, in this choppy darkness, I was committing murder. I had routed the engine's exhaust into the main cabin and now its fumes were filling the boat. The exhaust system's cooling water was collecting in the shower tray and being expelled, but the poison gas was staying below.

At four in the morning, while it was still dark, I shut off the engine. It suddenly seemed very quiet.

I steeled myself to open the companionway and was

greeted with a belch of foul, warm gaseous air. I gagged, coughed, and backed away. The smoky gas streamed and swirled out of the saloon to make a dissipating haze in the thin light. I could just see Gerry slumped on the table, his fingers curled either side of his cropped hair with its ridiculous pigtail. He was not moving.

I took a deep breath of fresh air, then went down into the choking saloon and put a finger on Gerry's neck. He was still warm. There was no pulse. I went into the forecabin where Liam lay on his back with his open eyes staring sightlessly at the closed hatch. His sleeping bag stank of urine. His pale, pimpled skin had been reddened by the effects of the carbon monoxide, while a trail of vomit had hardened on his cheek and pillow. I put a finger to his neck to find that, just like Gerry, he was quite dead. I pushed the forehatch open to let a gust of welcome chill air stream into the boat's foetid interior.

I tried to manhandle Liam back into the saloon, but his dead weight and the boat's clumsy motion made the task impossible, so I spent an hour rigging a system of pulleys and lines with which I hoisted both dead men out of the boat's reeking interior. I used the spare jib halyard to hang the twin corpses beside the mast where they hung like butcher's meat, supported by cords I had looped under their armpits. Suspended like that it was a comparatively simple job to pull their sleeping bags up around their bodies. I worked by the light of the navigation lamps, ballasting the sleeping bags with the lead weights that il Hayaween had so thoughtfully provided, then I lashed the bags' necks tight around the dead men's throats. Liam's aggrieved eyes reflected the green starboard light as I struggled to truss the cords tight. I wrapped yet more cord round and round the down-filled bags, expelling as much air as I could, then I lowered the halyard and draped the two bodies on the starboard rail. I untied the cords that had held the corpses, secured the halyard safely, then heaved the weighted sleeping bags overboard. There was a splash, a flurry of foam, then nothing. There was just enough wolfish grey light in the dawn sky to show that the two bodies sank instantly.

I fetched their two guns and hurled them into the sea, then disconnected the flexible tubing and threw it overboard. Afterwards, exhausted, I made coffee and folded a slice of bread over a chunk of tinned ham. The breakfast made me feel sick.

I reconnected the exhaust, then, with the sunlight streaming between a watery chasm of the dissipating clouds, I began to jettison the boat's supplies. Three months' rations went into the sea, and with them went the materials I had used to hide the gold; the rest of the resin, the hardener, the mats and the brushes. I kept two brushes and the unused can of white paint, but everything else went overboard. A trail of garbage followed *Corsaire* as gulls fought over the packets of bread and biscuits.

I cleaned the filthy exhaust deposits from the shower tray, then searched the boat for every last trace of Gerry and Liam. I tossed overboard their tawdry plastic holdalls and their cheap changes of clothes and the brand-new toothbrushes that neither had ever used, and their pathetic hoard of Cadbury's chocolate bars and the empty lager can Gerry had saved as a souvenir of his very first aeroplane flight. I jettisoned their brand-new Irish passports and their postcards of Monastir that neither man had bothered to send home, though Liam had got as far as writing half a misspelled message on the back of one card: 'Dear Mam, its great crack so far. Foods terribel. Give my love to Donna and Gran.'

I searched the pathetic relics before I threw them overboard, and found what I expected on a slip of cardboard that had been folded into the breast pocket of Gerry's suit jacket. It was an Irish telephone number which Gerry had doubtless been told to call collect once he reached America. The number would probably belong to an IRA sympathiser whose home and telephone had never before been used by the Provos, thus minimising the danger that the Garda Siochána, the Irish police, would be tapping the line. I memorised the number, then added the cardboard scrap to the sea's filth. Afterwards, with the boat rinsed clean, I stared behind and tried to frame a prayer to atone for my night's work, but no prayer would come. I told myself that Liam and Gerry had died in the service of their new Ireland. It would never have occurred to either of them that an Ireland fashioned by their kind would not be an Ireland worth living in, but all they had ever known was an Ireland that they could not endure and so, crudely, they had tried to change it. Now their trussed bodies were on the ocean floor while I, with Saddam Hussein's gold, sailed on.

I had murdered two men. I had done it in cold blood, with much planning and forethought, and solely for my own gain. I had not killed them to stop the slaughter of the innocents which il Hayaween's questions about airliners and ground-to-air missiles had implied, but instead I had killed Liam and Gerry for five million dollars. I did plan to stop il Hayaween's slaughter, but I also planned to steal the coins, indeed I had intended to right from the moment in Miami when I had first heard about the gold. The problem was not stealing the gold, but living to spend it. My story would be simple; that the badly overloaded boat, wallowing in rough seas, had been pooped by a bad wave. That she had sunk. That I had tried to rescue Liam and Gerry, but failed. That the gold, with the boat, was lost. That I had survived in a liferaft, alone. When I reached America I would hide for a few weeks, then, when the IRA found me, I would brazen the story out. Liam and Gerry would have destroyed my lie and so I had murdered them.

I tried to justify the murder by telling myself that they would have killed me if I had finished the voyage. Or if they were not to have been my killers, others would have killed all three of us. I told myself that if you sup with the devil you need a very long spoon, and that Gerry and Liam should have known what dinner table they were sitting at. I tried to justify their murder, but it remained murder and it was on my conscience as I sailed on to Barcelona. That too was part of the plan.

It was a hellish journey. I was single-handed in a busy sea, so I dared not leave the cockpit. Instead I catnapped at the helm and snatched the odd hour of sleep whenever it seemed safe or whenever sheer fatigue overwhelmed me. One night I was startled awake to hear the throbbing crash of a steamer's engines pounding not far off in the darkness and, when I turned in panic, I saw the lights of a vast ship thundering past not a hundred yards away.

The next day, during a lull from the cold winter winds that were sweeping south from the French coast, I buckled on a lifeline and, with *Corsaire* safe under the control of her self-steering, I crouched on the swimming platform built into her sugar-scoop stern and, using the pot of white paint that I had listed as an essential part of the false floor's disguise, I painted out the name *Corsaire* and the French hailing port, Port Vendres. I then took all *Corsaire*'s papers, shredded them, and committed them to the deep.

On the following day, when the second coat of white paint was dry and the old lettering completely hidden, I unrolled the transfer names I had ordered by mail in Belgium. Carefully, all the while balancing myself against the sluggish pitch of the overloaded boat, I rubbed the new names on to the fresh paint. Thus *Corsaire* became *Rebel Lady*, and Port Vendres became Boston, Mass. Then, using an epoxy glue, I fastened the old *Rebel Lady* maker's plate on to the side of *Corsaire*'s coachroof and, leaning dangerously out under the pulpit's lower rail and using commercial stick-on letters and numbers I had bought in Nieuwpoort, I put *Rebel Lady*'s Massachusetts registration number on either bow. I finally replaced the French tricolour with the Stars and Stripes, and thus *Corsaire* ceased to exist and in her place was Dr O'Neill's forty-four-foot boat, *Rebel Lady*, ready to go home.

Two days later I delivered *Rebel Lady* to the commercial docks in Barcelona. I spent a busy day knocking down her topworks; taking off her sails, craning out her mast. Then, with her spars safely lashed to her decks, she was hoisted out of the water. The crane driver slid open a window of his cab and shouted something through the thin dirty rain. I shrugged to show I did not understand, but the foreman translated into French for me. "He says she weighs as much as a sixty-footer!"

"I prefer heavy boats."

"Like women, eh?" he laughed and repeated the joke in Catalan to his crane driver who, with an exquisite skill, was lowering *Rebel Lady* into an open-topped container.

Once she was safely cradled I borrowed an electric drill and, using templates I had brought from Nieuwpoort, I etched *Rebel Lady*'s Hull Identification Number on to her transom and, as American law required, in a concealed place below. I chose the new false floor for the hidden number, then, that last job completed, I locked her hatches, signed her over to the shipping company, paid the balance of my account in cash and walked out of the docks to find a taxi. In a day or so *Rebel Lady* would be loaded on to a container ship, then, as deck cargo and with her secret hidden deep in her dark belly, she would be carried west across the winter Atlantic, bound for America.

And I too was going to America, but not across the Atlantic. Fear of il Hayaween made me circumspect and so I took a train to Nice, another to Paris, then took the metro to the airport. I telephoned Brussels again, told a lie, and caught a plane for Singapore. I was vanishing, going east about the world, but running, just like the newly christened *Rebel Lady*, for the refuge of home.

I stayed one night in a hotel near Singapore's Changi Airport, then, in a hot humid dawn and still groggy with sleeplessness and jetlag, I flew north to Hong Kong where I waited two hours before catching a plane to San Francisco. There, using my false American passport and carrying a stained sea-bag and my bright yellow oilskin jacket, I came home.

My flight to Boston was delayed so I bought a clutch of newspapers. The Iraqis were still refusing to withdraw from Kuwait despite the mass of coalition troops assembling in Saudi Arabia, and Saddam Hussein was still promising his enemies the mother of all battles. He sounded confident enough to make me wonder whether perhaps il Hayaween's plans were not so ramshackle after all. Perhaps there were saboteurs in place throughout the world, preparing to slaughter and maim and destroy in the names of Allah, Saddam and Palestine. I thought of fifty-three Stinger missiles and of a man with a maimed hand asking how easy it was to shoot down airliners, and I felt a tremor of fear at the thought of taking another plane, then told myself not to be so stupid. Whatever evil the Iraqis had planned would not be unleashed till after the shooting began in the desert.

The Boston plane should have left San Francisco at half past one in the afternoon, but it was nearer six in the evening before the aircraft at last climbed over the bay and headed east across the Sierra Nevada, which meant we did not land at Logan Airport till the small hours of the morning. It had been snowing and the temperature was way below zero. The last sleep I had enjoyed was somewhere over the western Pacific, and if I had been sensible I would have stayed the rest of that night in a Boston hotel, but by now the jetlag and adrenalin were combining to keep me awake and all I really wanted to do was reach my house on Cape Cod, so I rented a car and drove myself through the banked snow that lined the Massachusetts roads.

The drive took just over two hours. I was aching with tiredness, but the thought of the waiting house filled me with a feverish expectancy and, like a hunted beast seeking a secret lair, I wanted to recuperate in the safety and reassurance of home. There was a risk, a very small risk, that my enemies might be watching the Cape Cod house, but I doubted it for I had not seen the place in seven years, and Shafiq and his friends did not even know the house existed. As I crossed the Cape Cod Canal the clouds slid apart to reveal a clean-edged moon cut sharp as a whistle in a sky of ice-bright stars. The moonlight revealed yellow ribbons tied to trees and mailboxes and fences. A big illuminated sign outside a hardware store asked God to bless our troops. The radio, even at four in the morning, was filled with the threats of war, then it played 'God Bless America' and I felt tears prick at my eyes. It had been so long since I had been home, so very long.

It was ten past four in the star-bright morning when I turned on to the dirt road that led east towards the ocean and, as I breasted the pine-clad sand ridge that edged the marsh, I could suddenly see for miles and it seemed that every frost-edged blade of grass was needle sharp in the winter air. The far Atlantic was silver and black while the nearer waters of the bay glistened like a sheet of burnished steel. The snow had hardly settled on the salt marshes, but there was just enough to streak the dark shadows with bands of white. I braked the car to a stop on the ridge's crest and, with the radio and lights turned off, I sat and stared at the view in which, dead-centre and ink-black under the scalpel moon, my waiting house lay silent. The house and the sweeping beams of the Cape's lighthouses were the only new things in this view since the days when the Pilgrim Fathers had first stood on this ridge, or indeed, since the more ancient time when the wandering Indian tribes had dug for clams in the shoals of this sandy promontory that stuck so deep into the Atlantic.

I rolled down the car window to catch, on the surge of freezing air, the shifting sound of the distant ocean breakers. The sound brought with it a sudden rush of love for this place. It was home, it was safety, it was mine. My father had bought this house fifty years before as a refuge from the whores and pimps and lawyers who plagued his business, and now it would become my refuge. Here, I told myself, I could at last live honestly. No more secrets. I had come home.

Home. I sat there for a long time, letting the cold fill the car, thinking. Thinking and watching. Nothing moved in the salt marsh; I did not expect any of my enemies to be here, but old habits keep a man alive, and so I watched and waited.

I watched the house and listened to the sea. I felt no instinct of fear. This place was too far from the hatreds of the Middle East or the bitterness of Ulster to bear danger. This was the refuge where I would hide until *Rebel Lady* reached America, then I would give myself up to the government for questioning. My telephone calls to Brussels had merely been to warn them of Stinger missiles, il Hayaween and my conviction that a terrible series of airliner massacres was planned as a revenge for America's thwarting of Saddam Hussein's plans. I had given the CIA as much information as they needed to stop the Stingers being deployed, but they would want more. They would want all the information I had gathered and remembered since first they had sent me out, as an agent without strings and without provenance, twelve years before.

For Roisin had been right. I was one of the agents who did not exist. I was one of the CIA's secrets. I had been turned out into the world and told to stay out until I had something worth bringing home. I was one of the agents who would leave no tracks and make no footprints. I would be paid nothing, offered nothing, and my name would appear on no government list, no computer record, and no file. I did not exist. Simon van Stryker, who had recruited me to the programme, called us his 'Stringless Agents' because there would be no apron strings or puppet strings to lead our enemies back to Langley, Virginia. Now I was going back there of my own accord, but in my own time and I would not give them everything. *Rebel Lady* and her cargo were mine. Saddam Hussein's gold would not go towards paying off America's deficit, but to keep me in my old age.

What old age? I sat in the freezing, dark car and gazed at the moonlit marsh and I remembered how I had once dreamed of bringing Roisin to this house; I had even dreamed, God help me, of raising her children on this shore, but she had scorned that dream as the sentimental witterings of a dull and unimaginative fool. I remembered her eyes after her execution, all fierceness gone, then I thought of Liam's eyes that had been so accusing in the green lamplight. Poor Liam. After I had wrestled the sleeping bag about his corpse I had found his dried vomit on my hands and I had panicked as if I had been touched by a foul contagion. I remembered my childhood, and how Father Sifflard had told us of the one sin against the Holy Ghost that could never be forgiven, which sin no one seemed able to define, and I wondered if we all defined it for ourselves and if I was already guilty and thus doomed to the horrors of eternal punishment.

I rolled up the window, let in the clutch, and drove towards my house, which had been built 150 years before by a Captain Alexander Starbuck who, retiring from the profitable pursuit of whales in the Southern Ocean and quarrelling with his family on Nantucket, had come to this Cape Cod marsh and built himself a home snug against the Atlantic winds. My father had bought The Starbuck House from the estate of the Captain's great-granddaughter and had dreamed of retiring to it, but the dream had never come true. Now I would make it home. I drove slowly up the driveway of crushed clam shells that splintered loudly under the tyres, and stopped on the big turnaround in front of the house where my headlights shone stark on the silver-grey cedar shingles. It was a classic Cape Cod house: a simple low building with two windows either side of its front door, a steep staircase in the hallway and a snug dormer upstairs that must have reminded old Captain Starbuck of a whaling ship's cabins. The house's only addition since 1840 was the garage, which had been clad in the same cedar shingles as the house itself and thus looked as old as the rest of the building. It was a home as simple as a child's drawing, a home at peace with its surroundings, and it was mine, and that thought was wondrously comforting as I killed the headlights and climbed out of the car. I took the sea-bag from the boot and found the house keys that I had kept safe these seven years, then walked to the front door.

My key scraped in the lock as it turned. There had never been electricity in the house, and I had no flashlight, but the moon shone brightly enough to illuminate the hallway. My sister Maureen, who used the house as a holiday home, had left some yellow rain-slickers hanging on the pegs by the door, but otherwise the shadowed hall looked just as I had left it seven years before. The antique wooden sea-trunk with its rope handles that I had bought in Provincetown still stood under the steep-pitched stairway, and on its painted lid was a candle in a pewter holder. I fumbled in the holder's dish, hoping to find a book of matches.

At which point an electric light blazed about and dazzled me. I started back, but before I could escape something terrible struck my face and I was blinded. The pain made me want to scream, but I could not even breathe, and, vainly gasping for air and with my hands scrabbling like claws at my scorching eyes, I collapsed.

PART TWO

The police arrived five minutes later; their two cars rocking and wailing down the dirt track, then skidding ferociously as they braked on the clam-shell turnaround. A young excited officer, his pistol drawn, burst through the open front door and shouted at me not to move.

"Oh, go away and grow up," I said wearily. "Do I look as if I'm about to run away?"

My sight had half returned and, through the painful tears, I could just see that the girl who had attacked me was now sitting on the stairs holding an antique whaling harpoon that used to hang on my bedroom wall. She had not used the vicious harpoon to cripple me, but a squeegee bottle which now stood beside her on the steep stairway. "He broke in," the girl explained laconically to the three policemen who now piled excitedly into the hallway. "He says his name is O'Neill. Dr O'Neill." She sounded scornful. In the last few moments I had learned that this was one very tough lady.

"Do you want me to call the rescue squad?" the first policeman asked, while an older officer knelt beside me and gently pulled my hands from my face.

"What did you do to him?" The older man asked the girl.

"Ammonia."

"Jesus. Did you dilute it?"

"No way!"

"Jesus! Get some water, Ted. Can we use your kitchen, ma'am?"

"Through there."

"You used ammonia?" the first policeman asked in awed disbelief.

"Squirted him good." The girl showed the officers the liquid soap bottle that she had used to lacerate me through the banister rails. "I used to know a policeman in Los Angeles," the girl explained, "and he taught me never to piss a psychopath off, just to put the bastard down fast. Ammonia does that, and it's legal." The last three words were added defensively.

"Sure is." One of the policemen had fetched a saucepan of water from the kitchen. My breath was more or less normal now, but the pain in my eyes was atrocious. The officer poured water on my face while outside the house the police radios sounded unnaturally loud in the still, cold night air.

"We'll take him away in a moment, ma'am," the older policeman, a sergeant, reassured the girl.

"Then bury the bastard," the girl said vindictively.

"What did you say your name was, mister?" the sergeant asked.

"My name," I said as grandly as I could, "is Dr James O'Neill," and I fumbled in an inside pocket for my false passport.

"Careful!" The sergeant moved to restrain me, then relaxed as he saw I was not pulling a gun. "I know you!" he said suddenly.

I blinked at him. My sight was still foully blurred, but I recognised the sergeant as Ted Nickerson, a guy I had last seen in twelfth grade. Damn it, I thought, but this was not what I had planned! I had planned to disappear in Cape Cod for a few weeks, hidden from sight while my ship came home, and the last thing I needed was for the word to spread that I had returned to America as bait for Michael Herlihy or il Hayaween.

"You're Paul Shanahan!" Ted exclaimed. "Which means –" He stopped, glancing at the girl.

"Which means this is my house," I confirmed.

"It's not his house," the girl insisted. "I rent this place! I've got a five-year lease!" She was shivering in a night-dress and an old woollen bath robe. My old woollen bath robe. She had bare feet, long black hair, and an Oriental face.

"This is the Shanahan house." Ted Nickerson confirmed the ownership uncomfortably. He was still frowning at me. "You are Paul, aren't you?"

"Yeah."

"Bullshit!" the girl said with an explosively indignant force on the second syllable. "The house belongs to a guy in Boston, a guy called Patrick McPhee."

"McPhee's my brother-in-law," I told her. "He's married to my sister Maureen. Maureen holds the keys to the place while I'm away, that's all! She uses it for summer vacations and odd weekends, nothing more."

The girl stared at me. I guessed that by using Maureen's name I had convinced her I was not your usual rapist breaking and entering, but might in fact be telling the truth. Ted Nickerson was still frowning, perhaps thinking about my false name. "How's your face, Paul?"

"Hurts like hell."

"Ammonia's bad stuff," he said sympathetically, "real bad."

"How was I to know?" The girl was on the defensive now. "He doesn't knock, he just comes into the house . . ."

"Like he owns it?" I finished for her.

"Oh, shit!" she said angrily. "Then why the hell are you calling yourself Dr O'Neill?"

"None of your damned business," I snarled, then struggled to my feet. My eyes were still streaming with tears and my throat felt as if I had gargled with undiluted sulphuric acid, but I was recovering. "Who the hell put electric light in here?"

"I did," the girl said defiantly. "I'm a painter. I need decent light to work."

"Did you put in the telephone as well?" Ted Nickerson asked her.

"Sure did."

"Mind if I use it?"

"Help yourself. In the kitchen."

The girl edged tentatively down the stairs that Captain Starbuck had built as steep as the companionways on his old whaling ships. One policeman was out in the car, and the other two were hovering nervously by the open front door. "Can we close the front door?" the girl demanded. "I'm kind of chilly."

"Sure, ma'am."

I went through into the living room from where I could hear Sergeant Nickerson grunting into the telephone in the kitchen. I found the new light switch and, in the glow of a lamp, saw a box of tissues on a table by the low sofa and plucked out a handful which I used to scrub my eyes. The tissues helped, though the remnants of the ammonia still stung like the devil.

The room, except for the electric light and the paintings, had not changed much. It was panelled in old pale oak and its low beamed ceiling was formed by the pine planks of the dormer storey upstairs. It was a shipwright's house with a main floor of pegged oak that the girl had thoughtfully protected from paint drips with a dropcloth. The wide stone hearth was filled with ash on which I threw the crumpled tissues.

"Do you really own the house?" The girl had followed me into the living room.

"Yes."

"Hell!" She said angrily, then, with her arms protectively folded across her breasts, she walked to one of the small windows that stared eastwards towards the ocean. "The mailman told me he didn't think Patrick McPhee was the owner, but I thought that was just troublemaking gossip."

"McPhee's always been full of shit," I said savagely. "Marrying him was the worst day's work Maureen ever did. So how long have you been here?"

"Three years, but I don't live here permanently. I come here whenever I need to, but I've got a place of my own in New York."

"Manhattan?"

"Sure, where else?" She turned to glare at me, as though the night's misadventures were all my fault. "I'm sorry about your eyes." She spoke grudgingly.

"Blame Patrick," I said. I dislike my brother-in-law intensely.

"But I've invested in this place! I put in the electricity, and the phone!" She spoke accusingly. "I even had an estimate for central heating, but Maureen said I shouldn't waste my money. I thought that was kind of weird, but I didn't ask any questions. I was dumb, right? But I like this place too much. It's the light." She waved a peremptory hand at the window to explain herself.

"I know," I said, and I did know. In fall and winter the light on the Cape is so clear and sharp that it seems like the world is newly minted. Thousands of painters had been drawn by that light, though most of them merely wasted good paint and canvas trying to capture it. Whether the girl was good or not I could not tell, for my eyesight was still smeared. In the dim electric light her canvases seemed full of anger and jaggedness, but that could just have been my mood.

"My name's Sarah," she said in a placatory tone, "Sarah Sing Tennyson."

"Paul Shanahan," I said, and almost added that it was nice to meet her, but that courtesy seemed inappropriate, so I left it out. "Sing?" I asked instead. "That's a odd name."

"My mother was Chinese." Sarah Sing Tennyson was tall with very long, very straight and very black hair that framed a narrow, almost feral face. She had dark slanted eyes above high cheekbones. A good-looking trespasser, I thought sourly, if indeed she was a trespasser, for God only knew what the lawyers would make of this situation.

"When did you put the electricity in?" I asked lamely, supposing that at the very least I should have to reimburse her for that expense.

"Two summers ago."

"I didn't see any wires outside."

"I had to bury the cables because this is all National Seashore land so you're not allowed to string wires off poles. It was the same with the phone line." She gave me a very hostile look. "It was expensive."

More fool you, I thought. "And how much rent are you paying Patrick?"

"Is it your business?" She bridled.

"It's my Goddamn house," I bridled back. "And if my Goddamn brother-in-law lets my Goddamn house to some Goddamn girl, then it is my Goddamn business."

"I am not a girl!" Sarah Sing Tennyson flared into instant and indignant hostility. I could allow her some irritation for being woken in the middle of the night, but even so she seemed to have an extraordinarily prickly character. "I am a woman, Mr Shanahan, unless you wish to accept the appellation of 'boy'?"

Oh sweet Jesus, I thought, the insanities that old Europe was spared, then I was saved from further linguistic tedium when the kitchen door opened and Ted Nickerson, still holding the telephone handset, stared at me. "Paul?"

"Ted."

"I'm talking to a guy named Gillespie. Peter Gillespie. Does that name mean anything to you?"

"Nothing at all," I said truthfully.

Nickerson had been staring oddly at me ever since he recognised me, and now his puzzlement only seemed to deepen. "He says he expected to see you in Europe. Does that make sense?"

Christ, I thought, but the CIA had been far quicker than I had expected. They had responded to my warning calls by putting out an alert. "We got a warning to look out for you two days ago, Paul," Ted Nickerson said.

"Tell Gillespie I'll call him in a few weeks."

Ted shook his head. "I've got orders to hold you, Paul.

114

Protective custody." He moved his free hand to his holstered pistol, making Sarah Sing Tennyson gasp.

I half raised my hands in a gesture of supplication. "OK, Ted, no need for drama."

"You're not under arrest, Paul," Ted said carefully, "just under police protection." He spoke into the phone, telling whoever was at the other end that I was safely in the bag.

Which meant I had screwed up.

I met Peter Gillespie next morning. He came to the police station with an agent called Stuart Callaghan who was to be my bodyguard. "We guessed people might want to stop you talking?" Gillespie explained the bodyguard's presence. "The guys with the missiles, right?"

"I guess they might too," I said, though I suspected the people who wanted to stop me talking were more worried about the five million bucks in gold that should have paid for the Stinger missiles.

"You've had breakfast, Mr Shanahan?" Gillespie had very punctiliously shown me his identification.

"Sure."

"Then if you're ready?" Gillespie was plainly eager to begin my debriefing. I was carrying, after all, over a decade of secrets that would feed the agency's data banks. "We have a plane waiting at Hyannis Airport." Gillespie tried to usher me towards the door.

"Hold on!" I protested. It was not yet eight in the morning, I had snatched two hours' indifferent sleep in a holding cell, and I felt like death warmed over. "I've got to see someone before I leave. I want to use the telephone, then go back to my house."

"If you need a razor or a toothbrush –" Gillespie began.

"I have to make a telephone call," I interrupted him, "then visit home."

Gillespie was plainly unhappy, but he was uncertain how best to handle me. I was no prisoner, despite being locked up overnight, yet I was certainly something very exotic. I might have been one of the CIA's own, yet I had still come from the shadowy and unknown world of international terrorism, and that made me into a mystery. Perhaps they thought I had been contaminated by the vengeful creatures that came from the slums and refugee camps of the old world to give the new world its worst nightmares? Gillespie himself was very straight arrow; tall, fit, punctiliously courteous and businesslike, and clearly reluctant to let me use the phone, but he seemed to recognise my determination and so waved me towards a desk.

I needed to talk to an old friend. I would have much preferred to have talked with him in private, for I regarded my business with Johnny Riordan as an entirely personal matter and I doubted whether the CIA would agree with that view, but Gillespie's presence was giving me little choice. I would have to risk the CIA knowing about Johnny.

Johnny and I had been friends since childhood, when his father used to look after the Cape house for my father. Old Eamonn Riordan was a fisherman, and a good one, but his son was an even better one. Johnny had a natural talent for boats, the sea and for living. He was a great man, a raw force of nature, a muscled lump of goodwill, common sense and kindness, but he was also a man I was loath to involve in any trouble for Johnny Riordan was a father, happily married, and without a mean fibre in his body except perhaps towards those politicians who constantly interfered with his livelihood. Johnny tried to scrape a bare existence from lobstering or scalloping or tub-trawling the seas about the Cape, but in the lean months, all twelve of them most years, he was forced to keep his family· fed by taking on other jobs like stocking grocery shelves. Johnny thought the sacrifice worthwhile so long as he could continue fishing, for he loved the sea and was probably the finest seaman I had ever met. I had not spoken with Johnny in seven years but I knew, if only he was home, he would not blink an eyelid if I did call. Nor did he. "So you're back at last, are you?" he laughed. "Which means you'll be wanting a meal."

"No," I said, "I want to meet you at my house. Now. Can you make it?"

"Sure I can make it. The politicians won't allow us to go fishing these days just in case we catch something. I tell you, Paulie, those congressmen couldn't catch their rear ends with their own bare hands, not even if you painted it scarlet for them. Did you hear about the new catch restrictions? Courtesy of Washington?"

"Just meet me!" I interrupted him. "Please, Johnny, now!"

Johnny's pick-up truck was already parked in the driveway when Gillespie and Callaghan drove me home. Two golden retrievers wagged their tails in the back of Johnny's truck, for no pick-up truck on Cape Cod was complete without at least one dog. I thought Johnny might have been waiting in the truck's cab, but instead I found him ensconced before Sarah Sing Tennyson's hearth where he was telling my tenant tall tales of prohibition; how the Cape Codders used to run rings round the federal agents, and how there were still forgotten caches of Canadian whiskey in some of the cranberry bogs and trap sheds. Sarah Sing Tennyson, like everyone else, was entranced by Johnny who had a natural and contagious enthusiasm. "Well now, look who it is!" he greeted me ebulliently. He was a big man, with a shock of black hair, a broad black beard and an open cheerful face.

"You've met my tenant?" I gestured at Sarah.

Sarah Tennyson smiled thinly. "Don't you knock before going into other people's houses?"

"This is my house," I said.

"It's good to have an artist living here, isn't it?" Johnny tried to defuse the atmosphere with happiness. He gestured at Sarah Tennyson's paintings which were mostly of the Nauset Lighthouse, but rendered so gloomily that they might have depicted a watch-tower in hell. "I was telling her how they tried to teach me to do art at school! What a waste! I couldn't even draw a box, not even with a ruler to help. And good morning to you!" This last greeting was to Gillespie who had followed me into the house.

I hurried Johnny into the kitchen before he could start a general conversation about the weather and the fishing and the beaches. "Make free in my house, won't you, Shanahan?" Sarah Sing Tennyson called after me.

"Mr Shanahan!" Gillespie seemed to be worried that I might try to make a bolt out of the back door.

"This is family business," I said firmly, then I dragged Johnny into the kitchen and slammed the door shut.

"What's going on?" Johnny asked me. "She told me she's renting the place! I knew she was here off and on, but I thought she just borrowed it from Maureen at weekends. But I haven't seen Maureen for months, so I couldn't ask her. I know Maureen's husband is here sometimes, but –"

"It doesn't matter," I cut Johnny off. I knew I would have only a few moments before Gillespie interrupted us and I dared not waste a minute. "Listen," I told Johnny, "there's a boat being delivered to you. She's coming from Spain and I had her sent to you. She's coming deck cargo from Barcelona, and a customs agent will call you from Boston. I don't know when she will get here, but probably in about six or seven weeks, OK? There shouldn't be any customs duty to pay on her, because she's registered in Massachusetts. These are her papers." I took the original *Rebel Lady* papers from my oilskin pocket and shoved them into a bemused Johnny's hands. "If there are any problems, this will help." I began peeling hundred-dollar bills from the roll I had collected when I closed down my bank accounts in Belgium. "I paid for her carriage through to the Cape, but you'll need to hire a big crane to get her off the truck." I peeled away yet more bills. "She weighs damn nearly eighteen tons. Don't ask me why she's so heavy, but her original owner was probably nervous of tipping her over in a strong wind. Her new owner's name is on those papers, and he asked you to take delivery, understand? You agreed to store her here for the winter."

Johnny riffled through the hundred-dollar bills, then gave me a very disapproving look. "This isn't drugs again, is it, Paulie? Because if it is, I'm not helping. Don't even ask me." He held the money back towards me.

I pushed them back again. "I swear to God, Johnny, this has nothing to do with drugs. On my mother's grave, there's nothing illegal inside the boat."

"Nothing?" He was still suspicious.

"There's gold aboard her," I told him reluctantly, "which is why I don't want anyone to know about her. If anyone asks what we're talking about in here, you're agreeing to look after this house while I'm gone. You understand, Johnny? The boat's a secret."

"Gold! In her hull?" Johnny seemed cheered by that thought, then watched in amazement as I slipped the rest of the hundred-dollar bills inside my false passport, added Teodor's other false papers, then reached up to raise one of the spare bedroom floorboards that comprised the kitchen ceiling. Johnny supported the floorboard while I fumbled along the top surface of one of the kitchen's old black beams. Eventually I found the cavity I had long ago hollowed into the beam, and into which I now dropped the passport, papers and money.

"There shouldn't be any problems with the boat," I told Johnny. "Her papers are in order and I'll probably be back before she arrives anyway."

"You're going away again?" Johnny sounded disappointed, which was flattering after so many years.

"I'll be away for a few weeks, no more. But listen!" I rammed a finger into his chest to reinforce what I was saying. "There might be some real bastards looking for this boat. I've covered her tracks pretty well, but if anyone wants to argue about her, back off. Give them what they want and leave well alone. These are nasty guys, Johnny, real nasty. They're friends of Michael Herlihy, and worse, so if Michael asks questions, just tell him I asked you to look after the boat and you don't know any more about it than that, and if he wants the boat, or if anyone else wants it, just let it go! You understand me? I don't want you or your family to be hurt."

My mention of Mick Herlihy had made Johnny very unhappy. "This is IRA business, isn't it?" Johnny, like most of the American-Irish, had always insisted that the Irish Troubles were best left on the far side of the Atlantic. His own father, like mine, had loved to work himself into a lather about the injustices of Irish history, but Johnny had no belly for disliking anyone, not even the Brits.

"How is your dad?" I asked Johnny, rather than answer his question about the IRA's involvement.

"He died last year, God rest him."

"Oh, my God." I crossed myself. "Poor Eamonn."

"After Mom died he didn't have much interest in anything," Johnny said. "I couldn't even get him out on the boat! He was living with us by then, and Julie would try and keep him interested, you know, ask him to take the kids down to the beach or whatever, but he just wanted to be left alone. Father Murphy said some people just know when their time's come, and I reckon Dad decided his had."

"I never heard about your mom either," I confessed. "I'm sorry."

"You should have stayed in touch, Paulie," Johnny chided me, but gently, then he asked me again whether the gold on board the boat had anything to do with the IRA.

I was saved from answering because a very suspicious Gillespie pushed open the kitchen door. "What's going on?"

"Paulie's just telling me what he wants done with the house while he's away." Johnny, bless him, told the lie with all the conviction of a guileless man. "Are you sure you don't want aluminum siding?" he asked me. "The salt plays havoc with shingles, Paul, you should think about it."

"God no! No aluminum. Keep the cedar." I, a practised deceiver, sounded much less convincing, but Gillespie seemed reassured.

"If you're through?" he invited me to accompany him.

"And for God's sake, Johnny," I went on loudly enough for Sarah Sing Tennyson to overhear me, "make sure the girl gets the hell out of here."

Sarah Tennyson's anger flared to instant meltdown level. "Don't you dare come here again, Shanahan!" she shouted over Gillespie's shoulder. "I've already talked to my attorneys this morning and they say I signed the lease in good faith and I've paid the rent on time, so this place is mine." Johnny, ever a peacemaker, tried to calm her down, but she pushed the big man aside. "Do you hear me, Shanahan? This is my house for as long as the lease lasts, and if you break in here once more then so help me God I'll sue you and I'll take this house in lieu of damages and you will never set foot inside this place again. Never! Do you understand me, Shanahan?"

"Jesus," Gillespie muttered in awe, and no wonder, for Sarah Sing Tennyson in full strident flow was a classy act.

"What I understand," I said, "is that your lawyer can play let's-get-rich with my brother-in-law's lawyer, but I'm not involved, and I don't care to be involved. So you get your money back from Patrick McPhee and you send me the bill for the phone and the electric installation, and then you can take away your finger paintings, give me back the front-door key, and vanish."

She pointed to the front hall. "Get the hell out of my house, all of you!" Her scornful gesture encompassed Johnny, Gillespie and myself. "Out!"

"You pack your bags, and you get out!" I shouted as I was evicted from my own house. It was not the most effective of retorts, but it was the best I could manage and it left Sarah Sing Tennyson the undisputed victor of the hour.

"Let's just do as she says," Gillespie muttered. We scuttled ignominiously out to the driveway where Stuart Callaghan waited in the car. The hire car I'd rented at Logan Airport was also there, which hardly worried me. I had used the French prisoner's credit card to rent it and I guessed its owners would eventually get it back.

I looked back as we accelerated up the clam-shell drive and I saw Sarah Tennyson, her face a mask of outrage and anger, watching to make certain we really did leave my property. I blew her a kiss, received a rigid finger in reply, then we were over the sand ridge and into the scrub pine, and gone.

"I don't like Sarah Tennyson," I told Gillespie, "but someone should warn her that she's in danger if she stays in that house."

"I'll look after it." Gillespie made a note in a small book, then glanced out of the airplane window at the monotonous cloudscape that unreeled beneath us. We had driven to the small municipal airport at Hyannis where our six-seater plane had taken off into a sudden flurry of wet snow. Gillespie had already told me that the agency intended to keep me out of harm's way for as many weeks as it would take to empty me of secrets. "We're kind of excited to have you back," he had coyly confided as the plane had climbed through the clouds over Hyannis. "Not everyone thought that the Stringless Programme would work."

"It's still called that? The Stringless Programme?"

Gillespie glanced at the pilot, fearing that he could overhear our conversation, but the man was insulated with heavy earphones. "It's still called that."

"And you reckon it will take weeks to debrief me?"

"I'm sure you have a lot to tell us."

I thought of *Rebel Lady* and hoped to God that Johnny had no difficulties with her. Gillespie had gone back to his notebook, Callaghan was snoozing and the plane was droning through a winter bright sky high above the grey clouds. At Hyannis Airport I had bought a newspaper that told of war preparations on either side of the Kuwaiti frontier. The paper also reported on last-minute bids to prevent the fighting. Congressman O'Shaughnessy's house bill forbidding the use of American armed forces for one year had failed, yet the Congressman still preached his message of doom; he claimed now that the Pentagon had shipped fifty thousand body bags to the Gulf and said yet more were on order, and he was urging the President one last time to give economic sanctions a chance to bite. On an inside page was an article about the world-wide precautions against Iraq's expected terrorist onslaught; there were armoured vehicles patrolling European airports, air-passenger numbers had fallen drastically, and Western embassies throughout the world were mounting special guards. Saddam Hussein, happy to be in the spotlight of the world's nervousness, swore that he would never surrender, but would instead swamp the coalition forces and their homelands in infidel blood.

"Strap in!" the pilot called back as the plane suddenly banked and dropped. Raindrops streamed sternwards on the windows as we sliced into the clouds. The plane buffeted, dropped hard in an air-pocket, then reared back on a vicious up-current. An alarm beeped, then the servo-motors whined as the flaps extruded. "A bit rough, fellas!" the pilot apologised. "Sorry!"

Another lurch, another beep of the alarm, then we were out of the clouds and flying just feet above a dun-black and snow-streaked countryside. For a second I thought we were going to crash, then wet tarmac appeared beneath us, the wheels bounced, smoked and squealed, and we had come to earth. "Wilkes-Barre Scranton welcomes you," the pilot said facetiously. "Hell of a Goddamned day to fly."

The aircraft did not go near the small terminal, but instead taxied to where two cars waited. One was a limousine with black tinted windows and the other a police car. Two State Troopers wearing Smokey Bear hats and black rain-slickers stood by the limousine. Both troopers held rifles. The CIA clearly believed il Hayaween had a long reach.

We took Interstate 84 eastward into the snow-streaked forests of the Pocono Mountains. The bare trees had been splintered by ice-storms and the rock embankments which edged the road were thickly hung with icicles. We drove fast, our way cleared by the State Troopers. Deep in the mountains we turned off the Interstate and twisted our way up ever narrower roads until we reached a big painted sign that read 'US Department of Agriculture, Rabies Research Station, Absolutely NO Unauthorised Entry.' The State Troopers, their siren at last turned off, pulled on to the road's shoulder and waved the limo through.

I grinned. "I'm your mad dog, am I?"

Gillespie shrugged. "It keeps out the inquisitive."

The limousine stopped at a checkpoint manned by uniformed guards. A high fieldstone wall topped with coils of razor wire stretched into the forests either side of the gates. The guards peered at me, examined Gillespie's credentials, then the steel gates were mechanically opened and the limousine accelerated into a wide parkland studded with snow-shrouded rhododendrons. We passed between ploughed snow-banks, across a stone bridge that spanned an ice-locked stream, and into view of a massive, steep-roofed house that looked like some French mansion unaccountably marooned in a North American wilderness.

This was evidently to be my home for the foreseeable future. Here, under the mansion's coppered roof, I would be emptied of secrets, and it was not a bad place to be so emptied. The grand portico led into a palatial entrance hall that was furnished with a massive carved table, leather upholstered chairs, and a stone fireplace. Three stuffed mooseheads peered down from the dark panelled walls. A wooden staircase curled round three sides of the hall, embracing an intricate brass chandelier. I suspected the house had been donated to the government by the bewhiskered magnate whose varnished portrait hung gilt-framed above the stone mantel. It was the house of a nineteenth-century robber-baron; lavish, comfortable and bitterly cold. "Don't say the central heating's failed again!" Gillespie complained peevishly as he closed the heavy front doors.

"I'll find out," Callaghan said, and dived through a side-door.

Leading off the entrance hall was a library, its shelves, I later discovered, crammed with the collected writings of the founding fathers which was just the sort of dutiful yet unreadable collection one would expect of a patriotic millionaire. There was also a dining room, a kitchen, and an exercise room. The mansion's scores of other rooms were locked away. Other activities were conducted in the house, for during my stay I would sometimes see strangers walking in the grounds, and once I heard women's laughter coming from the other side of the bolted door in our dining room, but my interrogation was conducted in the isolation of the few rooms opening off the main hall and its immediate landing upstairs. My quarters were on that second floor; a private bathroom, a small kitchenette and a lavish bedroom which held a wide bed, a sofa, a desk, rugs, a bookcase full of thrillers, a reproduction of a drab Corot landscape and a television set. Unlike the downstairs rooms the heat here was working only too well. In my bedroom a steam radiator hissed and clanked under a barred window that could not be opened. I stooped to the thriller-packed bookcase. "A nice collection."

"Not that we hope you'll have much time for reading,"

Gillespie said. "We expect to be holding conversations with you most days and for quite long hours, though there will be some evenings when you will be unoccupied. The refrigerator is stocked, but let us know, within reason, if there is any particular food you'd like added to the stock. There's beer, but no spirits. The television works."

"And the telephone?" I gestured at the phone beside the bed.

"Of course."

"And it isn't bugged?" I teased him.

"I couldn't truthfully tell you either way." Gillespie actually blushed as he half admitted I was under surveillance, but only a complete fool would have assumed otherwise. He ushered me towards the door. "We have a lot to do, Mr Shanahan, so shall we go downstairs and begin?"

To unpick the past. To tell a tale of bombers and gunners, girls and boys, heroes and lovers. Confession time.

I was tired, dog tired. "We won't take a lot of time today," Gillespie promised, "but your messages to our people in Brussels were kind of intriguing." He was being very tactful, not asking why I had appeared in America when I had promised to walk into the Brussels Embassy, nor asking why I had used a false name. "You talked about Stingers? About a meeting in Miami? You suggested a connection with Saddam Hussein? With il Hayaween?"

That was the urgent need; to discover just what evil Iraq had planned, and so I told Gillespie everything about the meeting in Florida where Michael Herlihy and Brendan Flynn had introduced me to the two Cubans named Alvarez and Carlos though I suspected they might as well have called themselves Tweedledum and Tweedledee for all those names signified. I described how the Provisional IRA had negotiated the purchase of fifty-three Stinger missiles for one and a half million dollars.

Gillespie wrote the sum down. I was certain that the library must be wired for sound, and that somewhere in the mansion tape recorders were spooling down my every word, but Gillespie was the kind of man who liked to make notes. "And why were you invited to the meeting?" he asked.

"Because I used to be the Provisionals' liaison officer with outside terrorist organisations. I was the guy who fetched them their goodies. I was their money-man."

Gillespie's head came up from his notebook and for a second or two I thought he was actually going to whistle with astonishment, but he managed to suppress the urge. Nevertheless my words, if I could back them up with chapter and verse, meant that the CIA's Stringless Programme could chalk up one stunning success. "You liaised with all outside terrorist organisations?" he asked.

"So far as I know, yes, although in effect that was mainly the Palestinians and the Libyans. We did some business with the Basques as well, but they were never as important as the Middle Eastern guys."

"Red Army Faction? The Baader-Meinhof people?" Gillespie asked.

"Never saw them."

"The South Americans?" he asked hopefully.

I shook my head. "The IRA used to receive fraternal greetings from Cuba and Nicaragua, but no material support. We didn't need it. We were getting enough weapons from the Libyans and enough money from America, so why should we bother with a bunch of half-crazy Nicaraguans?"

"Even so!" Gillespie was impressed by the Middle-Eastern connections, though I rather deflated the good impression by telling him how the IRA had ceased to trust me four years before which meant that much of my information was out of date.

"Why did they stop trusting you?"

"That's kind of a long story."

"We'll get to it, I promise." He tapped his notebook with the eraser end of his pencil. "If you've been inactive for four years, why did you stay? Why didn't you come home?"

"Because I always hoped they'd reactivate me. They never cut me off entirely."

"We're fortunate they didn't." We were sitting in the lavish library, either side of the massive oak table. It was a comfortable room, supplied with a fire and a drinks cabinet and enough oak mouldings to have hidden a thousand microphones. Despite Gillespie's notebook I knew the surveillance devices existed, not just in this room but in my bedroom as well, for the Agency would want to analyse my answers for the slightest indication of stress. Gillespie was chasing a commodity as rare as rainbow's gold, the truth, and he wanted to make sure I was not bringing him fool's gold. Maybe my return at this critical time had happened because the enemy had turned me? Maybe I was telling lies to make them look in one direction while il Hayaween attacked from another? I might be a hero of the Stringless Programme come back from the world's darkness, but that did not mean they would trust me.

Nor did I intend to trust them. I had my secrets, chief of which was the existence of five million dollars in a renamed yacht. The five million dollars were my pension, my security, and I had no intention of ever letting the government know that such a sum had even been discussed. The money was not important. What was important were the Stingers, and il Hayaween, and Saddam Hussein's plans to spread terror world-wide.

"You say il Hayaween talked about bringing down an airliner at Heathrow with a Red Star?" Gillespie asked.

I nodded. "It's much easier than trying to smuggle a bomb aboard."

"But why a Russian missile? Why not the Stingers?"

"Because the Stingers are in America. I'm guessing that they never did mean to send all the Stingers to Ireland, but to deploy them in the States."

"You mean . . ." Gillespie stared at me.

"I mean that if we attack Saddam Hussein's forces in Kuwait then he'll bring down planes in Washington and Miami and New York and anywhere else he can."

Gillespie blanched at the thought of guarding the vicinity of every major civilian airport in North America. "And do you believe the Provisional IRA would co-operate with such an action?"

"No," I said firmly, "because the IRA wants American support. Part of their income and a lot of their respectability depends on Americans thinking of the Irish as harmless little leprechauns inhabiting an idyllic little island which is being unjustly treated by the nasty English, and blowing up American civilians with IRA weapons tends to sour that fairy-tale image. So I suspect the IRA are being used by il Hayaween. The Palestinians aren't in a position to travel to Miami to buy the missiles, but the Irish are. However, once the missiles are paid for, then God knows what il Hayaween has in mind."

"How were the Stingers paid for?"

"The usual method," I said, "is electronic transfer. I never handled the money itself, just the request, but I know the Libyans liked to use a bank called BCCI . . ."

"We know about those bastards," Gillespie said meaningfully, then shrugged an apology for interrupting me. "Go on, please."

"There isn't much more to tell. I requested the payment from Shafiq, he told me it was all OKed, and then I telephoned a number in Ireland to say that everything was on line and their money would be coming. They'd already paid a half-million deposit, so I only asked Shafiq for the one million."

"You have the telephone number in Ireland?"

I gave him the number that had been in Gerry's suit pocket, but warned him that it would almost certainly belong to a message-taker who would have no inkling of what the messages were about.

Stuart Callaghan, whose bodyguard duties seemed exhausted now that we had arrived at the safe mansion, had lit a fire in the library's big hearth. Now, at Gillespie's bidding, he took away the new details of the Stinger trade, doubtless to telephone them through to Langley so that the search for the missiles could be intensified. Gillespie still worried at my story. "What about the two Cubans. Were they Cuban-Americans? Or Cuban-Cubans?"

"I've no idea."

Gillespie tapped the pencil softly on the table. "Comrade Fidel must be itching to do his bit for Brother Saddam, mustn't he?"

"I guess so. I don't know."

"BCCI." He drew a pencil round the bank's initials. "You say the Libyans usually transferred money by wire?"

"Almost always. It's heavy stuff to carry around in a suitcase."

He half smiled at my half-jest. "So there should be a record of the transaction?"

"Bound to be."

"And of the half-million dollar deposit. Where would that have come from?"

"Boston, I guess, but I don't know. Herlihy must use a dozen banks."

"Look for the money," Gillespie said softly, "it's always the same. Look for the money." He looked up at me. "One last question before we break. Why did you use a false passport to enter the country?"

"How do you know I did?"

"Because we had an all-ports watch alerted for you."

"Maybe I walked across the Canadian border?"

"The Canadians co-operate with our all-ports watch alerts," Gillespie said softly. "And what about your hire-car? You used a French name and credit card? But it seems the card really belongs to a prisoner?"

"Habit," I said, "just old habit. I guess I wanted to use false papers one last time. A whim."

"You still have the passport and credit card?"

"I tossed them. I told you, it was my last time. I won't need false papers again, will I?"

"No, you won't." Gillespie pretended to believe me. He closed his notebook and carefully snapped a rubber band around its leather covers. "I guess that's the immediate business taken care of. What I'd like you to do now, Paul, is take a rest. You look bushed. Maybe we'll pick up this afternoon? There'll be someone with me by then."

"Van Stryker?" Simon van Stryker had recruited me into the Stringless Programme and I had liked him. I had spent years looking forward to meeting him again, hearing his congratulations.

"Van Stryker's rather exalted these days. But you will meet him in due course. He takes an interest in you." Gillespie paused and had the grace to look somewhat embarrassed. "We've asked one of the Agency's psychiatrists to sit in on future sessions. It's normal practice."

"To find out if I've gone mad?" I asked lightly.

"Something like that, yes," he replied just as lightly. In fact the shrink would be there to detect my lies.

"Fine by me!" I said.

"Great." Gillespie smiled. I smiled. Just great.

The psychiatrist surprised me because her appearance suggested someone who ought to have been knitting baby socks for a grandchild rather than monitoring a debriefing about terrorism, but doubtless she was a lot shrewder than her motherly, plump exterior suggested. She was a middle-aged black woman who smiled pleasantly at me, then shook the snow off her overshoes and settled in the bay window at the far end of the long library table. "Terrible weather," she said cosily, "just terrible. Do you mind if I call you Paul? I'm Carole, Carole Adamson."

"Paul's fine."

"Don't you mind me, Paul. I'm just here to listen." She was wearing a thick wool cardigan, wooden beads, and had a comfortable smile. She also frightened me for I was only too ready to believe that psychiatrists possessed arcane powers, and that my every little lie and evasion would telegraph themselves to Carole Adamson's shrewd and watchful eyes. I could not see her without turning in my chair, but I was very aware of her scrutiny.

Gillespie began the afternoon session by saying FBI agents had begun their search for the Stinger missiles and for their Cuban vendors. In the meantime, he said, he wanted to explore my history of terrorist connections. "I want to go back to the very beginning," he said. "Who introduced you to the IRA?"

"A guy called Joey Grogan."

"Was that in America?" Gillespie asked. "Or in Ireland?"

"In Boston," I said, and felt a flicker of annoyance. I had

come here to talk of il Hayaween and Stingers and the Palestinian training camps, and instead Gillespie wanted to plough this old field. "Why don't you just look up the file?" I asked.

"Because the Stringless Programme keeps no files," Gillespie said in a tone which suggested I should have known that. "All we know about you is what we can read in police records, but as far as the agency is concerned, Mr Shanahan, you have never existed. So we have to begin at the beginning. Where does Mr Grogan live?"

"He's dead." Poor Joey had died of emphysema in 1986 and Peggy, his widow, had immediately absconded to a trailer park in Florida with sixteen thousand dollars collected from Boston's Irish bars by the Friends of Free Ireland. The Friends ostensibly collected money to support the widows and orphans of IRA soldiers, which was hardly necessary considering the generosity of the British government's social security system, but everyone assumed the donations were for buying guns anyway. In practice much of the cash never went further than Boston's Irish bars, and what little did reach Ireland was a hundred times more likely to end up in a pub's cash-till than in the hands of a gunman's widow.

"You were recruited into the IRA before you met us?" Gillespie asked. "Before you met van Stryker?"

"I was supporting them, sure, but I didn't join the IRA proper till I went to live in Ireland."

"But you're confirming you were a long-time supporter? Was that for ideological reasons?"

"Ideological?"

Gillespie shrugged. "The Provisional IRA is a self-professed Marxist organisation, is it not?" He was being very prim.

I laughed. "Come on. Get real!"

"Well, isn't it?" He had very pale blue eyes that were not quite as friendly as his diffident manner suggested.

I shook my head. "The IRA says it's Marxist when they're dealing with socialist supporters like Colonel Qaddafi, and they say they're good Catholic boys when they're treating with the American-Irish in Boston. Most of them wouldn't know a Marxist if one raped them with a hammer and a blunt sickle. Two or three of the Army Council are probably Party members, but the IRA itself is either just a good old-fashioned patriotic liberation movement, or else a more than usually ruthless criminal organisation, depending on just how close to it you happen to live."

"So why did you join?"

"Because the Irish are my tribe! Because I learned about Wolfe Tone and Patrick Pearse long before anyone in my family thought to tell me about George Washington. Because I swallowed stories of the famine with my mother's milk. There probably isn't a family in South Boston that doesn't claim ancestors who were put to the sword by Cromwell, or massacred in the rising of '98, or starved in the famine, or beaten up by the Black and Tans. Those claims are our tribal badges!"

Gillespie wanted to know about my childhood, but there were no dark secrets there. I had been a happy child, dividing my time between our family's Boston house, my father's Cape Cod retreat, and his various business premises. Those premises ranged from the Green Harp Bar in Charlestown to a marina in Weymouth, but my father's real fortune was made from his brothels in Scollay Square.

"Brothels?" Gillespie asked painfully.

"They pulled them down," I said, "to build the new City Hall. Some people haven't noticed any difference."

"And your mother? What was her attitude to your father's businesses?"

"My mother worshipped the Virgin Mary. She believed every mother was born to suffer, and she wouldn't have wanted it any other way. She endured my father and adored her three children."

"But you must have been a trial to her?" Gillespie smiled to show he meant no offence. "We took the trouble to find your old police records."

"I told you, Mom believed women were born to suffer. That's what the priest and the nuns told her, and that's how she wanted it." Not that my police record held anything more sinister than the usual juvenile indiscretions. I had first been in court for beating ten kinds of living hell out of a man who had insulted my sister, and two years after that I did four months for receiving stolen goods.

"And your father died while you were in prison?" Gillespie observed.

"Yes."

"How did he die?"

"He was in the back room of a Southie Bar when some bastards decided to burn the place down. They shot him first."

"Why?"

"We were told it was an insurance scam."

"You believe that?"

"Maybe they didn't like his beer?" I smiled.

Gillespie stared thoughtfully at me. "It must have been upsetting for you."

"What?"

"Your father's death. You were only twenty-one, that's too young to lose a parent."

"What are you trying to prove?" I challenged him. "I thought I was here to help you guys, and instead you're trying to make out that I'm some kind of basket-case because my pa died? I don't need your counselling, Gillespie, or some crappy male-bonding session. I had a happy childhood, I thought Boston was a wonderful playground, and I think it's sad that my parents are both dead, but I don't suck my thumb or go in for pederasty or whimper in the night, so shall we move the fuck on?"

Carole Adamson tried to reassure me. "It's important

that we understand where you're coming from, Paul. Your life is the context for the answers you give us."

"What happened to your father's killers?" Gillespie had been entirely unmoved by my protest.

"Beats me," I shrugged, "the bastards were never found."

"I thought two of the suspected killers were found in the Charles River? Strangled?"

"Were they now?" I asked innocently.

"And a third man was found with his head thrust down a toilet in a Roxbury bar. He had drowned. The police believe that you and your brother were in that same bar on that night, but could find no witnesses to verify that belief."

"I thought you said I was in prison?"

"The parole board had released you on compassionate grounds before the funeral. And your brother was on leave from the Marine Corps."

I shrugged and spread my hands as though I knew nothing.

Gillespie turned a page in his notebook. "Your brother died in Vietnam?"

"Hue. And no, his death didn't make me angry at America."

Gillespie ignored the irrelevance. "So how did you earn a living after your father's death?"

"I took over his businesses."

"Including the brothels?"

"I told you, they pulled those down. No, all I kept was the marina at Weymouth and the Green Harp Bar in Charlestown. I sold everything else." I had been twenty-one, rich as a dream and cock of the Boston walk, but the money had slipped away like ice on a summer sidewalk. I let cronies use the marina slips for free, I ran a slate for friends in the Green Harp and I flew to Ireland to play the rich Irish-American to the admiring natives. I also made the bookmakers happy. On one day alone I dropped a hundred thousand dollars at Fairyhouse, a fair bit of it on a horse called Sally-So-Fair which started at a hundred to one and finished as dogmeat. I had sworn the horse could not lose, mainly on the grounds that I had spent the previous night with two whores, both called Sally and both fair-haired, but they were each a better goer than the horse.

I had to sell the marina and a half-share in the bar to pay my debts. I promised my mother I would be good, but the promise was easier to make than the keeping of it. My half-share in the Green Harp made money, but the money trickled away on girls and booze and horses. My mother wanted me to marry some good Catholic virgin, but I had smelt the milk-and-diaper stench of respectability and knew it was not for me. I needed the spice of danger, and Joey Grogan brought it me.

Joey was a passionate man, drunk with Irish myths and obsessed with liberating his ancestral home. I had first met him when he arrived at the Green Harp Bar to empty the Friends of Free Ireland collecting box that we kept alongside the Parish Fund box and the Multiple Sclerosis box and the Send the Kids to Camp box and the United Way box and any other charity box so long as it was not a Protestant box, but Joey scornfully swept all the other boxes aside and told me that there was only one cause worth supporting, and that was the cause of a united Ireland. I watched, amused, as he broke the other boxes open and poured their miserable harvest of dimes and pennies into his own pile. Later he recruited me to help him assemble an arms shipment for Ulster. The shipment was small stuff, mostly old handguns that we bought on the street corners of Boston, but still good enough, Joey said, to kill Brits. We sent them in a container load of panty-hose bound for Cork.

"Panty-hose?" Gillespie asked in disbelief.

Five years later, I said, Joey and I were sending big stuff; Armalites, Ingrams and even a pair of M60 machine-guns that had been liberated from a Massachusetts National

Guard Armory, but by then the Middle East had already overtaken America as the source of the Provisional IRA's weapons. We had become minor league, and Libya was the heavy hitter. "What year was that?" Gillespie asked.

"It was '76 when we sent the M60s. As a kind of reminder to the Brits of another '76."

"That was the year your mother died?"

"God rest her. She had cancer."

There was brief silence. A log spat angrily in the fire, arcing a spark that smouldered for a fierce and smoky second on the sacrificial coir rug that protected the library's parquet floor from just such embers. "Was it the death of your mother," Gillespie asked mildly, "that gave you the freedom to enter the drug trade?"

"I was never in the drug trade," I snapped. The debriefing had turned hostile because I resented this harrowing of my past. It seemed irrelevant to me. I had always been uncomfortable in the confessional because I hated to reflect on my actions. I was impetuous, generous and foolish, but not reflective. The truth was that I had smuggled drugs to make a quick buck, and a big buck, just as I had killed Liam and Gerry to make an even bigger and faster buck, but doing it did not mean I had to dwell on it, and I had small patience for my countrymen's love of self-analysis and self-absorption. My dad had taught me to live life at full throttle and not to worry about the rear-view mirrors, but these sessions with Gillespie promised to be long, uncomfortable bouts of mirror-gazing and I did not like it.

Gillespie turned a page in his folder. "In 1977 you were arrested in a boat called the *Fighting Irish* off the Boca Inlet in Florida, and the boat was carrying half a ton of marijuana. The Coastguard had tracked you from the Turks and Caicos Islands."

"I was charged?" I challenged him.

"Of course not." Because instead of going for trial I had gone underground, saved by a codfish aristocrat called

Simon van Stryker and his Stringless Programme. I had become legitimate.

Simon van Stryker was a WASP superstar; a man born to inestimable privilege, with immaculate manners and a gentle demeanour which nevertheless suggested that he could be as ruthless as a hungry rattlesnake. He was tall, elegant, beautifully spoken, and had pale green eyes as cold as the water off Nova Scotia. The moment I first saw him I knew his type, just as he knew mine. I was two-toilet Irish and he was the codfish aristocracy. The codfish aristocracy had never liked my kind for we were the incontinent, fecund, ill-spoken Papist immigrants who had fouled up their perfect Protestant America in the nineteenth century, but van Stryker still became my recruiter, my master, my friend. Van Stryker had saved me from God knows how many years in a federal prison in the depths of the Everglades surrounded by alligators, rattlers, coral snakes and Aids-riddled rapists waiting in the showers.

Instead he had taken me to a house in Georgia, not unlike the house where Gillespie now took my secrets apart. There, surrounded by camellias and azaleas, van Stryker and his team had probed me and analysed me and prepared me.

"Are you a patriot?" they had wanted to know, but they had hardly needed to ask for I had only to hear 'America the Beautiful' for the tears to start. We Shanahans had always been emotional. We were Irish after all, the cry babies of the Western world, and of course I was a patriot because America was my country. My love for it was laid down like the sediments of the seabed, dark and immovable, and however hard the wind blew or high the seas broke, still that ocean floor was as calm and still and unchanging as the farthest cold cinders of the universe. To me patriotism was bred in the bone, a part of the blood, etched till death. Show me Old Glory and I cry, play me 'The Star-Spangled Banner' and I weep.

So what did I feel about Ireland?

That was easy. Ireland was forty shades of green and smiling eyes and shamrocks and shillelaghs and the road ever rising to meet you and the St Patrick's Day parade when all South Boston went gloriously drunk. Ireland was dancing the jig and good talk and warm hearts and fellowship.

And England? they asked.

England was where the cold-hearted bores came from; the bank managers and the Republicans, the golfers and the Episcopalians.

And killing such cold fish was forgivable?

"I never killed one of the bastards in my life!" I protested.

But what about the work I did for the Friends of Free Ireland in Boston. Did I not collect money for the cause?

Sure I did, but so what if the money went to buy guns and bombs? It was for expelling the English from Ireland and hadn't the English been slaughtering the Irish for centuries?

Had I ever seen a child eviscerated by a bomb? Simon van Stryker asked me.

I had shrugged the question away, but Simon van Stryker had photographs of the child. She had been three years old, waiting with her mother at a bus stop in Belfast. The mother had died too, her legs torn off by the bomb blast. The bomb had been the work of the IRA. For a new Ireland.

And here were pictures of a woman tarred and feathered. Her hair had been cut off before the leprechauns jeered at her and smeared her with hot tar and chicken feathers, and all because her husband, who had made three widows and eleven orphans, was in jail for life and she had assuaged her loneliness by sleeping with another man. The woman was nineteen. Her lover had been a Catholic, and him they had beaten into a wheelchair. They were the IRA.

And here was a man whose kneecaps had been shot away.

A boy of sixteen had pulled the trigger and the victim would never walk again. The man was a Catholic and had been accused of giving information to the Ulster Defence Association which was one of the Protestant para-military groups, but in truth the victim had never talked to them. It had all been a mistake and the Provisional IRA had apologised for it. They made a lot of apologies because it helped convince Boston and New York that they were honourable men.

And here was another man, also a Catholic, whose kneecaps had been shot through. He had owned a hardware store, selling penny nails and epoxy glue, but he had refused to pay the IRA their protection money so one night they had come for him with a loaded gun and taken him into his backyard and shot him through the kneecaps while his wife screamed in the kitchen. Then they shot his dog to stop it barking and threatened to shoot the wife down if she did not stop her noise. They burned his shop down too.

Look at the photographs, Simon van Stryker had ordered me. Look at them. Look at them. I remember how the paths between the magnolias were drifted with fallen petals, thick as snowdrifts, the petals turning brown and curling at the edges.

Terrorism, Simon van Stryker told me back inside the Georgia house, is a means, not a cause. You can love the sinner, but you must hate the sin. Terrorism, by its very nature, is random. It must strike the innocent. Terrorism must kill the child if it is to shock the adult. Terrorism must hurt the helpless if it is to gain the world's attention. Terrorism, he told me again and again, is evil. It did not matter how noble was the cause that the terrorist served, the methods were evil. You could wrap terrorism in a flag of the most delicate green, but that did not make it right.

"They have no choice!" I tried to argue with him.

"They chose evil," he said. A terrorist chooses to use the bullet and the bomb because he knows that if he relinquishes those weapons then he is reduced to the level of ordinary politicians who had to struggle with the mundane problems of education, health, and unemployment. Terrorists, having no answer to those matters, talked in transcendent terms. They claimed their bullets would bring in the millennium and their bombs would make a perfect world. But in the end, van Stryker told me, it was still just terror, and if I wanted one creed to cling to over the years then I should remember that no matter how good the cause, it was wrong if it used terror as a means of achievement.

"What years?" I had asked.

"The years," he said, "that you would otherwise have spent in prison for running drugs. I saved you from those years, so now you will give them to me. And to America."

He explained that the CIA's Division of Counter-Terrorism used the usual weapons of espionage against the various terrorist and insurgent groups which threatened American interests, but those usual weapons were rarely useful. Terrorists were too cautious to confide their plans to telephones that could be wiretapped, and they were too experienced to share their information with a circle of people who could be suborned into treachery. Terrorist cells were wonderfully designed to resist intelligence operations. It was possible to smash one cell, but to do no damage to any others. Terrorism's secrets were protected by a wall of rumour and a moat of disinformation. Some terrorists did not even claim responsibility for atrocities they performed, preferring that the West should never learn who had inflicted the hurt.

"And the West is the target," van Stryker told me. "We Westerners are the possessors, so we must be attacked and hurt and mauled and bombed and humiliated. But we in the West have one terrorist organisation that is all our own, and which is trusted by the others, and if we can insert one good man into that organisation then it's possible, just possible, that he can travel far and deep into its darkness and one day, in his own good time, bring back news from that journey."

"You mean me."

"I mean you."

"You want me to betray the Irish?"

"Which Irish?" He had rounded on me scornfully. "The IRA claims to detest the Free State's Dublin government as strongly as they hate London. The Irish electorate doesn't vote for the IRA and most of the Irish people want nothing more than to see the IRA disappear! Besides, my enemy is not just the IRA. My enemies are the friends of the IRA; the Libyans and the Palestinians."

"So how do I reach them?"

"Let the IRA work that out. We'll merely equip you with the skills that will suggest to them that you might make a perfect courier. IRA activists can't move in Europe without the police of a dozen nations watching, but the Garda and the British Special Branch won't take any interest in an American yacht-delivery skipper."

We were walking along a damp path between the glistening leaves of the magnolias. "Supposing the IRA don't do what you think they'll do?" I asked van Stryker.

"Then I'll have wasted your time, and a lot of government money."

"And what do I make from it?" I had asked truculently.

"You're free, Paul. You're not in a Florida jail. You'll be taught a trade, given the capital to start your own business, and a ticket to Ireland."

"And when will you be finished with me?"

"When does a fisherman come home?"

"When his fish-hold is full."

"So bring me back a rich catch in your own good time."

We had stopped at the edge of the garden above a deep valley where a freight train wound its way northward. "Why me?" I asked him.

Van Stryker had laughed. "Because you're a scoundrel, Paul, a bad lot, a rogue, a rascal. I can hire any number of MBAs, straight-arrows, Rhodes scholars every one, but how often do I find a scoundrel who runs guns to Ireland and who murdered his father's killers? No, don't deny it." Van Stryker had offered me a quirky, almost affectionate smile. "When you sup with the devil, Paul, it is prudent to use a very long spoon and you're my spoon."

"And suppose I never come back?"

Van Stryker shrugged. "I didn't say there was no risk. Maybe you'll leave here and do nothing? Maybe you'll betray this programme? Maybe, probably perhaps, I'll never hear from you again. All I can do is offer you a new life and what you make of it is up to you. You aren't the only one I'm sending into the darkness, and if just one of you comes home it might be worth it."

And now I had come home to tell my secrets.

All but one.

Gillespie spent the first few days constructing a framework of my years abroad. He wanted names, places, facts, dates. Then, when he had the chronology straight and a rough idea of just what secrets I could tell, he brought in the experts who came to the mansion by helicopter to pick my brains. They were the agency's specialists on the Middle Eastern terrorist groups.

Gillespie imported no one to listen to my Irish tales, but instead took me through those years himself. I told him how I had gone to live in Dublin and then, at Brendan Flynn's request, to Belfast where I had started a yacht-surveying and -delivery service that acted as a marvellous cover for the smuggling of weapons, explosives and gunmen across the Irish Sea. I described how I had planted two bombs in Belfast, not because the IRA had needed another bomber, but because they wanted to see if I could be trusted.

"Did anyone die in the explosions?" Carole Adamson asked.

"No," I said. "We phoned in warnings."

"We?" Gillespie asked.

"A guy called Seamus Geoghegan led the unit. They brought him in from Derry."

"We know of Mr Geoghegan," Gillespie said. He told me Seamus was now in Boston, fighting off a British attempt to extradite him. Seamus's defence was that he was a political refugee entitled to the protection of the American Constitution, while the British argued that he was a common murderer; the American Anglophiles claimed he was an illegal immigrant and the Anglophobes said he was a hero. It was a tangle out of which only the lawyers would emerge enriched. Gillespie asked me about Seamus, but I could add nothing to the public record.

"How did you feel about the two bombings?" Gillespie asked. Outside it was snowing gently, covering the already snow-heaped bushes with a new layer of glittering white.

"I was doing what van Stryker wanted me to do. I was infiltrating the IRA." I said it defiantly.

"But did you enjoy it?" Gillespie probed.

"I got drunk after it. Both times."

"Did you enjoy it?" He insisted on the question.

"It was exciting," I allowed. "You take risks when you plant a bomb and you don't want the excitement to end, so when the job's done you go to a bar and drink. You boast. You listen to other men boasting." That was true, but I could just as easily have said that we got drunk because we did not want to think about what we had just done. Because we knew that nothing had been achieved by the bomb and nothing ever would be achieved. The only believers in terrorism were the fanatics who led the movement and their very youngest and most stupid recruits. Everyone else was trapped in their roles. I remembered Seamus Geoghegan shaking like a leaf, not out of fear, but out of a kind of hopelessness. "It's a terrible thing," he had told me that day, "but if you and I had been born in Liverpool, Paulie, we'd be fighting for the focking Brits, wouldn't we?" There was nothing ideological in the fight, nothing constructive, it was just a tribal rite, a scream, a habit, a protest. But it was also exciting, full of comradeship, full of jest and whiskey and daring. The cause gave our violence its licence and it salved our consciences with its specious justifications.

"You have a conscience about what you did?" Carole Adamson asked me.

"I was doing it for America, wasn't I?" I slid away from her inquiry.

And for America I had triumphed when, in 1980, the IRA asked me to be their liaison officer with other terrorist groups. They saw me as a man who could move about the world without attracting suspicion, and even suggested I move to Europe where my existence would provoke even less attention. I took the marine business to Nieuwpoort where I hired Hannah as my part-time secretary, rescued the cat from the alleyway opposite my house, and began trawling the dark seas for van Stryker's profit.

"What sort of business did you conduct with these other terrorist groups?" Gillespie asked in his mild monotonous voice.

I spread my hands as if to suggest the answer could go on for ever, but then offered a short version. "The Basques were after our bombing expertise, especially our electronic timers, while the Palestinians got a kick out of providing us with weaponry. I was a kind of procurement officer with them."

"And the weaponry is all of Communist origin?"

I nodded. "Most of the weapons came from Russia and the explosives from Czechoslovakia, but the Kremlin didn't want their involvement to be too obvious so they used Muammar al-Qaddafi as a middleman."

"And that was the extent of Qaddafi's involvement? He was just a middleman?"

I shook my head. "He's the IRA's Godfather."

"Godfather?"

"Whatever the IRA wants, Qaddafi will give them. Not

because he cares about Ireland, he probably doesn't even know where Ireland is, but because he hates Britain." Qaddafi's hatred had intensified following Margaret Thatcher's permission for the American bombers to use British bases for their attack on Tripoli. After that raid nothing had been too good for the Provisional IRA. They had become the beloved of Allah, warriors of the Prophet, Qaddafi's chosen instruments of vengeance.

"He gives more than weapons?" Gillespie asked.

"Weapons, advice, training, refuge."

"Weapons training?"

"The Provisionals don't need that. But I know they've sent at least two guys to Tripoli to learn interrogation techniques. Up till then, if they thought there was a traitor, they simply punched the poor bastard rotten and as often as not they killed the fellow before they got a squeak out of him. Nowadays, though, they use Libyan techniques. They're much more painful and much more certain." I paused as a great slough of snow slid off the roof and plummeted on to the walk outside the window.

"You arranged for this training?" Gillespie asked.

"Yes."

"And the names of the trainees?"

"I wasn't given their names. They were simply codenamed John and Michael." Later Gillespie showed me photographs of IRA men, but I found neither of the two I had escorted to Tripoli.

The first experts arrived from Langley. There was a small and excitable man with pebble-glasses who knew an extraordinary amount about how illegal immigrants were smuggled into the south of France, and wanted to know whether terrorist groups used the same routes. I gave him what help I could. Another man, dry as a stick, tried to trace the financial links between Libya and the various groups, while a third came to ask me about the East German training camp at Tantow which I had visited twice. Every day there were more photograph albums, more pictures, more dull hours turning stiff pages of expressionless faces.

A dark-haired woman arrived to talk about Libya and its support of terrorism. She showed me a photograph of Shafiq and I told her about his taste for pomade and his lust for French women, and about his grey elegant suits and his penchant for cachous and Gauloise cigarettes. She wanted to know about the methods Shafiq had used to contact me, and the places we had met and the codes we had devised for our telephone conversations. I talked about the Centre to Resist Imperialism, Racism, Backwardness and Fascism, then gave the name of the whorehouse in Marseilles that Shafiq thought was his private domain, and I wondered how long it would be before some Western agent dragged Shafiq from the brothel's front steps and into a waiting car. The car would have had the locks of its back doors removed so there could be no fatal last-second fumbling. Instead the doors would be tensioned with bungee cords that would swing shut as the car accelerated away. Or perhaps Shafiq would be seduced by some thin-boned French blonde who would suck him dry before releasing him to Qaddafi's vengeance.

"You met Qaddafi?" the woman asked. She was attractive, with a quick face and a sharp mind. It was she who told me about Shafiq's wife and three daughters in their Tripoli apartment. I never knew her name, nor those of any of the other experts who flew in from the CIA's Langley headquarters.

"I met Qaddafi," I said, and described his bitter anger after the American air raid on Tripoli. "He was especially mad at the Brits because Thatcher had allowed the bombers to take off from British airbases."

"So you negotiated the arms shipments he sent to the IRA as revenge?" she asked.

"I didn't have to negotiate. I had to stop him from shipping his whole arsenal. He would have sent everything he had."

"What about his plans for revenge on the Americans?"

"I suspect he brought down the jumbo jet over Lockerbie," I suggested, "but he didn't talk to me about that, only about the IRA."

"Now let us talk about il Hayaween," the CIA woman said vengefully. "God, but I'd like his hide nailed to my barn door."

I dutifully described his face, his clothes, his mastery of English, his sunglasses, his Blancpain watch, his injured right hand and his taste for American cigarettes. I had revealed most of those details in previous sessions with Gillespie, and the woman had come prepared with photographs of Blancpain watches so I could identify which exact model I had bought in Vienna. She also wanted some confirmation of the legends about him, but I had no knowledge of his sins. I had only heard rumours, such as the stories of his massacre of Israeli schoolchildren. "You believe that?" the woman asked.

"Yes, I think I do."

Gillespie, who sat in on all the sessions, shuddered. "How does a man live with the knowledge of a deed like that?"

"Maybe he has no imagination?" Carole Adamson suggested from her customary seat in the window.

I shook my head. "The best killers have imagination. To be as cunning as il Hayaween you must have imagination. That's what makes him so good. But he also thinks he's doing God's work."

"Do the IRA think they're doing God's work?" Gillespie asked without a trace of irony.

I laughed. "There's an old tale, Gillespie, of the aeroplane flying into Belfast and the pilot switches on his microphone and welcomes the passengers to Aldergrove Airport and says that the temperature is fifty-five degrees and there's a light rain coming out of the north and if they'd like to turn their watches to local time then they should wind them back three hundred years." The joke belly-flopped like a pregnant pole-vaulter. Gillespie and the CIA expert both frowned while Carole Adamson just shook her head to show she did not understand. "Three hundred years ago," I explained, "Europe was being torn apart by the wars of religion. Protestant against Catholic. Try and imagine a small island, three hundred years from now, where the natives will still be knocking technicolour shit out of each other in the name of communism versus the free market."

"So you do think the troubles in Ireland are about religion?" Gillespie asked. He was genuinely trying to understand. Terrorism, after all, was a very strange phenomenon to most Americans. It was a disease inflicted on the first world by crazed creatures from the slums of the old world and the refugee camps of the third, and Gillespie wanted me to explain the disease's origin.

I shook my head. "Religion in Ireland just defines which side you're on. The Troubles are about people who feel they have no control over their own lives, about people who live in public housing and have no jobs and eat bad food and smoke themselves to death and see their kids born to the same hopelessness and they just want to hit back against someone, almost anyone."

"So you're saying it's an economic problem?" the smart dark-haired woman asked earnestly.

"It isn't economic, but the Troubles are bound to feed off a bad economy. The IRA campaign of the 1950s collapsed because there was full employment, because no one felt deprived, because people were too busy paying off the instalments on their cars and television sets, but nowadays there are no jobs in Belfast, there's no future, there's no hope, so all that's left is the pleasure of revenge. What else can the poor bastards do? They know the south doesn't like them, and that the Brits would like nothing better than to get the hell out, and that in truth no one really wants anything to do with them at all, and so they fight back the only way they can; with bullets and bombs and the pleasure of knowing they're reducing other people to their own level of misery."

There was silence for a while. Outside the window the snow fell.

"Is there no conscience there?" Gillespie asked at last.

"The clever ones pickle it in alcohol, and the stupid ones put their trust in the clever ones." I gave the answer glibly, but I was thinking of Seamus Geoghegan and how I had once asked him if he felt the pangs of conscience, and he had thought about it for a long time and in the end he had just shaken his head. "I don't give a rat's toss," he had told me, "not a rat's toss." What he had meant was that it was best not to think about it, for thinking would only make him unhappy.

"I think perhaps conscience is over-rated by the West," the woman said musingly.

Gillespie seemed about to reply, but suddenly, shockingly, a telephone rang in the library. I had not even been aware that there was a telephone in the room and I jumped like a guilty thing, and even Gillespie seemed astonished by the bell's sudden shrill. He scrambled to his feet and hurried to a recess at the back of the room where he tentatively lifted the instrument. He spoke a couple of words, then put the phone down before coming slowly back to the table with a look of surprise on his face. "It's the war," he said aloud and to no one in particular. "It started last night. We're at war."

American and allied bombers were flying over the kingdom of Nebuchadnezzar. Tomahawk cruise missiles were hissing above the Land of the Two Rivers where Eden had once flourished and Babylon, the flower of all cities, had blossomed. "Dear God," Gillespie had murmured at the news, then he suggested we break off the debriefing to watch the television in the dining room. The news seemed impossibly optimistic, telling of incredibly accurate allied bombing, remarkably light aircraft losses, and burgeoning allied hopes.

There was no word yet of an Iraqi response, and certainly no news of terrorist attacks. I half expected to hear of civilian airliners falling from the sky or of dreadful bombs ripping open Western city centres, but instead, over and over, the screen showed the flickering of tracer rounds above Baghdad being punctuated by the sheet lightning of bombs exploding on the horizon. There were pictures of fighter-bombers screaming off Saudi runways, their wheels folding as the afterburners hurled the warplanes north towards the enemy.

I sat furthest from the screen. I was watching the allied planes attack Iraq but I was remembering the Israeli fighter-bombers over Hasbaiya. Usually their bombs or rockets struck before the Palestinians even knew the enemy was above them. There would be quick glints in the sky, a roll of wings and a billow of thunder, then the warplanes would vanish in the sky's hot brightness as their burning flares, voided to decoy the defenders' missiles, drifted slowly to earth. Afterwards, out of the smoke and rock-dust, a few stunned survivors stumbled.

I knew that sooner or later Gillespie would want me to talk about Hasbaiya. I wished he would spare me that. I half expected him to raise the subject after lunch, but instead, and after courteously asking the dark-haired woman if she would mind waiting a few moments before resuming her questioning, he asked me one more time about the fifty-three Stingers.

Gillespie's problem was that neither the FBI nor the CIA could find a single substantiating fact for my story of the meeting in Miami and the sale of the missiles. Gillespie brought me photographs of warehouses close to the Hialeah racecourse, but even when I identified the building in which I had seen the Stinger it had done no good. A search of the warehouse discovered nothing, and its records betrayed no Cubans called Alvarez or Carlos. Now, as Gillespie took me back to the library for the afternoon session, he told me that the telephone number in Ireland had proved to belong to an Enniskillen shop owned by a sixty-eight-year-old spinster who dealt in religious statuettes, while Brendan Flynn, taxed by the Irish police with my story of a meeting in Miami, blithely retorted that he had been attending a conference on the future of Ireland at the University of Utrecht. Gillespie told me that two distinguished professors of International Law and a minister of the Dutch Reformed Church had signed affidavits supporting Brendan's alibi. I had to laugh. Brendan had style.

"Such people wouldn't lie!" Gillespie reproved me.

"Those bastards will lie through their teeth. Come on, Gillespie! Academics and churchmen? They love terrorists! They get their rocks off pretending that terrorists are doing God's work. And especially the Dutch! I've been to those damn conferences in Holland. The Dutch are dull, so they love being on the side of the wicked. Say you're a terrorist in Utrecht and you'll have half a dozen priests and six academics all begging to lick your ass. That alibi's a piece of crap."

"And Michael Herlihy? He has two Boston lawyers willing to testify that he was taking depositions on that day."

"You trust American attorneys? What about Marty Doyle? Did you question him?"

"He claims to have been driving Michael Herlihy all day. In and around Boston."

"He's lying! He drove me to the warehouse, then he drove Brendan Flynn and me to Miami Airport. So pull the bastard in and slap him about. He'll tell you everything."

Gillespie sighed. "This is America. We have to use due process." He looked at me with silent reproof for a few seconds. "I also have to tell you," he went on, "that the British and Irish authorities have heard nothing about Stingers. Nothing at all."

"I saw one."

"So you say, so you say." But it was plain he did not believe me. "We'll keep looking," he said, though without enthusiasm, and then he turned to the dark-haired woman, who had waited patiently throughout the discussion of Stingers and alibis. "You wanted to raise a particular matter with Mr Shanahan?"

"Hasbaiya," she said bluntly.

I turned to her. The fire was snapping and hissing. "I'm sorry?"

"Hasbaiya."

Of course they wanted to know about Hasbaiya, but the very thought of the place made me go tense. I was very aware of Carole Adamson's scrutiny. "I've been to Hasbaiya," I said as easily as I could.

"How often?"

"Often enough."

"Twice? Ten times? Twenty?" The woman frowned at my generalisation.

"Eight times. My first visit was in '82 and the last in '86."

"You were attending training courses?"

Hasbaiya was the most notorious of the Palestinian training camps, a graduate school of death. It was not the only terrorist-training camp in the world, and not even the biggest. Indeed, in the old days, before their system collapsed, the Soviets ran a half-dozen such facilities, but Hasbaiya was the star in that dark firmament of evil.

"Did you train there?" the woman asked hopefully.

"No. My visits were just to introduce trainees."

I explained that no one could attend Hasbaiya, or any of the other Palestinian training camps for that matter, without being vouched for by someone the Palestinians trusted, and I had been the person who verified that the trainees I took to the camp were who they claimed to be and not some American or Israeli agent.

"And you introduced eight IRA men to the camp?" the woman asked.

"Four IRA men, one woman, and three Basques. The IRA didn't really think their guys needed outside training, but every now and then they'd send someone."

"So how long did it take you to make these introductions?" the woman asked. "A day?"

"Five minutes. I'd take the person to the commandant's office, say hello, and that was that."

"And then you'd leave?"

"Sometimes. Sometimes they invited me to stay a few days."

"Tell us about the camp."

I described it. Hasbaiya was built in the grounds of an old winery on the upper slopes of the Lebanon's Beka'a Valley. Most of its territory was used as a training ground to turn Palestinian refugees into storm-troopers, but at the top of the camp was a more secret area where terrorists came to perfect their skills of ambush, assassination and destruction. Hasbaiya's creed preached that death was the ultimate deterrent and that so long as the world feared death, so long was killing the terrorist's best friend, but for death to be useful it also had to be familiar, and so Hasbaiya used death as an integral part of its syllabus. Every trainee went there knowing that men and women died there, and that to be squeamish in the face of that slaughter was to demonstrate an unworthiness of the cause.

Gillespie broke in. "Let me clarify this. You're saying trainees died?"

"Sometimes, yes." I paused, and I was thinking of Roisin, but when I spoke again I talked of another American girl who had gone to Hasbaiya full of the fervour of one who would change the world. "Her name was Kimberley Sissons," I said, "and she came from Connecticut. I think she said her father was a corporate lawyer. She had a degree from Harvard."

"You're telling us they killed her," the Langley woman asked.

"Yes."

"For what reason?" Gillespie asked in his precise manner.

"They didn't have to have a reason." I hesitated again, wondering how to explain the inexplicable. "Were you ever in the army?" I asked Gillespie.

"The Marine Corps."

"Well I'm told that sometimes the army or the Marines will give a recruit a live rabbit and tell him it's dinner, but if the recruit doesn't have the guts to kill the rabbit then he goes hungry. I think that's how they treated the girls at Hasbaiya."

Gillespie and the woman stared at me for a few seconds. "Girls?" It was the dark-haired woman who asked.

"It was mainly the Western girls who were killed. Not always, but usually."

Carole Adamson intervened. "Was this a religious prejudice?"

"It was more to do with the fact that the Western girls argued."

"Argued?" Gillespie at last sounded shocked.

"Look," I tried to explain, "the Palestinians come from a culture that says a woman's role is to be subservient to the authority of men. Then these middle-class American girls arrived, full of revolutionary fervour learned from some Marxist professor at Stanford or Harvard, and there was bound to be friction. The girls were all feminists, all argumentative, and all deeply into inter-cultural bonding, and they found it quite difficult to understand that their ordained place in the revolution was to be bonded between a lice-ridden mattress and an unwashed Palestinian." I had sounded callous, but beneath the table my hands had been shaking. The dark-haired woman had gone silent and just watched me.

"So they were shot?" Gillespie asked. "For arguing?"

"Not always shot. Kimberley Sissons was strangled with copper wire."

"Just for arguing? For standing up for her rights?" Carole Adamson sounded horrified.

"I told you," I said, "it was a demonstration."

"So who was the demonstrator?" Gillespie asked.

"Another trainee was ordered to kill her, and if he'd hesitated or disobeyed, then he'd have been the next to die. It was their way of making the trainees rethink their attitude to death." I paused, knowing I had not given the real flavour of Hasbaiya; the febrile excitement that infected the place, the enthusiasm for killing and the triumph of mastering its dangers. "Maybe they were trying to destroy conscience?" I suggested.

"Did you kill anyone at Hasbaiya?" Gillespie asked.

"I told you, I wasn't a trainee. I just escorted people there."

"That doesn't answer the question," Carole Adamson said with an unaccustomed asperity.

"I did kill a man, yes," I admitted.

"Why? Were you ordered to?"

I shook my head. "It was a fight."

"Who was he?"

"A guy called Axel," I said, "just Axel. I didn't know his other name. He picked the fight, not me."

"When was that?" Gillespie asked.

"On my last visit."

"In '86?"

"Yes."

"And you'd simply escorted someone there?"

"Yes."

"And he picked a fight? Why?"

I shrugged. "God knows."

"How did you kill him?"

"With a spade," I said, "like an axe-blow." I had told the truth, but only a tiny shred of the truth, but the rest of the tale was my nightmare and not to be shared with Gillespie's notebooks or Carole Adamson's diagnosis or the dark woman's encyclopaedic knowledge of the Palestinians and Libyans.

Gillespie was consulting the early pages of his notebook where he had written down the framework of my story, the chronology. "Eighty-six," he said. "Was that when the IRA stopped trusting you?"

"Yes."

"Was that anything to do with Hasbaiya?"

I hesitated again. Outside the window the snow was dazzling, glinting with a billion specks of light. "Yes," I admitted, knowing that in the end I would have to tell a part of the story. "I took an American girl to Hasbaiya," I said, "and she accused me of being a CIA agent."

"The girl's name?" Gillespie was writing in his book.

"Roisin Donovan," I said as casually as I could. "I think she spelt her first name R-O-I-S-I-N."

"American, you say?" He frowned at me.

"Like me," I said, "tribal Irish. But she came from Baltimore."

"So tell me about her."

I feigned ignorance. "To be honest I didn't know too much about her, except that she'd moved to Northern Ireland and was very active in the Women's Section of the Provisional IRA." I could feel my heart thumping and I was sure Carole Adamson must be registering my discomfort. I myself was horribly aware of everything in the room; the crackle of the poor fire, the creak of my chair, the scrape of Gillespie's pencil on the pages of his notebook, the sceptical gaze of the dark-haired woman.

"Why did she accuse you?" Gillespie asked. "Describe the circumstances."

I took a breath. "I took her to Hasbaiya. We reached the camp and I took her to Malouk's quarters. Malouk was the commandant. She went inside, spoke with him, and ten minutes later he asked me to stay on in the camp. Which I didn't want to do because I had a boat-delivery job lined up for the following week, but Malouk wasn't a man you argued with, so I said sure, and that night he arrested me."

"Because Roisin Donovan had accused you?"

"Yes."

"What had she told him?"

"She told him," I said, "that the CIA was trying to infiltrate European terrorist groups, and that to preserve their agents' secrecy they were not using field controllers or letter drops or any other communication systems. She called them stealth spies because they were undetectable. They wouldn't report back to Washington until their whole mission was finished." I paused, staring out of the window. A deer stood at the edge of the far dark woods. It sniffed the air, dipped its head, then was gone with a flash of its white tail. "Then she said I was one of those stealth agents," I finished bitterly.

"Are you telling us she knew all about van Stryker's programme?" Gillespie asked.

"She knew about his idea of not using any form of communication in the field."

"Did she mention van Stryker?"

"No."

"Any other names?"

"No."

"So it sounds like a wild accusation." Gillespie was scornful.

I shrugged as if to suggest he must be right, though the truth was less pretty. Roisin and I had often talked about the possibility of the CIA infiltrating the IRA with an American agent. Their motives, we agreed, would be to do their British allies a favour as well as to eavesdrop on the rumours that were whispered through the European terrorist grapevines. We had embroidered the idea, suggesting how it might be done and how such an agent might avoid detection. It had not been Roisin who had dubbed such agents as 'stealth spies', but me. I had offered her that thought as if it had been mere idle speculation, but in reality I had been playing with fire; just like a cheating husband might get a stupid thrill from mentioning his mistress's name to his wife, so I had not been able to resist describing van Stryker's notion as a fantasy of my own. I could imagine just what psychological hay Gillespie and Adamson would make from such an admission, so I wisely said nothing.

Gillespie turned a page in his notebook. "And the Hasbaiya authorities believed her accusation?"

"They didn't know whether to believe her or not, but they were worried to hell by her," I said.

"So what did they do?"

"They sent a message to Ireland to discover whether anyone there suspected me, and that message saved me. It seemed that Seamus Geoghegan had taken refuge in Roisin's apartment, and on the very day she'd left for the Lebanon he'd been arrested by the Brits. They claimed to have been given information by an informer, and it could only have been Roisin. So it seemed that she was the traitor, not me, and that by accusing me she was merely trying to spread the guilt to confuse everyone." I made a rueful face. "But even so she'd tarred me with suspicion, and that suspicion was enough to make them cut me out of the game."

"What happened to Miss Donovan?" Gillespie asked.

"She was shot," I said bleakly.

There was silence. Carole Adamson had scribbled a note

which she now leaned forward to slide down the table. Gillespie unfolded the scrap of paper. In the fire a log collapsed in a shiver of cascading sparks. Gillespie screwed the note into a ball and tossed it at the flames. The ball missed the hearth, bouncing off the mantel and rolling on to the coir rug. "How much time did you spend in her company? I mean, on the way to Hasbaiya?"

"Three days. We met in Athens, flew to Damascus, then drove to the Lebanon."

"So you must have talked with her?"

"Sure."

"Did you become lovers in those three days?" Gillespie asked.

"No!" I tried to make my answer scornful.

"What did you talk about on your journey?"

"Nothing much," I said. "She wasn't very sociable."

"You must have discussed something!"

"The scenery, Irish beer, the heat. We chatted, that's all."

"Did you like her personally?" Gillespie pressed me.

"Like her? I don't know." I was feeling excruciatingly uncomfortable. "Hell! She isn't important."

There was silence again. The light was fading outside. It was deep winter and the days were short. The dark-haired woman looked at her watch. "I should be going, Peter." She spoke to Gillespie. "I kind of hate driving in the dark."

"Of course." The spell was broken. I felt myself relax. People round the table moved, stretched, made small talk. The woman thanked me for my time, said I had been helpful, then followed Carole Adamson into the hall to find her coat. Gillespie said he needed to visit the bathroom.

They left me alone in the library. I was thinking of Hasbaiya, of Roisin. Seamus had once told me that conscience could be diluted in alcohol. "I'll drink to that," I had said, and now I helped myself to a bottle of rye whiskey kept in the drinks cabinet and carried it back to the deep library window. There I watched the snow, drank, and watched the snow again. Then I remembered the ball of paper lying on the coir rug, the one on which Carole Adamson had scribbled her note to Gillespie, so I turned and picked it up, uncrinkled the paper, and read her urgent words. "He's telling lies! Telling lies!" And no wonder, by Christ, no wonder.

Roisin had been lucky in one thing only; she had died swiftly.

I later heard that Brendan Flynn had himself requested the act of mercy. He claimed that Roisin had been given neither the time nor the opportunity to betray the Palestinians, only the Irish, and that the Irish should therefore set the manner of her death and he wanted that death to be quick. I had always wondered if Brendan asked the favour because he too had been one of her lovers. Whatever, Roisin was taken to a dry gully beyond the camp and there shot. She took one bullet in the head and her blood had sprayed against the white heat of the sky and splashed on to the yellow, sulphurous rocks. I remembered her look of outrage and defiance as she had died. Her skin had been very red, burned by the fierce sun. She had very fair skin and burned easily.

I was ordered to bury her on the hillside where she had died. A German called Axel Springer offered to stay with me, though he did precious little to help as I hacked a shallow scrape with the long-helved spade. He talked instead, telling me he was a theology student at Heidelberg, but that his real religion was the Red Army Faction. I wondered why he had volunteered to help me, and only began to understand when he stopped me from rolling Roisin's thin corpse into the stony grave. "I want to look at her," Axel said in his heavily accented English, "she was very pretty."

"She was beautiful," I corrected him. Roisin had never

been pretty, she had been too fierce and too committed and too scornful of weakness to be called pretty.

"It is a sexual thing, you see," Axel said.

"What is?"

"Why girls like this become involved in terrorism."

"You're joking," I said.

"I have never joked," he said in all seriousness. "Work has been done by American feminists on the correlations between sexuality and terrorism, and they maintain a direct linkage between sexual desire and terrorist activity. It has to do with the relaxation of inhibitions, both in society and in bed. I can offer you the reading list, if you would like?" He smiled and held out a pack of cigarettes. In those days I had smoked so I took a cigarette, stooped to his light, and gratefully sucked in the comforting smoke. "Of course," Axel went on, "the camp authorities recognise the sexual linkage. That is why they encourage girls like this one to attend. These girls are hardly good pupils, but they have their uses."

"Their uses?"

"It is obvious!" Axel blew a plume of smoke that whirled away down the valley. "The Arabs want the white girls. It is their revenge for colonialism. But they would not have enjoyed this one." He jerked his head at Roisin.

"Why not?"

"Too thin! Look at her!" He leaned down and ripped Roisin's flimsy shirt open. "See? Just pimples!" He gestured at her breasts, which were very white and very small. "Pimples!" Axel said again, but he could not keep his eyes away from them, and it was then that I understood exactly why he had stayed behind to help me bury her.

"Cover her up," I said. "It isn't right to bury her half naked."

Axel had squinted up at me. "What is your name?"

"Paul."

"Paul. I think you have American bourgeois inhibitions. You should deal with that. It isn't healthy."

"I said cover her up!" I snapped.

"OK! OK!" But instead of pulling the torn shirt over her body he caressed her small white breasts with his right hand, and it was at that moment I had hit him with the edge of the spade. I hit him so hard that the steel blade sank three inches into his skull, but even so the blow did not kill him straightaway. He was still making an odd noise, half pain and half protest, as I pulled him off Roisin's body and he remained alive all the time that I took to bury her and to cover her shallow grave with a heap of stones to keep the beasts and birds away from her flesh. Axel could not speak, but his eyes watched me and he made the strange noises as I told him he was going to hell and that for the rest of eternity he would suffer an unimaginable agony. In the end he died, but I did not bury him. Instead I left him to the wild-winged creatures that screamed in the night, then I carried my bloodied spade back to the camp where I confessed my deed, but no one cared that Axel had been killed, for in Hasbaiya death was a creed.

Outside the window the snow fell with the coming night.

The air war in the Gulf blazed on, yet still no reprisals seared America. No planes tumbled from the sky, no bombs slashed at city centres. Indeed it seemed that my story of Saddam Hussein taking a terrorist revenge on America was just that, a story, a fantasy. Gillespie still questioned me about the Cubans in Miami, and the million and a half dollars, but I sensed he no longer believed a word of my tale.

The days passed in a blanket of snow. I turned the pages of photograph albums and dredged up memories of meetings years before. The days began to have a dull rhythm. I watched the breakfast television news every morning, always expecting to hear that the allied ground troops had attacked the Iraqi army, but the air war went on and on. One morning I saw Congressman O'Shaughnessy expressing his concern that a ground campaign would cost thousands of American lives. It would be better, Tommy the Turd said, if the bombing campaign was given several more months to do its work. I was about to switch the set off when a news bulletin told of a bomb attack in London. The Provisional IRA had parked a roofless van in Whitehall, and the van had concealed a battery of mortars that had launched their bombs against Downing Street. The new Prime Minister and his cabinet had narrowly escaped injury. The news footage showed the burnt-out van standing abandoned in a sleety rain. Later that morning, just as I had anticipated, Gillespie asked me about the attack, but I could only offer him my strong suspicion that the spectacular operation had been planned as a strike against Margaret Thatcher, whom the IRA detested, but that the plan's execution had been delayed to become a part of Iraq's world-wide terrorist revenge. That delay might have cost the Provisional IRA their chance of killing Margaret Thatcher, but it had doubtless pleased Colonel Qaddafi and Saddam Hussein.

Two more terror bombs struck London, both random attacks at train stations. One commuter was killed. The bombs had been left in rubbish bins and had exploded in the rush hour. They were primitive attacks, far removed from the sophistication of the Downing Street bombs, and I suggested to Gillespie that the Provisionals had been driven to such crudities by their eagerness to convince Saddam Hussein that they were truly co-operating. None of the London attacks had brought a united Ireland one day closer, but they had undoubtedly preserved the IRA's standing with their most generous sponsor, Libya.

In the days following the IRA attacks, and probably in response to questions coming from London, Gillespie pressed hard about my knowledge of IRA active-service units, but I knew nothing that could help him. The only top

IRA men I knew were Brendan Flynn and Seamus Geoghegan. The rest were already dead, or else I had never met them. Gillespie thought I was hiding them, but he was wrong. I was hiding gold coins, not men.

I knew the debriefing was coming to an end when Gillespie asked about my future, offering to give me the benefits of the Federal Witness Protection Programme. "We'll give you a new name, a new social security number, a new job, and a settlement grant somewhere far away from your old haunts. No one could possibly trace you."

"You'll make me a school janitor in North Dakota? Thank you, but no. I'm going back to the Cape."

He frowned. "Is that sensible?"

"Probably not, but it's home."

He was still troubled. "You'll have made enemies. They'll know where to find you."

"I don't want to hide."

He half smiled. "You need the risk, is that it? You can't bear to think of spending a dull ordinary life?"

"I like the Cape, that's all."

"Then so be it," he agreed reluctantly.

Next evening, at long last, Simon van Stryker came to offer me his blessing. I received no warning of his coming, though Gillespie had shown an air of expectancy all day and, when we gathered in the library before dinner, I found a tray had been placed on the table with an ice-bucket, crystal glasses, an old-fashioned soda-syphon, two kinds of Scotch and a half-bottle of sherry. "Is this a celebration?" I asked.

"In a way, yes," Gillespie said, then he turned to the window as the sound of a helicopter thumped through the library's double glazing. A brilliant beam of light swept across the darkening snow then shrank as the helicopter descended and a cloud of wind-stirred white crystals made a fog of the beam, then the machine itself appeared in the sparkling white cloud and settled on to the snow-covered lawn. The landing lights went out. None of us spoke.

A log tumbled on the fire, spewing sparks. Carole Adamson frowned into her sherry while Gillespie surreptitiously patted his hair. A moment later the heavy front door banged hollowly and there was a mutter of voices in the hall. "That will be him," Gillespie said unnecessarily.

"Who?" I asked. Then the door was thrust open to reveal a tall, smiling man clothed in faultless evening dress and it was suddenly hard to imagine Simon van Stryker dressed in any other way. His hair was whiter than I remembered and I guessed he must be in his sixties by now, but he looked very fit and his face was still lean and animated. He strode across the room. "Paul Shanahan! You kept the faith! Well done!" He held out his hand. I shook it awkwardly.

Van Stryker greeted Carole Adamson. "I never had a chance to congratulate you on your paper in the *New England Journal of Medicine*. I have two points to debate with you, but perhaps they should wait? And Peter!" He held out his hand to Gillespie. "You've had a long task, well done." He smiled at us, filling the room with an air of vibrant intelligence. He held his hands to the fire, shivered, then nodded acceptance of a whisky. "But a very small one, Peter. I'm expected at a rather rigorous dinner at the White House tonight. I shall be late, but that's better than not showing up at all." He stood in front of the fire, staring about the high-ceilinged library with its rows of indigestible reading. "Some extraordinary men have told us their life stories in this room, Paul. I like to think of it as America's confessional."

"Do I get absolution now?"

Van Stryker laughed at my question, then thanked Gillespie for his whisky. He took one sip then placed the glass on the mantel and I sensed it would not be touched again. "Help yourself." He waved me towards the tray of drinks. Outside the window the helicopter's engine grumbled. Van Stryker was clearly not staying long, but I was glad he had made the effort to come to this strange mansion in the snowbound hills. I had needed to see him. For fourteen years he had been my mentor. "So what on earth happened to your Stingers, Shanahan?" van Stryker asked me now.

"I don't know."

"Maybe they never existed?"

I shrugged. "Maybe, but I held one of them."

He looked at me with his pale, clever eyes. "Have you told us everything?"

"At least three times, it seems."

"Good for you, Paul," van Stryker said, then frowned down at the coir rug. "If there were no Stingers, Shanahan, or only one of the beasts, why did they send you to Miami?"

"I don't know."

"We know you went there. We found your footprints in the airline's computer." He still stared down at the floor. "So why?" he asked softly.

"Maybe it was an operation that went sour," I suggested, and did not add the suggestion that it might have gone sour because some clever bastard had purloined the purchase price. "Most operations do," I said instead.

Van Stryker's gaze snapped up to me and I knew he was wondering if I was one of his operations that had gone sour. "What's happened to the rest of Saddam Hussein's terrorist revenge?" he asked. "Has that gone sour too?"

"Maybe," I said.

"All but for the Provisional IRA," he said bitterly. "Of all Saddam Hussein's allies only they have drawn blood. One dead civilian on London's Victoria Station. Is that the very best il Hayaween can produce?"

Everyone seemed to be waiting for my answer. I shrugged. "Il Hayaween told me that the Syrians and the Iranians were not supporting Iraq's terrorist campaign," I said, as if that explained everything.

"Nor are they," van Stryker said impatiently, "but one dead rail commuter? Is that Saddam Hussein's best effort?"

168

"They almost got the British Prime Minister," I suggested.

Van Stryker shook his head. "Our analysis shows the Provisionals had that attack planned for months. They just delayed it to please their Arab masters. No! There has to be something more!" He sounded angry. "Have you really told us everything, Paul?"

"Of course." Though articulating the lie gave me a stab of guilt which I assuaged by telling myself that all I had held back was the real price of the missiles and the method by which the Libyans had tried to pay that price. The gold was mine. Yet I still felt guilty for hiding it, but that was the effect van Stryker had. He was a man who inspired loyalty, but I reassured myself that the gold was as harmless as a cheque, or a bank transfer. What mattered were the things the gold had been intended to buy. "Maybe," I proffered, "the two Cubans were trying to rip off the IRA?"

"A rather dangerous game," van Stryker replied with a humourless laugh.

"Not if you're far enough away from them. They've never mounted an operation over here."

"And they'd better not!" van Stryker said, then looked at his watch before turning to Gillespie. "What's your evaluation of Shanahan, Peter?"

"I think the debriefing's been very useful," Gillespie said, though without enthusiasm. "I don't think he's told us everything he knows about the IRA, but that was never our prime target. We haven't solved the Stinger story, and maybe never will, but what he's told us about the Palestinian groups and Libya has proved most valuable."

"The Israelis are pleased with us, you mean?" Van Stryker looked at me, but still spoke to Gillespie. "So you think Mr Shanahan's life has not been wasted?"

"Not at all," Gillespie said stoutly.

"Dr Adamson. What is your considered judgment of Paul Francis Shanahan?"

"I'm not sure I have one yet. He hasn't permitted us to see him yet. He's been protecting himself because he resents being questioned, which is why he treated this debriefing like a contest."

"And who won?" Van Stryker asked lightly.

"I lost score." Carole Adamson was suddenly no longer motherly and comforting, but sharp. "He's hidden his real self behind a mask of flippancy."

"You mean he's a deceiver?" Van Stryker was still equable. "But isn't that why we chose him in the first place?"

"But who is he deceiving? Because I tell you he's hiding more than his personality behind that slippery mask. Whatever Mr Shanahan sees as being in his own best interest will be kept good and private from us."

"Paul?" Van Stryker turned courteously towards me.

"I've hidden nothing," I said with wondrously feigned innocence.

"You entered America with false papers, did you not?" Van Stryker seemed unperturbed as he asked the question.

"For old times' sake," I said happily. "I'll never do it again. Promise."

Carole Adamson gave me a disinterested glance. "I wouldn't worry about his papers. I'd ask him a few hard questions about Miss Roisin Donovan instead. That should lift a corner of his mask."

Van Stryker held his hands towards the fire. "We know you lied about her, Paul. She lived with you in Belfast, yet you claim not to have known her?"

"Aren't I allowed some privacy?"

"Not in America's confessional, no." He smiled, glanced at me, then looked back to the fire. "You were lovers?"

"Yes."

"She had a lot of other lovers. Did you know that?"

I wondered how much they knew about Roisin, but I did

not want to ask. I did not want to talk about her. "I know she had other lovers," I said defensively.

"Does that hurt you?"

I had no intention of answering that question, or any damn question like it. I had been sent into the dark to bring back information, not the raw materials of psycho-analysis, so I said nothing. Van Stryker held his hands towards the fire. "Not that it matters," he answered his own question blithely, "because she's dead and you're very much with us. But you always were a survivor, Paul. A rogue and a scoundrel, but an undoubted survivor." He smiled at me. "I came here to thank you."

"To thank me?" His gentle courtesy took me by surprise.

"You're my first stringless puppet to come home. You've brought your cargo of information and I thank you for it. And we owe you money." He held up a hand to still my exclamation of surprise. "I know we said you would not be paid, and officially we owe you nothing, but I'll make sure the agency diverts some funds. Just as a token of our thanks. It will take time, maybe some months. And, of course, we may have more questions for you. In fact I'm sure we'll have more questions for you. Questions are the one thing that never end. Peter knows where you'll be, does he?"

"I'm going back to the Cape," I told him.

"I envy you. Nancy and I have a summer cottage on the Vineyard, but we never manage enough time there. Life is too busy. We do some sailing as well, when we can."

"You've got your own boat?" I asked him.

"A Nautor Swan," he said casually. "A sixty-one-footer named for Nancy. We keep her at Edgartown, but of course she's ashore now, on jackstands in our yard."

It would be a Nautor Swan, I thought, and doubtless Nancy was beautiful and their children successful and the summer cottage on Martha's Vineyard a waterfront mansion. This was the codfish aristocracy.

Van Stryker took a business card from his breast pocket.

"If you do dredge anything up from your sub-conscious and want to talk to me, then that number will always reach me." He held the card towards me. "And thank you, Paul, for taking the risks you did."

I took the card. I felt awkward because I had told lies. They were not important lies, but still I felt I did not deserve van Stryker's generosity, nor his thanks. Then I told myself that of course I did. I had been the poor bastard who dared the Beka'a Valley and the back streets of Tripoli. I was a hero, and I deserved thanks, peals of trumpets, and a boat's belly filled with gold. I deserved it all.

"Now I really must go!" Van Stryker smiled a courteous farewell to Gillespie and Adamson, shook my hand one more time, and then was gone. Gillespie let out a long relieved breath. Outside the window the helicopter lights dazzled us as the machine hammered up into the darkness.

They let me go next morning. Gillespie gave me five hundred dollars in cash and an air ticket to Boston. It was Sunday and somewhere in the valley a church bell was tolling like a tocsin. It was a cold still morning and a new fall of snow glittered under the wintry sun. I pulled on my yellow oilskin and stepped into the bright new day, a free man again. And going home.

I knew how badly Michael Herlihy would be wanting to discover the truth of the missing gold; he would be wanting it badly enough to have its location beaten out of me. Yet Michael was a lawyer, and a careful one, and he had never done anything in his life without massive forethought and a hedge of precautions, so I reckoned that if I swanned into Boston unannounced and took him by surprise there was a good chance that I could be away before he had a chance to react, maybe before he even knew I was in Massachusetts.

Yet, at the same time, I knew I could not avoid a confrontation with Michael for ever, because if I was to live the rest of my life on Cape Cod, free to waste each day on its circling seas, then Michael and his henchmen would need to be faced down or bought off. I would also need to make sure that Sarah Sing Tennyson was safely evicted from my property, which meant I had to twist the tail of the bombastic ape who had married my sister.

The bombastic ape was called Patrick McPhee. He was a big-bellied man with a hair-trigger temper and a face like a steam shovel. He was a drunk, a failure, a bully and a lout. Everyone had warned Maureen against marrying him, but in McPhee my sister had seen a tall handsome young baseball player who boasted of his glorious future in the major leagues, and Maureen had first insisted on marriage then made it inevitable by becoming pregnant. My father raged at her, provided her generously with a dowry, then had walked her down the carpeted aisle of Holy Redeemer. Maureen had worn a lace-edged frock of glorious white, and within days she had the first black bruises to show for her trouble. "The screen door banged into me when I was carrying some shopping," she told our mother, and a month later she had tripped across a kerbstone, then it was a fall she took while stepping off a bus, and so it had gone on ever since.

Patrick had duly gone to the minor leagues and there

failed. His pitching arm that was so good at raising bruises on Maureen turned out to be muscled with noodles. He came home to Boston where he drank, put on weight and lived off past glories and Maureen's money.

That money had long been frittered away and all Maureen had to show for her impetuous romance was a crumbling house and five sullen sons who, God help them, took after their father. Christ, I thought as the taxi drove me down the wintry and rain-sodden street, but we had been a wicked family.

Maureen herself opened the door to my knock and, for a moment, just stared. "Oh, my little brother," she finally said. She had put on weight and there was a bruise next to her right eye, suggesting she had turned away too late from a blow.

"Can I come in?"

"You've come this far, so why not the last step?" She pushed the screen door open and stepped aside to let me into the kitchen. "You remember Terence?" Terence was Maureen's youngest and was now twelve or thirteen years old. He was sitting at the kitchen table stuffing his face with a peanut butter and jelly sandwich. He wore a Desert Storm T-shirt stretched tight across his huge gut. "Say hello to your Uncle Paul," his mother told him, but the kid's mouth was too stuffed with sandwich to let him say anything so he just raised a languid hand in greeting. In the kitchen corner a television blared, while another television, showing a different programme, was just as loud in the living room next door.

Terence slumped off his chair and dragged open the fridge door. He stared bemused into its well-stocked interior, then delivered his verdict. "No soda."

"I'll get some, honey," Maureen said.

"Why don't you go and get it yourself?" I asked Terence in a reasonable voice.

"Leave him alone!" Maureen intervened, clearly practised

in defending her children from the wrath of adult males. "Go on upstairs, honey," she told her son. "Take something to snack on."

"Where are the other little charmers?" I asked when Terence had shambled out of the room and Maureen had switched off both televisions.

"Probably at Roscoe's, playing pool. His lordship's at the Parish of course, where else?" Maureen sat at the table and lit a cigarette. The ashtray was overflowing with butts and her fingers were the colour of woodstain. She studied me for a while. "You look good. Where in God's name have you been?"

"In the last seven years?" I dropped my sea-bag by the door and ran myself a cup of water from the tap. The sink was piled with unwashed dishes. "Mostly in Belgium. But here and there. I really came to see Patrick."

"About that girl?"

I nodded. "Sarah Sing Tennyson."

She shrugged. "I told his honour not to rent the house to her, but things have been tight these last few years. When were they not? You want a cigarette?"

"I gave up."

"Good for you. I tried quitting and put on thirty pounds, so I started smoking again, but the thirty pounds stayed with me just the same. You're in trouble, aren't you?"

"No."

"I can smell it off you like the smoke off a bonfire. You know they've been asking about you?"

"Who has?"

"Herlihy and his friends. They're fair mad at you, Paul. Are you going to tell me why?"

"No."

"Why do I even ask?" She struggled to her feet, crossed the room and reached into a high closet for a fifth of gin and a fifth of Jameson's. I noticed how thick she had become in the waist and ankles. My God, I thought, but she was

175

only forty-two or -three yet she looked twenty years older; all but for her hair, which was as lustrous and thick as ever. "Help yourself." She sat and pushed the whiskey bottle towards me.

"Patrick's going to have to get rid of that Tennyson girl," I said.

Maureen laughed. "Some chance! You know Patrick. He's terrified of any woman he's not married to. He'll tell you that he'll deal with her, but he won't."

"How much rent is he taking off her?"

"Five hundred a month, and even then he gets to use the house when she's not there. God knows why she lets him."

"Five hundred?" I was astonished. The house was certainly worth five hundred dollars a month; indeed, in the summertime, I could have let it for five hundred dollars a week, but Sarah Sing Tennyson had to be crazy to pay that much for part-time occupancy.

"Not that I get to see any of the money," Maureen said bleakly. "His eminence takes it all for himself."

"Is he in work?"

"Not so you'd notice. A bit here and there." She shrugged and I guessed that nothing had changed. Patrick had pimped for a time, then worked as an enforcer for a debt-collector in Roxbury, but mostly he lived off what small income there still remained from Maureen's inheritance and, evidently, off the rent he illegally took for my house.

I poured myself a generous finger of my brother-in-law's whiskey, then grinned at the health warning printed on the label. "When did they start putting this shit on bottles?"

"About the same time the telephones stopped working." She gave me the flicker of a smile, a hint of the old Maureen. "You've been away too long, Paul. You even sound like a foreigner."

"I'm back now."

"To Boston?"

"The Cape. When were you last there?"

"It must be all of four years. His excellency doesn't approve of my going down there. He takes his Parish friends down if the girl's not there, but not me." She drew on the cigarette. I had given Maureen the keys to the Cape house so she could have an escape hatch, but I had never intended Patrick to take the place for his own amusement.

"What does he do there?"

She shrugged. "They play at being men, you know? They lose money at cards, drink beer, and shoot duck in the fall."

"He won't be doing it any longer," I said, "I'm moving back in. Have you seen Johnny Riordan lately?"

She shook her head. "Not for three years. The last time he came here Patrick picked a fight with him. It didn't come to blows, but they fair shouted the tar out of each other, and Johnny hasn't visited with us since."

"What was the row about?"

She sighed. "The usual, you know?" She explained anyway. "Patrick had just got back from Ireland, so he was sounding off about the Brits. How they were worse than the Nazis, and Johnny wouldn't take him seriously."

"Patrick went to Ireland!" I could not hide my astonishment.

"The Friends of Free Ireland arranged the trip. They had one week in Dublin and one week in Belfast. Father Shea went from Holy Redeemer, and Michael Herlihy travelled, of course, and some young fellow from the Congressman's office went with them. Patrick was full of himself when he got back. He was ready to fight England single-handed! I wish to hell he would sometimes. So now he's on the committee. A big man, he is, and busy! He's planning wars against England when he isn't drinking whiskey or losing money on the horses." She lit another cigarette from the stub of the first. "Are you really moving back home?"

"Yes."

"And with a sack of troubles." She was silent for a few seconds and the smoke of her new cigarette rose in a smooth

177

column that suddenly tumbled into chaos a few inches above her hair. "Is it a woman?"

I shook my head. "I lost my last girlfriend. She reckoned I'd never make her rich so she went off with a Frenchman."

"Good for her. What happened to that girl you were sweet on in Ireland?"

"She died."

"Poor thing." Her right hand sketched the sign of the cross. "Be careful, Paul."

"I always am."

She grimaced. "Is it drugs again?"

"I'm long out of that."

"I'm glad, Paul. That was a cruel business. So what are you going to do?"

"I don't know. Maybe I'll buy a fishing boat? Run after the tuna? I hear the Japanese buyers wait at the Cape wharves to buy fresh tuna. Cash on the nail, ten or even fifteen bucks a pound and no questions asked. I could make a good living with a tuna boat."

"Sure you could, sure." Maureen knew all about dreams that never came true. She was probably the expert.

I picked up my bag and went to the door. "You say Patrick's at the Parish?"

"All day. I wish he'd stay there all night, too." She got to her feet, walked to me, and put her arms round me. She said nothing, but I sensed she was crying inside, but whether at her wasted life or whether for relief at my homecoming I could not tell.

I drew back slightly and very gently touched the raw, yellow edged bruise beside her right eye. "Did Patrick do that?"

"No, it was Mother Teresa who hit me. Who the hell do you think did it?"

I kissed her. "Look after yourself," I said, then I looked up and saw that Terence had come to the kitchen door from where he was staring aghast at us. I guess he had never seen anyone show affection to his mother and he was consequently in culture shock. I gave him the finger. "She's my sister, punk."

"Where are my trainers, Mom?"

"I'll look for them, honey." She pulled away from me.

"And you said you'd get me some soda, right? And these chips are stale."

I let the door bang shut and walked fast away.

The hall was always called 'the Parish', though in fact it was not the parish hall at all, but belonged to one of Boston's many fraternal orders who were happy for their big brick building to serve as a church hall, a social club, and as a meeting place where the local Irish community could vent its joys, sorrows and political indignations. During the hunger strikes, when the IRA men were dying inside Long Kesh, the Parish had been the scene of passionate gatherings, just as it had in the mid '70s when Boston's bussing crisis had turned the city into a battleground and the men of the neighbourhood had sworn that not a single black child would ever cross their local school's threshold. That battle had long been lost, but the older struggle went on, evidenced by two enthusiastic slogans which were hugely painted in green letters on the Parish's side wall. 'Brits Out of Ireland' and 'Support the Provos!' the slogans read and were supported on either flank by gaudily painted arrangements of Irish tricolours, harps, and assault rifles.

The other enthusiasm of the Parish was sport, which meant basketball, and specifically the Celtics. The Parish was where men came to watch the Celts on a giant TV projection screen, and when the Celts were playing even the politics of old Ireland took second place.

Yet, that Sunday, when I pushed through the Parish door, there was no basketball on the big screen. Instead the crowd was watching a news channel. The land war in the Gulf had at last begun, and Saddam Hussein's mother of battles was being joined on the sands of western Iraq. "We're kicking ass!" a man I had never seen before greeted me ebulliently. "We are kicking ass, you bet! Kicking ass!"

I pushed through to the bar. The place was crowded and noisy, filled with smoke and the smell of beer. I glanced round, saw no sign of Patrick, so instead cocked a finger towards Charlie Monaghan behind the bar. Charlie stopped what he had been doing, stared at me, looked away, struck his head, looked back, grinned, then abandoned his customers to march down the bar with an outstretched hand. "Oh, Mother of God, but is it yourself, Paulie?" He reached across the bar to embrace me. "I thought it was a ghost, so I did! Paulie! It is you, is it not?"

"It is. How are you?"

"I'm just grand! Just grand! No complaints, now. Have you been hearing the news? We've been kicking ten kinds of shit out of the shitheads. And I'm not talking about Iraq, I'm talking about the basketball, so how will you celebrate it?"

"Give me a Guinness."

"It's on the house, Paulie." He let his assistants take care of the other customers while he gave me the vital news that Larry Bird had recovered from the operation on his heel and was running, as Charlie Monaghan put it, like a buck deer in the springtime. "He's playing like a hero! Like a hero! And last year they were saying he'd never step on the parquet again, not with his foot and being thirty-three and all, but now the other teams are having to double-guard him. Can you imagine that, Paulie? Double-teaming Larry Bird! It's just like old times, Paulie!" Charlie had grown up in Letterkenny, County Donegal, yet to hear him talk about the Celts was to think he had lived his whole life in the shadow of Boston Garden. "I tell you, Paulie," he went on, "but we're going to be world champions this year, no trouble at all!"

I managed to check the ebullient flow long enough to ask where I would find Patrick.

"Patrick Ewing? He's playing for the Knicks these days, but surely you knew that, Paulie?"

"Not that Patrick. I mean my brother-in-law."

"Oh, Padraig? That's what he calls himself these days. Patrick's not good enough for him. It's Padraig or nothing, so it is." Charlie laughed, and no wonder, for using the Gaelic form of his name was an extreme affectation for a man like my brother-in-law who could barely speak his own language, let alone the Erse tongue. "He's in the snug," Charlie went on, "but he's busy, so he is." The snug was a back room of the Parish, much given to private business.

"Busy doing what, for Christ's sake?"

Charlie scraped the head off the Guinness with a knife, topped up the glass, then slid it across the bar. Then, with a conspiratorial wink, he touched the side of his nose with the frothy blade. "He's got Tommy the Turd in there."

"The Congressman?" I sounded astonished.

"Aye! The cretin who wanted to give Saddam Hussein a whole year to get his army ready. Too dumb to succeed but too rich to fail." A columnist in the *Boston Globe* had delivered that scathing verdict on Tommy the Turd and it had stuck like a hook in a cod's gill, but the congressman's scatological nickname had inadvertently been invented by Charlie himself who, with his lovely southern Irish accent, turned every soft 'th' sound into a hard 't'. Thus 'thus' became 'tus', 'three' became 'tree', and House Representative Thomas O'Shaughnessy the Third had forever been transmuted into Tommy t' Turd.

And Tommy the Turd was now in conference with my brother-in-law? "Good God," I said. For however dumb Congressman O'Shaughnessy might be, he was still mighty exalted company for Patrick McPhee. Thomas O'Shaughnessy the Third was a thousand-toilet Irish, a Boston aristocrat whose family was one of the richest in Massachusetts. Tommy's grandfather, Tommy O'Shaughnessy Senior, had been an immigrant from County Mayo who had made his fortune in cement manufacture. Tommy's father had more than doubled the family's wealth but, fearing for the company's profits if his son ever took over the family business, Tom O'Shaughnessy Junior had purchased Thomas the Third a seat in the House of Representatives instead. Rumour had it that the safe Boston constituency had cost the family well over eight million dollars, but at least they had put Tommy the Turd where he could do no direct damage to the cement profits. "So what in the name of God is Tommy doing here?" I asked Charlie.

"Plotting, of course."

"Plotting what?" The Guinness was far too cold, but that was something I would have to learn to live with now I was home again.

Charlie leaned across the bar and lowered his voice. "You know Seamus Geoghegan?"

"Of course I know Seamus. We're old friends."

"Well, you know he's right here in Boston? And that the Brits are trying to extradite him? They failed at their first try, but now they're having another go in an appeal court. So we need money to defend him."

"We being the Friends of Free Ireland?" I guessed, remembering that my brother-in-law was now an official of that group.

"You got it, Paulie. Patrick's on the committee of the Friends now, so he is. Michael Herlihy really runs it, of course, but Michael needs someone to tally up the cash and keep the membership list in order, and Patrick volunteered after he visited Ireland. Did you hear about that? Jasus, but Patrick came back from Belfast with steam coming out of his ears and there's nothing he won't do for Ireland these days." Charlie chuckled and settled his elbows on the bar ready for the pleasure of telling a good story. "Last September he even hired a bus and drove a whole party of us down to Meadowlands in New Jersey. Two British Army bands were putting on a show in the Brendan Byrne Arena, and Patrick had the bright idea of slashing the tyres of all the cars in the parking lot. When we reached the place he told us it was a blow for a free Ireland, so it was, but the moment a police cruiser came by, Padraig was running faster than loose shit off a hot shovel!" Charlie laughed. "Mind you, if you listen to him tell the tale now you'd think we won half the battle for Ulster that same night."

"So now he's touching Congressman O'Shaughnessy for Seamus's legal aid?"

Charlie nodded, then held up a warning hand as he saw me turning to leave. "But he says he doesn't want to be disturbed."

"To hell with that. He's family, isn't he? You think he won't want to welcome me home?" I winked at Charlie, picked up the Guinness and my sea-bag, and went to the snug.

There were five of them in there. Two were strangers, but I knew the other three well enough. There was Patrick himself, Tommy the Turd and, to my surprise, though I should not have been surprised at all, the bright boy of Derry, Seamus Geoghegan himself.

"Who the fuck . . ." Patrick started to protest when I pushed through the door, then he recognised me and his jaw literally fell open.

I dropped my sea-bag at the door. "Patrick. Congressman," I greeted them with a nod apiece, then smiled at Seamus. "Hey, you bastard!"

"Paulie!" He stood, grinning, arms spread. "Paulie!" He came round the table and embraced me vigorously.

"Watch my fucking Guinness, you ape!" I protested at his greeting.

"You're in dead trouble, you know that?" He whispered the urgent words in my ear, then stepped back and raised his voice. "You're looking grand, so you are! Just grand."

"And yourself," I said, then placed what was left of my

Guinness on the table. "How are you doing, Patrick? Or is it Padraig now?"

"We're in executive session here," he said very pompously.

"Fock away off," I said in my best Belfast accent. Tommy the Third looked vaguely worried, but that was his usual expression for the Congressman had always gone through life with only one oar in the water. "You remember me, Congressman?" I asked him.

"Of course," he said, though he did not use my name, which suggested he did not know me from George Washington. "Might I introduce Robert Stitch?" Tommy went on with his customary politeness. He used courtesy as a defence against cleverness, and it worked, for he had a reputation, especially among women, of being an appealingly well-behaved and well-brought-up boy. "Robert is one of my Congressional aides," he explained now.

Stitch was pure Boston Brahmin, a young codfish aristocrat, who offered me a curt unfriendly nod. He was reserving further judgment till he knew whether I would be a help or a hindrance to his cause.

"And that's my lawyer, my solicitor like." Seamus jerked his head towards a wild-haired, bearded and bespectacled man who stood and held out his hand.

"I'm Chuck Sterndale," the lawyer said with a smile, "it's good to meet you, whoever you are."

"I'm Paul Shanahan," I said.

"Paulie was with me in Belfast, so he was," Seamus told the room happily. "The first time I did a runner from Derry and the fockers were all over my backside, Paulie put me up in his flat. We had a grand time, didn't we, Paulie?"

"We had good crack." I used the old Belfast expression.

"It was good crack, right enough."

"You're Irish, Mr Shanahan?" Stitch asked cautiously.

"By ancestry, but I was born not a mile away from this room, but unlike some I can mention I actually went to

Ulster to do my bit for the cause. Of course, I know that slashing tyres in the New Jersey Meadowlands advances the struggle gloriously, but it's not quite the same as pulling a trigger in Belfast."

That got to Patrick, as I had meant it to. "What the fuck do you know?" His mouth was half full of potato chips that sprayed out across his beer glass as he bellowed at me. "I was in Belfast three years ago, and I fought when I was there! I did my bit! I got beaten up by the fucking Brits! You want to see the fucking scar?" He jerked up his left sleeve where a barely discernible white scratch showed against his *Erin Go Bragh* tattoo.

"Oh, that's terrible!" I mocked him. "What happened, Patrick? Oh no! Don't tell me you mugged another Salvation Army girl?"

"Fuck you!" He scooped up a handful of chips that he crammed into his mouth as if to show that he had nothing more to say to me. A cigarette was burning in a full ashtray beside him.

Tommy the Turd raised a pacifying hand. "I can vouch for Mr McPhee's story. Mr Stitch was with Mr McPhee on that day and he will testify that they suffered a clear case of unprovoked British brutality; clear, unprovoked, and blatant."

"So what happened, diddums?" I asked Patrick.

Patrick glared at me while he tried to decide whether or not to indulge my curiosity, but immodesty got the better of him. "I had a meeting arranged, right? Me and Mr Stitch were personally invited to meet with some soldiers of the Provisionals. Fellows like Seamus here, the real heroes of Ireland! They wanted a chance to thank us for our support. They're good fellows, they are, good fellows. So we were told to go to this abandoned house in Ballymurphy, and we went there in broad daylight, broad daylight! Just me and the Congressman's aide, and you'll never believe what happened! Never!"

"Clear, unprovoked, blatant brutality," Tommy the Turd interjected solemnly.

Seamus winked at me while Robert Stitch, who seemed a good deal less proud of the war story than Patrick, stared at the table. "So tell me what happened," I invited Patrick.

"There must have been a security lapse," Patrick said, "because we hadn't been waiting more than five minutes, not five minutes, and the IRA soldiers hadn't even had time to arrive, when a British patrol came to the house. They knew we were there all right! They shut off the back entrance and attacked through the front. Attacked! Isn't that the right word, Mr Stitch?"

"They rushed the house," Stitch said gravely.

"They didn't ask who we were," Patrick said indignantly, "they just attacked!"

"Blatant, unprovoked, clear brutality," Tommy the Turd assured me. Stitch visibly winced.

Patrick shook his head modestly. "We fought back, of course. We were just defending ourselves, nothing more, but I tell you, those Brit bastards won't forget meeting Padraig Aloysius McPhee of Boston, no sir! But there were too many of them, just too many."

"Naked, unprovoked, blatant brutality," Tommy the Turd told me, while Seamus held his breath in an attempt not to laugh.

"So tell me what happened next?" I asked. I had adopted a wide-eyed expression, full of astonished concern. "Did they take the two of you to the Royal Victoria Hospital?"

"We refused to accept any of the enemy's medical help," my brother-in-law said proudly. Stitch was examining the table-top even more closely.

"But surely the enemy arrested you!" I exclaimed. "I mean, sweet suffering Christ, Patrick, but hadn't you just beaten the living shit out of a whole Brit patrol? So where did the surviving soldiers take you? The Castlereagh Police Station? The Silver City? Falls Road Police Station?"

"They realised their mistake," Patrick said with immense dignity.

"You mean they apologised?"

"They discovered we were Americans," he said, "and were forced to let us go."

"Oh, it's a rare tale," I said, sounding deeply impressed.

"Shocking," Seamus somehow managed not to laugh as he spoke, "nothing short of focking shocking."

"Clear, naked, blatant brutality," Tommy the Turd said. He was a dazzlingly handsome youth, stern-faced, machine-tanned and immaculately groomed. His father had recently bought Tommy an expensive blonde wife, which had started speculation that the Congressman was being equipped and coached for a run at the Presidency. "And unprovoked!" he added.

"So you can stuff your mockery, shitface," Patrick said to me with a triumphant leer.

"I apologise, Patrick, I really do. I had no idea you'd fought so bravely. Now tell me why you rented out my house?"

"Is this relevant?" Robert Stitch intervened.

"Shut up," I told him, then walked to the back of Patrick's chair. "A five-year lease, Patrick? Five hundred a month? That's thirty thousand bucks. You want to write me a cheque?"

"We'll talk about it later, Paulie."

"We're talking about it now, you fuck. So how much money have you got on you?"

"Not now, Paulie!" He tried to stand up, but I put my hands on his shoulders and held him down.

"How long has the bitch been there, Patrick? Three years? That's eighteen thousand bucks you've taken already! Have you got it handy?"

"Please, Paulie!" He heaved up, but I slapped him hard across the side of his head and he gave a gasp and sat down fast.

I reached into his inside jacket pocket and found his billfold that held a stack of twenty-dollar bills, maybe two or three thousand dollars' worth. "I'll take it as a down payment, Padraig, but I'll be back for the rest. And in the meantime just tell Miss Sarah Sing Tennyson that you made a mistake and that she's to get the hell out of my home. Do you understand me, Padraig?"

"You can't take that money!" Patrick said nervously. "That's not mine."

"But nor is the rent you take off Miss Tennyson, Padraig." I shoved the stack of bills into my pocket.

"But that was for the cause!" Patrick insisted.

"And so's this," I said, and I bent down and whispered in his ear. "I'm back home for good now, Patrick, and if I find another bruise on Maureen I'll cut your balls off and feed them to the crows, so help me God." I could see the sweat beading on his great shovel of a face. I straightened up and belted him across the right side of his skull again, this time so hard that he squealed with pain and almost fell off his chair. I grinned at Tommy the Turd who was looking terrified. "Naked, unprovoked, blatant brutality, Congressman. It's the way of the Irish. Hey, Seamus, come and have a drink at the bar. We'll plan some fishing trips, eh? Maybe catch a few blues and stripers."

"Sounds grand, Paulie."

I walked to the door. Robert Stitch was frozen, fearing an explosion of violence. Patrick was shaking like a leaf while Tommy the Turd looked as if he'd just pissed into his Brooks Brothers pants. Only Seamus and his lawyer were grinning. "Keep Seamus out of the hands of the Brits," I told Chuck Sterndale.

"I'll surely do my best, Mr Shanahan. But some of that money you just took off Mr McPhee would help me do it."

"Mr Padraig McPhee owes me thousands more, councillor, and it's all yours, OK?" I looked at Patrick. "I'm having another drink with Charlie Monaghan now," I told him, "and after that I'm catching a bus for the Cape. So if you want to make something out of what just happened, then you'll know where to find me. See you in a minute, Seamus."

I picked up my bag and went to the bar where Charlie Monaghan, who had a perfect sense for when trouble was brewing, gave me a Guinness and an apologetic shrug, then went to find something to do in the stock room. A group of kids was playing darts, but most of the room was still watching the big screen for war news. I saw Marty Doyle, Herlihy's gopher who had driven me in Miami, scuttle across the far side of the room and I guessed he was going to inform his master that I had appeared in Boston. I waved at him, but he ignored me like a healthy man avoiding the gaze of someone stricken by the Black Death.

Seamus waited a few minutes before joining me at the bar. A couple of men who wanted some of the hero's fame to rub off on them offered him a drink, but Seamus told them to get lost, then settled beside me and placed his foot on the brass rail. He was a man as tall as myself, with black hair and scary pale eyes. Except for the eyes it was a good face, bony and gaunt, a real portrait of a gunman. "What the fock's going on, Paulie?" he asked quietly.

"I'm having a private row with Patrick about my Cape house."

"I don't mean that, and you know I don't. Hey, you!" This was to one of Charlie's bar assistants. "Give us a hot Powers!" His Northern Irish accent was so strong that it sounded like a 'hot Parrs'. He watched as the hot water was poured over the sugar and cloves, then as a healthy slug of whiskey was added. He was not expected to pay for his drink; no real IRA man ever had to pay for a drink in the Parish.

Seamus lit a cigarette and squinted at me through its smoke. "Either you're mad to come back here, or you're wearing bullet-proof underpants. Your brother-in-law's talking about you on the telephone in there and wee Marty Doyle is screaming that Michael Herlihy will cut you off at the knees, and you're drinking a Guinness like you haven't got a care in the world. You do know you're in trouble, don't you, Paulie?"

"Is that what you hear, Seamus?"

"Even the bloody Pope must have heard! Jasus! They're saying prayers for you already."

I laughed. I liked Seamus, really liked him. He was good crack. "You know it's been the best part of ten years since we met," I told him. "Can you believe that?"

"As long as that?" He shook his head in disbelief, then shot me a wary look. "But I'm hearing stories about you, Paulie, and they're not good."

"What are you hearing?"

"That you did a runner with some money. A lot of focking money."

"Only five million bucks," I said, "in gold. Be reasonable, Seamus."

"Mother of God!" He almost choked on his hot Powers, then, because I had admitted my guilt so cheerfully, he grinned. "You're mad! And they'll never let you get away with it!"

"Who said I had it?" I demanded. "The boat sank."

"And so it did, Paulie," Seamus said, "and the Brits are giving us back the six counties for Christmas, and the Pope is giving me a cardinal's hat. Who do you think you're talking to, eh? Jasus, Paulie, if that boat had gone down then you were a fool not to sink with it."

I shrugged. "It wasn't their money, Seamus. It came from the Libyans or the Iraqis. It had nothing to do with Belfast, not a thing."

"That's not what I hear. I hear stories about Stingers."

I gave a reluctant nod. "Fifty-three of them."

Seamus grimaced. "I hear they paid half-a-million bucks as a deposit on the Stingers. And that you told them you were bringing the balance!"

"Herlihy should keep his damned mouth shut," I said.

"He didn't tell me!" Seamus said. "I heard it from Ireland, so I did. I reckon Brendan Flynn wants your guts for garters."

"Fuck Brendan," I said savagely.

"That's not how it works, Paulie, and you know it. You can't just do a runner with the money." Seamus had turned to watch the big room with his pale, wary eyes. "You want me to talk to them? I'll say you'll bring the money in soon. I'll say it was all a misunderstanding and that none of us wants any trouble. You want me to talk to them?"

"You don't know the half of it," I said grimly.

"You mean those two who vanished? Liam and Gerry? Brendan told me about them. Are they dead?"

I hesitated, then nodded. "They're dead."

For a second I was tempted to confess to Seamus that I had murdered them in cold blood, but Seamus evidently did not care for he just shook his head. "Brendan doesn't give a fock about those two. They were just supposed to look after the taxi trade and the butchers' shops. All they had to do was slap a few faces and keep the miserable fockers in line, but no, they had to go into business for themselves, didn't they?" Seamus meant that Gerry and Liam, despite their big tales of dead soldiers and flattened city buildings, had only ever been enforcers for the Provisional IRA's protection rackets. Their contribution to the new Ireland had consisted of beating up Catholic barmen, shopkeepers and taxi-drivers who were late with their weekly donation to the Provos. By far the largest part of the IRA's activities was spent in running its protection rackets, just as the Protestant gunmen did in their parts of Ulster. "But Liam and Gerry weren't content with looking after trade," Seamus explained. "They decided to raid a couple of sub-post-offices in Ardoyne and Legoniel and they beat the shit out of a fellow who was married to Punchy O'Neill's sister, so Punchy complained, of course, and Brendan turned their names in to the Brits, only they managed to reach the Free State before they were ever arrested, so naturally Brendan had to look after them. But they were never any good! All they did was collect the money. Jasus, Brendan's not going to mind them going down the drain. He'll probably thank you for switching them off, so he will! For God's sake, Paulie, let me talk to him. Let me make it right."

"Have a try," I said, though only to make Seamus happy. There was going to be no deal over the money, none at all.

"What shall I say?" Seamus asked. "That you'll bring the money in soon?"

"Sure," I said, not meaning it at all.

"Five million, eh?" Seamus laughed. "And I remember when you and I couldn't find a quid between us."

"We were never that skint," I said, "but they were good days."

"Aye, they were. Better than these."

"You don't like it here?"

"Aye! I like it well enough. Boston's OK." He dropped his cigarette on to the floor and killed it with the toe of his boot. His skin was pock-marked, but that blemish had never stopped the girls chasing after him, though Seamus, who seemed to have ice-water in his veins when it came to guns or bombs, was rendered helplessly nervous by women. If Roisin were alone in our Belfast apartment Seamus would sit on the back stairs rather than try to talk to her without my help. It was not that he disliked women, just that he was simply terrified of their beauty and power. "Boston's OK," he said again with a wry tone. "Beantown. What kind of a focking name is that for a city? Beantown."

"So what's wrong with Beantown?"

"There's nothing wrong with it. People are nice enough, so they are, but it isn't like home, is it? The beer's focking freezing, the summers are hotter than hell, and they're always watching focking netball on the telly! Focking men's netball! It's a focking girls' game, I tell them."

"It's called basketball," I said, as if he didn't know, "and it's Boston's religion."

He laughed, then shook his head. "I miss Derry, Paulie. I really miss it. I mean I know it's not much of a place, not worth a rat's toss really, but I miss it."

"I miss Belfast," I said, and I did too. I loved that city. It was a dirty, ugly, battered city and I had never been happier than when I had lived there. The city's first impression was dour; all bomb damage and hopeless dereliction, but the brick streets crackled with wit and were warmed by friendship.

Seamus grimaced. "I sometimes think that if they'd just let me go home for one short day I'd kiss a focking Apprentice Boy out of sheer gratitude." He gave a brief and bitter laugh. "I told that to some fellow in here and he didn't even know who the focking Apprentice Boys are! He'd not even heard of the Orangemen!"

"Don't blame them," I said. "They love Ireland, right enough, but they don't want to know how complicated it is. You can't blame them, Seamus, and their hearts are in the right place."

But Seamus wasn't listening to my explanations. "They had a fellow give a talk in here, what? Six months back? Something like that, and he said the focking Brits had built a focking gas chamber in Long Kesh, and that they were systematically murdering the whole Catholic population!" Seamus grimaced. "I mean, shit! I don't like the focking Brits, but they haven't got that bad. Not yet, anyway. I didn't say anything, of course, what's the focking point?"

"None."

He laughed. "And your brother-in-law, eh? Getting slapped about in Ballymurphy! So the lads are still pulling that stunt, are they?" He shook his head happily. "What a prick Patrick is! I know he's your family, Paulie, but what a prick!"

"I know. He's a creep."

"And family, that's another thing! My da died last year and I couldn't be with him. It isn't right, a son not being at his father's grave. And my mam's not well. Something with her chest, her breathing, like. My brother wrote and told me, but what can I do?"

So there was a brother, and Kathleen Donovan had not lied to me, and I suddenly wondered what the hell use was five million bucks without someone to share it with? "Go back to Ireland," I suggested to Seamus. "Your ma can cross into Donegal and see you there, can't she?"

"She can, but the focking Garda will have me in Portlaoise Jail before you could spit. They want me for a wee job I did in Dundalk." He grinned apologetically. I knew it would be no good asking what the wee job was, though it was almost certainly a bank raid. Seamus was a much wanted man, though nowhere was he wanted more avidly than in Northern Ireland where he had made his bloody and infamous escape from Long Kesh. The Provisionals had lost two men in the breakout, but they reckoned the propaganda value of Seamus's freedom was well worth the price. But now, as an illegal immigrant in America and a wanted felon in Britain and Ireland, the battle for his political asylum was filling newspaper columns on both sides of the Atlantic. "They say I'm a focking symbol," Seamus gloomily told me. "They say I'll be Grand Marshal of their St Patrick's Day parade next year. They want to give me a medal of freedom on the State House steps. They're even talking about making a focking film of me! Can you believe that? Some prick little actor in Hollywood says he wants to make a film of me! But I don't want to be in a focking movie, Paul. I want to go home."

"Go and see a plastic surgeon," I suggested.

"I was thinking of doing that," he said softly. "I tell you, with all the focking money they're spending just keeping me out of jail I could have looked like Marilyn Monroe by now, tits and all." He blushed for having dared say a rude word, and for a second I thought he was going to cross himself, then he just shook his head sorrowfully. "Shit, Paul, I just want to go home. I don't want any more trouble. The younger lads can do some of the fighting now, eh? I've put a few quid away, so I have, and there's a scrap of farmland near Dunnamanagh that would do me just grand. A few cattle, some arable, and a tight little house. That'll do me right enough." He paused, his eyes far away, then he lit a new cigarette. "I was thinking of Roisin the other day." He had reddened with embarrassment, and I wondered just how badly she had humiliated him.

"I often think of her," I admitted.

"I had a letter from her sister a few weeks back. It came to Chuck's office, my lawyer, right?"

"Did you write back?"

He shook his head.

"What did the letter want?"

"She wanted to know what happened to Roisin, like. Christ, what was I to say?"

"The truth?" I suggested, though in my mouth the word tasted like ash.

"Who the fock knows if Roisin even had a sister?" Seamus asked me. "And Chuck said I shouldn't write back, in case it was a set-up by the focking Brits. You know, to get information? So he chucked the letter away."

"It's just as well," I said vaguely.

"And what was I supposed to tell the sister?" Seamus asked indignantly. "That Roisin was shot by the focking Arabs?"

"Right."

"Focking maniacs, that's what those Arabs are. Hanging's too good for the fockers." Seamus stared at the green cut-out shamrocks that decorated the bar's back-mirror. "She never did betray me, Paulie. No one did. The Brits said they had the information off her, but they never did. They were just making trouble, and I reckon their trouble worked for they got her a bullet, right?" He frowned. "And she was a rare girl. She had a tongue on her though, didn't she just? Never heard a woman speak like it." He suddenly froze, his eyes staring at the mirror which reflected the far side of the room. "Are those two boys after you, you think?"

Two men, both wearing plaid jackets buttoned tight up to their necks, had appeared at the far side of the hall. They were young, broad-chested, and convinced of their own toughness, and neither was trying to hide their interest in me. I suspected that Patrick had whistled them up in the hope that they could retrieve the money I'd just lifted from his pocket. "They're looking for me, right enough," I told Seamus.

"Why?"

"Personal. Patrick wants that money back I just took off him, and he doesn't want to ask me for it himself."

"Are you sure it's not political?"

I shook my head. "There wouldn't have been time to get the orders."

"What about Michael Herlihy? He's got the authority, hasn't he?"

"Not for this sort of trouble, Seamus. Any orders for my killing would have to come from Belfast or Dublin. For Christ's sake, you think Brendan will have me chopped up before he knows where the gold is? No, this is personal, Seamus. This is between me and Padraig."

He grinned. "Then I'm on your side, Paulie. Two of them and two of us, eh?" He drained the last of his hot whiskey. "Poor wee fockers. Do we finish them off?"

"We just frighten them."

"You go first then. I'll be twenty paces behind." He made a great play of shaking my hand and saying farewell, then I picked up my bag and pulled on my oilskin. A cheer greeted the abandonment of the war news and the beginning of a televised basketball game. The two men watched me go to the side door, saw that Seamus was ordering another drink, and so followed me towards the winter afternoon.

It was game time.

In the old days the Parish's side door had opened into an alleyway that ran between the hall and an Italian bakery, but the bakery had long been pulled down to leave an abandoned lot which the Parish used as a place to hide stolen cars and the truckloads of merchandise that disappeared from Logan Airport's bonded warehouses. The lot was hidden from the road by a high fence that acted as a neighbourhood bulletin board. The fence's outer face was a mass of posters which currently advertised a teach-in on British propaganda techniques in the United States, auditions for the American Children of Ireland Marching Band and Twirlers, classes in spoken Gaelic, an announcement about the St Patrick's Day parade arrangements, and twin appeals for contributions to help mark the tenth anniversary of the hunger strikes and the seventy-fifth anniversary of the Easter Rising in Dublin.

The fence made the lot a fine and private place in the middle of which a police cruiser was now sitting with its engine running, its front doors open, and its emergency lights whipping an urgently lurid glow across the handful of parked vehicles. The car was empty, except for two discarded police caps that lay on the back seat. The cruiser explained why the pair of young men had appeared with their plaid coats buttoned to their throats. It was not that police uniforms would have scared anyone in the Parish, which had Boston's Irish cops well under control, but inevitably the appearance of two policemen would have caused a stir and the two men had wanted to take me quietly. Besides the police cruiser there were two trucks parked in the lot, a red Lincoln Continental and a black Mercedes sports car that must have belonged to Tommy the Turd for it had a special Congressional licence-plate.

I cut right, going past the Mercedes towards the gap in the fence which would lead me towards East Broadway. There was a cold wind and a light rain in the darkening air, making me glad that I was wearing my thick yellow oilskin. I heard the Parish side door bang open behind me and felt the adrenalin warm my veins. "Shanahan!" someone shouted.

I turned, but kept walking backwards.

"Freeze there!" The two youngsters were nervous, but were determined to play the scene tough. They fumbled under their tight buttoned plaid coats for their pistols.

They were still trying to extricate their guns when Seamus came out of the Parish door. The two policemen, embarrassed by the unwanted witness, straightened up. I had started walking towards them, feigning innocence. "You wanted me, boys?"

"Don't mind me, lads," Seamus sauntered down the steps.

The cops tried to lose Seamus. "We just wanted a word with Mr Shanahan. Something private."

"Private, is it? But Paulie and I are old friends. We go way back, lads. There's no secrets between us, are there, Paulie?"

"You can talk in front of Seamus," I said, "so what is it? A parking violation? Or a donation for the police orphanage?" I was six paces in front of them and Seamus was three paces behind, and the two cops were both sweating despite the chill wind, and no wonder, for Seamus had a certain reputation among the Irish. "So what do you want of me?" I asked them, and heard the Ulster lilt in my voice. I had caught the accent when I lived there, and at moments of stress it came back. Behind me the police car's lights whirled in the gloom.

"It's nothing." One of the two cops had decided to back out of the confrontation. He held his hands palm outwards towards me. "Nothing at all. Forget it."

"You're disappointing me, boys." I took a step closer. Seamus jerked his head to his left, telling me he would take that man, and I took another pace forwards when suddenly the Parish side door banged open again and an agitated Michael Herlihy appeared on the top step. "Stop it! Now! You hear me? John Doyle? O'Connor? You back off, now, both of you!" Herlihy's voice was sharp as ice. He must have been close by, perhaps in the back room of Tully's Tavern that he used as a South Boston office, when Marty Doyle had told him of my appearance in the land of the living. Herlihy, hearing that Patrick was having me beaten up by the Parish's tame police, saw the small matter of five million dollars being complicated. Michael Herlihy wanted to find out just what attitude I was taking to the missing gold before he saw me tenderised, and so he had come full pelt out of his lair to head off the trouble. "Whatever you were doing," he ordered the two policemen, "stop it!"

"Just what were you doing?" I asked the relieved policemen.

"Nothing, Mr Shanahan, nothing. We were just leaving! It was all a mistake."

They moved to walk past me towards their car, but I put out a hand to stop them. "Hadn't you heard, boys? The Parish has got valet parking these days. Isn't that right, Seamus?"

"Right enough, Paulie."

The two policemen dared not move for Seamus radiated a capacity for mind-numbing violence and was standing hard behind them. He was not restraining the policemen, but neither cop dared move a muscle as I climbed into their squad car, took off the parking brake and shifted it into reverse. I smiled through the windscreen, then rammed my foot on to the accelerator. The police car shot backwards, smack into the brick side wall of the neighbouring hardware store. "Sorry, boys!" I shouted. "I'm more used to boats than I am to cars!"

Seamus was laughing. Herlihy, whose office pallor had turned even whiter than usual, glared but did not try to stop me, while the two police officers just stood like whipped children. I pulled forward, hearing the tinkle of broken brake lights falling to the ground, then rammed the accelerator again, this time aiming the car at Tommy the Turd's Mercedes. Herlihy flinched when he saw what I was doing, then closed his eyes as I rammed the police cruiser hard into the flank of the sleek black sports car. There was a horrible mangling noise. "It's been so long since I've driven a car, boys!" I shouted. "But I'll get it right, don't you worry!"

A dozen men had come out of the Parish, attracted by the squeal and crash of tortured metal. Herlihy, tight with fury, turned and ordered them back inside. Seamus's lawyer ignored the order and stood laughing while Tommy the Turd and his Waspy aide were wondering if the world had slipped gears. Patrick McPhee, knowing he had started this madness with his ill-judged summons for police help, fled in panic from Michael's anger.

"Here goes!" I shouted. "I'll get it right this time!" I shifted into reverse again, slammed my foot on the accelerator, and crashed the car back sickeningly hard into the brick wall. My head whiplashed on to the grille that protected the front seat occupants from whatever prisoners they had in the back seat. I killed the engine and climbed out, to see that the boot lid was spectacularly buckled. The cruiser also had a crumpled bumper and had lost a headlight and the best part of a wheel arch, while the expensive body panels of the Congressman's Mercedes were horribly dented and gouged. "Replace it with an American car, Congressman," I called to him, "a man like you shouldn't be driving a European car, should you now?"

Tommy the Turd's aide hurried the Congressman back into the Parish as the two policemen stalked past me. "Fuck you, Shanahan," one of them muttered, then they pulled off their plaid hunting coats, climbed into their wrecked cruiser and, with a foul scraping sound, drove out of the lot.

Seamus applauded me. Michael Herlihy, looking more

than ever like a beardless Lenin, spat at me. "That wasn't clever, Paul," he said.

"It wasn't meant to be clever, Michael, just a scrap of fun. Did you never have fun, Michael?" I looked at Seamus. "He was always the class nerd, Seamus. Altar boy, chalkboard monitor, nuns' favourite. Michael's idea of a good time is to run in the Boston marathon, or have you even given up that small pleasure, Michael?"

Herlihy picked his way through the puddles of the parking lot until he was standing close beside me. "Where have you been these last few weeks, Shanahan?" He had waved Seamus aside, wanting to speak privately with me.

"I've been chatting to the CIA, Michael." I smiled seraphically.

"You've done what?"

"You know I spilled the beans. Was it the FBI or the cops that talked to you?" I smiled down into his thin, bloodless face. "I got worried that the Arabs weren't sending the Stingers to Ireland, but planned to use them here. I knew you wouldn't have wanted that to happen, Michael, it would have been bad for the movement's image, wouldn't it now? So I played the patriot game."

He ignored my blarney. "Where in God's name is the money?"

"It's funny, isn't it," I said, "how you lawyers always ask that question."

"Where is it, Shanahan?" He was intense, hissing his words, his body tight as a whip.

I clicked my fingers ruefully, as though I had misplaced something. "I should have told you, Michael, the boat sank. It was a rotten boat, a real clunker. It went down off Sardinia. I tried to save the two Belfast boys, but they panicked and the boat went down like a stone with them still inside. And with all that gold weighing the boat down, they never stood a chance. Straight down. Nothing but a few bubbles and a floating lifejacket."

"Don't tell me lies." Michael spoke menacingly.

I knew he was never going to believe the story, not in a thousand years, but it was worth a try all the same. "As God is my witness, Michael, just south of Sardinia. There was a sudden squall out of the north, a brute of a sea running, and –"

"No!" He snapped the denial, cutting me off. The rain flecked his glasses as his voice gathered intensity. "You've gone too far, Paul, and Ireland wants you to answer some questions."

"No," I said, "you're the one who'll have to answer questions, Michael. That money didn't come from Libya, it came from Saddam Hussein, the bastard who's doing his level best to slaughter American boys right now. So what you're going to do now, Michael, is you're going to forget the money, you're going to forget the Stingers, and you're going to forget me."

"You're insane!" Michael's voice rose to a sudden shrill intensity.

Seamus crossed the lot to act as a peacemaker. "I'm taking care of it, Michael," he said soothingly. "Paulie will find the money, won't you, Paulie?"

"Leave this alone, Seamus!" Herlihy snapped, then looked back to me. "I'll have your killed, so help me! I'll have you killed!" Michael rarely displayed any emotions for he was one of nature's Jesuits, a tough sinewy little son of a gun under a pale, thin and clerical exterior, but now, behind his rain-obscured glasses, he had lost his self-control. "You bring me the money, Shanahan, all of it, or you'll wish you'd never been born."

"Boo," I said to him.

"Damn you!" He turned and stalked across the parking lot, then stopped at the Parish's side door for a parting shot. "There's a British Consulate in Boston, Paul."

"You want me to go and tell tales to them, is that it?"

He pointed at me. "It takes one phone call, just one, and

I can have the Brits on your back. You'll end up like Gallagher." Brian Gallagher had been an arms dealer who had been acquitted in a Boston courtroom of illegally exporting arms to Ireland, and two weeks after his acquittal his body had been found in a cranberry bog near Waltham. He had not died easily. No one knew who had killed him and, though rumour blamed Gallagher's partners whom he was said to have cheated out of their money, Michael Herlihy was convinced that the Brits had sent a special forces undercover team to reverse the jury's decision. "I won't weep for you, Paul," Herlihy called as a parting shot as he went inside.

"The Brits wouldn't focking dare come here, would they?" Seamus asked.

"Christ, no! Michael's always seeing Brits under the bed. He thinks he's on their wanted list and it makes him feel like a hero. But Michael's biggest danger is that he'll get a shock off his electric toothbrush. Just forget him. He's a jerk."

"But a dangerous one." Seamus picked up my discarded sea-bag and tossed it to me. "Look after yourself, Paulie. And don't worry about Michael or about Belfast. I'll clear you. I'll say it was all a misunderstanding and that you'll be bringing the money."

"You're a grand man, Seamus."

"And fock the Brits, eh?"

"From here to forever," I gave him our old refrain, then walked away, and I hoped to God that the Brits did not have a team in New England for I was already playing two sides against a third and I did not need a fourth.

But those worries could wait. Instead, through the spitting rain and with Patrick's money in my pocket, I walked to the bus and was carried home. To Cape Cod.

It was dark when the taxi dropped me off. I could have phoned Johnny Riordan from Hyannis, and he would certainly have come and collected me from the bus depot, but I could not be sure that some nasty surprise would not be waiting at the house and so I had caught the taxi and told the driver to drop me off at the convenience store close to the dirt track which led over the sand ridge. I bought myself some milk, a tin of Spam, some bread and margarine, then walked back to the track which twisted through the pine woods and so led to my house on the salt marsh. I stopped on the sand ridge and watched the marsh and the house for a long time, but all seemed innocent under the high scudding clouds and so I finally walked down to the clam-shell driveway, found my house keys, then discovered that the half-Chinese differently gendered person called Sarah Sing Tennyson had changed the Goddamn locks. "Hell!"

I went to the kitchen window, found a decent-sized rock, and broke through one of the glass panes. No alarm shrieked. No one called out in warning, so I guessed Miss Sarah Sing Tennyson was not in residence.

I reached up, found and unlatched the window catch, then heaved up on the sash window. It did not move. The bitch had put in sash locks too, so I took the rock and smashed through the whole window: glass panes, nineteenth-century mullions and all, and, after knocking out the remaining shards from the old putty, I crawled through on to the draining board. I ripped my jeans and cut my thigh on a scrap of glass I had failed to dislodge, then pushed two cups and a plate off the draining board to shatter on the kitchen floor, but at least I was home. I groped around the kitchen until I found the newly installed light switch, then set about reclaiming my house.

I had made more enemies than Saddam Hussein in the past few weeks so my first necessity was the ability to defend myself. I went into the empty garage and found that most of my old tools were still under the bench. I took the crowbar back into the living room where Captain Alexander

Starbuck had built a broad hearth out of four massive stone slabs. I lifted the right-hand slab, shifting it aside to reveal a deep dark hole in front of the fireplace. The hole was the best of all the many hiding places constructed in the house during Prohibition. At very high spring tides, especially if an easterly wind was holding the water inside Pleasant Bay, this hiding place could flood, but those rare tides had never affected the whiskey hidden inside the hole, nor had they pierced the layers of thick plastic sheeting that I had wrapped and sealed around the long wooden box that I now wrestled up from the damp sandy hole and on to the hearth. I had last seen this box seven years before, when, just hours before leaving the house, I had wrapped and hidden it.

The telephone rang.

I swore.

It rang four times, then there was a loud click in the kitchen and suddenly Sarah Sing Tennyson's voice sounded. "I'm sorry I can't speak with you right now, but if you'd like to leave a message after the tone I'll get back to you just as soon as I can." Another click, a beep, and I assumed the caller had rung off, but then a man's voice spoke. "Where the hell are you, Sarah? I've tried the loft. Listen, baby, just give me a call, OK? Please? This is William, just in case you've forgotten who I am." The last few words were spoken in a petulant whine, suggesting that William had been severely pussy-whipped by Ms Tennyson. I grinned in sympathy for poor William, then laughed as I thought of the FBI or the CIA trying to decode the lovesick fool's message. The phone, I was sure, had to be bugged. I might have been thanked by van Stryker, but that did not mean I was trusted.

I carried my unearthed box over to the long table that was littered with twisted paint tubes, sketch books, pads and magazines. I made a space, then used a pair of Sarah Tennyson's scissors to slash through the plastic wrapping. I levered the top off the box and found the contents just as I had left them.

On top of the box was a US Army issue Colt .45 automatic dating from the Second World War. Its magazine held a paltry seven rounds, but they were powerful. I cleaned the pistol meticulously, dry-fired it a few times to make sure that everything was working, then pushed one of its magazines home. I dropped the gun into a pocket of my oilskin jacket, and, feeling a good deal safer, went to open my tin of Spam.

I made myself some crude sandwiches, enlivened them with Sarah Sing Tennyson's mustard, then, before eating and because the broken kitchen window was filling the house with bitterly cold air, I lit a fire with Sarah Sing Tennyson's kindling and logs. I found some of my tenant's cardboard and masking tape, which I used to make a crude repair to the window, and afterwards used her coffee and grinder to make myself a pot of fresh-brewed that I carried with the sandwiches to my fireside.

Food had rarely tasted better. It was like the magic moment at the end of a sea watch, after a bitter trick at a frozen wheel in a stinging spray and a cold wind, when the worst of junk food thrown together in a pitching boat's galley tastes like a banquet. It made me wonder why more five-star restaurants did not feature Spam and mustard sandwiches on their menus.

I also wondered what had happened to modern art for, as I ate, I stared in puzzlement at Sarah Sing Tennyson's paintings. Two or three of the canvases were recognisably pictures of a lighthouse, and the rest were recognisably like the two or three that had some remote relationship to reality, but beyond that the canvases were a drab mess. She did not seem to brush the paint so much as trowel it on like rough plaster, yet clearly she was some kind of recognised artist for she had claimed to make a living from her painting. Her most puzzling effort was a splatter of purple and brown and white paint which, when I turned it round on its easel, bore a small and helpful label on its reverse: 'Sunset, Nauset, October 1990.' If that was a sunset, I thought grimly, then the environment was in a worse state than the most fearful doomsayers suspected. I turned off the electric lights and carried the coffee to the big window.

The wind gusted at the black panes. Over its fretful noise I could just hear the roar of distant water where the ocean breakers tumbled on the outer face of the barrier beach. Closer, in the cold darkness, a thousand rivulets of salt water were creeping up from the bay, flooding the salt marshes and rippling the eel grass where the most succulent scallops grew. There were oysters out there too, and the best clams in the world, and mussels, and lobsters to make an appetite drool. And when a family tired of lobster there were cod cheeks or fresh swordfish steaks or bluefish or herrings, and in the old days it was a rare house that did not have a whole deer carcass hung up at winter's beginning, and in the fall there were ducks and beach-plums and cranberries and wild blackberries. It was a good place to live. And to die, I remembered, and so, the sandwiches finished and the coffee drunk, I went back to my unearthed box.

I took out the Colt's remaining magazines, then lifted out my second gun, my favourite, a semi-automatic M1 Carbine. It was a simple battle-ready rifle, also dating from the Second World War, yet it felt balanced and it fired beautifully.

I cleaned and loaded the M1 which, like the Colt, had been stolen in Boston for eventual delivery to the IRA. I had kept both guns back from their shipment, wanting them for myself, and now they would help protect Saddam Hussein's gold. Thinking of the gold reminded me that in the morning I must find a public telephone to discover if Johnny had any news of *Rebel Lady*.

In the meantime I carried the two guns upstairs. Sarah

Sing Tennyson had installed no electric lights on the second floor so I had to find a candle to light my way to the bedroom where I discovered my antique whaling harpoon back on the wall. The harpoon was a nasty piece of work; its rusting iron head was six feet long, wickedly barbed, and socketed on to a wooden pole handle that gave it another six feet of reach. I used the harpoon to brace the door in case an enemy tried to surprise me in the night, then I undressed, laid the guns close to hand, climbed under Sarah Sing Tennyson's patchwork quilt, and slept.

I slept like the dead. I slept through the dawn and into the morning, I slept through the night's rising tide and through the forenoon's ebb and I did not wake till the seas were pushing in again to the marsh channels. A bright winter sunlight streaked the yellow panelled wall and lit the stripped-pine chest of drawers on which Sarah Sing Tennyson had placed two Staffordshire dogs. I could smell the ocean, and I could smell her scent on the sheets and pillowcases. It had been so long since I had smelt that in a bed, a woman's smell, and I immediately, predictably, thought of Roisin.

There had been women enough since Roisin, but none like her. Sometimes I told myself that I had romanticised Roisin's memory as a shield to protect myself from other entanglements, yet in truth I wanted entanglement. I wanted to be like Johnny. I wanted to wake to a house full of noise and children and dogs and muddle. I wanted a wife. I wanted what passed in this world for normality, and yet was such a rare privilege for it was only made possible by love.

I rolled over. Sarah Tennyson had hung four prints on the wall which divided the bedroom from the stairwell. They were old prints of faraway cities, all domes and spires and arches. Where had she bought them? With whom? And what men had come to my house and lain on these sheets and shaved in my bathroom and taken their evening drinks on to the deck to watch the shadows lengthen across the marsh? Had browbeaten William slept here and wakened to the sound of tidewaters creeping through the marsh? I smelt the woman-smell on the warm sheets and was jealous.

I turned on to my back. The bedroom dormer faced east towards the sea and once, when the bay's tide had been unusually high, I had seen the water's dappled ripples reflected by the rising sun on to this bedroom ceiling, though usually the high tides stayed a hundred yards off in the intricate channels beyond the deck. I had always dreamed of putting an old duck punt in the closest channel and, at the bay's deep-water edge, where a secret tideway wriggled past Pochet Island, I had planned to moor a small cat-boat that a child could sail down past Sampson Island and Hog Island and Sipson Island and Strong Island and so to the new raw cut where the great Atlantic had ripped the barrier beach apart and clawed the houses off from Chatham's foreshore. This was a place for kids to grow, for this was God's adventure playground. It was a place where a child could play wild and yet feel safe. It was a place to romp with dogs along the tideline and to scratch for clams in the mud and to climb on fallen trees and to take a canoe across the bay to where the ocean beaches stretched empty. It was a place where God had so arranged matters that television reception was bad and a child could therefore grow without the worst corrosion of all.

Except I would raise no children here. I was forty, I had never been married, and Roisin, whom I had thought to bring here because she would love the bay and the beaches and the sea beyond, was dead. God, I thought, forty years old! In the trade of terror that made me an old old man. Most kids started in their teens and were burned out by their early twenties. They met girls who wanted babies, and mothers do not like their babies' fathers to be serving life imprisonment in Northern Ireland's Long Kesh or in Eire's Portlaoise Jail, and so the milky new brides would nag their menfolk into giving up the gun. A few men, like Seamus Geoghegan, survived longer, but only because they had never been henpecked out of the business. I smiled, thinking of Seamus watching the Celts play netball.

There was a sudden noise above me. I froze, then slowly reached out with my right hand for the carbine. The noise was a scuttling sound, sudden and fitful, and I realised it was nothing but a squirrel come to the roof from its nest in the scrawny stand of pines that stood to the north of the house. I relaxed, resting the rifle's stock on the patchwork quilt so that its muzzle faced the ceiling. I stared at the gun's lean and efficient lines.

That was my fate, I guessed. Just as my brother had died in Vietnam, so I would die with a bullet in my guts, or in my heart, or exploding the blood vessels in my skull. I would die in a rage of adrenalin, snarling and shooting back at my enemies, but shot down like a dog all the same. But better to die of a bullet, I told myself, than to die alone and old and unloved. I had chosen my path, though now, smelling the smell of a woman in my bed, I doubted that the choice had been wise or even fair, for there would have been nothing drab about raising children in this good place.

But now I would face my enemies here. Like a beast seeking refuge, I had come home, but only to play for the biggest stakes of all, gold and life. If I won I would be left here alone with all the money a man would ever need, and a deep-water sailing boat and a high-bowed fishing boat and what else? Bed-sheets losing their scent? A cat-boat no child would ever learn to sail? But they were just maudlin regrets for the long nights, and now, in this light-flooded morning, I had to think ahead and see where danger lay.

Brendan Flynn was dangerous. But Brendan was far away and he would be loath to set an operation on American soil, for the first commandment of the IRA was Thou Shalt Not Upset The Americans With The Truth. Brendan would therefore leave things to Michael.

Michael was angry, because I had stung him and a stung Michael Herlihy was a relentless enemy, but he was not a fool. I knew he would make some effort to retrieve the gold, but the effort would be subtle and, in the end, like the lawyer he was, he would probably agree to a settlement. Maybe one million? That seemed fair, and certainly I could make the price of all five millions much too steep for Michael's taste.

The Brits? I doubted they were in the game. Michael Herlihy liked to imagine that the British kept a team of killers on the American coast, but that was Michael's wishful thinking. He did not like to think of other men facing danger each day in the slums of the Bogside or across the hedgerows of South Armagh while he lived easy in the New World, and so he wove a fantasy that he too, in his city office or in his bleak apartment near Boston Common, faced the horror of a knock on his door in the night's black heart. But there were no SAS killers patrolling the streets of Boston looking for Michael. I could forget the Brits.

Which left the most dangerous enemy of all, il Hayaween, but would he really come for me in America? This was not his turf. There were no Palestinian slums to hide his men in America. America was an unknown land to il Hayaween, it was a glittering heaven that would dazzle a Satanic archangel. I dared not underestimate him, but I had come to the one place that would give him pause for, though the Palestinians understood Europe, America unnerved them. Besides, van Stryker would always help protect me if he thought there was the slightest chance of il Hayaween pursuing me into the New World and so, for the moment, I felt safe.

Then tyres suddenly crunched loud on the clam-shell drive and I flung back the bedclothes, pulled the harpoon away from the door and, taking the safety catch off the loaded carbine, ran down the steep stairs. I was crouching behind the front door even before the approaching vehicle had come to a halt. My heart rate had doubled in just fifteen seconds.

I listened. The crunching sound of the tyres stopped and I heard the ratchet of the parking brake. A click as the vehicle's door opened, then I too ripped open the house door and aimed the carbine straight at the intruder's chest.

Straight at Kathleen Donovan.

Who stared at me, and I suddenly knew there was no one else I had rather see, for I had so much unfinished business with her, and if my conscience was ever to be clear then she was as good a person as any to begin the process. Then I saw her eyes widening in alarm at the sight of the gun. "No!" she said. "No!"

"I'm sorry." I made the gun safe, put it aside and straightened up. "I'm sorry," I said again, for she was still looking horrified, and then I realised I had come downstairs stark naked. "It's all right," I said, "you just woke me. Come on in. I'll get dressed. Come in. I'll only be a minute," and in that utter confusion I ran back upstairs and prayed to God that this time I would not miss my chance. Not this time, not now that I was home at last and so utterly alone.

She waited outside the house, refused my offer of coffee, refused even to come into the house, but instead asked to walk towards the sea. She was nervous, but perhaps that was hardly surprising for she must have known I had lied to her in Nieuwpoort and it must have taken real courage for her to come and accost me in my Cape Cod retreat. "How did you know I was here?" I asked her.

"I didn't. I was just hoping." She walked ahead of me on the narrow track, staring down as she walked. "If you must know" – she finally turned and looked defiantly back into my face – "I hired a private detective to discover more about you, and he found this address."

"So you just came here?" I asked.

"Because I want to know why you lied about Roisin," she said. "Or do you still insist you never knew her?"

"I knew her," I admitted.

We walked on in silence. The sand on the path had been bleached white as bone by the dry winter air and by the day's bright sun. Small streaks of snow lay in the shelter of the far dunes and shards of ice glinted at the margins of the small pools between the brittle pale grasses. The wind was light, coming cold from the north-east. Kathleen wore a black overcoat edged with red cuffs and a tall collar that stuck up to meet her tasselled woollen hat. "Is she dead?"

"Yes. Four years now." We were speaking very stiffly.

"How?"

I could feel myself shaking, and I only trusted myself to answer with one word. "Shot."

"In Ireland?"

"No."

"Then where?"

I sighed. My breath misted in the air, blew away over the salt marsh. "She died," I said, "in a Palestinian training camp called Hasbaiya. She'd gone there to learn about bombs and killing, but instead they killed her."

"Why?" A terrible intensity in the voice.

"Because they thought she was a CIA agent."

"Oh, my God."

I thought for a second Kathleen was going to sit down on the path, and I held out a hand to steady her, but she shook my help away and walked on alone. We were threading the path that twisted erratically about the head of the bay between stands of reed and clumps of grass and which led eventually to the great stretch of beach where the Atlantic rollers crashed against the strand.

She turned after a few paces and raised her green eyes in a challenge. "Why didn't you tell me this in Belgium?"

"Because . . ." I began, then faltered into silence. The truth would sound so stupid, but I had promised myself I

214

would tell this girl the truth and so I launched myself into the lame excuses. "I know it'll sound stupid, but I kind of thought you might be working for the Brits."

She laughed. Not with amusement, but in bitter scorn. "First Roisin is the CIA, now I work for the British?"

I tried to explain. "Concealment's a way of life. Lying is a response to any question. I'm sorry, I really am. I wanted to tell you, but I dared not."

"So why tell me now?" She had begun walking again.

"Because I'm out of it now. It's all over for me."

"Out of what?" she asked derisively. "The IRA?"

"I was in the IRA," I said carefully, "but only because this country asked me to join." No, that was not true. I would have joined anyway because it was tribal, because it was adventure, but would I have stayed? Could I have stayed after seeing an adult shrunken to the size of a child by a bomb made from gasoline laced with soap-flakes that make the fire stick to flesh like blazing napalm? "I worked for the CIA," I told her.

She glanced at me, looked away, and I saw that she did not believe me, although she was too polite to say as much. "And Roisin?" Kathleen asked. "Was she in the CIA as well as the IRA?"

"She wasn't in the CIA."

"Then why did they shoot her?"

So I told her about Seamus's betrayal, and that too sounded lame, and I was beginning to wish Kathleen Donovan had not come to see me on this bright dry morning, but then I went back to the beginning, right to the very beginning in the smoky Dublin pub when Roisin had come in from the night with raindrops glistening in her hair, and on through to the day when I had piled the stones on her grave. I left Axel out of the tale, and I sketched over the end of our relationship, but the rest was truthful enough.

"So she has no gravestone?" Kathleen asked when I had finished the story. "No memorial?"

"I paid for masses to be said for her in Dublin," I told her truthfully.

Kathleen shrugged, as if doubting that the masses would do a scrap of good. She walked in silence for a long time, then suddenly spoke of her elder sister, saying how even as a child Roisin had been obsessed by Ireland. "She didn't go there till she was fourteen, but by then she already spoke Gaelic and she could tell you the name of every county, and the name of every street between St Stephen's Green and Phoenix Park."

"I remember watching the television news from London with her once," I said, "and at the end they would always give the weather forecast, and that day they said it was going to be a lovely sunny day over England, Scotland and Wales, but there'd be clouds and rain over Ireland, and Roisin got so angry because she thought the English meteorologists were just being anti-Irish."

Kathleen smiled in recognition of the story and I thought how like Roisin she looked, and I turned away because I did not want to betray anything, not on this cold day when, at last, I was confessing most of my sins.

We walked on, heading south now. To my right I could see my house across the bay's headwaters while to my left the ocean seethed beyond the dunes. "I always wanted Roisin to come and live here," I confessed to Kathleen. "I had this dream of raising children and of going shopping on weekends and of sailing on the bay."

Kathleen looked up at me, surprise on her face, and for a second I thought she was going to cry, but then she offered me a rueful smile instead. "Roisin was never very motherly, not unless she changed when she reached Ireland?"

I shook my head. "She never changed. She was Cathleen ni Houlihan till the very day she died." Cathleen ni Houlihan was the great fighting heroine of Irish legend.

Once again Kathleen smiled in recognition. "When Roisin was eight she offered to pay me her allowance for the rest of her life, all her allowance, mind you, the whole weekly dollar, for ever, if I would just change names with her. She so wanted to be called Kathleen." We had reached the innermost dunes and now threaded them towards the sea. "She wanted me to sign our name-changing pact with drops of real blood. She even had one of Mom's kitchen knives all ready." Kathleen laughed at the memory, then gave me an accusing look. "Did Roisin join the IRA because of you?"

"Not because of me, no, but I introduced her."

"Did she kill anyone?" It was a hostile question.

"Not directly, at least I never heard that she did." I walked in silence for a few paces. "I tried to stop her getting involved, but it was no good. And after I left Belfast she stayed on by herself. I know she never shot anyone, but that was because she couldn't use a gun. She used to shut her eyes before she pulled the trigger, and it made her a lousy shot. But she did what she could. She told me about going into a bar once, looking for a man, and she pretended to be an American journalist, and when she found the guy she went back and told the gunmen exactly where they could locate him. That way they were able to walk straight to his table and not risk drawing attention to themselves by asking questions. But she was frustrated too. They didn't really trust her, not like their own people. They used outsiders like us when we could be useful, but they never really trusted us in Belfast. I think that's why Roisin wanted to be trained at Hasbaiya, so she could equip herself for a campaign in London. An American doesn't stand out in London the way they do in Belfast or Derry."

Kathleen still walked with her head down. We crossed the sand track that led to the summer shacks at the far end of the beach, then climbed the last line of dunes before the sea. "Did you betray her?"

"Me?"

"You said you were CIA. So you must have informed on

her along with everyone else." Her voice was hostile, her accusations wild.

"It didn't work like that." I knew I dared not describe van Stryker's Stringless Programme. "I didn't inform on her. I loved her."

"Did you want her to live in Belgium with you?"

"More than I wanted anything else." I walked past a dead gull's feathered bones and I spoke of a love's ending. "Roisin thought my job in Belgium would be dull. It was too far from the armed struggle, you see. I was still doing a job for the IRA, but it wasn't a job she could help with, and she desperately wanted to be involved at the heart of things and I was going to be at the edge, and so she refused to come with me. We used to meet whenever we could, or whenever I could persuade her. Sometimes I'd fly to Dublin, and sometimes she'd come to Belgium. She once helped me deliver a yacht from Spain to Sweden, and I thought she was so happy during that voyage." I stopped, remembering Roisin's real happiness, the sound of her laughter, the gentleness that was surprising in her when she could be eased away from her hatreds. Except it had been her hatreds that made her feel alive. She had enjoyed the voyage, but felt guilty for being away from the fight. "I wanted to marry her," I told Kathleen, "but she wasn't interested."

I stopped at the crest of the dunes to see a ragged sea breaking and foaming and spewing a winter's spray along the endless sand.

"Was there another man?" Kathleen asked with a cruel acuity.

"Yes." The great breakers crashed unending on to the cold deserted beach.

"Who?" Kathleen asked, and waited my silence out, so eventually I went on, even though I did not want to.

"The first I knew of was before I left Belfast. He was called John Macroon. He was younger than Roisin, a hothead, a wild boy. God, he was wild. He would dare anything. And he was also a good Irish Catholic boy, scared witless of women, but I knew Roisin had broken his fears. I just knew from the way she talked and from the way he looked at me, but I never dared ask her, just in case she told me the truth. Once she came to me with a bruised face and I knew he'd hit her, but she wouldn't tell me what the bruise was. And I didn't want to believe she was being unfaithful, so I pretended everything was good between us. Then Macroon died, shot by a soldier in an ambush. He was on his way to plant a bomb at a country police station and the soldiers knew he was coming and they just shot him. No warning, no questions, just bang. And that night she was weeping fit to flood all Ireland with tears, and she told me about him."

I crouched at the foot of the dunes on the beach's edge. The sea was empty of boats. There were tears in my eyes and I blamed the wind that smelled of salt and shell. "Macroon was very rough with her, but she said that she did not want him to die without knowing a woman. Christ!" I blasphemed aloud, and Christ, but how I hated to remember, yet I remembered only too well. I remembered my pain, and my need to hear every last damned detail of what I saw as a betrayal and Roisin claimed was a gesture of comfort to a hero. I remembered her defiance, her anger at me, her hatred for my tenderness, though later, in the night's tears, she had wanted my comfort.

"You say Macroon was the first?" Kathleen asked.

"There were others," I said, then was silent for a long time, or for as long as it took for a dozen great waves to break and shatter along the empty shore. "I'm sorry I didn't tell you any of this in Belgium. I guess I should have written to your family when she died, but somehow Roisin wasn't the kind of person you thought of as having family."

Kathleen had found some tiny scraps of shell that she was lobbing idly on to the beach. "I think we all knew she was dead. You can sense it, can't you? She'd usually remember to send a Christmas card, or a card for Mom's birthday, but when we didn't hear for so long . . ." She shrugged. "But we wanted to know, you understand? We wanted to be certain one way or the other. Mom doesn't have too long, and Dad's kind of frail too, so I promised I'd find out for them." A gull screamed overhead and Kathleen pushed a strand of dark red hair out of her eyes.

"What will you tell your parents?"

She was silent for a long time, then shrugged again. "I guess I'll lie to them. I'll say she died in a car accident and that she was given the last rites and a proper Christian burial. I don't think Mom and Dad want the truth. They don't approve of terrorism. Nor do I." She said the last three words very forcefully, then lobbed another scrap of shell that skittered along the sand. "I've had to think about terrorism," Kathleen went on, "because of Roisin. Even before she went to Ireland she believed in violence. She collected money for the cause and she used to collect newspaper clippings about dead British soldiers and dead Irish policemen. Mom hated it. She thought Roisin was sick, but Dad said it was just the Irish sickness and a good reason to live in America."

"But what if you can't live in America?" I asked. "What if you're a Catholic living in Protestant Ulster?"

"That's not an excuse for murder," Kathleen said firmly. "And if the IRA can't wear a uniform and show themselves in battle, then they're not real men, they're just arrogant people who think they know better than the rest of Ireland, but the truth is they'll burn in the same dreadful hell as whoever put that bomb on the Pan Am plane, or the men who shot the nuns in El Salvador, or the terrorists who killed our Marines in the Lebanon." She turned and looked defiantly at me. "I suppose you must think I'm very naïve? Or very stupid?"

I stared at the sea. "The British did terrible things to the Irish."

"And we did terrible things to the native Americans, so you think that the Cherokee or the Sioux should be able to bomb shopping malls or ambush American servicemen?"

"No," I said, "I don't think that."

"So what do you think?" she challenged me.

I knew that only an answer of the most rigorous honesty would serve my purpose here, and my purpose was not to feed a proud tribalism, nor to be defiant, but to match Kathleen's truthfulness with a genuine response. "I think," I spoke slowly, "that terrorism is wrong, but I also think it's seductive because there's a glamour in the men and women who fight a secret war, but at the very heart of it, and God I hate to admit it, but at the very heart of it we all know that the British would do almost anything to be free of Ireland. Yet everyone agrees there'd be a bloodbath if the Brits left, that the Catholics would set on the Protestants, or the Protestants on the Catholics, and that threat of violence is the only justification the British troops have for staying in Ireland, and so every bomb and every bullet the IRA uses only makes their justification stronger. So the IRA and the INLA and the UVF and the UDA are the only people keeping the British there, because the British sure as hell don't want to be there. They hate the place! They quite like the Free State, but they dislike Ulster, and they detest Ulster's Protestants! But who in the whole wide world does like the Northern Irish Protestants? Do you think Dublin wants to swallow those one million God-drunken stiff-necked bastards? And if the British won't protect them, who will?" I paused, gazing at the grey horizon. "I don't think any of it makes a blind scrap of sense, because I don't think a single bomb has brought a free Ireland one day closer, but even so I still can't see how any self-respecting lad growing up in Ballymurphy or Turf Lodge or the Bogside has any choice but to go on making the bombs. I think it's a tragic, miserable, gut-wrenching mess. That's what I think."

"And the CIA wants to be involved in that mess?" she asked me, showing her incredulity at my claim to have worked for the American government.

"I don't know." I was feeling cold. "I was never a proper agent. I mean I didn't take an oath or anything like that. They didn't even pay me, but they asked me to find things out, and I did. But not about the IRA. They just used that as a kind of introduction." It sounded lame, but it was the best I could do. "For me it was a kind of game, but not for Roisin. For her it was a cause. That was why she wanted to go to Hasbaiya. She wanted to learn how to kill without flinching. She wanted to win Ireland all by herself, and I just wanted to have a good time." Which is why I had killed Liam and Gerry, because they stood between me and the gold. They had not died for Ireland or for America or for anything. Just for me. It made me feel shallow, but I did not know how to make myself profound. I remembered Liam's eyes glazed with the green light and shuddered.

Kathleen stared at me for a long time. "Roisin really hurt you, didn't she?"

How pale the sea was, I thought, and how cold. "More than I ever thought possible," I admitted, "more than I ever thought possible."

"I'll take that coffee now," she said in a small forced voice, "if it's still on offer."

"Yes," I said, "it is."

We walked away from the sea, our shadows long and dark against the white winter sand.

We did not talk much as we walked back around the head of the bay. I was nervous of Kathleen's disapproval, while she had too much to think about. We made small talk; how good it was to live near the sea, that it was cold, but that the winter had nevertheless been mild. As we neared the house I asked where she lived, and she told me in Maryland not far from her parents. She said she had trained as a dental hygienist. "But I'm out of work right now."

"I wouldn't have thought teeth were affected by the recession?"

"They are, but that isn't why I'm jobless. I was stupid enough to marry the dentist, you see, and now we're divorced. It's kind of messy." She sounded resigned to the mess. "At least we didn't have kids."

"Ah," I said, which was inadequate, but about as much as I could manage. I was nervous, because I so wanted Kathleen to like me. Indeed, I suddenly felt as though my whole future happiness depended on Kathleen's approval of me. I saw in her a quieter, gentler Roisin.

"David ran off with one of his patients," Kathleen went on, then shook her head. "I sometimes wonder why we all make each other so unhappy. It wasn't meant to be that way, was it?"

I thought of my dreams of bringing up Roisin's children beside the water. "No, it wasn't meant to be that way." And I thought of Johnny Riordan and knew that there was at least one happy person among my friends, then I remembered I had to telephone Johnny, though not from the telephone in my house, and I wondered if Kathleen would give me a lift up the road to the public phone booth in the small shopping complex. But first I had to make coffee. "I've only got caffeinated," I said as we walked about the side of the house, "and it isn't even my coffee. It belongs to someone who was squatting in the house."

"Maybe I won't have any then." She stopped at the corner of the house and gave me a very nervous smile. "Maybe I'd just better be going."

"That's fine by me." I hid my disappointment. "But can you give me a ride up to the main road?"

She nodded. "Sure."

"I'll just get some small change for the phone," I told her, and I pushed open the kitchen door which I had left

223

unlocked because Sarah Sing Tennyson had not thought to leave me a new key when she changed the locks, and there she was. Sarah Sing Tennyson was standing in my kitchen with a squeegee bottle in her right hand.

I began to twist away. I had the Colt .45 hidden in my oilskin pocket, but she was much faster than me. She squeezed. and my hands flew to my burning face and I half heard Kathleen scream with fear, then a figure ran out of the kitchen, past Sarah Tennyson, and told Kathleen not to worry, that I wasn't being hurt, then something hit me viciously hard across the skull. My knees began to give way, a man's voice grunted as he hit me again, then all went dark.

PART THREE

I recovered consciousness in a moving vehicle. That it was moving was about all I could tell for my head had been shrouded in a sack or bag and I had been thrust down into a foetal position on the carpeted floor of the van or car. My eyes were in terrible pain, my face was smarting and my nostrils filled with the stink of ammonia. I tried to stretch out, but discovered that I had been trussed into immobility. For some reason, though, I had not been gagged. "Who the hell —"

I had begun the question before I screamed. A terrible pain stabbed up from my kidneys. The pain was fearful; a sobbing, aching, dreadful lance of horror that seared through my abdomen. It seemed to take minutes for the pain to subside. I gasped for breath, half gagging on the bilelike taste of vomit in my mouth. I kept my eyes screwed shut for to open them was to invite a visitation of the stinging pain left by the ammonia. Then I remembered Kathleen and had a sudden terror that she would be hurt just because she had been visiting my house when these bastards ambushed me. "Please . . ." I spoke with a deliberate humility, but no sooner had I opened my mouth than the pain sliced into my back again and my screams sounded like the terror of a wounded animal.

The car, if it was a car, swerved round a corner, throwing me sideways against a pair of legs. Once the subsiding pain allowed me to think half clearly I decided I had to be in the back of a car, rather than in a van, and hard down on the car's floor where I was wedged between the front and back seats. The sound of the transmission told me the car was an automatic. I knew one person was on the seat to my right, so now I edged to my left to discover whether a second person hedged me in, but as soon as I moved a hand slapped me hard round the head. They wanted me to be still and they wanted me to be quiet, and the pain already inflicted me on persuaded me that their wishes were best respected. I stayed very still and very quiet.

I was also very scared, if that word could do justice to the bowel-loosening terror that trembled in me. Whoever these people were, they were experts. They had taken me with a skill and efficiency that spoke of long practice. I had suspected nothing, but had simply walked into their ambush like a child. They had immobilised me in seconds and now they were carrying me away and I was helpless. If I moved, I was hurt. If I made a noise, I was hurt. They were training me like a dog, making me subject to their control, and there was nothing I could do to stop it. Not one thing. And if these people decided to kill me, then I would die like a dog, because these people were good.

The car pulled off the road. I felt the vehicle sway as it crossed a kerb-cut, then I heard the tyres scrunch on gravel. I had no idea how long we had been driving. I had no idea if we were even on the Cape still.

The car seemed to drive into an enclosed space. I could hear its exhaust echoing loud, then the engine was switched off and I heard the doors open. Four doors.

A hand reached down, grabbed one of the ropes that pinioned me, and yanked me with extraordinary force out of the car and on to a cold hard floor.

I sensed someone kneeling beside me. Something cold touched my ankle, a knife blade I imagined, and I whimpered with fear, but the blade merely cut the bonds that trussed my legs.

A hand yanked me upright. I swayed, but managed to stand. My wrists were still bound and the thick sack was still over my head, but otherwise I had been freed of the ropes.

A hand pushed me forward. I stumbled, hardly able to walk. My feet were bare on the concrete floor. I had been wearing boots and socks when I had been ambushed, but they, like my oilskin jacket, had been stripped off me and, as far as I could tell, I was dressed only in jeans, underwear, a shirt and a sweater. My gun was gone, everything but those few items of clothing was gone. I was pushed again and I dutifully tried to hurry, but succeeded only in stubbing my bare toe against a stone step. I cried out, fell, then scrambled up before they could hit me again. I seemed to have entered a thickly carpeted passageway. It was warm suddenly.

A hand checked me. I heard a door open. The hand turned me to the right, pushed me slowly forward, very slowly, and I sensed I must use caution, and sure enough I found my foot stepping into thin air, and I gasped, thinking I was going to pitch forward into a terrible void, but a hand steadied me, and I realised they had simply steered me on to a flight of wooden steps.

I went down the steps into what had to be a cellar. The footsteps of my captors were loud on the wooden stairs, then echoed from the bare concrete floor. At the foot of the steps I was pushed a few paces forward, then checked again. They wanted me to stand still.

I obeyed. I was shivering. The cellar was cold. I could hear nothing.

Then, suddenly, a knife sawed at my wrists and the ropes fell away. I gasped, half expecting the knife to swing up at my belly, but nothing happened. I rubbed my wrists, then raised my hands towards the bag tied around my head.

A club or cosh hit my kidneys.

I screamed and half fell, but hands held me upright. I wanted to be sick again. The pain swelled in me, receded, swelled again; a pain that came in red waves. The pain reminded me that they wanted me to stand still.

So I stood still.

Hands gripped my sweater and jerked it upwards. Without thinking I stepped back and immediately the pain whipped at me as I was hit again, expertly hit so that the agony slammed up my back. I half crouched to escape the pain, but the hands on my sweater pulled me upright.

They wanted my sweater off. Weeping, unable to resist, I

raised my arms and they tugged the woollen sea-jersey off. The bag over my head had been tied at my throat and so stayed in place.

Fingers touched my throat. The touch of the fingers was warm, light and fluttering. The very lightness of the touch terrified me, then I realised that the fingers were merely undoing the buttons of my shirt. I was shaking with fear as the fingers slid down my chest and belly, then as they tugged the shirt-tails clear of my jeans and pulled the flannel sleeves off my arms.

I gasped as the fingers caressed my belly. Only it was not a caress, but rather the touch as the belt of my jeans was unbuckled, then the jeans were unbuttoned and unzipped. Hands pulled my jeans down, then my underpants. Obediently, eager to help, wanting these remorseless captors to like me and to stop hurting me, I stepped out of the clothes.

I was naked and I was cold. I was hurting and I was frightened.

Hands touched my throat again. I whimpered softly, then realised that the warm fingers were merely untying the lacing of the bag that shrouded my head. I sensed the person take a backwards step, then the bag was whipped off and, though I was instantly dazzled and though my sight was still smeared and my eyes smarting from the ammonia. I could at last see where I was and who was with me.

Facing me was Sarah Sing Tennyson. She was holding my clothes. Standing beside her was a tall and well-built man wearing a black balaclava helmet like those which the IRA favour when they are photographed by journalists. The knitted cap hid all but his eyes and his mouth. I could see he had a moustache, and that his eyes were blue, but otherwise the man's face was utterly masked. He also wore black leather gloves, a black sweater, black shoes, and black trousers. I sensed that there was at least one other person behind me, but I dared not turn round in case they hit me.

The cellar was stone-walled and completely bare of any

furnishings except a coiled garden hose that had been attached to a tap which served a metal sink fixed to one wall. The ceiling was big, suggesting a large house, while its bareness spoke of an abandoned one. The wooden stairs were to my left, climbing steeply to a closed door. The cellar was lit by a single light bulb which, though dim, had been sufficient to dazzle me in those first seconds after the hood had been removed from my eyes. The cellar floor was a screed of bare cement with a single drain in its very centre, a feature which, in these circumstances, was as menacing as the garden hose.

Sarah Sing Tennyson had my clothes draped over one arm. She was also holding a pair of shears. They were tailor's shears with black handles and steel blades a foot long.

She said nothing, but, when she was certain that the sight of the shears had captured my attention, she began to slice my clothes into shreds. She first cut the shirt, then the jersey, then my underpants, then the jeans. She worked slowly, as if to emphasise the destruction, and looked up frequently as though to make sure that I was aware of what she was doing. One by one she reduced my clothes into a pile of frayed patchwork at her feet. The sound of the shear-blades sliding against each other made a sinister metallic sibilance in the echoing cellar. The message of that hiss, and of the dumb show that ruined my clothes, was to emphasise my vulnerability. I was naked, and I had no hope of escaping without the help of my captors. They had reduced me to a shivering, frightened, naked dependant. Each slice of the blades reminded me that I was totally at the questionable mercy of Sarah Tennyson and her companions and, as if to stress that dependence, when she was done with my clothes and the last cut scrap had fluttered down to her feet, she dropped her gaze to my shrunken groin and opened the shear-blades wide so that the light slashed off the steel in a glittering angle. I felt myself shrivel even further. She smiled, my humiliation assured and complete.

"You're going to answer some questions," the masked man beside Sarah Sing Tennyson said suddenly, and his voice gave me the first clue as to who my abductors were for he spoke in the sour accent of Northern Ireland, so harsh and ugly compared to the seductive cadence of the southern Irish voice. "Where's the boat?"

I had to prevaricate. Christ, but I could not just give in! "What boat?" I asked, and then I screamed, because there was not one man behind me, but two, both of them masked like the first man, and both of them had hit me at once. I fell, and this time no one tried to hold me up, but instead the man who had asked the question kicked me, then all three were working me over, using short, sharp blows that pierced and shook and terrorised me with pain. I could control neither my bowels nor my bladder and, when they had finished, I was both weeping and filthy.

Sarah Sing Tennyson had not joined in the beating, but just watched with a half-smile on her face. The three men were all masked, all gloved, and all dressed in black. They were experts at pain and humiliation and I suspected they had not been trained by torturers, but by psychiatrists. I remembered the nameless men who had gone from Belfast to Libya to learn the modern techniques of interrogation, and I knew that I would have no choice but to tell them what they wanted to know. Of course I wanted to be brave. I wanted to emulate those men who claimed to have resisted the interrogations in the cellars of Castlereagh Police Station, but all Belfast had known that such stories were bombastic rot. They had all broken; the only difference being that some had told their secrets in awful pain and some had told them quickly to get the ordeal done.

"Stand up," the man ordered me. There was no emotion in the voice, nothing but resigned tones suggesting that this was a man doing a routine job.

I staggered to my feet. I was weeping and moaning, because the pain was all over me like a second skin. One of the three men went to the wall and uncoiled the hose. He turned on the tap, then triggered the jet of water at me. The ice-cold soaking was not a part of their brutality, but designed to wash me down.

By the time I was clean, I was also shivering. My teeth chattered and my voice was moaning very softly.

"Be quiet!" the man next to Sarah Sing Tennyson said.

I went very quiet. The cellar stank of faeces and urine.

"Let me lay down the rules of this interrogation," the man said in his quiet, reasonable voice. "You're going to tell us what we want to know. If you tell us, then you'll live, and that's a promise. If you don't tell us, you'll die, but you'll suffer a lot in the dying. None of us enjoys inflicting pain, but pain has its uses. So where is the boat?"

"She's travelling deck cargo." My teeth were chattering and I could not finish the sentence.

"Going to Boston?"

"Yes," I said eagerly, "that's right, going to Boston."

"When will it arrive?"

I hesitated, distracted by the small sounds of the two men behind me, but they were merely shifting their feet. "They didn't give me a date, but they thought the voyage should take about six weeks!" I hurried the last words, not wanting to be hit.

"They?"

"The shippers."

"Their name?"

"Exportación Layetano."

"In Barcelona?"

"Yes."

A dozen rivulets of water trickled away from my shivering body towards the drain. There was no blood in the water. These men had hurt me, but without breaking my skin. They were experts.

"You arranged for the boat's shipment?" The Ulster voice was curiously flat and neutral, as though he were a bored bank manager asking tedious details of a customer in order to determine whether or not a loan would be a wise investment for his bank.

"I arranged the shipment."

"The boat's name?"

"She used to be called *Corsaire*. I changed it to *Rebel Lady*."

"Describe her."

I stammered out the description: A forty-four-foot sloop, centre cockpit, sugar-scoop stern, with a deep heavy keel, red anti-fouling under her bootline, white gelcoat above.

"How much gold is on board?"

"Five million dollars."

Was there a second's hesitation of surprise? Maybe, but then the metronome-like voice resumed. "Describe how the gold is stored aboard the boat."

So I described the saloon's false floor, and how the cabin sole lifted to reveal the slightly discoloured fibreglass that needed to be chipped away to reveal the mix of sand and gold.

"Does the boat have registration papers?"

"Yes."

"Well, where are they!" A hint of impatience, promising pain.

"They're at my house." I told the lie because I could not expose Johnny to these bastards. Then I screamed, because something thumped hard and sharp in my tender kidneys, and I was falling as another slash of pain seared down from my neck. I hit the wet concrete, whimpering.

"Get up."

I slowly struggled up. A small, red, atavistic part of my brain counselled a sudden counter-attack, a whirling slash at the tormentors behind me, but I knew such an assault would be doomed. They were ready for me, they were fitter than me, they were better than me, and I was weakened, slow, shivering and so horribly vulnerable.

"Lies will be met with pain," the man said in a bored voice. "The boat's papers are with Johnny Riordan, yes?"

So they had known all along and had just been testing me. "Yes."

"How much money did you give Riordan?"

I had almost forgotten giving Johnny any money, and I had to think quickly before anyone hit me. "About a thousand bucks."

"Why?"

"To hire a crane to get the boat off the truck. Or in case the longshoremen at Boston need a bribe."

"Who's the importer?"

"I don't know. Exportación Layetano decide that."

"The name of your contact at Exportación Layetano?"

"Roberto Lazarraga."

The questioner had been holding the black hood that had covered my eyes. He now tossed it to me, but I was so feeble and shaking that I muffed the catch.

"Pick it up."

I picked it up.

"Put it on."

I obeyed.

"Stand still. Hands at your sides!"

The blindness and my nakedness combined to make me feel horribly vulnerable. I could hear my four captors moving about in the cellar. Footsteps climbed the stairs, then came back. Something scraped on the floor, filling me with the terror of apprehension. There was silence for a few seconds, then feet banged hollowly on the wooden stairs again.

"Take the hood off," the voice ordered, and as I did so the door at the top of the stairs slammed shut and I found myself alone. The scraps of my clothes had been taken away and the scraping sound had been merely the noise of a metal camp bed being placed by a wall. Three blankets were folded on the camp bed and a zinc bucket stood at its foot. I just had time to notice those amenities when the light went out.

I staggered to the cot bed, pulled the blankets about me, and lay down. I curled up. I was wet, cold and shaking.

God alone knows how long I stayed there. I was no weakling, but I could not fight these men. Their silence and their discipline spoke of their professionalism. I had watched an interrogation in Belfast once; sharing with Seamus Geoghegan a privileged view of some poor bastard being questioned about the betrayal of a bombing mission. The questioners wanted the name of the boy's contact in the security forces and, in their desperate attempts to get it, had beaten the lad into a raw, red, sodden horror. The interrogators had argued amongst themselves as they worked, daring each other to inflict more hurt, accusing each other of being counter-productive, and finally they had abandoned their attempts with nothing to show for their work but blood-bubbling denials from the crippled twenty-year-old. He had lost one eye, most of his teeth and was sheeted with blood. He never recovered his full sight, and would never again walk without a dipping limp, and the IRA later learned it was the boy's sister who had telephoned the security forces. By then she had moved to England and had married her soldier lover, while her lacerated, dribbling, stammering brother still declared his pathetic allegiance to the Provisional IRA and their heroic freedom fighters.

But my questioners were different. This team had been trained to give pain in measured doses and to reward answers by granting freedom from that pain. This team worked as a disciplined unit, without hesitation and without any need to speak. The only words used were those addressed to me, and those I offered back. There was no fuss or noise to distract me from the main business of the proceedings, which was to elicit what poor Gillespie had so signally failed to discover; the whereabouts of the gold.

But their very knowledge of the gold's existence told me who they were. They believed that their anonymity conferred menace, and so it did, but as I lay in the shivering dark I retained enough sense to realise that the only people who knew about the gold were those who had despatched it. The CIA did not know, the Brits did not know, only the IRA and the Libyans and the Iraqis knew.

So either I was in the hands of il Hayaween's men or in the grip of the Provisionals, and the evidence was overwhelming that it was the latter. No Palestinian or Libyan terrorist would dare try to enter the United States while the war in the Gulf raged, but any number of Irish could have come here. I had defied Michael Herlihy, and now he was striking back. I had underestimated him and I had misunderstood Sarah Sing Tennyson. She had to be a terrorist groupie, a hanger-on to the movement. I knew she was an acquaintance of my brother-in-law, who in turn was associated with Herlihy, which tied her in neatly with the Provos. Had she been left in my house expressly to raise the alarm when I came home? And she had met Johnny, which would explain their knowledge of his involvement. God, I thought, but let these bastards spare Johnny. And what had they done to Kathleen? Or was she a part of it? Had she been sent to lure me out of the house while they prepared their ambush? That thought was the worst, the last straw of despair, yet why should I be surprised? I had lied to her in Belgium, so what possible consideration did Kathleen owe me?

I shuddered in the dark. I had taken a risk, a vast risk, five million dollars' worth of risk, and it had left me in the hands of the Provisionals' trained interrogators. Professionally trained interrogators. Colonel Qaddafi had seen to that; dreaming of the days when his pet Irishmen would make some Englishman or Scotsman or Welshman shriek in a Belfast cellar in repayment for the American bombers screaming over Tripoli.

I shivered under the thin blankets. By staying very still I

could somehow hide from the pain. A small, brave voice nagged me to struggle off the camp bed and crawl up the wooden stairs to see if the door at the top would open, but I did not want to move, nor draw any attention to myself. I just wanted to huddle under the blanket. I wanted to shudder by myself in the dark womb of the cellar listening to the heartlike rhythm of the sea.

My God, I thought, but it was the sea I could hear. It was not the thunder of huge ocean rollers, but the susurration of smaller waves breaking on a soft beach which suggested I was held in a house either close to Nantucket Sound or on Cape Cod Bay. Weymouth, perhaps? The town, south of Boston and nicknamed the Irish Riviera, would be a good place for a Provisional IRA interrogation team to hide.

And the fact that this team was from the Provisionals was good for me. I did not for one moment believe my questioner's seemingly earnest promise that I would live if I told the truth. Every interrogator holds out that hope, but when these people heard my truth they would let me live, simply because they would not dare kill me. They thought I was a renegade and thief, and they were about to discover I was something far more dangerous; a legitimate American agent.

And if I was wrong, then my best hope lay in my trust that professionals like these did not inflict a slow death, but would want to be rid of me quickly.

And so I lay in the dark, shivering, trying to remember prayers.

The door at the top of the stairs crashed open. There was no light. I shouted, expecting pain, still half asleep. I had been dreaming of Roisin. "Hood on! Now!" the Northern Irish voice shouted from the stairhead. "Put it on! Put it on! Hurry! Hurry! Hurry!" Feet clattered on the stairtreads. "Hurry! Hurry! Hurry!"

I frantically fumbled for the black hood, discovering it on the floor beside the cot. I pulled it on.

"Stand up! Move! Move! Move!"

I scrambled in agony off the cot. Light suffused the black weave of the hood.

More footsteps hurried loudly down the stairs. I thought I detected all four of my tormentors, but I could not be certain. I wondered how long I had been asleep. I sensed it was now nighttime, but I guessed my sensations were quite useless as a gauge of the passing hours.

"Drop the blanket," the voice snapped.

I dropped it.

"Step forward. Stop there! Hood off."

I pulled the hood off, blinking in the light.

"Hands to your side!"

I obeyed, exposing my vulnerable nakedness. As before the unmasked Sarah Sing Tennyson faced me while, to her left, my questioner stood in his sinister head-to-foot black. I guessed the other two men had taken their positions behind me.

"What was the purpose of the five million dollars?"

"To buy Stingers." My speech was thick with sleep.

"How many Stingers?"

"Fifty-three," I answered. They knew the answers, but they did not know I knew who they were and so they would ask me questions to which they knew the answers just to keep me from guessing their identity. A game of mazes and mirrors. Of undoing knots while blindfolded.

"Who was selling the missiles?"

"A Cuban consortium in Miami."

"Describe the Cubans."

I had little to tell, but did my best.

"The missiles were meant for Ulster?"

"Yes."

"Was the trade arranged in America or Ireland?" The Ulster accent was toneless, suggesting that the questioning

239

would go on and on and that nothing I could do would stop it. It was all a part of the well-planned interrogatory technique. They wanted me to feel I was trapped in an unstoppable process that was beyond the control of anyone, and that the only way out was to give the machine what it wanted; the truth.

"Both, I think."

"Explain."

I assumed the questioner was running over known ground to test my responses and lull my suspicions as he moved imperceptibly towards the questions he really wanted answered. I told him about Brendan Flynn and Michael Herlihy, and even about little Marty Doyle. I described Shafiq's part in the arrangements, and how il Hayaween had taken over the mission. I admitted that I had deliberately broken il Hayaween's instructions by renaming *Corsaire* and shipping her to America as deck cargo.

"Why did you break those instructions?"

"Because I wanted to return to America quickly to report on the missile sale to my superiors."

"Your superiors?" Was there a hint of puzzlement in my interrogator's voice? "Explain."

I kept my voice dull and listless. "Van Stryker and his people."

"Who is van Stryker?"

"CIA, Department of Counter-Terrorism." I inserted an edge of desperation in my voice, as though I was aware of revealing things that were truly secret and sensitively dangerous.

There was a measurable pause, and a detectable uncertainty when my interrogator spoke again. "You're CIA?"

A half-second of hesitation as though I was reluctant to answer, then, "Yes."

"Since when?"

"Since 1977."

I could see Sarah Sing Tennyson's reaction clearly enough. Till now she had done nothing but keep a supercilious and careless expression, but now there was a genuine worry on her face.

"Describe your mission in the CIA." I sensed my interrogator was off his script. He was winging it, wondering where my surprising admissions would lead.

"To penetrate Middle Eastern terrorist groups." I spoke dully, mouthing the words I had rehearsed in the cellar's creeping dark. "I was instructed to use the credentials of IRA membership as an introduction to such groups."

"The CIA ordered you to join the IRA?"

"Yes."

"How were you to achieve that?"

"I was already collecting money for Ireland and sending weapons from Boston, so the IRA knew of me and trusted me."

"How did the CIA discover you?"

"I was arrested for running drugs into Florida."

"And the CIA ordered you to spy on the IRA?"

"No. They didn't need me for that."

Silence. There was a soft explosion nearby, making me jump, before I realised that the noise had come from an adjoining cellar in which a heating boiler had just ignited with a thump of expanding gases.

"Why would the CIA not be interested in the IRA?"

"I'm sure they are, but I was ordered to concentrate on the Middle Eastern groups, and my standing with those groups depended on my being totally trusted by the Provos, so I was ordered not to risk that trust by informing on them." This was the story that Roisin had told in Hasbaiya, and which had so terrified the Palestinians. Now, four years later, I was using its truth for my survival.

"Have you reported back to van Stryker?" the interrogator asked.

"Yes."

"When?"

"The whole of last month. I was being debriefed in the Pocono Mountains."

"So van Stryker will collect the boat from Boston."

I hesitated, and a foot shifted menacingly behind me. "No!"

"Why not?"

"Because I was going to collect it."

"You planned to steal the money?" My questioner sounded amused.

"Yes."

"Did you tell van Stryker about the boat at all?"

"No. I just told him that money was being telexed from Europe."

"And how much money does van Stryker think is involved?"

"One and a half million, of which a half-million has been paid."

"Is Herlihy looking for the boat?"

"Of course he is."

"Put the hood on."

They had left me holding the black bag which I now pulled obediently over my face. I heard them go upstairs and the cellar door scrape shut. I dragged the hood off my head, feeling a sudden exultation. I had worried them! I had unbalanced them! I had unbalanced them so much that on this visit they had not laid a finger on me. The truth was making me free. It had changed the script and altered their reality!

I turned to see a paper bag had been left on the floor by my bed. The bag contained a cold cheeseburger in a styrofoam container along with a cardboard cup of tepid coffee. I ate hungrily. The light had been left on and I could see that the cellar seemed to have been cleared out recently; there were dust-free spaces on the floors and walls that suggested boxes and furniture had been stored down here and had recently been taken away to make room for my interrogation.

Then, suddenly, the lights went out. In the next-door cellar the dull roar of the boiler was switched off, to be replaced by the softer sound of the sea. I lay down. I waited. I dared to think I had won. I dared to think I might live. I dared to feel hope.

I stayed in the cellar for days. I lost track of the time. I tried to keep a tally by scratching marks on the wall by my cot, but the meals came irregularly and my sleep periods were broken by sudden insistent demands that I put the hood on, stand up, stand still, answer, and so I had no regular measure by which to judge the passage of the days.

At first I had pissed blood in my urine, but the blood stopped coming as the days passed and I received no more beatings. The questions went on, mostly now about my debriefing and just what I had told the CIA about the IRA. They even asked me about men I had never mentioned to Gillespie, and I hid nothing from them for there was always the threat of violence behind the questioning, but even so I knew I had driven a deep wedge to widen the great chasm of loyalties that besieged the Provisional IRA. The Provos, like all terrorist organisations, wanted the respectability of external support and though like every other leftist guerilla movement they could count on the endorsement of socialist academics and liberal churchmen, they wanted more, much more. The twin endorsements that the Provos craved were those of America and the Middle East; that of America because it endowed them with respectability, and that of the Middle East because it provided them with their most lethal toys; but their quandary was that their two supporters hated each other, which made it even more important that each should be decried to the other. The Provos never boasted of their Libyan connections to the Americans, but rather painted that connection as a sporadic, unwanted and unimportant acquaintanceship, while to the Libyans, who were now their main sponsors, they declared that the donations of the American-Irish were the gifts of fools who did not understand the Marxist imperatives of revolution, but who could nevertheless be constantly gulled into supporting Libyan aims.

My interrogators, who had begun by assuming I was a traitor to the Provisionals, had now learned I was something far more dangerous, an agent of the United States, and that to kill me might risk the enmity of the United States. There was a chance my death could be publicised, provoking a dangerous drop in financial support from America. Thus, in fear of that exposure, they were treating me with a delicate caution. They had already abandoned hurting me and, as the days passed, they brought me better food, though never served with metal knives and forks or on china plates that could be broken to make a weapon. I drank from the garden hose, or else from the cardboard cups of coffee. I was given a pillow and thicker blankets, and my interrogators even let me ask a question of them without rewarding me with pain. What happened, I asked them, to the girl who had been with me when they abducted me?

"Nothing. She merely agreed to help us by taking you away from the house while we set up your reception committee."

"She's with you?" I could not hide my disappointment.

"Of course, and why shouldn't she be, considering who her sister was? Tell us about Roisin, now."

So I told the wretched story once again, and as I told it I thought what a fool Kathleen had made of me and I almost blushed when I remembered the hopes I had dared to make in my mind as we walked back from the beach. I had seen her as Roisin's replacement and all the time Kathleen had been a part of Michael Herlihy's attempt to get even with me. Christ, I thought, but how I had underestimated that garbage lawyer!

The days passed. My initial euphoria at having changed the rules of the interrogation gave way to a quiet despair. I might be spared the pain, but I became convinced that the easiest way the Provos could dispose of any possible embarrassment was by killing me secretly, and thus the best I could hope for was a swift bullet in the back of my skull. I had long given up any hope of opening the locked door at the top of the cellar steps. I had explored that option only to discover that the door was made from thick pieces of timber, and my only house-breaking equipment was the feeble legs of the camping cot that would have buckled under the smallest strain.

So I waited. My mind became numb. I tried to exercise, but there seemed such small hope of continued living that I invariably abandoned my efforts and crawled back to the small warmth of the cot and its blankets. I began to welcome the noisy irruption of my interrogators because talking to them was at least better than staring at the stone cellar walls or gazing into the impenetrable blackness when the light was off. They even began to let me talk sitting on the cot, wrapped in the blankets. My masked questioner stayed for hours one day, talking of Belfast and its familiar streets and the people we had both known and for a time that day I felt a real warm bond with the man because of the love we shared for that decried, battered and rain-sodden city.

Then came a day, or at least a long period, when I was awake and listening alternately to the sea and the central heating boiler and during which no one came to question me. The house, it seemed, was oddly silent. The cellar light was off.

I rolled off the cot and crouched on the floor. There was something unusual, something unsettling in the silence. I had become accustomed to the small sounds of the house; the squeak of a door, the scrape of a foot, the chink of metal against a plate, the distant noise of a toilet flushing; but now there was just a profound silence in which, with a horrid trepidation, I edged my way to the stairs and then climbed slowly upwards. I was naked and the small hairs on my arms and legs prickled. I had goose-bumps.

I reached the top step. I stopped there, listening, but there was nothing to be heard. I groped for the door lever, pressed it down and, to my astonishment, the door swung easily open.

Light flooded into the cellar. It was a dim light, like daylight enshrouded by curtains.

I stepped out of the door to find myself in a long, beautifully furnished and deeply carpeted hallway. A brass chandelier hung in the centre of the hallway, while a balustraded staircase curved away to my left. There was a lovely oil painting of a barquentine on one wall and a nineteenth-century portrait of a man dressed in a high wing collar hanging on the opposite wall. The wallpaper was a Chinese design showing birds of paradise among leafy fronds. Beside the front door was a wind gauge that flickered as an anemometer on the house roof gusted in the breeze. The only incongruous feature of the elegant entrance hall was a stack of boxes and bikes piled against a washer and a dryer; all the things, I guessed, that had been taken from the cellar to make space for my bare prison.

To my right an open door led into a vast airy kitchen, tiled white, with a massive fridge humming in one corner. Copper pans hung from a steel rack. Two paper plates had been discarded on a work-top along with a pot of cold coffee. I went back into the hallway, selected a random door and found myself inside a lavishly appointed living room. The room was hung with delicate watercolours, the sofas were deep and soft while the occasional tables gleamed with the burnish of ancient polished wood. Old magazines lay discarded on the tables and, more incongruously, a pile of empty hamburger boxes was stacked in the marble fireplace, suggesting my kidnappers had sometimes eaten in this lavish room. The shuttered windows were framed by plush drapes of antique tapestry corded with red velvet. An old-fashioned brass-tubed spyglass stood on an elegant tripod before one of the windows. I crossed the deep-carpeted room and pulled back the wooden shutters.

"Christ!" I was suddenly, wonderfully dazzled by the reflection of a full winter sun streaming from a glittering winter sea. This house, so lavish and rich and huge, was built on a mound almost at the sea's edge. The small waves flopped tiredly on to a private beach not twenty paces from my window. There was a tarpaulin-covered swimming pool to my left, a balustraded timber deck in front of me, and a boathouse and an ice-slicked private dock to my right. A yacht was berthed at the dock while out to sea there was a red buoy with a number 9 painted on its flank. I guessed I was in one of the big estates near Hyannisport or Centerville, or perhaps I was further west in one of the great beach-houses of Osterville.

Then I forgot all that speculation for I had suddenly noticed what name was painted on the sugar-scoop stern of the yacht berthed at the private dock.

I had last seen her in Barcelona, stowed safe in an open-topped container. Before that, in a lumbering winter sea, I had committed murder in her saloon. Now she was here, docile and tame, in the deep winter's sun.

She was the *Rebel Lady*.

I stumbled upstairs, flinging open closet doors as I searched for clothes. In the master bedroom, where the rumpled sheets suggested at least one of my interrogators had slept, I found a walk-in wardrobe filled with summer clothes. There were checked trousers, and trousers embroidered with spouting whales, and trousers bright with golfing motifs, and three pairs of trousers printed with emerald shamrocks, but at the back of the closet I found a plain, undecorated pair of jeans which fitted me well enough. I pulled on a shirt decorated with a polo player, a white sweater that purported to be the livery of an English cricket club, and a pair of blue and white boat shoes. There was a slicker in the wardrobe. I grabbed it and ran downstairs.

Then, before going out to explore *Rebel Lady*, I spotted a telephone on the kitchen wall.

For a second I hesitated, torn between my desire to search the boat and my worries about Johnny, then I picked up the phone and punched in his number. I could scarcely believe that the phone worked, but suddenly it rang and Johnny himself answered and I felt a great wash of relief pour through me. "Oh, Christ," I said, and slid down the wall to sit on the tiled kitchen floor.

"Paulie?" Johnny's voice was tentative, worried.

I was crying with sheer relief. "Johnny? Are you all right?"

"Of course I'm all right. I've been trying to reach you for two weeks!"

"Two weeks?" I gazed around the kitchen. My mind was in slow gear, stumbling and lurching. "What day is it, Johnny?"

He paused. "Are you drunk, Paulie?"

"Tell me. Please."

"Sunday."

"Christ," I said. "Who's winning the war?"

"That finished days ago! It was a walkover." Johnny paused. "What the hell's happened to you, Paulie?"

"Did someone come for the boat papers?" I asked him.

"The girl, of course. You know? The pretty Chinese girl?" He chuckled. "You dog."

I climbed to my feet and leaned my forehead on the cold window glass and stared out at the berthed yacht. "She told you that we were lovers?" I guessed that was what his chuckle meant.

"I can't blame you. She's a real hot one." Johnny must have sensed that something was wrong, for his tone suddenly changed. "Are you saying you didn't send her?"

"In a way I did." Not that it mattered now, I thought. The main thing was that the bastards had not snatched Johnny and given him the treatment in some raw cellar.

"Are you OK, Paulie?" Johnny asked.

"Not really."

"So where the hell are you?"

"Big house, I'm guessing it's somewhere on the Cape shore of Nantucket Sound. Does a red buoy with a number nine mean anything?"

"Not off the top of my head."

"Hold on, Johnny." I had spotted a pile of junk mail that someone must have collected from the mail-box and piled indiscriminately on a work surface.

I pulled the top piece towards me and saw it was addressed to 'The Occupier'. I read the address to Johnny, who whistled. "You're keeping rich company. Centerville, eh? That number nine buoy must mark the Spindle Rock. I'll come and get you in the truck. Be there in forty-five minutes, OK?"

I put the phone down, pulled on the slicker, and tugged open the kitchen door. I saw that the alarm system which should have been triggered by the door's opening had been ripped out. I pulled the thin slicker round my shoulders and stepped into the brisk and freezing wind. I shivered as I walked gingerly along the frozen path to the private dock which had pilings fringed with thick ruffs of ice left by the falling tide. A gull screamed a protest as I approached the dock, then flapped slowly away across the glittering sea. I paused beside the boathouse, scrubbed frost from a window pane, then peered inside to see a beautiful speedboat suspended on slings above the frozen water. The sleek boat's name was painted clear down her flank in huge green letters, *Quick Colleen*. She had a pair of monstrous two-hundred-horsepower engines at her stern, making her into a pretty, overpowered toy for the summer; a fitting accessory to this pretty, overpriced summer home that my captors had used as their temporary base. I walked on to where *Rebel Lady* fretted at her lines.

Those docklines, like the yacht's rigging, were thick with ice. The wind stirred *Rebel Lady*, jarring her against her frozen ropes and quivering her long hull. I stepped cautiously down into her cockpit and found that her companionway was unlocked. I pulled the boards free, slid back her main hatch, and ducked inside out of the wind.

To find the gold was gone. I had not really expected anything else, but a mad optimism had lurked at the back of my thoughts ever since I had glimpsed *Rebel Lady* at the wintry dock.

The saloon was a shambles. My interrogators had taken axes to the false floor, ripping and tearing away the fibreglass to expose the gold beneath. Then they had taken my hoard. Five million dollars' worth of gold, all gone, or all but one krugerrand that I found lost in a heap of sand and fibreglass chippings. I picked the coin up, span it on my palm, then pushed it into a pocket as a souvenir of a wasted voyage. I thought I saw another coin glinting in the rubble, but when I cleared the sand and shreds aside I saw it was just the shiny head of one of the keel-bolts.

I went back to the cockpit. My interrogators had done well. They had got exactly what they wanted. The gold would pay for the Stingers, and I did not doubt that some of the Stingers would stay in America to be used for Saddam Hussein's revenge against the United States. That revenge was the true purpose of il Hayaween's operation. The Brits would lose some helicopters over South Armagh, but the real targets were the great lumbering wide-body passenger jets struggling up from American airports with their cargoes of innocence.

I climbed back to the dock and walked slowly back towards the house.

Then I stopped because I heard a car's tyres grating on the gravel drive. Voices sounded happy and loud. "Let's use the back door!"

There was nowhere to hide, so I stayed still.

First around the corner was a pretty slim young woman in a long fur coat. She was running and her breath was misting in the cold air. She had golden hair, a wide mouth and blue eyes. She saw me and suddenly stopped. "Darling?" She was not speaking to me, but to Congressman Thomas O'Shaughnessy the Third who followed the woman around the side of the house. He just stopped and gaped at me.

Then two men appeared. One was the Congressman's waspish aide, Robert Stitch, the other was Michael Herlihy.

Congressman O'Shaughnessy still gaped at me, but Stitch was much quicker on the uptake. "Shall I call the police, Congressman?"

"I wouldn't, Congressman, I really wouldn't," I advised Tommy the Turd.

The Congressman suddenly recognised me. "You're Shannon, isn't that right?"

"Shanahan," I corrected him, "Paul Shanahan."

"This is my wife, Duffy." Tommy, playing as usual without his full deck, resorted to his inbred courtesy.

The pretty Duffy smiled at me. "Hello."

"You already know Mr Herlihy?" O'Shaughnessy enquired of me as though this was a pleasant meeting in his golf club. "Mr Herlihy is the Treasurer of my Re-election Campaign Committee."

I ignored Herlihy. "Nice house, Congressman." I nodded at the huge mansion.

"Thank you," he said happily. "Really, thank you."

"Just what the hell are you doing here?" Stitch intervened in the pleasantries.

"Do we really need to have this conversation in the yard?" Mrs O'Shaughnessy, who looked horribly wasted on the Congressman, asked plaintively. "I'm freezing!"

Herlihy walked towards me as Tommy the Turd escorted the delicious Duffy into the house. "What are you doing here, Shanahan?" Herlihy spat the question.

"There's your boat," I pointed at *Rebel Lady*. "That's what you wanted, isn't it?"

"That?" He stared astonished at the yacht.

"That! You bastard!" I grabbed him by the collar of his coat, ran him along the dock and pushed him down into the cockpit. "There! Look! That was where your precious money was!"

A gust of wind shook the boat, and a sluggish wave heaved up the wounded hull and Michael Herlihy immediately paled, swore, and dived for the gunwale where, with a gut-heaving wrench, he voided his expensive brunch into the sea. "Oh, God," he groaned, "oh, God." The very smallest movement of *Rebel Lady*'s wind-stirred hull had instantly provoked his chronic seasickness. "Oh, my God," he said again, and leaned over the sea to throw up once more.

I left him there. "Bastard," I shouted at him, then stalked away.

Stitch moved to confront me. "Can you give me one good reason why I shouldn't call the police?" he asked me nastily.

"Yes," I said. "Try explaining to the police why the Congressman allowed his cellar to be used by a Provisional IRA hit squad for the last two weeks."

"He did what?" He backed away from me, not sure I was telling the truth, then decided that he had better employ some quick damage control just in case I was. "It isn't true! We've been researching the trade deal in Mexico. We haven't been here." He was scenting an appalling scandal and was already rehearsing the excuses that would leave his Congressman unscathed.

"Just bugger away off," I told him.

"Who on earth moved the cellar things into the hall?" I heard the delectable Duffy O'Shaughnessy ask from inside the house. Robert Stitch, fearing some new mischief, ran through the open kitchen door, as Michael Herlihy, his face as white as the ice-slicked rigging, managed to clamber up from *Rebel Lady*'s cockpit on to the dock's planking. I paused at the corner of the house and watched as Michael staggered feebly away from the sea. He was reeling. I had forgotten just what a terrible affliction his seasickness was.

"Herlihy!" I called.

He looked at me, but said nothing.

I fished the single gold coin from my pocket. "Here's the rest of your money, you bastard." I tossed it to him.

He let the bright coin fall and roll along the path. "Where are you going?" he called as I turned and walked away.

"Home. And leave me alone, you hear me?"

I walked down the long gravel drive and out through the high fence to the road. Johnny arrived twenty minutes later and we drove away.

Miraculously, I was alive.

"Who struggles by in that little house?" Johnny asked as we drove away from the high-hedged mansion on the beach.

"House Representative Thomas O'Shaughnessy the Third."

"Tommy the Turd lives there!" Johnny sounded surprised, though he must have known that Tommy's only qualification for high office was his inordinate wealth.

"And don't forget the Back Bay mansion," I said, "or the house in Georgetown, or the ski-lodge in Aspen."

"I'd like someone to tell me one day," Johnny said sourly, "why the bastards who want to put up my taxes are always so rich." I offered no response and he shot me a sympathetic look. "So what happened to you back there?"

"I screwed up."

"Meaning?"

"I thought I was cleverer than I am." I hoped that evasion would suffice, but Johnny deserved better from me. "I guess I was falling out with the IRA."

"You shouldn't have had anything to do with them in the first place."

"They have a good cause," I said mildly.

"If it's that good," he demanded flatly, "then why do they need to murder for it? No one bombs people to solve world hunger. No one kills to save a kid from leukaemia, and those are good causes."

"I won't argue."

"And the gold?"

"All gone."

He laughed. To Johnny the only rewards worth having were those that had taken hard work, the rest was dishonest at worst and meretricious at best. Johnny and his kind were the backbone of America, the good heart of an honest country that somehow contrived to put men like Tommy the Turd into Congress. "You want the money back you gave me?" Johnny asked me. "I haven't spent it."

"Keep it," I said. Christ, I thought, but I would have to get a job now. I would have to join the nine-to-five. I would have to become like the rest of the world, and that was one of the great terrors of the secret world, because belonging to a sanctioned organisation of killers gave a man the feeling of being special, of being apart, of being above the petty cares and constricting rules that hampered other people, but now, after years of arrogance, I would have to earn my bread. I wondered how much money van Stryker planned to give me; not enough, I suspected, to pay for the years of lotus-eating idleness I had planned beside the Cape Cod waters. I wondered what the yacht-delivery business was like in the States and supposed it mainly consisted of taking plastic powerboats up and down the Intracoastal Waterway either side of winter. I doubted it would be easy to break into such a business, but what else was I good for? "I had dreams of buying a tuna boat with that gold," I confessed to Johnny. "Now I doubt I could even afford a can of tuna."

He chuckled. "You don't want a tuna boat. There are too many of them already, and they're all using aeroplanes as spotters. When the fish are running it's like the Battle of Midway out there. Ten years ago you could harpoon a big fish every week, but now you're lucky if you see a decent sized fish all summer."

Another dream dead, I thought, and I leaned my head on the window at the back of the cab. So what was I going to do? Had the last fourteen years been for nothing? "Is there much of a market for boat surveying?" I asked Johnny.

"Not that I know of." Johnny drove placidly on. "But young Ernie Marriott's met a girl in New Bedford, which means I need a crewman every so often."

"Are you offering me a job?"

"I'm offering you freezing hands, a wet ass, hard nights, and maybe the chance of a penny or two if the government lets us catch a fish when we're not filling in forms."

"You're on," I said.

"But it isn't a career," Johnny warned me. "I can hardly keep my own family in bread. Still, it's better than working in one of these places, right?" He waved his hand at a crazy-golf park which, though boarded up for the winter, still betrayed a drab gaudiness designed to bring in the summer customers. We were driving east on Route 28, the Cape's southern artery and a showplace of shoddy businesses and cheap motels; proof that when mankind arrives in paradise he will drown the glory of the angels with neon signs and honkytonk bars. "Another few years," Johnny grumbled, "and this will all look like Florida." He brooded on that sorry fate for a few miles, then turned a frown on me. "Did you really tell Sarah Tennyson to fetch the boat for you?"

I shook my head. "She lied to you, but I guess it doesn't matter."

"So there was nothing between you two?"

"Me and that ballbreaker? You've got to be joking."

He laughed. "She was convincing to me. So who the hell was she?"

I shrugged. "I don't know, Johnny. She's probably a terrorist groupie. Some girls get their kicks by hanging around killers." And did that include Kathleen Donovan? God, that hurt, that she had set me up for the snatch.

"So she isn't an artist?" Johnny sounded disappointed.

"Not with paint," I said, "but I think the Provos put her in my house to act as a tripwire." And she had played that part so cleverly! By acting shocked and being tough when I returned she had convinced me that she was an innocent bystander. Christ, I thought, but I had even asked Gillespie to warn her of trouble, and she was a part of that trouble all along.

"So did she get the gold?" Johnny asked.

"The Provos did. It was meant for them anyway."

He shook his head in disapproval, then, being Johnny, he

found a silver lining on the cloud. "But at least you got the electricity put into the house, didn't you?"

"But why?" I asked that question aloud, suddenly struck by an incongruity. Sarah Sing Tennyson had been in my house three years already. That made no sense, not if she had merely been placed there as a tripwire for my return – for who could have foreseen the Gulf War three years ago?

"Why what?" Johnny asked.

"God knows." I was suddenly disgusted with myself and with everything I had done in the last few weeks. What did it matter whether the girl had been in my house three months or three years? I had played the game and lost. It was over.

I stayed that night with Johnny, and next day went home and began clearing out my house. I took Sarah Tennyson's daubs, piled them on a patch of sandy ground beyond the deck, splashed them with gasoline and slung a match at them. The oil paint burned well, making lovely colours in its flames as the black smoke plumed thin across the marshes.

I took the dust-sheet off the oak floor, then sanded and waxed the boards. I scrubbed the kitchen, dusted the stairways, and aired the bedrooms. I had lost the Colt .45 when I was snatched, but I found the carbine under the bed. I hid it away, then replaced the broken kitchen window and put new locks on the doors. When a telephone bill arrived addressed to Ms Sing Tennyson I sent it to Herlihy's law office, then had the telephone disconnected. I neither wanted it, nor could I afford it.

I lived spare. What small supplies I needed I could buy every day at the convenience store. On the days when the tides were slack I went trawling for cod with Johnny and he paid me wages from the pile of money I had given him for *Rebel Lady*. I used a chunk of my own cash to buy myself a cheap pick-up truck and debated whether I should equip it with a golden retriever or a black labrador. I was one of at least a hundred people who applied for a mechanic's job at an Upper Cape marina, but at forty I was reckoned too old for the position. My remaining cache of money dwindled and it was painful to remember that, just a year ago, I had been sole proprietor of Nordsee Yacht Delivery, Services and Surveying, with a handy cash flow and profit enough for my needs if not for those of the unlamented Sophie. Now, thanks to my own greed, I was down to my last few bucks, though I still owned the renamed *Roisin* in Ireland and, come the spring's revival in the boat market, I decided I would order her sold and use the money to eke out a few more months on the Cape.

One fine March morning Sergeant Ted Nickerson, the policeman who had rescued me from Sarah Sing Tennyson's ammonia on the night of my return to the Cape, dropped by the house. "Just keeping an eye on the place," he explained as he climbed out of his cruiser. "So you're home for good now, Paul?"

"Yes."

"The CIA finished with you?"

"Ask them, Ted." I was not feeling sociable.

"But you're OK, Paul?"

"I'm fine," I said.

Nickerson walked to the edge of the drive and stared southward across the bay. He noticed the remnants of the bonfire on which I had burned Sarah Tennyson's canvases. "I could probably arrest you for lighting that fire. You must have broken at least a dozen federal regulations, not to mention the state laws and the national park rules and the town ordinances." He spat in disgust. "A man can't even piss over the side of his boat these days without breaking the law." He took a cigarette from a pocket and shielded the lighter with his free hand. "We got a telephone call a while back. From a young lady called Kathleen Donovan. She was kind of distressed. Said she thought you were being kidnapped. Were you?"

"Yes," I said, but did not add that she had been a part of it.

"But we had orders not to interfere with you. If anything happened we were to talk to a guy in the Washington office of the FBI. So we did, and he seemed to think you could look after yourself. And if you're here now then I guess he was right?"

"I guess so, too." The FBI, I surmised, had acted for the CIA who had sensibly not wanted a small-town police force to tangle with international terrorists. But I also noted that neither the CIA nor the FBI had seemed unduly worried by my disappearance. No one had inquired about me since, evidently no one had looked for me while I was gone, and I could only surmise that van Stryker or Gillespie considered that I deserved whatever mischief came my way. I had been useful to them, now I was useless and discarded.

"But I thought you ought to know about the young lady," Ted went on, "especially as she sounded kind of upset. She particularly wanted me to let her know if you were OK." He took a scrap of paper from a pocket. "That's her phone number. Of course I could give her a call myself, but if you want to speak to her then you'll be saving the police department the price of a long-distance phone call." Nickerson held out the piece of paper.

I took it. "Thanks, Ted."

"Just being neighbourly, Paul." He hesitated. "I suppose you're not going to tell me what this is all about?"

"One day, maybe."

"Yeah, and maybe one day the Red Sox will win the Series." He climbed into his car and wound down the window. "The Goddamn town wants to declare police cars a public facility and therefore smoke free. Fuck 'em, I say." He waved his cigarette at me, reversed the car, then drove away.

I stared at the piece of paper. It felt like one last chance. Or, of course, it could be another trap to snare a fool, just as Kathleen's last visit had been, but my future was not so golden that I needed to take care of it and so I drove the truck up to the main road and, with my last few quarters, placed a call to Maryland.

Kathleen Donovan lived in a small house on the ragged outskirts of a one-street country town. The house had two storeys, a wide verandah, and a windbreak of scrub pine. Behind it was a meadow with an old tobacco drying shed decaying in its centre. "None of it's mine," she said. "I just rent it."

"It's nice," I said with as much conviction as I could muster.

"Not when the wind's in the south. Then you can smell the chicken farm beyond the swamp." She laughed suddenly, knowing I had lied out of politeness. "I just wanted to get away from Baltimore."

"To be near your folks?"

She shook her head. "To get away from them. I spend three or four nights a week up there, and it's good to get away. It's real nice here in spring, you know, when the dogwood is out?"

"And in summer?"

"Hot. Too hot." She sounded resigned. "I don't know. I guess I won't renew the lease. This was an experiment. I always wanted to live in the country, and I thought once David and I were divorced that it would be a real good time to do it, but it isn't all it's cracked up to be. Not one of my carrots came up, not one! And the deer ate all the lettuce and the bean bushes had bugs and there were worms in the tomatoes."

"That's why God made supermarkets."

She laughed. Then looked up at me. "I'm sorry."

"Why?" We were standing beside my pick-up. I had only just arrived, and we were both feeling awkward, and I guessed she was regretting her impulsive agreement to let me visit her. I was nervous, and the ten-hour drive from Cape Cod had given me too much time to anticipate the failure of this meeting. I wanted to fall in love with Kathleen, maybe I had half convinced myself that I was already in love with her, and I had even half convinced myself that it was not simply because she was her sister's ghost. I had not been truthful about my reasons for visiting, but instead had told her I had business in Washington and could I perhaps take the chance of dropping by? She had hesitated, then agreed, and now I asked her once more why she was apologising to me. "Why?"

"For agreeing to help those people. Who were they?"

"You didn't know them?" I asked.

"Not really." She turned away. "That's why you came, right? To find out about them?"

"Yes," I lied. I had come because I wanted to resurrect Roisin in her sister.

"You want to walk?" Kathleen asked.

"Sure."

"If you go five miles down that track you come to the Chesapeake Bay." She pointed eastwards. "I had this idea that in summer I'd bike down there and have lazy days on the water."

"You and a million mosquitoes, right?"

She nodded. "And the ticks." She led me to the road and we walked slowly towards the small town. The landscape was very flat, accentuating the sky and reminding me of Flanders. "It was the girl who came to me, Sarah Sing Tennyson?" Kathleen said. "She said you'd thrown her out of the house, and that she wanted to get inside to rescue her paintings, and that if I took you for a walk then she knew she'd be safe." Kathleen blushed slightly. "She was very persuasive."

"I can imagine." I kicked a dry pine cone ahead of me. "I wonder how she found you?"

"That was easy. You remember I hired a private detective

261

to find out about you? Well he visited the house when she was there, and I guess he and she talked. But she never told me she was taking men with her, or that they planned to beat you up. I couldn't believe it!" Her voice rose in innocent protest as she remembered the violence. "I phoned the police!"

"I know, thank you."

"So what happened?"

"They locked me up for a while."

"Who were they?"

"They were from Ireland," I told her.

"So what happened?"

I shrugged. "They were looking for something. And when I told them where it was, they let me go."

She looked up at me. "I felt badly. I didn't feel badly when I agreed to help Sarah Tennyson, because I thought she was being real straight and you'd been a pig to me in Belgium and I thought I'd enjoy getting back at you. But you were different on Cape Cod."

I walked in silence for a few paces. The bushes beside the road looked dead and dry, the meadows were pale. "I wanted to tell someone the truth," I said, "and I'd decided to trust you."

She nodded, then laughed as she realised that I had trusted her when she had been deceiving me, and vice versa. She bit her lip. "What fools we all are."

"I thought that after so many years of lies it would be a change to tell the truth," I explained, "like giving up smoking, or going off the booze."

"And is it a change?" she asked.

"It makes life less complicated."

"Like I thought small-town life would be, only it isn't really less complicated, there's just less of it. This is it." She nodded at the main street. "Two churches, a town office, a bank, feed store, convenience store, coffee shop, and a post office. The movie house closed down, the service station moved to Route Five, but you can buy gas from Ed's feed store if he really likes you and his son isn't watching."

"What's wrong with Ed's son?"

"He's in the State Police and he can't stand his dad, not since his mom told him about his dad's fling with Mary Hammond who used to deliver the mail before Bobby Evans's dog bit her leg and it went septic. The leg not the dog."

"And you like living here?" I asked.

"I hate it."

We both laughed. "And you're too stubborn to admit you've made a mistake," I challenged her, "because you're so like Roisin."

"Am I like Roisin?" she asked. We had stopped in the main street and were facing each other. "Am I really?"

"Yes. In looks, anyway."

She frowned. "Does that make it hard for you?"

I hesitated, then told the truth. "Yes."

"Don't," she told me. She was frowning.

"Don't?" It seemed the world trembled on an edge, and I knew it was not going to fall my way. I had built a dizzying scaffold impossibly high and had dared to think she would want to share it with me.

"I've got a guy, Paul," Kathleen said gently. "He teaches school in Frederick."

"I didn't mean that," I said, but I had meant it, and she knew I had meant it, and suddenly I felt such a fool and just wanted to be out of this damn chicken town.

"He's a good man," she went on.

"I'm sure he is." I felt as though my dizzying scaffold was collapsing all around me in splintering poles.

"Let's have a coffee," she said, and we sat in the coffee shop and she told me about her trip to Europe, and about her adventures in Dublin and Belfast, but I was not really listening. I did a good job of pretending to listen; I smiled at the right places, made intelligible comments, but inside I was desolate. I was alone. Roisin was gone for ever. I had thought she could be clawed back from the past, out of her Beka'a grave, but it was not to be.

"I hope you found out what you wanted to know," Kathleen told me when we walked back to the truck.

"I did, thanks."

"I guess you won't see Sarah Sing Tennyson again?"

"I guess not."

She put her hand on my sleeve when we reached the truck. "I'm sorry, Paul."

Me too, I thought, me too. "Good luck with the teacher."

"Sure. Thanks." She smiled. "Good luck in Washington, eh?"

"Sure," I said, "sure," and drove back to Cape Cod.

It was past one o'clock when I reached the house. It was a dark night and the moon was hidden by high flying clouds. I was too tired to open the garage so I just left the truck on the clam-shell turnabout then walked to the kitchen door. I was weary and I was disgusted with myself. I had made a fool of myself. Dear God, I thought, but I had really believed I could fall in love with a ghost. I unlocked the door, pushed into the kitchen, and froze. I could smell tea. It was not an overpowering smell, just an aroma, but unmistakable. Tea.

My MI carbine was hidden in the living room so, for a weapon, I pulled out my fish-filleting knife that had a wicked sharp blade and then, very slowly, I edged towards the living-room door.

It was jet dark in the house. I could hear the wind and the eternal beat of the far waves, and I could still smell tea. Had Sarah Sing Tennyson dared come back here? I had an idea that women drank more tea than men, but the Irish also drank tea, so had Herlihy sent someone to kill me after all? I reached the living-room door. For a second I contemplated turning on the light, then decided that darkness was probably a better friend than the sudden dazzle of the electric bulb.

I pressed down the door lever, crouched, and pushed the door open. It swung into the living room's darkness. I was crouched low, the knife in my right hand. The M1 was hidden four paces from me, held by strips of duct tape to the underside of the long table. I was gauging just how long it would take me to free the weapon when a man's voice sleepily spoke my name. "Shanahan?" The voice came from my right.

My heart leaped in panic, but I managed to stay still and to say nothing.

"Shanahan?" the man said again, and this time I heard the fear in his voice. I suspected he had been dozing and was now scared of what the darkness had brought into this cold room. "I'm going to turn a light on, OK?" the man said, and I suddenly recognised the voice of my CIA interrogator.

"Oh, Christ. Gillespie? Is that you?"

"It's me, yeah."

I felt the tension flood out of me. "Jesus. Did you have to wait in the dark? I could have filleted you."

"To be honest I fell asleep. But I didn't want to leave a light on in case you got scared and thought the ungodly were waiting for you. Which is why we left our car up at the post office."

"How the hell did you get in?" I was still crouched, but now leaned my back against the door jamb.

"Stuart Callaghan picked the lock of the front door. He's good at things like that." Gillespie was moving cautiously across the dark room. He had been sitting in the old settee in the bay window and now he shuffled towards the hall door beside which Sarah Sing Tennyson had put the main light switch.

"So what the hell are you doing here?" I eased the filleting knife back into its sheath.

265

"We need to know about the boat, *Rebel Lady*? And about the money on board her." He sounded very disapproving, as though it was bitterly unfair of me to have deceived him.

"How the hell did you find out about *Rebel Lady*?" I asked.

"It's our job to find things out," he said in a pained voice, then he found the switch and suddenly the room was filled with light. Gillespie must have been cold for he was wearing one of the yellow plastic rain-slickers that had been hanging in the hallway.

"How did you know I'd be here?" I asked him.

"The police told us you were in residence. A guy called Ted Nickerson?"

"I assume you're not alone?" I asked him.

"No. Callaghan is upstairs. I decided one of us would wait for you while the other slept. But I didn't mean us both to fall asleep." He yawned, then walked to the table where he had left his cellular telephone. "You look kind of bushed," he said. "What happened?"

"I just drove ten hours there and ten hours back to be stiff-armed by a girl. I thought I was in love with her."

"Ah." He seemed embarrassed by my revelation and uncertain how to respond. "I'll just report that you've surfaced," he said and picked up his telephone.

I was still leaning against the kitchen door and Gillespie was pressing a number into the telephone when he suddenly coughed and looked up at me with a puzzled expression.

At least I think he coughed. It was hard to tell because at the same time the whole room was shockingly filled with the sound of a gunshot and the splintering crash as the bullet shattered a pane of the bow window behind Gillespie. The CIA man jerked forward and I realised the cough was the sound of the air being punched from his lungs by the violence of the bullet's strike. He staggered, but managed to stay upright. The bullet which had hit him had been deflected and weakened by the window glass. He blinked. I was taking a breath to shout at him to get down when a second bullet, fired through the broken window and thus undeflected and unchecked, struck him in the back, and this time Gillespie was hurled violently forward and I saw a vent of bright blood mist the room's centre, then he crashed to the floor and I heard the air sigh from his lungs as he slid forward on the polished oak boards. His cellular telephone spun into the kitchen where it lodged against the rubbish bin.

I edged back into the kitchen shadows. Gillespie was not moving. I could just see his back. Two bullet holes. The first shot had hit him high on the left shoulder, the second must have shattered his spine. There was the faintest trickle of blood; a surprisingly small amount considering the sudden spray that had reddened the living room's air. I could see some blood on the floor, and more on the edge of the table that concealed my carbine.

Callaghan was surely awake now? Two bullets? The sound of the gunshots was reverberating in my ears. The marksman had to be in the marshes beyond my terrace. Should I stay where I was, or try to run into the dark? Or should I try to fetch the gun hidden under the table? But to reach the gun would mean going into the light that had made Gillespie a target. I slid the knife free again. It was a feeble weapon in the face of this night's savagery, but the best to hand.

A footstep sounded outside the house. Not by the kitchen, but beyond the bow window. Someone was on the deck. Christ, I thought, but the bastard is coming inside to make sure of his work! I edged back out of the wash of light which came from the living room and I thought I saw a shadow at the far window. A black shadow. Il Hayaween? Please God, I prayed, but let this not be il Hayaween. Maybe the shadow was just my imagination? Then the shadow moved, grunted. The gunman was looking through the window to see what his bullets had accomplished, but Gillespie's body had slid across the floor and was half hidden from the window by the heavy table.

I gripped the filleting knife's cord-wrapped handle. The killer was working with a high velocity rifle, so what chance did I have if he came indoors? None. What had Sarah Sing Tennyson said? Never piss a psychopath off, but put him down fast. I needed an ammonia squirt, not a damned fish-gutting knife.

The shadow had gone. Maybe I should run for it. No, not with the killer still outside. So wait, I told myself, wait.

Gillespie's hands made small scratching noises as his fingers contracted into claws. That was not a sign of life, but a natural process as the body relaxed in death. The wind at the broken window stirred the brown drapes.

Footsteps sounded sudden and loud on the steep stairs from the bedrooms. The stairs, built in the nineteenth century, were pitched far more steeply than twentieth-century building regulations would allow and the hurrying Callaghan tripped on them, stumbled, then hit his shoulder against the wall at the bottom. "Shit!" he swore, then shouted. "Mr Gillespie? Sir? Are you there, sir?"

I sat utterly still.

"Jesus Christ!" Callaghan had come into the living room. He could not see me for I was deep in the alcove beside the stove and Callaghan was staring at Gillespie. "Jesus Christ!" he said again, and whirled round, dragging his gun from his shoulder holster. He was wearing a shirt and trousers, but no jacket, tie or shoes. He must have been sleeping upstairs, and now he had woken to nightmare.

"Jesus!" He was in shock. He saw the broken window and ran towards it, then sensed that danger might lie on the other side so ran back to the room's centre, then he changed his mind again and went back to the window where, like a cop in a movie, he flattened himself against the drapes so he could peer round the corner into the salt darkness. He stood there, muttering to himself. I knew I would have to announce my presence, but I had to do it very carefully or else he would whirl round and shoot at my voice. He was twitchy as hell. I took a breath, readied myself to speak, when suddenly he turned, gasping, and I heard the rifle fire, its sound dreadfully loud in the confines of the house, and in the very same instant Callaghan fired back and I saw the muzzle flame of his pistol bright against the dark window.

Callaghan fired a second time, but the second pull on his trigger was merely a reflexive spasm of his fingers as he went down. He had been hit. I had seen the rifle bullet jar his chest like a seismic shock, and I saw the life flit out of him in that very instant and I knew that the gunman was a marksman of genius for he had exploded Callaghan's heart with a single lethal shot.

Callaghan slumped to the floor. His second bullet had struck the ceiling to leave a bright splinter of raw wood protruding from a beam.

There was silence.

The killer was in the house. He had come into the house for what? Probably to determine the outcome of his night's work. So in a second or two he would turn over Gillespie's body and find he had killed the wrong man. He had surely been after me, no one else.

So what would he do? Flee? Or search the house? Either way I knew I should move. Get out! Into the dark wetlands where this lethal marksman could not see me. Yet to move would be to make a noise and attract his attention. Christ! Why had I not hidden the carbine in the truck? I tensed myself ready to move, but fear kept me still. If I gave the man a half-second to react I would be dead because this assassin was good, very good.

Then I heard an odd scraping noise from the far end of the living room. I was unsighted, nor did I intend to move and see just what was making the noise. Was the man dragging Callaghan's body away?

Then there was a terrible splintering crash, and a moan, then silence. I waited. The cold wind sighed at the broken window and I could smell the bitter smell of propellant in the house.

"Oh, fock," said the voice, and groaned.

I moved. Very slowly. First I stood, then I took a half-pace forward so I could see into the living room.

And there he was; slumped against the far wall. He had collapsed and his rifle had fallen a couple of feet from his right hand. He was wearing a black sweater, black trousers, black leather gloves, black shoes and a black balaclava helmet which showed only his eyes and mouth. The black sweater and trousers seemed to glisten at his belly, and I realised that Stuart Callaghan, with his first dying shot, had badly wounded the killer.

He saw me and his hand twitched towards the rifle, but the movement gave him a spasm of pain. He cursed, not in anger, but in resignation. "Oh, fock," he said again.

"Hello, Seamus." I crossed the room and kicked his rifle away, then stooped and picked up Callaghan's fallen automatic.

"This is a focking mess, Paulie." Seamus made an enormous effort to reach up with his right hand and pull off the black woollen balaclava helmet. It left his black hair rumpled. "Focker got me in the belly."

"You were after me."

"I thought that focker was you." He jerked his chin towards the fallen Gillespie. From the outside, in the sudden light and with his back turned and wearing the yellow slicker he had found in my hallway, Gillespie must have looked very much like me. "Who the fock are they?" Seamus asked.

"The law. They came to question me." I crouched in front of Seamus and tried to assess his injury. I was no expert, but it looked bad. The bullet, as best I could see, had struck Seamus low on his left hip, then must have ricocheted off the pelvic bone to splinter and mangle his guts. He was bleeding horribly. If I had used Gillespie's cellular telephone to call an ambulance Seamus might have lived, but he understood why I did no such thing. Those who live by the sword must die by it.

I crossed to Callaghan, but without turning my back on Seamus. Callaghan lay on his back, his mouth brimming with glistening blood above which his teeth were bared in a feral snarl. "That was a good shot, Seamus."

"I was always a good shot. I remember in Strabane once, waiting in a burned-out house, and a Brit soldier almost got me. Surprised me, he did. He came through the back door, see, and I was watching out the front, but I hit him the same way. Fired from the hip." His speech was slow. Occasionally his breath would catch, interrupted by pain, but he was making sense. "I got away then."

"You were only ever caught once," I said.

"That was so focking ridiculous," he said. "It was all a focking accident, Paulie, just bad focking luck. I'd left the flat not five minutes, and this wee girl jumped a red light, so she did, on the corner of Ormeau Avenue. You know, where the television place is? And I hit her smack on, and there was a bloody police Land-Rover right there and the fockers recognised me." He had been heading south, making for Dublin with a stolen driving licence in his pocket. The Army Council had reckoned he would have been safer in Dublin than in the north, even though he was wanted in both parts of Ireland. "The focking Brits said they were acting on information," Seamus said bitterly, "but it was all an accident, nothing more. And that's why she died, eh? Just because the focking Brits lied."

"That's why she died," I agreed, but I did not want to talk about Roisin's death. "Who ordered me killed?" I asked instead.

"Michael Herlihy, of course. He said you'd nicked the money, and you had to be punished." Seamus drew in a terrible, shuddering breath. "I wouldn't do it till I got confirmation, but it came, right enough."

"From Brendan Flynn?" I guessed sourly.

"Aye." Seamus tried to grin, but failed. "I'm sorry it had to be me, Paulie."

"You're not given much of a choice in these things." I squatted in front of him. "Is it hurting, Seamus?"

"It's sort of dull now, Paulie. Not so bad, really." He sat in silence, his head against the wall. "Focking shame it had to be you. I always liked you."

"I liked you, Seamus." Already we were using the past tense.

"I remember Brendan Flynn telling me you were a dangerous one, but I reckoned you were all right."

"I thought Brendan trusted me?"

"He wouldn't trust the Pope, that one." He sighed. "Why did you steal the money?"

"I didn't. I wanted to, but I didn't."

"They say you did, but I suppose they're nicking it for themselves. Just like they always do." Blood was puddling under his buttocks. He was weakening so much that he could hardly lift his right hand. "There's some ciggies in my shirt pocket," he said. "Would you mind?"

I held the automatic close to his face as I groped under his sweater. I found the cigarettes and a lighter, put a cigarette between his lips and clicked a flame.

"You used to smoke, didn't you?" Seamus asked.

"I gave it up."

"Don't you miss it, Paulie?"

"Smoking? Sure I do." I eased away from him. "The day I get to heaven, Seamus, St Peter's going to be waiting at the Pearly Gate with a packet of twenty and a book of matches."

"You think you'll get to heaven?" The cigarette twitched in his lips as he spoke.

"We'll all meet there, Seamus. You, me, all the boys. No

Brits, though. And the hills will be green as emerald and the streams full of salmon and the sun ever shining."

"Like Dunnamanagh, eh?" That was a dream that would never come true; the wee house in the fold of the good green hills of County Derry. Seamus blinked rapidly, maybe because the smoke was in his eyes. "There was even a girl in Lifford."

"You? A girl?"

"I always wanted one. I was sweet on her. Her da said I could ask her out, so he did."

"But you never did ask her?"

"Never had time, Paulie. I wasn't like you. I wasn't one for the girls." He seemed to be aware that something had been amiss in his life, but he could never have articulated it, nor known how to correct it, and I wondered what demons, born of a mother's fears and priestly spite, had chased him through the long dark corridors of his lonely nights. "You remember that fellow we shot in Dunmurry?" he asked.

"Of course I do."

Seamus laughed. "So focking scared. So focking scared. You remember where he hid?"

"In the roof tank, you told me."

"Like a drowning focking rat." The boy had been accused of rape. He was twenty-one or -two, and there was no evidence that would have stood up in court, but the community had no doubts of his guilt and so the Provos had stepped in. Seamus had been staying with me and had been asked if he wanted to do the honours, and I had driven him up to the housing estate. It was a Sunday evening in November and there had been a hint of snow in the darkness. The boy's mother knew why we were there and she begged us to go away, but the father growled at her to hold her peace. The other kids were crying. The boy ran up the stairs. "Watch the focking windows," Seamus told me, then he had followed the boy into the attic. The panicked kid had taken refuge in the header tank where Seamus shot him. Seamus laughed again. "There must have been blood coming out of their focking taps for days!" He was silent for a few seconds. "Head shot, it was."

"Do you remember them all?"

"Every one, Paulie. Like they was on films in my head." He frowned, I thought with pain, then he chuckled again. "Did I ever tell you about Danny Noonan's big bomb?"

"No."

"So focking silly." He was laughing, and I think the laughter was hurting him, but the tale was in his head now and he had to get it out. "It must have been the first or second bomb I ever saw set. In a big focking cardboard box, it was. Danny Noonan built the bomb. He'd just been made the explosives officer in the South Derry brigade and he wanted to make himself known. Wanted everyone in the world to know a new man was on the job like, so he put every scrap of focking explosive he could find into that damned box. I tell you, Paulie, that bomb would have blown the ceiling clean off Africa, it was so big. But Danny wanted it big, see? He wanted something that would make the papers, you know?" He paused to suppress a moan.

"Take your time," I said stupidly. Time was the one thing that was fast running out for Seamus.

"So Danny decides we'll take out the BBC transmitter. You know the one? That focking great mast outside Derry? Must be a thousand feet tall if it's an inch! That would make the papers, Danny said, so we all get in the car and off we go, Big John MacAnally was our driver. Daft as a clock, he was, but he could drive right enough. So off we go and we get in the compound easy enough and there are all these engineers just pissing themselves with fright. There's Danny, Big John and me, all masked up, two of us with guns, and Big John holding the focking bomb in a focking great cardboard box. So Danny tells Big John to put the bomb by the mast, right underneath it like, but Big John gets all worried. He asks your top engineer man how long it will take them to repair the damage if he sets the focking bomb off under the mast, and your man says it'll be all of six months. And Big John says, 'You mean if the bomb goes off I can't see *Kojak* this Saturday night?', and the fella says, 'Ye'll not be seeing *Kojak* for six months of Saturday nights!'" Seamus stopped, and his breath came in horrid rasping gasps for a few seconds. The cigarette fell from his lips, bounced off his thigh, and hissed to extinction in the blood puddling beside him. I thought he was not going to be able to finish the story, but he made a huge effort to take in a breath.

"So Danny's going berserk, he is. Put the bomb down, he orders, but Big John won't. He wants to know where he can put it so he can still see *Kojak* on Saturday night, so the engineer tells him to knock off the sub-station in the laneway. Danny's screaming at Big John, but Big John tells Danny to shut the fock up because he wants to watch *Kojak*. In the end we put the focking bomb by the sub-station, down on the laneway like the man said, just to cut off the electricity like, and just so Big John could see his *Kojak* on Saturday night. Christ, but you should have seen that bang! Jasus, but we scared rooks out of the trees three counties away! There was smoke rising to the moon, so there was. We flattened a hundred yards of hedgerow, but it never made the newspapers. And that was Danny Noonan's big bomb, just to knock out one focking sub-station in a focking hedge." He tried to laugh, but was in too much pain. "And Big John got to see his *Kojak*, so he did."

"It's a good tale, Seamus." That was why he had told it. He came from a race that still told tales and still took pride in the telling.

"So many good tales, Paulie." He blinked a few times, then looked beseechingly at me. "I'm cold, Paulie."

I wanted to tell him it would not be long now, but I said nothing. Out beyond the barrier beach the waves seethed and growled like the world's heartbeat.

"They said they'd give me a medal," Seamus said after a long silence. "They said there's a Massachusetts medal of freedom. They said they've given it to other IRA men. They said they'd pin it on my chest on the State House steps."

"Michael Herlihy told you that?"

"Aye, but I had to kill you first. He said you'd betrayed the movement and that he'd give me money if I killed you, but I told him I didn't want any money. Then he said they'd give me the medal like, and all the newspapers would show it. My mam would have been pleased, Paulie, to see me with a medal. She was always nagging at me to do something in life, know what I mean? And she'd have liked a medal. And the Brits would have been pissed off." He was quiet for a bit. He had gone very pale. His hands scrabbled and I thought for a second he had come to his moment of dying, then I realised he was trying to reach for his cigarettes. He abandoned the effort. "Give me another ciggie, Paulie."

I lit one for him, resisting the sudden strong temptation to drag down a lungful of smoke. "There." I put it between his lips.

He sucked on the smoke, then nodded at Gillespie's corpse. "I thought that fellow was you." The mistake clearly worried Seamus. It was a blot on his record. "It was the yellow coat that fooled me."

"How long were you waiting for me?" I asked.

"Since teatime. Herlihy had Marty Doyle drive me out here."

"Where's Marty now?"

"Waiting up by the shops." Seamus grinned weakly. "He's driving a focking flower van. Can you believe it? It's like the time we tried to take a focking hearse to put a bomb outside the Guildhall. Full of flowers, it was, and Malachy O'Brien had the focking hay fever. Can you believe it? He was sneezing so much he couldn't drive! We had to abandon the focking bomb, so we did!" He laughed weakly. "Those were the days, Paulie."

"Weren't they just?"

Seamus drew deep on the cigarette. "You remember the big flats on Rossville Street. And William Street. I'll never see them again, will I? And what was that pub on the Lecky Road?" He was asking about landmarks in Derry, a city I did not know. "And then we used to drink in that big bar off the Creggan Road. It was so focking cold in there in winter. That landlord was a mean bugger. Short arms and deep pockets, he had, so one night Big John MacAnally said he'd warm the place up and he lit a fire on the floor with focking newspapers. He was a focking mad bugger. They shot him, so they did."

"The Brits shot him?"

He shook his head. "Our own fellows. Big John was a risk. Mad as a priest without a woman or a whiskey, so he was. Did you ever know Father Brady?"

"No."

"He told me it would be a bad end." He breathed hard. "Can you not get me a priest now, Paulie?"

"No, Seamus, I can't." Because what had happened this night had to be hidden, buried as Roisin was buried, which meant there could be no priests and no rescue squad and no local police. That was the rule of the secret world and Seamus knew it.

He nodded acceptance of my refusal. "Whose side are you on, Paulie?"

"Yours, Seamus."

"You're not a focking Brit, are you?"

"No."

"Roisin always thought you grassed on Wild John Macroon."

"I wish I had." Macroon had been the boy she had slept with before we parted. "But I didn't. I didn't need to, he was always going to get himself killed."

"That's true enough." Seamus pulled on the cigarette. "She was a fearful strong girl, so she was."

"I know."

"What was that record she was always playing? About Sandy Row and throwing pennies?"

"Van Morrison," I said. When I had lived in Belfast it had sometimes seemed that Van Morrison's album *Astral Weeks* was the city's theme music. It was played everywhere, seeping subliminally through the city's brickwork; sad anthems for wounded tribes.

"She got mad at me," Seamus said sadly.

"Because you wouldn't go to bed with her?"

"Aye." He looked at me with astonishment, amazed that I had known such a thing. "I should have done, shouldn't I?"

"Probably."

"But it wasn't her that betrayed me," he said, "the Brits just said that to get us all worked up." The British ploy had clearly rankled in him. He went quiet again. A half-inch of ash dropped down his sweater's front. "So she was shot?" he asked.

"Yes," I said, knowing I could not avoid the subject.

"In that Arab place?"

"Yes."

Seamus's pale knowing eyes looked at me. "It was you, wasn't it?"

"Me, Seamus?" A thousand acts of contrition had not let me deliver those two words with any conviction. "Me, Seamus?"

"It was you," he said, "that shot her."

I hesitated, not sure whether I even trusted a man on the lip of eternity, but then I nodded. "Yes. But she didn't know it was me. I was wearing a head-dress, see, and they just gave me the gun."

"And then you shot her?"

"Once through the head. Quick." I wondered how Seamus had known, then guessed it was written on my soul for all the damned to read, and I wondered how I could ever have hoped for happiness with Kathleen after what I had done to her sister on that yellow hillside in the Lebanon.

"You poor focker, Paulie," Seamus said, then he suddenly tensed and his whole back arched with the onslaught of a terrible pain. "Oh, Jasus," he wailed.

"Is it hurting?"

"Like the fock, it is." He was crying now. "Oh, Jasus," he said again, and the second cigarette rolled out of his mouth and I heard him muttering, and at first I thought he was saying a Hail Mary, but before I could decipher the prayer his voice had dribbled away into incoherence. I rescued the fallen cigarette from a fold of his sleeve and stubbed it on the floor. I thought he had died, but suddenly he opened his eyes and spoke with an awful clarity. "It's hard to kill someone you know."

"It is, yes."

"But you don't have much choice, do you?"

"No." If I had not shot Roisin, then I would have been shot. But did that make it right?

Seamus had gone quiet. I rocked away from him, but he twitched a hand towards me as though he needed my proximity. "Just tell me it's going to be all right, Paulie."

"It is," I said.

"Tell me." His hand twitched towards me again.

I held his hand to give him the solace of human touch. He had known so little love, while his talent for rage had been used by lesser men.

"Tell me," he demanded again.

"Ireland will be one," I told him, "united under God, ruled from Dublin, and there'll be no division left, and no more tears, and no more dying."

"Oh, God, yes," he breathed, then tried to speak again, and his tongue seemed to rattle in the back of his mouth, but his willpower overcame the spasm of death to let him quote a line of verse. "'Life springs from death,'" he said, but he could go no further, and I waited and waited, and still he said nothing more, and so I edged even closer to him and put my face down by his face and there was no breath in him at all, nothing, and so I touched his eyes shut with my right hand and finished the words for him. "'And from the graves of patriot men and women spring living nations.'"

Seamus Geoghegan, the bright boy of Derry, was dead.

My house was a disaster. It held the corpses of two CIA men and an IRA gunman, and if the newspapers ever got hold of that poisonous stew then the fuss would never stop. What I needed now was a piece of efficient housekeeping.

I took Callaghan's automatic, the money and the passport from the hiding place in the beam, then left through the kitchen door. I climbed into the pick-up. The engine started first time. I rammed it into gear, slewed the steering wheel round, and accelerated up the track. I flicked the headlights on, scaring a rabbit out of my path.

I turned left on to the main road. I could see the white-painted panel van in the parking lot of the abandoned shopping precinct. The main shop was a seasonal outlet for cheap beach accessories like inflatable dolphins, plastic buckets and parasols. Next door was a shed that used to sell good ice-cream but now advertised frozen yoghurt. I pulled up in front of the yoghurt shop where my pick-up's headlights illuminated the legend on the van's body: 'Shamrock Flower Shoppe. Blooms for all Family Occasions. Weddings our Specialty'; then I killed the lights, left the engine running and ran across to the white van.

I rapped on the driver's door, startling Marty who had evidently been fast asleep. He unlocked the door. "Is that you, Seamus? Jesus, I must have dropped off."

I ripped the door open and dragged Marty out of the seat. He yelped in panic as I spun him round to the dark side of the van, away from the road, and he screamed as I slung him down on to the gravel where I rammed my knee into his belly and the muzzle of the pistol into his throat. "Say a prayer, Marty."

"Jesus! Is it you, Paulie?"

"No, it's Cardinal Bernard Law, you shithead. This is our new way of making converts. Who the hell do you think I am?"

"Where's Seamus?"

"He's dead, Marty."

"Oh, Mother of God." He tried to cross himself.

"Now listen, you fuck." I thrust the gun's cold barrel hard into his Adam's apple. "You're not going to give me any trouble or else Mrs Doyle will be collecting the life insurance and moving to a Century Village in Florida and you'll be nothing but a framed photograph on top of the television set. Is that what you want, Marty?"

"No, Paulie, no! I'll do whatever you want!"

"Then get in the back of the van."

I dragged him up, hustled him round, and pushed him through the van's rear door. The body of the van was filled with flower boxes fastened with lengths of green wire which I used to pinion Marty's wrists and ankles. I gagged him with a strip of cloth I cut from his sweater, then felt through his pockets till I came up with some small change. "Now just wait here, Marty, and don't make a peep or I'll use you for target practice."

There was a telephone beside the frozen yoghurt shop. I pulled a visiting card from my pocket and punched in the numbers. It was an 800 number, a free call, but when it was over I needed Marty's quarters to call Johnny who sounded pissed off at being woken in the middle of the night, but he recovered quickly enough when I told him what I wanted. "I'll meet you by the dinghy," he told me, "in half an hour, OK?"

"I'm sorry, Johnny," I told him.

"Who needs sleep?"

I went back to the van. Marty mumbled something through his gag, but I told him to shut up, then slammed the van's rear door and went back to my pick-up. I drove south on Route 28. It began to sleet as I arrived at Stage Harbor where I parked beside a trap-shed and switched off the pick-up's engine. I waited.

Johnny arrived ten minutes later and I followed him down to where his dinghy was tethered. "Give me the boat keys," I said.

"Forget it, Paulie, I'm coming with you."

I did not argue. Everything had gone wrong this night and I needed help. So we rowed out to Johnny's trawler, the *Julie-Anne*, started her up, and went to sea.

We motored westward, guided through the shoals of Nantucket Sound by the winking lights of the buoys in the glassy-wet darkness. The big diesel motor throbbed comfortingly away. It was warm in the wheelhouse. Johnny steered with one hand and held a coffee mug with the other. "So what's it about?" he asked.

I did not answer. I just stared through the glow of the *Julie-Anne*'s navigation lights and I thought how many had died. Liam, Gerry, Gillespie, Callaghan, Seamus. And they were probably just the beginning.

"At least tell me whose side I'm on?" Johnny insisted.

"The angels. But don't go near my house for a few days."

"It isn't drugs?" Johnny asked.

"I swear to God, Johnny, it isn't drugs. Someone wanted to punish me for taking the gold."

"I thought you said the IRA had got their gold back?"

"I guess they wanted me dead as an example to anyone else who had a mind to rip them off. But just stay clear of the house, Johnny."

We travelled on in silence. Rain slicked the deck and spat past the glow of the red and green lamps. The fishfinder's dial glowed in the wheelhouse dark. About three hours after we had left Stage Harbor I watched the lights of a small plane drop from the clouds and descend towards Martha's Vineyard. Johnny turned on his radar and the familiar shape of Cape Poge formed on the green screen. The eastern horizon was just hinting at the dawn as we slid past Chappaquidick Point. The water was smooth and slick, pocked with the rain and skeined with a thin mist that hazed the lights of Edgartown as Johnny, with a careless skill, nudged his huge trawler towards a pier. "They'll probably charge me a hundred bucks just to land someone, let alone breathe their precious air. Greediest town in America, this one. Do you want me to wait for you?"

"No. But thanks."

"Look after yourself, Paulie."

"I've not been very good at that, but I'll do my best."

I jumped ashore, then walked into town. I was looking for a big house with a Nautor Swan called *Nancy* parked on jackstands in her front yard. I had come for van Stryker's help, because everything had gone wrong.

"Shanahan." Simon van Stryker opened his door to me, grimaced at the weather, then ushered me inside. He was dressed in an Aran sweater, corduroy trousers and fleece-lined sea-boots, but he looked every inch as distinguished as the last time we had met when he had been rigged out to dine at the White House. "I've got a team heading for your house." The 800 number I had called had been the number on the card van Stryker had given me in the Poconoes. The call had been answered by a young man who had calmly listened to my description of three dead bodies and my desperate appeal for help. I had held on while he called van Stryker who, in turn, had ordered me to meet him at his summer house where he now opened a closet to reveal a shelf of bottles. "Laphroaig?"

"Please."

He took the seal off a new bottle, poured me a generous slug, then placed glass and bottle beside me. "So tell me exactly what happened." I told him the story of the night, of my coming home, of Gillespie and Callaghan dying, of Seamus bleeding to death. While I talked van Stryker emptied the contents of a canvas sailing-bag on to the kitchen worktop. He had brought eggs, ham, cheese, milk and tomatoes. "Nancy thought we'd be hungry," he explained, "and this looks like being a long discussion. Do go on."

"There isn't much more to tell," I finished lamely. "I left the bodies there and called for help."

He found a bowl and whisk. "That was wise of you, Paul." He began breaking eggs, while I looked through his windows across the rain-stippled harbour to the low dull heathland of Chappaquiddick. Dawn was seeping across the cloudy sky, making the harbour's water look like dull gun metal. "So tell me," van Stryker ordered, "what you think this is all about."

"It's about Stingers," I said firmly. "It's about men at the end of runways. Men hidden in the woods near Washington's Dulles Airport or on boats in Jamaica Bay near JFK's runways. Men in vans near Boston's Logan Airport or in the warehouses near Miami International. It's about dead airliners. Il Hayaween loves to kill jumbo jets. He wants bodies floating in Boston Harbor, and on the Interstates and across the perimeter roads of a dozen airports. He wants one day of revenge, one day of slaughter, one day to make America pay for Saddam Hussein's humiliation."

"You don't believe the Stingers were meant for Ireland?"

"Some, yes, but only a few. Those few were the IRA's reward for negotiating the purchase. It would have been impossible for the Palestinians to come to America and negotiate the sale, so Flynn did it for them."

"And the money in *Rebel Lady*," van Stryker suggested, "was the purchase price of the Stingers?"

I coloured slightly, but nodded. "Yes."

"Why didn't you tell us about *Rebel Lady*?"

"Because I planned to steal the money. That was my pension plan and my health insurance and my future income all wrapped up in one Arab package." I paused, sipped his good whisky, then looked up at van Stryker's thin, clever face. "How did you find out about *Rebel Lady*?"

"Gillespie found out."

"How?"

He stirred the eggs. "A wiretap, of course. Good old-fashioned illegal bugging." Van Stryker smiled at me.

"Oh God, of course. You had my house bugged before I even left Europe?" I suddenly realised that of course van Stryker would have taken that precaution, which meant that the very first time I had talked to Johnny Riordan about collecting *Rebel Lady* the hidden microphones must have been hearing every word I spoke.

"No," van Stryker said.

"No?"

"Your house is certainly wiretapped. My guess is that there are microphones covering the downstairs, and a voice-activated tape recorder concealed in the attic. That's how they usually do it if they've got access to the premises."

"They?"

"We prefer using the telephone to carry the wire-tapped signal away" – van Stryker ignored my question – "but that's difficult if you're not operating legally. So I suspect your eavesdroppers used a tape recorder. Which means, of course, that they must have had access to your house to collect the tapes."

"Sarah Sing Tennyson," I said, and felt as a blind man must feel when given sight or, much more aptly, like a fool given reason. "Jesus Christ!"

"The first is the more likely culprit, though in fact her name isn't Tennyson. It's Ko, Sally Ko. Her father is Hong Kong Chinese and her mother's from London. Miss Ko is British Intelligence, though naturally the British say she's a cultural attaché, but that's what all the spooks say these days. It's a harmless convention, we do it too."

"Oh, God," I said, "oh, Christ," and I thought what a fool I had been, what an utter, Goddamn, stupid fool. "And she wasn't even after me," I said, "but after Patrick and his friends?"

"Your brother-in-law? Yes. I'm told he sometimes used your house to plot arms shipments, which the Brits rather gratefully intercepted. Gillespie only discovered all this when his people went to put in their own wiretaps and found the British microphones in place."

My God, but what a fool I had been. Why else would a tenant pay to have a telephone and electricity installed? The phone system probably disguised the basic wiretap while the electricity powered the hidden tape recorder, and every time my dumb-ass brother-in-law plotted another arms shipment to Ireland, British Intelligence had gleefully listened in. Then they must have heard me talking to Johnny about a shipment of gold, and suddenly their humdrum intelligence operation had turned into a triumph. And what a triumph it had proved for the Goddamn Brits! Five million in gold and fifty-three Stingers neutralised, and all for the price of a few hidden microphones and a voice-activated tape recorder. "The bastards," I said feelingly, "the bastards."

Van Stryker took two plates from a dresser. "It was clever of them to use Congressman O'Shaughnessy's house!" He laughed. "That's a very elegant touch, Paul. I shall congratulate them on that."

"Elegant like hell. I thought they were going to kill me!"

"I'm sure Gillespie warned them against anything so drastic."

And of course it was Gillespie who had set me up for the Brit bastards. They had snatched me on my first morning back home, and how had they known I would be there if Gillespie had not told them? And that would also explain why the FBI had told Sergeant Nickerson not to worry when Kathleen Donovan had made her nervous protest at my kidnapping, because Gillespie had known all along who had snatched me, and why, and what they were probably doing to me. "The bastards," I said again, remembering my humiliation. And remembering too how I had spilled so much information about Belfast to my Irish questioner. Who was he? A Protestant? I looked at van Stryker. "You set them on to me, didn't you?"

"Gillespie felt you had been less than honest with him at the debriefing," van Stryker admitted, "and your tale of Stinger missiles just didn't make sense, Paul. I could have made things much tougher for you, but we all thought this way would be much quicker. And so it proved. You were right about the Stingers all the time, you just didn't think to tell us that you'd fouled il Hayaween's plans by stealing his money."

"But the Brits," I said bitterly.

"Better them than the Libyans, and better them than Brendan Flynn's men." Van Stryker was bland. "Was it a bad beating they gave you?"

"Like having a root-canal without an anaesthetic."

"I'm sorry, truly. But if I'm dealing with a creature like il Hayaween then I can't take chances. I needed to know what you were hiding, and I found out. You were hiding one million dollars."

"Is that what Miss Ko told you?" I asked.

"She did more than tell us. She even shared the million with us, or rather we permitted them to take one half. Thanks to you, Paul, Her Majesty's Secret Service is now richer to the tune of half-a-million dollars."

"No," I said, and relished thus puncturing his equanimity. "They're richer to the tune of four and a half million dollars. Miss Ko lied to you. There were five million bucks on that boat, van Stryker, all in gold. Your Goddamn allies have screwed you."

"Five?" He was astonished, shocked, incredulous. "Five!"

"Five million," I said, "in krugerrands and maple leaves. One thousand pounds gross weight of fine gold. I know! I glassed the coins into the boat. She was a brute before the gold went in and after it she sailed like a pregnant pig. Five million. The Brits lied to you."

"Oh, dear God," he said, then turned away to concentrate on the omelette. He was not really thinking about the eggs or the skillet, but about the money. He was adding it to the equation, thinking, trying to discern his enemy's mind. "Isn't five million dollars rather a lot of money for fifty-three missiles?" he asked me after a while; then, suspiciously, "If the missiles even exist?"

"I saw one of them."

"Just one?" Van Stryker turned the heat down under the omelette pan, suggesting that our hunger must wait on his puzzlement. "I don't like that one Stinger. It all sounds too convenient. So just tell me everything, Paul, and this time make it the truth."

So I told him the truth, the whole truth. I spoke of Brendan Flynn, Michael Herlihy, Shafiq, il Hayaween, Liam, Gerry, *Rebel Lady*, Sarah Sing Tennyson, the British interrogators, the gold and Seamus Geoghegan. I described my act of murder in the Mediterranean, I told him about Teodor, I told him everything. Van Stryker listened to it all in silence and, when I had no more to tell, he said nothing, but just stared at me, thinking, when suddenly the telephone rang, startling us both. Van Stryker answered it, spoke softly for a few moments, then put it down. "Your house is secure. My people are there."

"What will you do with the bodies?"

"We'll take Gillespie and Callaghan a long way away and fashion a car accident."

"And Seamus?"

"He will disappear."

"Just like that?"

"Just like that." Van Stryker tipped the omelettes on to the plates. "I rather suspect the British will be blamed. Now, eat." He put an omelette in front of me and I devoured it as though I had not eaten in weeks. Van Stryker ate his more fastidiously, then wiped the skillet with a paper towel before hanging it from an overhead rack. "I wish you'd told me about the five million dollars at the very beginning, Paul." He was not reproving me. I think van Stryker understood human cupidity well enough not to blame me. He had gone to the window from where he stared at a fishing boat that was throbbing towards the sea leaving a wake to ripple across the grey harbour water like widening bands of crimson light. "It's simply too much money!" van Stryker protested, "and I don't like the idea of Stingers being launched at the end of American runways. It's too complicated. For a start, where would il Hayaween find the men to fire the weapons? And why gold? Why not a simple bank transfer?"

I thought about it. "Maybe Herlihy demanded gold?"

"And why send two punks to guard you? Why not use two or three of their top men? Were Liam and Gerry the very best that the Provisionals could find?"

"No way."

"So why them? And why involve you? And why Stingers?" He turned to me as he asked that question, then he repeated it forcefully, as though the clue to everything lay in the choice of weapon. "Why Stingers?"

"Because they're the best."

"But you don't need the best to knock down an airliner. Airliners are lumbering great targets that wallow around the sky without so much as a single counter-measure on board. They're not agile like a ground-support helicopter or fast like a low-level fighter-bomber. A cobbled-together Russian Red Star could knock out a Boeing 747, and the Palestinians must have hundreds of Red Stars! So why Stingers? And why you?"

He had utterly confused me now. "What do you mean? Why me?"

"Why did they want you?"

"To bring the boat across"– I spoke as if the answer was obvious to the meanest intellect –"of course."

Van Stryker shook his head. "No!" he protested fiercely, "no! Why would they bring a boat to America with five million gold dollars they don't need, to buy fifty-three

Stingers they don't want, and which probably never even existed? For God's sake, Paul, the FBI have spent weeks looking for those missiles and there isn't even a whisper of confirmation that they exist! So forget the missiles, think about why they wanted you."

"To bring the boat across," I said again, but this time in quite a different tone; a tone of slow revelation.

"Because the boat is hiding something," van Stryker carried on the thought. "And they showed you a Stinger and they showed you money because they knew you'd buy that story because you of all people know just how the IRA has been lusting after Stingers for years, but this isn't about Stingers, Paul, it never was! This is about the boat!"

"Oh, Christ," I said. "Where's the boat?"

He shrugged. "The damned Brits said it was empty, finished, useless. We believed them."

"Oh, Christ," I said again. "I gave the boat back to them!"

"Gave it back to who?"

"Herlihy."

"Who has disappeared," van Stryker said. "So what's in it, Paul? What were they hiding under a coat of gold?"

"I don't know, I don't know." But whatever it was, I had given it back to them. "Oh, God," I said, "oh, God," because it wasn't over, not by a long way.

"We'll find the boat." Van Stryker snatched up the phone. "We'll search the whole damned coast and we'll find it. Give me the description again?"

"Find Herlihy first," I suggested, "because he'll know where *Rebel Lady*'s hidden."

"I told you, Herlihy's vanished."

"I can find him."

"You can?"

I would have to. Because Saddam Hussein had sent America a present, and I had lost it, so now I would find it again.

*

Herlihy was still not at his home. FBI agents broke in to find his apartment empty. Neither was he in his office, the Parish, or in the back room behind Tully's Tavern. He had disappeared.

"The money was never important!" van Stryker shouted at me. "The gold was a blind to dazzle you! To disguise the truth! And that's why Herlihy sent Geoghegan to kill you, to protect that truth. He's retrieved the boat, after all, and your telling tales was the one danger left. Is that it?" He pointed down.

He was shouting because we were in a Coastguard helicopter that had been summoned to Martha's Vineyard on van Stryker's authority. Once on board we had flown fast and low across the wintry waters of Nantucket Sound and were now hovering above the shopping precinct where I had left Marty Doyle.

"That's it!" I could still see the white Shamrock Flower Shoppe van. With any luck Marty would still be in the van, undiscovered by an inquisitive policeman. I reckoned that if anyone knew where Herlihy was hiding, then it had to be Marty Doyle.

"Down!" Van Stryker gestured the order at the crew chief who passed it on to the pilot. We were in the rescue compartment, a cavernous metal space behind and below the control cabin. A winch and a rescue basket filled one side of the rescue chamber where van Stryker and I, muffled against the cold, sat on a metal bench. The pilot returned a message protesting that a federal regulation prohibited landing on unapproved sites unless it was an emergency.

"Tell him this is an emergency! To his career!"

The machine settled slowly down. Shingles blew off the frozen-yoghurt shop's roof and a passing motorist almost swerved into the woods as the vast helicopter threaded its precarious way between the electricity and telephone wires to settle in a swirl of dust on the empty parking lot.

"Be quick!" van Stryker ordered me.

I ran to the flower van, yanked the back door open, and there discovered a terrified and half-frozen Marty Doyle. I dragged him out and, because his ankles were still tied with the green wire, I carried him like a child to the throbbing helicopter. I slung him on to the metal floor, then clambered in after him.

"Up!" van Stryker shouted.

As we rose into the air I saw the first blue flicker of a police car's light coming south to discover why a helicopter was disturbing the Cape's frosty morning, but the patrolman was arriving too late for the helicopter was already tilting over and racing out towards the open Atlantic. We passed over my house, and over the iced puddles in the marsh, and out across the dunes where I had sat with Kathleen Donovan, and out across the tumultuous smoking rollers that hammered incessantly on the frozen sand.

I pulled the woollen gag off Marty's face. "Morning, Marty."

"I'm so fucking cold, Paulie!" He was shivering. Both doors of the big helicopter were wide open and the morning was freezing. "Where are we going?" he asked.

"To find Michael Herlihy," I told him. "So where is he?"

"I don't know, Paul. Honest!"

I smiled at him, then cut off his wire bonds. "Put this on, Marty." It was a safety harness. The poor wee man was shaking with cold, but he managed to get his arms into the harness which I buckled tight across his chest. "So where's Herlihy?" I asked again.

Marty looked at me with his doglike gaze. "As God is my witness, Paul, and on my own dear mother's grave, I swear I don't know."

I pushed him out of the door.

He screamed and flailed, then jerked as the safety line I had attached to the back of his harness caught hold. He hung twenty feet beneath the helicopter and three hundred feet above the heaving grey seas that were being lashed into a spume as the freezing wind whipped their tops frantic.

I hauled him back into the helicopter's belly. "I don't think you heard me, Marty. Where's Herlihy?"

"He's at the Congressman's summer home. Oh, God, please don't do it again! Please! For the love of God, Paulie! Please!"

I gave him a cup of coffee instead, but he spilt most of it as the big rescue helicopter tilted its rotors west and sped us back towards Nantucket Sound and towards the last dark secrets of the *Rebel Lady*.

"I am constrained by rules," van Stryker reprimanded me. "If I'd known you were going to pull that stunt in the helicopter, I'd have stopped you, and if we interrogate Herlihy then it has to be done according to regulations. If we arrest him, we must have a warrant and he must have his rights read. If he wants to have a lawyer present during the interview, then he must have one."

"No footprints, you said, no apron strings. I'm still running free, van Stryker. You turned the Brits on me to avoid the rules, so now turn me on to Herlihy."

His thin face betrayed a flicker of a smile, then he offered me a raised hand in mock blessing. "No bruises, no broken bones, no cuts, no evidence of violence. Can you keep those rules?"

"Better than the Brits, believe me."

"Then go." He waved me out of the car. We had flown to Otis Air Force base at the inner end of the Cape, then driven through the early traffic to Centerville. It was still not yet nine o'clock and we were already parked close to Congressman O'Shaughnessy's beach house.

I opened the car door. "I'll be back by eleven."

"It takes longer than that to squeeze the truth out of a man."

"Not really." I smiled, and climbed out of the car.

The wind was cold. The street had the joyless, deserted feel of a resort out of season. Nearly all of these houses were the vacation homes of the very rich who needed sea-front 'cottages' to escape from the stifling summer heat of Boston or New York. It was a good lair for Michael Herlihy, for who would dream that a US Congressman would shelter an enemy of the people? Even a Congressman as moronic as Tommy the Turd could usually be reckoned above such foolishness.

I clicked open the gate. The house appeared shuttered and empty. I walked round to the back, bruising the frosted grass beneath my boots. There was no one in the kitchen and, as I had expected, the door was locked. I knew there was an alarm system that the Brits had circumvented and which I assumed the Congressman would have had repaired, but so long as there was someone in the house then there seemed a good chance that the system would be switched off. In which hopeful belief I rammed my oilskin-padded elbow hard against a pane of the door's glass. Nothing. I rammed again, but only succeeded in bruising my elbow through the thick layers of oilskin. They made windows tough these days.

I picked a big rock from among the stones which edged the border of a flower bed and smashed through both layers of glass. The noise seemed appalling, but no bell shrilled its hammer tone into the dawn. I reached through the hole, found the latch, and let myself in. The heat was on in the house and a dirty plate lay unwashed in the kitchen sink.

I still had Callaghan's gun. I took it from the oilskin's deep pocket and stalked into the main hallway, which had been emptied of the cellar's encumbrances. I stopped and listened at the foot of the stairway, but heard nothing. The living room was deserted and its tall windows securely shut-tered. I edged through another half-open door into a huge dining room which held a table that could seat twenty guests. Silver shone on the shelves of a mahogany hutch. Another door led from the dining room's far end. It was ajar and I edged it further open to see that it led into a leather-furnished and book-lined den with one wall smothered in framed diplomas and awards. This was evidently the room where Tommy the Turd came to pretend he was educated, and it was also the room where Michael Herlihy, still fully dressed, was fast asleep.

I put the gun barrel under his nose. "Morning, Michael."

"God! What! No!" The last syllable was prompted by the pain he had felt as I rammed the gun into his upper lip.

"Be very still, Michael," I said, "and very quiet."

"Paul?"

"Be quiet, Michael!"

He had clearly waited in this comfortable room for news from Seamus. He had waited in the Congressman's leather recliner, drinking the Congressman's whiskey out of the Congressman's crystal tumbler. Now, woken to a bad dream, he was shaking.

"Seamus is dead, Michael."

"I don't know anything. Nothing!" He tried to get out of the chair, but the gun persuaded him to stay still. I ran a hand over his rumpled clothes and found a small automatic in one pocket.

I took his gun and put it into my pocket. "You sent Seamus to kill me."

"Don't be ridiculous, Paul."

"Marty Doyle told me."

Michael stiffened. "I have no knowledge of these matters."

"That's very formal, Michael, very legalistic. Where's the boat?"

"What boat?"

"*Rebel Lady*."

"I don't know. The Congressman arranged to have her towed away from his property. Why don't you ask him yourself? He's in Washington." He pulled a telephone towards him, then gasped as I slashed the gun barrel across his bony nose.

"No telephones, Michael. So where's *Rebel Lady*?"

"I told you, Paul, I do not know!"

"Then let's find out if you're telling the truth, shall we?" I reached down and yanked him out of the chair. I tripped him as he lurched forward, throwing him face down on to the room's Oriental rug. I folded the rug over his head so he could see nothing. "If you move," I said loudly enough for him to hear, "I'll blow your fucking brains out."

The room's heavy velvet drapes were tethered by tasselled silk cords. I slashed the cords free, then tied Michael's hands behind his back. That done I pulled him to his feet, picked a sturdy poker from the collection in the hearth, then pushed Michael out of the den and into the luxurious dining room. "This is a comfortable hiding place, Michael."

"I'm not hiding," he protested. "This is where I'm planning O'Shaughnessy's re-election campaign."

"Don't take me for a fool, Michael. The Congressman is always re-elected. Daddy's money sees to that. If the Congressman was a pox-ridden baboon and his opponent was the Archangel Gabriel, he'd still be re-elected. You don't have to work at Tommy's re-election, you just have to wheel him out and point him towards Washington. No, Michael, you were hiding here, that's what you were doing. Tell me, have the Arabs sent you more money?"

"You'll regret these allegations!"

"The five million was your price, wasn't it? You and Brendan?"

"I don't know what you're talking about, and I demand that you release me! I demand it!" He turned and shouted the words into my face.

"As we non-lawyers say" – I smiled sweetly at him – "fuck away off." I rammed him with the poker, forcing him to stumble on down the hallway into the kitchen, then out through the broken kitchen door and down the brick path to the locked boathouse. Michael was dressed in his lawyer's three-piece suit and began to shiver in the bitter wind. "Please?" he said.

"Where's *Rebel Lady*?"

"I have no idea where the boat is. Can't we talk about this inside?"

"Why not in here, Michael?" The boathouse door was secured by a padlocked hasp that yielded to the leverage of the poker. I kicked the broken door open, then pushed Herlihy inside and tethered him to a stanchion with the free end of the curtain cord.

"No, please!" He suddenly understood exactly what I intended doing.

"Where's *Rebel Lady*?" I asked in a very reasonable tone.

"I don't know what you're talking about!"

"I think you do, Counsellor, I really think you do." I went to the far wall where two control boxes operated the twin hoists holding *Quick Colleen*. I pressed the green buttons and the machinery hummed smoothly as it lowered the sharp-prowed boat into the frozen dock. The ice splintered noisily under the hull's weight, then the speedboat settled in the water, her bow inwards.

Herlihy made a futile lunge for freedom, but his tether held. "Paul! Be sensible!"

"But I am being sensible. It's a nice calm day, the waves aren't more than a foot high, so think of this as a treat! Do you remember when we were teenagers and I took you out for a boat ride?"

"Please, Paul!" He was shaking.

"Where's *Rebel Lady*?"

"We sank her, out there!" He jerked his head towards the frigid waters of Nantucket Sound.

"I wonder why I don't believe you? But we'll soon see if you're telling the truth." I stepped on to *Quick Colleen*'s foredeck, unbuckled the forward hoist strap and unclipped her cockpit cover to discover her ignition key was still in the dashboard. I tossed the cover on to the dock, released the second hoist, then pressed the switches that tilted the big two-hundred-horsepower engines into the water. The batteries still had power and the twin engines whined down into the icy waves that lapped soft against the low racing transom. I checked the big fuel tank and found it full, primed the engines, advanced the chokes, and turned the key.

The cold engines coughed a couple of times, then, one after the other, they caught and fired. I ran the throttles up so that an ear-shattering bellow reverberated in the boathouse, then let the twin beasts idle. Smoke hazed the boathouse entrance.

"Fun time," I said happily as I climbed back on to the dock.

"No!" Michael clung desperately to the stanchion. I slapped his hands free, kicked his feet out from under him, then hurled him on to the white leather seats of *Quick Colleen*. "No!" he protested again. His face had already turned a deathly pallor. "Please, Paul!"

"Where's *Rebel Lady*?"

"I told you! We sank her."

"Then let's go look for her!" I rammed the throttles into reverse and the expensive boat slashed backwards. I swivelled her, rammed the twin levers forward, and screamed straight out to sea. Within yards the hull was planing and before we had even reached the Spindle Rock *Quick Colleen* was splintering the wintry sea at fifty miles an hour. At that speed even the smallest wave banged and shook the lightweight racing hull. She crashed across the grey waters, quivering and hammering like a live beast and leaving behind her a twin cock's comb of high white water that glittered in the early sunlight.

"Isn't this fun!" I spun the wheel, forcing *Quick Colleen* to turn like a jet-fighter. She skidded sideways as the huge engines tried to counteract the centrifugal force, then I wrenched her back, gave her full throttle, and let her run loose and fast towards far Nantucket. "I said, isn't this fun!"

Herlihy had vomited on the leather seat. He was retching and heaving, bringing up nothing but a mixture of bile and water. The boat thumped on the waves, banging like a demented hammer. A fishing boat had left a long gelid wake a mile ahead and I steered straight for it, slamming into the bigger waves at full speed. The sound of the seas hitting *Quick Colleen*'s hull was like the crack of doom. The boat bounced in the air, came down in an explosion of white water, slammed up again, shook down once more, and Michael was grovelling and sliding around in his own vomit as he desperately tried to keep his balance.

I turned the boat hard, accelerated again, and rammed her back through the fishing boat's wake. Michael stared up at me, a terrible look on his pale face, then shook his head as if to tell me he had taken enough torment.

I cut the throttles, letting *Quick Colleen* idle in the cold, gentle water. "So where's *Rebel Lady*?" I asked him.

"In Washington, DC."

"Where?"

"At the Virginia Shore Marine Depot."

"Where's that?"

He heaved, brought up a trickle of mucus, then groaned. Even the small rocking of the boat was murder to him.

"Where's that?" I asked him again.

"It's at the northern end of Washington National Airport. Go into the city from the airport and it's the first turning off the Mount Vernon Memorial Highway. Now, please, Paul! Take me back! Please!"

"Who took her there?"

"I hired a delivery firm in Cotuit."

I gave the engines a tad of power, throwing Michael back on to the fouled cushions. His face had a green tinge now.

"What's hidden inside her, Michael?"

"I don't know. Truly! Nothing perhaps. You were bring-

300

ing the money, that's all! Then she was to be left at that yard."

"Il Hayaween ordered her taken to that particular yard, yes?"

"Yes!"

"And he sent you more money?"

"Yes!"

"How much?"

He was reluctant to say, but I gunned the throttles slightly and he yielded immediately. "Five million again." He slid sideways, heaving and retching.

"He wired it, right? To where, the Caymans?"

He nodded. "Yes."

"And the five million is for you and Brendan to share, yes?"

"Yes."

"And no one else knows about this, do they?" I suddenly saw it clearly. That was why Brendan had sent me two punks, because he dared not ask the Army Council to allocate good men. "This operation was never cleared by the Army Council, was it?" I accused him.

Michael gazed up at me. That question scared him, but he was too cowed, too miserable and too wretched to dare tell a lie and so he shook his head.

Which meant he was freelancing. He and Brendan. None of this had been approved by the Provisional IRA's Army Council. The whole thing was an unsanctioned operation. "There never were any Stingers, were there?" I asked.

"There would have been!" Michael pleaded. "We could have bought every Stinger on the market! That's what we were going to do, Paul! Don't you understand? We had to make money! I wanted Boston to be more important than Tripoli again! I wanted to see Ireland free!" The last word was a despairing cry as another spasm of illness wrenched him forwards.

"So who were those Cubans?"

"The Arabs provided them. We had to convince you that there really were Stingers."

Oh Christ, I thought, but Carlos and Alvarez had probably been the genuine articles; straight out of Cuba with Fidel's cigar-smoke reeking in their nostrils. "Bastard," I told Herlihy, then I gave *Quick Colleen*'s throttles a thrust, driving her fast on to the plane before whipping her into some fast S-turns, spinning and flogging her through the merciless sea. Herlihy was screaming and sobbing. I had never known the exquisite punishment of seasickness, but I had seen enough sufferers to know that its misery could prise the truth out of the most secretive of sinners.

I cut the throttles again, letting the sleek hull settle into the small waves. The shore was a mile away now. Michael was gagging and moaning; a man in anguish. "Tell me," I demanded, "what is in that boat and worth ten million dollars of Saddam Hussein's money?"

"I don't know. They just asked us to deliver the boat to Washington."

"And what were you to do with me?"

"Nothing." He looked up at me, tendrils of vomit trailing from his blue lips. "Honest!"

I put a hand to the throttles.

"You were to be killed!" He said it pathetically, begging me not to touch the throttle levers. "You and the two boys."

"Because the *Rebel Lady*," I said, "was never to be associated with the IRA, is that it?"

"Yes!" He gazed beseechingly at me. His rumpled suit was flecked with vomit and seawater.

"And you and Brendan were willing to help Saddam Hussein attack America?"

"We didn't know what it was about!" he protested.

"Oh, you did, Michael. You may not know what's inside *Rebel Lady*, but you knew damn well she isn't carrying a goodwill card for the President."

"She brought us money," he said, "and I'll give the money towards the cause. Ireland will be free!"

"Oh it will," I said, "I promise you that, but it won't need your help, because Ireland doesn't need traitors like you."

"I'm not a traitor."

"You're a piece of shit, Michael, a piece of legal shit." And I pushed the throttles forward, gave the boat two punishing and gut-wrenching turns, then headed hard for the shore.

And wondered just what lay in the dark belly of the *Rebel Lady*.

Washington, DC lies ninety-five miles from the mouth of the Potomac River. *Rebel Lady* would probably have done most of those miles under power after her delivery crew had sailed her south from Cape Cod. The weather had been kind, so they had probably taken the outside route to Sandy Hook, then down to Cape May where they would have taken her by canal and river into the Chesapeake Bay. Then, once into the Potomac, they would have motored her up to the nation's capital and, if they had remembered the old tradition that honoured George Washington, they would have sounded the ship's bell as they passed Mount Vernon.

Once in the city itself they would have taken the Virginia Channel where, just south of the Pentagon and north of the airport, the Virginia Shore Marine Depot lay. In winter the dilapidated yard was a storage place for cruisers and dismasted yachts. It was a dispiriting place, nothing but a mucky run-down yard hedged behind by the expressway looping off the river bridges and in front by the gantries and pylons that stood in a bay of the Potomac to hold the approach lights for Washington National Airport's main runway. The big jets screamed overhead.

"Of course we're not as well known as the Sailing Marina to the south of the airport," the yard's manager shouted to me as a passenger jet thundered above us, "but we've got more depth of water than the Pentagon Lagoon." The smell of kerosene settled around us in the wake of the huge plane. I could see the Washington Monument across the river and beyond it, to my right, the last gleams of reflected sunlight from the Capitol Dome. The Capitol, like the White House, was a little over two miles away while the Pentagon was just one mile north. *Rebel Lady* had been brought like a plague bacillus right into the very heart of the Republic. "So what's all this about?" the manager asked and, when I said nothing, he tried to prompt me. "They paid good money for her storage. Cash!"

"I'm sure they did."

Once she had reached the yard *Rebel Lady* had been craned out of the water and cradled among a score of plastic-wrapped yachts. Her hull had been supported by metal jackstands and her thick keel rested on big wooden blocks. On Herlihy's orders her new name had been painted out, making her just one more anonymous boat among the hundreds of craft stored in Washington's boatyards during the bitter winter months.

Now, at dusk on the day which had started with *Quick Colleen* in Nantucket Sound, I stood where *Rebel Lady* had been hidden away. *Rebel Lady* herself had already been taken away to have her secret excised, but I had wanted to come to the boatyard to see for myself just where Saddam Hussein's revenge on America would have been triggered.

"Shame what they did to her," the manager said. "Wrecking an interior like that."

"Wicked," I agreed.

"Funny thing, though. She had a Florida manufacturer's nameplate on her coachroof, but she wasn't built in the States."

"No, she wasn't." The real *Rebel Lady*, now called *Roisin*, waited for me in Ardgroom. I had decided I did not like that new name. I would change it back. Or find another name. *Scoundrel* perhaps? Then I would go and claim my boat and sail her back across the Atlantic.

"One of my guys reckoned she was French-built," the manager told me, "but she was a hell of a lot heavier than any French boat I've ever seen."

"I know. I sailed her." That crossing of the Mediterranean seemed so long ago now. I suddenly remembered Liam's dead eyes gleaming emerald with the reflected lamplight.

"You sailed her? So what was it all about?" the manager asked eagerly.

"Smuggling. Cocaine." I offered him the answer which he would find most believable.

"I reckoned as much. The stuff was hidden in that big keel, eh?"

"I guess so."

"I know so!" he said happily. "I was here when they X-rayed her. They got excited, I can tell you! Excited!" He gestured towards the vacant hard-standing where *Rebel Lady* had been parked and where all that was now left of her presence were abandoned keel-blocks, jackstands, and the cumbersome X-ray equipment that was used to survey the health of hidden keel-bolts. "You think we'll be on the TV news?" the manager asked me hopefully.

I shook my head. "You don't want to be on the evening news, believe me, not with that boat. But thank you for letting me see the place."

"You're welcome." He tried to hide his disappointment. "And if you ever need boat storage in the nation's capital, Mr . . .?" He hesitated, inviting my name, but I shook my head again and walked away. It was nearly dark and the runway's approach lights shimmered their reflections in the river's hurrying water. A plane roared close overhead as I climbed into the back seat of the government car and slammed the door.

It had all been so close. And so clever. Whatever it was, which now, in the city's evening traffic, I went to find out.

*

Rebel Lady had been taken to one of the military reservations close to Washington where, in a great empty hangar, she stood forlorn under massive bright lights. I found van Stryker in a glass-walled booth from where he intently watched the white-garbed team that worked underneath the jacked-up hull. "It's in the lead keel," he told me without taking his eyes off the boat and without saying what 'it' was.

The huge bulbous keel had already been taken off *Rebel Lady*. Like most ballast keels it had been secured to the fibreglass hull by long silicon-bronze stud bolts. Van Stryker's team had loosened the bolts and gently lowered the keel to the hangar floor. Standing beside the exposed keel, which was now hidden from my view by the men and women in their protective clothing, was a bright yellow flask as big as a compact car and decorated with the three-leaved insignia of the nuclear industry. "It was a bomb?" I asked in horror as I recognised the symbol.

"No. He doesn't have the technology to make a bomb, not yet." Van Stryker looked tired. His job was to preserve the republic from the attacks of terrorists and he knew just how close this attack had come to success, and now he was thinking of the other attacks that would doubtless come in the future. "Someone's going to make the bomb, Paul, someone who thinks they can change the world in their favour by setting it off. But not this time."

"So what is it?"

"A small sliver of Chernobyl."

"Chernobyl?"

Van Stryker sipped at a brown plastic mug of coffee. "We think the Iraqis hollowed out that keel and filled it with around four tons of uranium-dioxide. That's the nuclear fuel you put in ordinary commercial power stations like Three Mile Island or Chernobyl. They chopped the fuel rods into pellets and mixed them up with powdered aluminum and what looks like ammonium nitrate. That means they mixed the uranium into a huge firebomb. Then they added a detonator and a timer. Simple, really, and comparatively cheap."

"And what will that lot do?"

"The firebomb would have reached a temperature of over seven thousand degrees Fahrenheit, and once the nuclear fuel caught fire it would have spread a miniature plume of radioactivity just like the Chernobyl plume." Van Stryker offered me a sudden sympathetic glance. "Don't worry, Paul, my experts say you probably weren't exposed to excessive radiation. By sheathing that horror in lead and keeping it under water they gave you protection. Then you made yourself even safer by piling the gold on top."

I stared at the white-dressed figures. "What would the bomb have done to Washington?"

"If the wind had been southerly then their toxic bonfire might have made the Pentagon untenable for years to come, or even the White House. What a revenge for Baghdad that would have been." Van Stryker fell silent for a few seconds. "Think of a city contaminated with radioactive isotopes; strontium and caesium. Think of the birth-defects, think of the cancers. That's why they wanted the boat out of the water when the detonator triggered, so the fire could start properly. If she'd been floating it would have been snuffed out and at best just contaminated a few miles of river, but on dry land, and with a good wind, they might have smeared a hundred square miles with lethal poisons."

"This wasn't the IRA's doing, you know that?" I told van Stryker.

"Your IRA," he said flatly, "was the only organisation to support Saddam Hussein with bombs. Don't make excuses for terrorism. Don't try to tell me they're just misled heroes."

"I just said . . ."

"I heard you what you said, Paul, and I understand your mixed loyalties." He stared at the bright arc lights and the busy men and the bright yellow flask. "Did you know that when George Washington couldn't find uniforms for his men he made them place scraps of white paper in their hats? He was saying, these are my warriors, these are your targets. He didn't hide them, he didn't send them home to hide behind women's skirts at day's end. He was a man."

I said nothing, but just stared at *Rebel Lady*. A rope's bitter end hung from her gunwale and I wondered if she would ever sail again. I doubted it, and I thought how unfair to a boat that her last voyage should be under such false pretences. She deserved one last romp through high seas with full sail and no unfair ballast slowing her down.

"The Garda arrested Flynn this afternoon," van Stryker said.

"Will you extradite him?"

"No. The less the public know about this, the better. Nuclear matters seem to bring out the most hysterical aspects of the American people so I shall try very hard to keep all this secret. But Flynn will be taught that Uncle Sam is not easily mocked. The Garda will find something with which to charge him, and a few years in Portlaoise Jail should teach him to respect us."

"And Herlihy?"

Van Stryker shook his head. "There's too many lawyers round him to make a trumped-up charge stick, but I think the Internal Revenue Service could be persuaded to make his life a misery."

"And what of me?" I asked.

"On the whole," he said, "you've been on the side of the angels. We'll give you some back pay, Paul. Say a hundred thousand? You can make a new start with that."

"Yes." I sounded sour. "But it isn't five million, is it?"

"Which the Brits have suddenly agreed to turn over to us," van Stryker said grimly. "I have spoken sternly to Miss Ko." A telephone suddenly buzzed, cutting off van Stryker's tale of how he had dealt with the perfidious British. He answered the phone and I saw one of the protectively clothed figures beside the gutted *Rebel Lady* speaking into the other handset. Van Stryker grunted a few times, thanked the man, then put the telephone down. "July 4," he said slowly. "The timer was set for noon on Independence Day. It's a fair bet Washington will be crowded that day. Maybe a victory parade for Desert Storm? Maybe a nation's street party?" Van Stryker sounded angry, and no wonder, for who among the crowd celebrating America's independence would have thought twice about a plume of smoke across the river, or would have sensed the invisible fall of deadly isotopes seeping across the Mall and Pennsylvania Avenue?

"I very nearly brought it about, didn't I?" I spoke in bitter recrimination.

"Did you?" van Stryker asked in a tone of mild disbelief. He was again staring at the crippled boat and the bright flask.

"By not telling you about *Rebel Lady.*"

"Oh, we knew something was up, and I suppose we'd have discovered the boat eventually." He still spoke mildly, and I remembered his stricture that everything should be done according to the rules, unless, of course, a man was outside the rules, and that surely included the British team that had abducted me? And how could terrorism be fought strictly within the rules? Due process was a feeble weapon compared with a firebomb laced with soap-flakes or a Kalashnikov in the hands of a bitter youth. I remembered an IRA man complaining in a Lifford pub how he had just lost two men to an SAS ambush. "There used to be rules," he had told me bitterly, "but now the focking Brits are fighting just like us." Could terrorism only be defeated by terror? That was a horrid question, as horrid as the scene in the brightly lit hangar where a small crane was lowering a pallet loaded with what looked like mounds of dull silver powder into the flask. "A toxic nuclear cocktail," van Stryker explained.

"But it isn't over, is it?" I said. "Il Hayaween won't stop with this failure."

"But he's lost the initiative, Paul, and we'll be setting traps for him and, thanks to the Gulf war, he's lost some of his old hiding places. This is a victory, Paul." He gestured at the broken boat. "It isn't the last victory, because you can't beat terrorism, only contain it, but my God this feels good, and maybe it will feel better soon? We're going to make the bastards who sent us that present dance to Uncle Sam's tune for a little while, and who knows? We might even dance them into an early grave."

"I suppose," I said slowly, "that I should thank you for keeping me out of an early grave?"

"You don't have to thank me." Van Stryker did not look at me as he spoke, but instead watched as men uncoiled hoses with which to wash down the hangar. "When I sent you out fourteen years ago I never expected to see you again. We sent others, don't ask who, and so far you're the only one to come back. Two others certainly won't return and a third might have joined our enemies. It wasn't an easy job you did, and I don't suppose you feel clean about it, but you served your country, Paul. You have preserved the republic from evil, and for that it is my duty to thank you." He turned and held out his hand. "So, as far as I am concerned, you can go with a clear conscience."

It was a bright night, the sky ablaze with stars above a clean country that was safe from harm. I walked to the car, breathing a cold air, and I wondered what the hell would happen now.

"The airport, sir?" the driver asked.

"Please," I said, and we drove away, leaving behind us the bright facility with its parked helicopters and low loaders and armed men and yellow lamps and warning signs. The sentries waved us through the guardpost, and the brilliant lights disappeared behind as we drove through the dark woods towards the small safe towns of America. The small towns of decent folk who are so hated by the terrorists.

I would go home now to my own small town, but I guessed, after all, that I would not stay there. There would be no peace for me, not yet, for ghosts still stalked my world and I did not know how to exorcise them; nor would il Hayaween abandon me, for I had made a fool of him and he would want me dead. I thought of Roisin's eyes in the instant before I had pulled the trigger. Oh dear God, but the paths we choose so heedlessly. The lights of Washington smeared the sky ahead, and I thought of a fire blossoming in a city, of death dropping soft as snowflakes across wide avenues. I closed my eyes. In the spring, I thought, I would go to Ireland, and I would take my boat to sea and I would let her take me somewhere, I did not know where, I did not care where, just anywhere that a scoundrel might find refuge.

read more 🐧

BERNARD CORNWELL

If you enjoyed this book, there are several ways you can read more by the same author and make sure you get the inside track on all Penguin books.

Order any of the following titles direct:

0140174583	STORMCHILD	£7.99
014017723X	WILDTRACK	£7.99
0140177248	SEA LORD	£7.99
0140177256	CRACKDOWN	£7.99
0140177264	SCOUNDREL	£7.99
0140231862	THE WINTER KING	£7.99
0140232478	ENEMY OF GOD	£7.99
0140232877	EXCALIBUR	£7.99

Simply call Penguin c/o Bookpost on **01624 677237** and have your credit/debit card ready. Alternatively e-mail your order to **bookshop@enterprise.net**. Postage and package is free in mainland UK. Overseas customers must add £2 per book. Prices and availability subject to change without notice.

Visit www.penguin.com and find out first about forthcoming titles, read exclusive material and author interviews, and enter exciting competitions. You can also browse through thousands of Penguin books and buy online.

IT'S NEVER BEEN EASIER TO READ MORE WITH PENGUIN

Frustrated by the quality of books available at Exeter station for his journey back to London one day in 1935, Allen Lane decided to do something about it. The Penguin paperback was born that day, and with it first-class writing became available to a mass audience for the very first time. This book is a direct descendant of those original Penguins and Lane's momentous vision. What will you read next?

He just wanted a decent book to read ...

Not too much to ask, is it? It was in 1935 when Allen Lane, Managing Director of Bodley Head Publishers, stood on a platform at Exeter railway station looking for something good to read on his journey back to London. His choice was limited to popular magazines and poor-quality paperbacks – the same choice faced every day by the vast majority of readers, few of whom could afford hardbacks. Lane's disappointment and subsequent anger at the range of books generally available led him to found a company – and change the world.

'We believed in the existence in this country of a vast reading public for intelligent books at a low price, and staked everything on it'
Sir Allen Lane, 1902–1970, founder of Penguin Books

The quality paperback had arrived – and not just in bookshops. Lane was adamant that his Penguins should appear in chain stores and tobacconists, and should cost no more than a packet of cigarettes.

Reading habits (and cigarette prices) have changed since 1935, but Penguin still believes in publishing the best books for everybody to enjoy. We still believe that good design costs no more than bad design, and we still believe that quality books published passionately and responsibly make the world a better place.

So wherever you see the little bird – whether it's on a piece of prize-winning literary fiction or a celebrity autobiography, political tour de force or historical masterpiece, a serial-killer thriller, reference book, world classic or a piece of pure escapism – you can bet that it represents the very best that the genre has to offer.

Whatever you like to read – trust Penguin.

read more
www.penguin.co.uk